Tequila
Mockingbird

◆

Tequila
Mockingbird

◆

Carter Ratcliff

Station Hill

of Barrytown

Published by Station Hill of Barrytown, the publishing project of the Institute for Publishing Arts, Inc., 120 Station Hill Road, Barrytown, NY 12507, New York, a not-for-profit, tax-exempt organization [501(c)(3)].

Online catalogue: www.stationhill.org
e-mail: publishers@stationhill.org

 This publication is supported in part by grants from the New York State Council on the Arts, a state agency.

Interior design: Susan Quasha
Cover design: Susan Quasha/Carter Ratcliff

The author gratefully acknowledges the encouragement of those who read this story in its early stages, especially Betsy Baker, Diane Burko, Phyllis Derfner, Marty Fisher, and Mary Curtis Ratcliff, as well as the exemplary presence of Maya Żmigrodzka.

Library of Congress Cataloging-in-Publication Data
Ratcliff, Carter.
  Tequila mockingbird / Carter Ratcliff.
     pages cm
  ISBN 978-1-58177-138-1
  1. Models (Persons—Fiction. 2. Female friendship—Fiction. 3. Russians—New York (State—Fiction. 4. Manhattan (New York, N.Y.)—Fiction. 5. Chick lit. I. Title.
  PS36183.A825T47 2014
  813'.6—dc23

                              2014010163

to Phyllis

.1.

Longer, thicker, stronger … some girls obsess about it, but I'm way more realistic. I mean, the last guy who really got me off was totally average in the dick department. He was pretty average all around, but nice. So we had a nice time, plus highlights in bed. He found me in Spain, Málaga, to be exact, and took me to Ibiza for a week. Which was ultra-nice. One afternoon, I swear, every pair of male eyes on the island was ogling me in my basically invisible bikini. At night, I went to parties with this guy, the one with the average dick. The general idea was, here she is. My gorgeous model girlfriend. Proof of the pudding, though he did all the eating, except for this lovely afternoon in one of those thatched-hut things with this girl with no tan line who couldn't get enough of me. Yummy.

Of course, the general idea is never quite what you think it is. Sooner rather than later I figured out that this very nice guy was giving people the impression that he was about to dump me. Just to show that he wasn't grateful to be with this hot number— namely, me—and to explain ahead of time why I would not be hanging on his arm like a total lamo the next time he showed up on Ibiza. He never let me in on this side of his plan, needless to say, but I'm pretty sure this was it because one of his supposed friends started sniffing around me the second time we met, at this party on a terrace that reached way out over the waves. Which were about a thousand feet below.

Scary, right?

Except that I was all giggly with bubbly and didn't care. It was fun to have this dope, the supposed friend, getting all insinuating around me. Lots of eyebrow action. I have to admit I considered it. He was terrible but not that terrible. But I decided against it. My friend Brenda the supermodel needed me back in New York and just in case I didn't know how much she needed me she would call every fifteen minutes or so.

Once she called when I was right on the edge and I knew it was her but I didn't answer. The girl with no tan line didn't even notice it, we were both getting off, getting into the timeless time you get into if you're the orgasmic kind, and I knew Brenda would be there when I got back to real time. She always is, that's just basic. Something I can count on. She'll be there in real time because she is the one who makes it real.

A few days later, I stopped by her place, this five-story townhouse on East Sixty-Third Street. She was still bummed, of course, and of course I began to feel the same way. Brenda is such a stunning presence, the moment I see her I start to get in sync. Not that she tries to be overwhelming or anything. It's just that she's way better looking than just about anyone else who was ever born. And so sweet. Kind of weirdly flawless, meaning she has this aura that draws you in. Whatever is happening, it's all about her, and that feels OK.

In fact it feels really great, because it's her, it's her moment, always, and you're lucky to be part of it. But it's not like she erases other people. Actually, it's the opposite. When I'm with Brenda, I'm like Popeye the Sailor Man. I yam what I yam, only more so, meaning, there she was, on her Vicente Soto sofa way longer than the average stretch limo, and I felt this terrible pang. She wasn't smiling her amazing smile. Her face was blank but she was obviously upset, so I was, like, what's up, sweetie? How have you been? You seemed so freaked on the phone.

She just groaned.

I just stared at her. Brenda is so amazingly beautiful. But she comes across as a touch dysfunctional. Sometimes, when people get to meet her, they're knocked out by her looks, really thrilled to see her up close and then afterward they're, like, hunh? What was that? She's really nice and all, but, er, um … the thing is, Brenda doesn't really focus on you if she doesn't know you and her circle of acquaintances is not what you would call extensive, thanks to the security that sprang up around her when she was about nine years old and the general public started drooling at the sight of her. Day to day, she sees her people and that's about it. She didn't even start dating until a couple of years ago.

Her first was a country and western singer. A Nashville type with a major career. Quite the peculiar choice. Even the tabloids were baffled. SUPERGLAM BRENDA FALLS FOR THIS??? And there'd be a picture of the guy in a cowboy hat with a look on his face like he just took a massive hit of ultra-bad meth. Then, for something completely different, there was this ancient English aristocrat. A real wit. He'd get this creepy little smirk on his face, to let you know he'd just said something funny but, major problem, I could never get the joke. Neither could anyone else. Then there was this other blueblood, Latin American Division, the proud possessor of vast acreage in Uruguay or Paraguay or somewhere. You'd say something about a three-bedroom apartment of a certain dimension and then, the subject of square footage having been introduced, Reynaldo would pipe up with a reminder that his family's hacienda was twice the size of Rhode Island.

There was a hedge-fund guy from Connecticut, a software genius from Vancouver, and then a mogul from Zürich. If there were any justice in the world, the guy from Zürich would have been king of the cuckoo clocks or maybe high-end chocolates but, no, he had a patent for some sort of sweat-absorbing elastic, perfect for sportswear, and I will never forget the balmy summer evening when he cornered me at one of Brenda's soirées and explained to me how the polymers or whatever absorb all the more odiferous components of human perspiration. Which made sense, no doubt, but left me with mixed feelings. I mean, I got the point, way to go, hard-working polymers, but, on the other hand, the only sweat I really know about is the work of the lovely, adorable bodies I get close to and that is just the icing on the scrumptious cake. So to speak.

After the Swiss mogul there were more moguls and aristocrats and a few Hollywood types, not to mention Bollywood types, and then an oligarch from the former Soviet Union. Then another. And another. You know that shop downtown, Cheese of All Nations? Well, Brenda's dance card had been sort of Jerks of All Nations, but now I was beginning to spot a trend. And I was getting worried. I mean, I like everybody. Even Americans. But these Russian oligarchs made me nervous.

I would call them Vladimirs and Brenda would get kind of hurt, telling me the exact name of the current one. Which I could never remember, though of course I was aware of the oligarch phenomenon. So I knew they were loaded. Ill-gotten gains up the wazoo. Fine. Get your share. Of course, Brenda didn't need to get her share. Her share was already bigger than she'd ever need, so I didn't really see why she put up with these guys. With their unbelievably shitty attitudes. And their vodka. Russians are the limpest studs on the planet, according to Brenda. Which is fine with her. She's not into cock all that much.

Of course, the worst is their idea of art. Like, they're international sophisticates, right? Which means they have to be high-profile patrons of the very best the contemporary art world has to offer. So far, so good, except that their idea of the very best is a balloon dog by Jeff Koons or somebody. And then, to show they're gazillionaires, they have to pay way too much. A record-setting price that guarantees just oodles of headlines. A major scoop about a bright, shiny balloon dog. It really is the worst. Except that it isn't. The worst, according to Brenda, is that one of these creeps has been calling her, telling her he's going to have her killed.

I hear this and I'm dazed. Major shock. Then I'm, like, sweetheart, darling, have you told anyone else about this? Well, um, no, she hasn't. She doesn't tell anyone about anything, except for me, the one person who actually talks to her, so when I heard about the death threats maybe I should have called 911. What is your emergency, Ma'am, and I'd be, like, er uh, I have this gorgeous friend and, well, and she keeps going out with these Russian oligarchs, and, uh … uh … not really a workable script. So maybe I should have called Brenda's dickhead lawyer. Ronnie, we have a situation.

But I wasn't sure we did have a situation. In other words, I didn't want to believe it. Besides, talking to Ronnie is like going to night school and taking a course in the law of diminishing returns. The more he talks, the less he says, and all you find out is your eyelids are getting heavier and heavier. Hypnosis works. But I have to talk to somebody, meaning Pam the personal manager, because, basically, there is no one else. The problem, of course, is that Pam hates me. Not really, it's just that she doesn't get what there is between Brenda and me. I don't get it, either.

Brenda is so vague that she really doesn't function like the usual gal-pal. She's just there, at the heart of my universe. Just completely there, being perfect, like this dreamy force of nature the branding and marketing people have turned into the definition of beauty for a global audience. Without Benda having to do much of anything. Not anymore. Before I had my recent spell of wanderlust, we spent a lot of time hanging out together. Fooling around in the exercise room on the top floor of her house, talking about stuff. Sometimes we'd wander through this huge closet of hers, looking at all the fabulous things people send her. Marc Jacobs. Oscar de la Renta. Valentino. Every high-end designer on earth and Brenda thinks that's how it is. You have this huge closet on East Sixty-Third Street and people send you things.

Then, because you are so sweet, you send them a silver-lamé bagful of items from the BXR line of cosmetics. Plus a bottle of BXR, your perfume, this ultra-pricey bestseller and supposedly the essence of you, Brenda Xavier Rawlings, the most gorgeous creature in the history of the world. Eat your heart out, Cleopatra. Not to mention Helen of Troy and Gisele Bündchen, who actually is not all that beautiful. Very striking, no doubt, but I've heard guys say that Gisele looks like a guy.

Of course, there could be advantages to looking like a guy. Or being one, because that might make it easier to deal with this Sergei person—that's his name, Sergei Propokoff—the one who's been calling Brenda, telling her he's going to have her killed. Or maybe this is one of those rare cases where gender doesn't matter. I mean, male or female, what am I going to do? Shoot him? I don't believe in violence, though maybe I would if I knew I could get away with it.

Which I could if I could be, like, male for a day and then switch back, so I'm thinking, OK, I'm a girl and then I turn into a boy and do all this boy stuff, like acquire a gun and shoot Sergei in the head, and then I turn back into a girl. The perpetrator is untraceable, even with DNA. Especially with DNA. The perfect crime. But why stop there? If you could switch back and forth, you could do whatever you wanted. Live the perfect life.

Aside from worrying about Brenda and Sergei, my main problem is my career. I mean, I did have one, not all that long ago. I had gotten beyond the beginner's luck stage and it felt like I was developing something solid. The magazine people liked me. At *Harper's Bazaar*, especially. I did a lot of editorial work for them, meaning my picture was appearing in their big feature spreads. Also in *W* and *Allure* and *Marie Claire* and a little at Italian *Vogue*, which went nuts about this photographer, Ian Vrdolyak, who had a thing for the American tomboy. That's my look. Not that I'm not curvy and girly when I want to be, like I was on Ibiza, it's just that I'm five-ten and I have this boy-next-door thing I can do on cue. Athletic stances, very straight-on, with my strong jaw looking very strong indeed and this gaze of mine—very level, very intense. Works every time.

Anyway, all that editorial exposure led to some pretty lucrative ad work. I got runway gigs, which kept me in the magazines, meaning the ad agencies were all the hotter for me. And so that's how it worked, a big, swirly circle of success, and eventually, nice surprise, I realized that I had accumulated quite a bit of loot. Not megabucks, like Brenda, but enough to take a breather.

That was over a year ago. Early summer in Manhattan, one of those unsweaty days which get you to walk around and look at things. Buildings. Even trees, in Herald Square, and guys in running shorts with those dorky Bluetooth things in their ears. Not that I remember any one day in particular. Or any one guy. Just the nice feeling of that time, when I decided I wouldn't be returning my booker's calls for a while. I was rethinking things, especially my sad little secret, which is that I'm not crazy about the modeling biz. It's too much like work.

So I dropped in at the agency and said a quick good-bye to my booker, the highly professional Abigail Worringer. Who was slightly flabbergasted. Then I sublet my place on West Twenty-Eighth and went to Europe and now I'm back here. As little as possible. It's basically a dump, OK for sleeping and showering and getting out the door in the morning. I never bothered too much with furniture, so the main features are my king-size bed and some dumbbells and a great big Pilates ball. A full-length mirror against the wall. Every girl should have one. Plus my prize possession, an all-stainless-steel coffee maker from Sweden.

Oh, and a couple of Katy Perry CDs left by my ex-tenant, this really nice guy who was always late with the rent. I never listen to them because, one, I'm not a Katy Perry fan—when is she going to stop acting sexy and just be sexy?—and, two, I don't have a CD player. I don't even have a TV, just a bunch of DVDs left over from when I did have one. Because everywhere you go in the fashion world, music is blasting and video images come at you, non-stop, like some kind of glitch in the optic nerve. By the time I was nineteen I had had enough of all that to last me a lifetime.

Except that tonight I'm going to be happily planted in front of this flat screen the size of a Ping-Pong table and it'll be great because I'll be with Brenda, watching whatever movie her people pick for her. She likes Olivia Wilde and Drew Barrymore. She likes Zac Efron. Anything pretty and cute and non-violent is fine with Brenda. For her, movies are the backdrop, she's the feature attraction, and we won't really be watching, we'll just be talking.

About clothes, mostly, and travel and after a while it'll be time for dessert, also known as the main course, that strawberry-rhubarb-mascarpone extravaganza she'll have sent over from JoJo, ultra-yummy, and we'll slurp some of the fizzy stuff ... or I will, because Brenda hardly ever touches booze of any variety. With or without it she gets sleepy, and maybe I'll help Rosalie the house-keeper tuck her in. Or maybe not.

Either way, it will be a lovely evening, a sweet interlude, just the way we planned it this afternoon, while Brenda was getting made up for a shoot. I was lying on my bed, the cell phone next to me on speaker, silently screaming at Abigail, my booker, return my call, you useless cow, I have to start making the rounds, but don't get back to me right now, at this very moment, while I'm still talking to Brenda. Arranging for something to look forward to.

Which is great. Because it always is. Except this time. About two minutes into the movie, she decided to tell me about Sergei. Why he wants to kill her.

His driver had picked her up, taken her over to his place. I ask her if it wouldn't have made more sense for him to show up here, at her house. She says, um, well, yes, but sometimes she meets her escort somewhere else. Which I don't quite get. It seems to depend on Mike the security guy's assessment of the paparazzi situation but, whatever, he and Pam the personal manager take care of all that. OK, so now I ask where Sergei's apartment is and she says it's on Park Avenue, somewhere in the seventies, she doesn't exactly know. Because why should she, the driver knows, so there she is, sitting in Sergei's living room, all alone. All dressed up. They're supposed to be going out. A reception at the American Wing of the Met. She's bored, just wandering around, and she opens a door and there's Sergei. Sitting at this big, shiny desk.

Across the desk from Sergei is somebody Brenda has never seen before and has never seen since. She has no idea who he is. She doesn't care who he is. Because if she doesn't know who he is, he's nobody, he doesn't exist. So why should she care? This is how Brenda's world works. But Sergei lives in a different world. Sergei is upset. Now that Brenda saw him with this other guy, Brenda has to be killed.

"So Sergei was steamed."

"He was furious, Fiona … screaming at me. I ran into one of the bedrooms and closed the door—"

"Did he try to get in?"

"No, and when I came out he was fine. We just went to the Met. Everything was fine."

"Fine?"

"You know …"

"Did he ever say anything about it later?"

"Um, no … just that I shouldn't have seen that."

"What about killing you?"

"What? Oh, um … that started a little later. I decided I didn't want to see him for a while and then he started calling all the time."

"Saying he was going to have you killed?"

"Yes."

Brenda looked up. An assistant to one of Pam's many assistants was standing in the doorway with a tray. Two servings of the eagerly awaited mascarpone thing and two flutes of champagne. Lowering it onto the coffee table, she kept her eyes lowered, like Brenda was this light you shouldn't look at too directly.

I watched the girl leaving, her awkward stride, so adorable, then I took a sip of champagne. Brenda sat there, facing the screen, not seeing it, even though there was this close-up of Olivia Wilde … then Olivia was kissing Ryan Reynolds … still nothing … I took one of Brenda's hands and she looked over at me. I didn't say anything but she knew what I meant, which in this case was the obvious. Don't worry, sweetie, everything's going to be all right. Just perfect. The way it always is. Because of who you are.

This morning, around dawn, it was raining and I was listening to it without actually waking up, then I fell back into a really deep sleep, it's one of my talents, so I was feeling totally wired when I headed out the door for an early meeting with Abigail from the agency, who wasn't just flabbergasted, she was seriously pissed when I took off a year ago, but is actually kind of nice to me when I show up. On time, I might add, and looking so fresh. My new go-getter attitude toward my career is having a great effect on my aura, I'm giving off all kinds of lovely vibes, if I do say so myself, having seen a really terrific version of Fiona in the huge mirror behind the receptionist as I waltzed in and announced myself.

Now Abigail is sitting at her desk, letting me stand, telling me my look-book is a perfect shambles. But not to worry, Fred is going to help me get it together.

"Fred?"

"Fred Galimberti, Fiona. Our media resource coordinator?" She tilts her head to one side and gives me this kind of laser stare, meaning, come on, Fiona, surely you've memorized our entire personnel directory.

Actually, I do remember Fred Galimberti, so I say, "Right. Fred. He took over from that other guy, the one who flipped out and took you hostage that time and—"

"Fiona. Please. This is serious. Fred is serious. And he has assured me he's very much looking forward to working with you."

"Terrific."

Really terrific, but first there is something we have to take care of, according to Abigail, who takes me by the wrist, like I'm six years old, and drags me past all the desks and light tables and all these screens crawling with news and some talk show and of course the fashion channel.

Along the way, I'm saying hi to secretaries and bookers and publicists and assistant publicists and people who do the sort of tech stuff that bores me to tears. They're all saying hi, telling me how great I look, and I bounce it right back, not skipping a beat, you too, great to see you, what's up … great to see you … you too … blah-blah-blah … Cora Burke is not one of the major agencies, but it has always been hot, always humming along on adrenaline and all the mad New Yorky energy that barges in through the wall of windows on the north side of the office.

I avoid a heap of boxes filled with who knows what, and who cares, and suddenly I'm alone in a dressing room with Abigail the over-size cow. The gigantic cow. She has put on quite a bit of weight over the past few years. Over the past decade or so, I imagine, ever since the modeling biz put her out to pasture. Which still pisses her off, so she hates me, hates all her girls, those scrawny cunts … of course, it's not true hatred, just total resentment.

Because she really loves all her girls, loves the whole idea of modeling, dealing with the photographers and designers and groupies and fans and the money people and the media and, above all, the girls. Not that she has ever been all that crazy about dealing with me and now she's telling me to strip.

Hunh?

"Fiona. Darling. If I'm going to put you up for this job, I have to know that you're in good shape."

"Are you kidding me?"

"Fiona. Just get undressed. This minute."

What bullshit. A second ago I was basking in the general warmth and now I'm being barked at, like those recruits in *Full Metal Jacket*. But … whatever … so I step out of my flats. I slip out of my summery dress, one of Ralph Lauren's true inspirations, and stand there, my arms crossed over my chest. Glaring at Abigail. She glares back and points at my chest with a quick jerk of her chin. Meaning show me your breasts.

Umm. OK.

So I unhook my bra and stand there, feet apart, hands on hips. Like those big, defiant broads in those great photos by Helmut Newton. Those big, defiant broads with big, defiant tits. Talk about genius! Helmut Newton figured out how to show how sexy they are, those lovely big slightly saggy tits. You grab one and it fills up your hand. To really hold it you need two hands … not that my tits are like that.

I cover them with my arms and glare some more at the cow. She grabs my wrist again, yanking me in her direction. Now she's inspecting my arm, like I'm one of those ninety-eight-pound imports from Slovakia or somewhere and she's going to find needle tracks. Which of course she doesn't and so, after a squint at my other arm, she says, "Show me your behind."

Oh, come on! This is total harassment, so I figure it's time for me to harass her. Instead of turning around, so she can scope out my butt, I begin to take off my panties, slowly, to this frantic chorus of no, no, really, it's not necessary, you really don't have to do that, Fiona.

Oh, but I do, because ever since I got back to town I have been going to the gym, religiously, the one over on the Chelsea Piers, and giving a lot of really special attention to my butt. Lunges, squats, lots of time on the glute machine. Meaning, this particular feature of my anatomy—which has been perfect ever since I was twelve—is now, at this very moment, more perfect than ever. So I'm thinking that Abigail, whose butt I'll bet was never perfect, really ought to get a high-focus, up-close look at this perfection of mine.

So I'm naked, facing away from her, arching my back. Like, here it is. Pretty amazing, right? Abigail takes off in a hurry, muttering about updating my contact information. Which I will do. In a moment. But there is something I want to do first.

Turning around, I look back over my shoulder. And down. At the mirror image of my well-maintained butt. My lovely ass. And guess what, it is. It really is … it is really and truly perfect.

If I didn't love Brenda so much I'd be maybe just a little bit annoyed that she made me her exclusive confidante on the subject of people who want to kill her. Of course that's why she did it, because I love her so much and she knows it in her strange Brenda way. Never in a million years would she have thought of telling anyone else about the Sergei problem. So now it's time to tell Pam the personal manager, and I really don't want to. Let sleeping dogs open their own can of worms.

Just kidding. I obviously have to do it and I know Pam is going to hate me all the more when she realizes, like, all she does for Brenda and Brenda still doesn't confide in her. She confides in that flaky Fiona person.

Pam is a good-looking thirty-five-year-old with straight black hair. Pam never smiles. Pam carries a clipboard and wears charcoal-gray suits. Not pantsuits, skirt suits. With hems way too high, making me think of those porn scenes that take place in an office setting. The babe in the charcoal gray skirt suit appears at the door. Do you have a moment, Mr. Long? There are a few things I'd like you to examine. How do I even know about the office scenario? Because of this shithead ex of mine. He was a defense attorney and I was starting to click, getting my first six-page spread in a major mag. *Harper's Bazaar*, not that it matters. Or mattered to my shithead ex.

He would sit and watch porn, like this is what guys do. The girlfriend, namely, me, walks in and he keeps on watching. Fortunately, I was so busy I hardly ever saw him. Which was his big excuse for running around on me non-stop. Another thing that guys do. What a jerk. Anyway, I think of him whenever I see Pam with all that thigh showing. Like she's about to bend over a desk and hitch her skirt up.

So. It's morning, a new day ... time to tackle the Sergei conundrum ... in other words, the Pam problem ...

Saved by the call-back. It's Abigail, and she's telling me I have a go-see tomorrow at ten-thirty. So, do I want to commit? That's how Abigail talks when she wants to let you know that she has her doubts about you. Do I want to commit to this appointment? I'm, like, sure. Absolutely.

"So that's a definite yes?"

I take a deep breath, to put a little distance between me and the impulse to scream, of course it's a yes, you fucking moron. Another deep breath and I say, "Yes. It is. Definitely. It's a definite yes."

"Great, Fiona. Very good."

So I give her a really sweet thank you. Thank you so much, Abigail, good-bye, I'll be there, ten-thirty sharp. Then I sit there, thinking. Should I call Pam? Or just show up?

I just show up and Pam is not only no problem, she is actually nice. Leading me into her office on the ground floor of Brenda's place, this zone of ruthless efficiency. As I sit down in the chair beside her desk, she asks me if I'd like coffee. Maybe a croissant?

"Mm, sounds good."

Pam nods to the girl who has been hovering at the door—an assistant-assistant, a sweet girl in creamy linen slacks. About a

minute later she's back with a tray featuring coffee in a Wedg-
wood pot, a matching cup, a plate with two croissants, butter,
blackberry jam. The silverware looks kind of Rococo, like Pam
had some other assistant borrow it from the design collection at
the Metropolitan Museum of Art. This is not exactly a shock. The
whole place is filled with museum-quality stuff.

My plan, of course, was to skip breakfast but I can't help
myself, I'm drowning a croissant in jam and realizing that Pam
is not just being nice. She's appreciative and not at all snotty or
defensive when I tell her about Sergei's phone calls, the death
threats, how scared Brenda is. Pam stares at her clipboard for a
while, her lips pursed, then she nods, saying, "I'm so glad you
came forward with this, Fiona. It's not always easy to know what's
going on with Brenda, and that can be frustrating. As I'm sure you
can imagine. And I'm sure you understand that, based on what
you have told me, we could have something of real magnitude to
deal with here."

I'm tempted to ask Pam how she could let a nasty customer
like Sergei get anywhere near Brenda, but I don't. I ask her who
he is and now she does get a bit defensive, launching this big
justification of herself and the entire organization, Brenda Xavier
Rawlings Incorporated, telling me that all this is a terrible surprise, a number of well-placed people spoke very highly of Mr.
Propokoff, there were follow-up enquiries, as with all of Brenda's
prospective escorts, and evidently he is quite prominent in public
affairs.

Meaning what? He gets his picture in the back of *W* magazine,
one of those shots of people at a charity event? Like that's supposed to prove something, a photo of this guy with a paralyzed
grin, his arm around a supermodel.

I am trying like mad not to come across as judgmental, but
Pam realizes I'm not buying her story, so she smooths her skirt for

a while and then looks up, saying, "Brenda's career is important, of course, but her welfare is the prime concern. We have a no-risk policy. Any sign of trouble and we circle the wagons."

Like the wagons aren't circled already, on a daily basis, business as usual. But I guess you can always circle them tighter. Or get more wagons. Anyway, Pam is beginning to repeat herself, telling me that any threat, no matter how small is taken with the utmost seriousness.

And I guess I must be this super-empathic person, just loaded with those mirror neurons I've been reading about, because Pam's monologue is going around and around, in these really boring circles, and my thoughts are doing the same thing, going around and around and around, telling me this is a truly fucked-up situation, no one is going to do anything, but something has to be done. So I have to do it.

And I don't have the slightest idea of what to do, but it better be something, because, as I may have mentioned, this is a truly fucked up situation, no one is going to do anything, and so on and so forth, over and over, and then Pam is asking me if I'd like to go upstairs, say hi to Brenda for a moment, which of course I did, that's kind of a given, and now I'm semi-running over to Fifth, got to get a cab, I'm late for my hair dresser, who is a fanatic about punctuality.

So this is terrific, right? I'm getting back to work and already I'm behaving like it's amateur night, Fiona the Airhead just sort of winging it. Not a good policy when your hairdresser is this gay woman who makes a big professional point of being immune to flirtation, meaning it's great when I turn up at her salon on Ninth Avenue, this shrine to stainless steel and clear nail polish, and it turns out that she's running late for once. Which doesn't mean anything, I know, but I decide to consider it a good omen.

It's bedtime, my hair looks fabulous, and I'm brushing my teeth, feeling these sweet waves of nostalgia for my year of living irresponsibly, flying into Florence with a bunch of phone numbers and getting hooked into this expat party circuit—not Americans but Brits, and not all fashion types, thank god.

There was this one guy, not English, actually, but Irish, Jack Halloran, a painter, and really so sweet. And good-looking. An Irish Al Pacino, if you know what I mean, with a studio in Umbria. Unbelievably charming, except for the road you had to take to get up the hill to the farmhouse-slash-studio. Pothole city, like Manhattan.

Anyway, once you got there, it was beautiful, scads of flowering vines, the golden dusk descending on the vineyards on the far side of the valley—travelogue stuff, which made it all the easier to play the artist's wife in Italy. It's a great role, highly recommended, though Jack wasn't much of a painter. All his energy went into fucking me, much to my delight, then it turned out that he was broke, no career at all.

So I helped him out and took off for Prague. For years and years, people had been telling me, oh, Fiona, Prague is such a beautiful city. You just have to see it. OK, terrific, let's get that out of the way. Which I did and, guess what, Prague really is a beautiful city. Then I wandered around on the Dalmatian coast for a while, checking out the undiscovered treasures of former Yugoslavia, and that was great. Then Greek island hopping, hop, hop, hop, then Kitzbühel, Venice in the dead of winter, really wonderful, then Normandy, very bleak and astounding. These huge tilted surfaces of wet sand. Like slabs of light. Then down to Provence, for a few weeks in a deserted pension.

Kind of a mindless itinerary, when I think back on it. Of course, I met tons of interesting people, but a lot of the time I was alone, seeing the sights or in my room, reading, which I love to do. And I would talk to Brenda on the phone every few days. I'd get her to tell me about her latest night on the town, always a major media event. Then she'd get me to tell her about the sights I'd been seeing. She loved to hear about that. But the stuff I was reading, not so much.

A couple of months ago, I zipped over from Provence to the Costa del Sol. More expat Brits and the realization that I was running low on money. There was this one evening on a terrace in Torremolinos when the Mediterranean charm of the harbor just wasn't doing it for me. I was getting even less help from my glass of Rioja. One sip and I felt hung-over. I must have been projecting a ton of doom and gloom, because suddenly a slim man in a lightweight blazer was looming up out of nowhere and asking me if everything was all right.

I said, no, not exactly, and he sat down at my table, saying, maybe he could help. And giving me this dazzling smile. He was handsome, mid-forties, and, long story short, we started pretending we were soul mates or something. It was easy, we liked each other in bed, and after a while he took a flight to Miami he had been mentioning at carefully spaced intervals. Just so I wouldn't get too used to the situation.

No chance of that, of course, the guy's conversation bored me silly after about three minutes. All this stuff about the people he had working for him in Florida, rewriting the zoning laws so this huge swamp could turn into a golf course complete with yoga and sushi … a team of plastic surgeons hot off the plane from Rio … whatever, this was his major obsession so naturally I'm also fascinated. Let's just take that for granted, right?

One good thing about blank men, they're so easy to replace. Before I knew it I was on Ibiza with the guy with the average dick and that was fun. But I was tired of missing Brenda. All the time. This constant ache. Our phone calls were nice but I missed her presence. Being in her presence. So it turned out that those threats from Sergei got me back to New York, meaning, I could see Brenda again. And start leaving messages with Abigail at the agency. Then there was all that wondering if and when the horrendous cow would ever get back to me. And feeling abandoned, even though I deserved it. I guess.

I mean, I had abandoned Abigail, right? Quite the fucked-up dynamic. Anyway, after she did get back to me I was heaving sighs of relief for about a week or so, telling myself I am now this brand-new person. Because of all these resolutions I started to make the moment I realized I actually did have a future.

Like, for example, I've been swearing to myself since I was eighteen that I would never to go to bed with anyone who wasn't at least eighteen. Then, last fall, when I was in Kitzbühel, I spent an afternoon with this beautiful blond who turned out to be sixteen. Yikes! I mean, she was taller than me, her tits were bigger. And, oh my god! Those hips! Those thighs! Also, she knew what she was doing. I guess I should have asked her for ID. Anyway, it was so sweet, up in the mountains, in this built-in bed … under the duvet … these bright yellow leaves sailing by the window like mad, for hours and hours. All afternoon.

Then it was evening and she told me her age, sort of bragging, but also hoping I wouldn't be pissed off, which I wasn't, not really, I forgave her and myself, too, because there really was no way to know. She was quite the grown-up, ready to go drinking in the dance halls at the big hotels. Which we did, getting hit on by wave after wave of males. Males of all ages. All shapes and sizes and every last one of them unsuitable. Until, in the third place we went, the fabulous Goldener Greif, there were these three ski instructors in training, really dreamy and, I don't know, virginal, unlike my new friend Gaby.

Anyway, we danced with them for a while and drank some more of this Alpine specialty, which you usually only get around Christmas-time but I guess this was Christmas in July because there we were, swilling it down, gallons of red vino essentially just ruined by cloves and honey and all sorts of stuff, and the rest is too blurry to be history. It's more like this wild, shadowy legend of getting lost in a labyrinth of bodies and eventually finding the treasure. Total satisfaction.

The moral of the story? You can pardon yourself for breaking a resolution when you don't know the facts. Like, Gaby looked about twenty-three. But when you do know the facts, there's no excuse, and if you do break your resolution you're just a weak, feeble person with no principles. No integrity. No nothing, which is how I felt, a total nothing, sitting on my bed and working myself up to put in a call to the office of my porn-loving ex—the one Pam's hemline reminds me of.

So I suppose I owe Pam's hemline a big thank-you for inspiring the bright idea of calling this shithead. After swearing that I would never talk to him again. Not ever. Not under any circumstances. So how could I even think of calling him? I mean, I knew the facts. Who he was. What he was. I knew everything about him, including the fact that he is the sort of person I should never have gotten mixed up with in the first place. Much less now.

So. To get back to the burning question, how could I be thinking of calling this jerk? Because of Brenda. Needless to say. Or it's because of Pam the personal manager and Sylvia the publicist and Ronnie the lawyer and Mike the security guy and the guy on the nightshift and the entire brigade of Brenda's people, who were doing, basically, nothing. I couldn't stand it.

Brenda had been so happy to see me when I went up to her room the other morning ... we talked about clothes, what Andrea Gil's new collection would be like ... she dedicated her spring line to Brenda, an unprecedented gesture, as everybody kept saying and saying. Then we went off on the subject of hair conditioner ... the usual stuff. But she was scared. I could feel it and, as I said, I couldn't stand it. There was a terrible Sergei problem and the brilliant solution of Brenda Xavier Rawlings Supermodel Inc., this well-oiled machine, was to go into hibernation. Stick its head in the sand and hope for the best. I really had to do something.

So here I was, leaving a message for my ex. Bennett Ross. Defense attorney extraordinaire and world-class dickhead. He got back to me in forty-five minutes. His voice was too loud, as usual, but his attitude was surprising. Almost bearable.

"Great to hear from you, Fiona ... Dinner? Sure. Who's paying? ... Whoa, hold on, babe. My idea of a joke ... Oh, come on, not JoJo again. You're stuck in a rut. How about Daniel? Pricey enough for you? ... Great. I'll make the reservation. See you then." Then being tomorrow evening at nine-thirty. Defense attorneys work late.

He showed up in his courtroom uniform, a Martin Greenfield suit, ten grand at a minimum, this bald-headed guy with a slightly phony tan and a good physique. I was wearing sandals and tight jeans and this really luxurious Dolce & Gabbana top made of light blue silk, my color right on the nose, with a bunch of buttons open and no bra. Meaning, I made a big point of leaning forward a lot more than I had to as I was sitting down. Thinking once again how you always can tell if a guy is ogling you even if you're not watching his face. Which I wasn't, at that moment. I was being demure.

He told me how great I was looking, so I said, you too. Then he started right in, taking up right where we left off, three years ago, asking me if I was still munching mass quantities of pussy.

"Bennett," I said, "don't give me this shit. Like I should feel bad about liking girls. You loved that. You tried to get in on it, you stupid prick. Sometimes I think the reason we broke up is that none of my girlfriends could stand you."

"We broke up, Fiona, because you were a compulsive shopper. Your career was taking off like gangbusters and you still managed to spend three or four times more than you were making. Which was quite a feat."

"Tough on the old wallet, right?"

"I could afford it. I could've afforded alimony. Which you didn't need. Supposedly."

"Supposedly?"

"Is that what this is about? You need money?"

"Fuck you, Bennett."

At that point, the waiter stopped by. Bennett grabbed the wine list and, all serious and decisive, ordered a bottle of St. Emilion. After which, he told me how much it cost. Nearly three-hundred bucks, adding, "You were a luxury I could easily afford. Babe."

"Along with all the other babes."

"Oh, like, I'm supposed to be faithful while you're downtown, setting world records for god knows what."

"You knew what, Bennett. It made your mouth water."

Suddenly, he laughed. It wasn't a mean laugh. Or a dumb laugh. It was borderline friendly. Another surprise. I smiled and leaned forward a bit.

"So," he said. "What is this really about?"

"I want to ask you a favor."

"No shit. What I meant was, what is the favor you want to ask me?"

"Right. Well. I want you to introduce me to somebody."

"Ah. OK. That's the quid. What's the quo? What you're going to do for me?"

"Guess."

"You're going to blow me."

"Uh …"

"Look. Fiona. Who am I supposed to introduce you to?"

"Somebody who can tell me all about Russians. Russian gangsters. Like, one of your cop friends."

"Shit. I can't believe this, Fiona. For Christ's sake. Don't tell me anything more. And let me tell you something. Forget about my cop friends. Cops don't talk to civilians."

"I'll blow the guy."

"Very amusing, Fiona. You were always a genuine wit. And now I'm going to be your pimp." He leaned back in his chair and looked into my eyes. Then he got this big grin on his face, saying, "This is about Brenda. Right?"

I kept my face blank. A useless move. Or a useless non-move. Because not only was he right on target, he knew it.

"OK," he said. "It's about Brenda. Which is great in a way. Because I know how you feel about the beautiful Brenda. So here is the deal. I'll introduce you to someone in the District Attorney's office. I know just the guy. Very nice, very bright. I'll introduce you to anyone you want, provided he's not a cop. The Dalai Lama. Spongebob Squarepants—"

"Spongebob Squarepants?"

"He's a cartoon character on TV. I'm seeing this woman with kids, they—never mind. What I'm saying is, I'll introduce you to Smokey the Bear, if that's what you want. Thomas the Locomotive. Anybody. All you have to do is this one thing."

He paused, staring at me, slightly bug-eyed.

"What, Bennett? What am I going to do?"

"You're going to get me a date with Brenda."

I almost choked on my wine. A date with Brenda? This total creep? Never happen, not in a zillion years.

So I said, "Sure, Bennett. No problem. I'll get right on it. First thing tomorrow morning."

First thing tomorrow morning is an appointment in the West Thirties, a cattle call. Which is usually a pretty well organized event, like hanging around the DMV, waiting for someone to acknowledge your existence, except a touch more glamorous. But this one is like rush hour reserved for cute girls, and just as hectic as the subway kind, meaning there's all this crowding and jostling and, actually, it's worse.

Because in the subway, which I never take unless I'm end-of-the-world desperate, you can sort of keep to yourself, but here I have to deal with the casting director and her amazingly pretentious assistants and a bunch of people I have no idea what their function is, and I'm having to balance my book on my knee and flip through it without losing my balance because there's no place to spread it out, what a total goat fuck … a phrase I got from Mike the security guy, who happens to be an ex-military type, so he has all this lingo left over from when he had a serious job. Like, AFI, another fucking inconvenience, and BFO, meaning a blinding flash of the obvious, something he gets from Pam on a regular basis. Then there's my favorite, oxygen thief, which is someone who just stands around and uses up air, like fifty percent of the girls on Brenda's staff. Fifty percent at a minimum.

Anyway, the whole experience was really crazy but worth it because they were casting for a show, and one of the pretentious assistants got all pleasant all of a sudden and took my comp card and my info and gave my arm this encouraging little pat-pat-pat, like I'm a total beginner in need of encouragement. Which was all right … great, actually, because it means I'm coming across as one of the new kids on the block, fresh meat, a girl with prospects, and then I'm on to my first real gig since I got back.

It's a shoot in this huge studio on North Moore Street, down in Tribeca, and there are seven of us girls and we're supposed to be standing on these pedestals. Not even elegant ones with lots of fancy detail, just these blocky white things, like in an art gallery. And very tall, so we need a ladder to get up there and of course there isn't a single ladder, one of the gofers is looking for the super or the engineer or maybe Mandrake the Magician, anybody who can come up with a bunch of ladders.

In the meantime, the stylist is explaining to us that this is not the daily grind, this is classy and exclusive and possibly even culturally significant. Even though it's catalog work. Because the client is trying something new, making their very best stuff available only to a very high-end segment of their mailing list, an upper percentile of an upper percentile, and I'm, like, great, let's just fucking do it, but there are no ladders on the horizon, which is really not great, it's giving the stylist this huge opportunity to let us know that she thinks of herself as an *artiste* of some sort.

A creative type, in a cashmere turtleneck and super-skinny jeans, who no doubt cries herself to sleep every night because she's not styling all these shoots for *Vogue* or something. Maybe *Marie Claire*, which she would settle for in a flash, and now she's saying all this stuff about the elegance and refinement of Sally Verstraaten, the designer whose things we're going to be wearing, and how Sally's inspirations will impart those qualities to us if our hearts are really in it. Oh, and the importance of being soigné.

That's her big word. Soigné, which is a nice enough word, but it's all so embarrassing. I mean, these girls know how they're supposed to be in front of the camera, but they're patient with all this bullshit. Because that is also part of how we are supposed to be. Nice and patient with the daily bullshit.

After the stylist finally shuts up and there are still no ladders, I go over to this table and get some coffee and suddenly I'm face-to-face with the photographer, this very young guy with a ridiculous haircut. Like, an uptown version of a neo-hippy non-haircut, and he's wearing a suede jacket with fringe about a yard long. Jeans and cowboy boots with silver toes. Before I can say anything, he introduces himself. Trevor Vrdolyak.

The brother of Ian Vrdolyak, my favorite photographer. I tell him he doesn't look anything like his brother Ian. Which he doesn't, and this gets his attention. He says something about a complicated family history.

"But," he goes on, "I suppose all family histories are complicated."

I say, "Not mine. My family history is simple. My parents were horrible, they abandoned me, and I turned out very badly."

"Right. You became a fashion model."

"Right." We're both smiling, not coming on to each other. Just smiling. Which is pleasant.

Suddenly he gets this look on his face, like, I'm a genius, I just got a dazzling idea, and he's saying, "Hold on. I love Sally but she did only one great piece this year, an evening dress with a puffed skirt, and now that I'm seeing you I realize we've got to get you some very high heels and into this dress. We were thinking of it for this other girl, in fact she's been fitted for it, but why make a decision unless you're ready to ignore it. Right?"

I smile like he's witty beyond words, I mean, he really is nice and it is also very nice to see the dress he's thinking of putting me in, a pinkish-ocher number in silk, with this skirt, flounced and not all that short, so it's not going to show as much of my legs as I'd like. But it has a tight bodice and it is nice, nicer, nicest, just nice to the nth degree, to have this delicious girl looking after me now, getting me hot as she fits me into the dress.

Which is definitely the best thing in this collection, like a second skin, and when the girl, Janie, gets done with it, you can almost see my girl-abs. And I'm thinking, Janie may or may not be into girls but she is definitely into clothes for girls. Then a whole bunch of ladders show up and Janie is giving me this sweet smile and hug, and I'm wondering, maybe girls and clothes for girls are the same thing for some girls.

Like, for Janie, clothes for girls is sex, even if she doesn't know it, but it's sex for just one part of her brain. The other part, which she does know about, is straight, so she has a husband, he's a stock broker or a guitar player or whatever, and everything is nicely compartmentalized. Which I can imagine, but, as Trevor screws around with his light meter, I'm imagining it in this completely theoretical way. I cannot feel what that would be like, I am so non-compartmentalized myself, and I try, I really do, but there are some things I really, truly do not get.

So I'm climbing up this ladder wearing heels, because they've told us a million times it would be too risky to try to put on our shoes once we get up there, and the whole concept of this shoot is becoming slightly tedious, not to mention obvious, like I'm going to be a stand-in for a statue, which is a stand-in for a living, breathing human being, which I also am, except I'm feeling pretty inhuman up here on my pedestal. Sort of like a Christmas tree ornament that Trevor keeps moving from one pedestal to the next.

Between pedestals, I'm drinking coffee and not even looking at the big plates of millefeuille and other gooey and-slash-or flaky stuff that no one is going to eat, it's there to test our will power.

Which I have plenty of, at this point, I'm not even overdoing the caffeine. I'm just standing around and giving off the right vibe, I guess, because this woman comes up to me, and pretty soon we're talking about the movies.

She loves Halle Berry and so do I, more as a precaution than anything else. I mean, we're all going to be in our forties some time, so why not love a totally tuned-up babe of that vintage? Actually, this woman is already there, looking great, and confident enough to dress down. Not in black but some dark non-color. Shapeless slacks on a shapely bod, a button-up sweater, like somebody's idea of a librarian. And the sweater a touch too tight … lovely big breasts … now she's giving me her card …

Hmm … Angela Auerbach, a booker from Alliance, saying she'd love to go over my pictures with me some time, maybe we should talk. Then she asks me how Abigail has been. I say, fine, and she says she and Abigail go way back, a lovely person, so professional … and of course she's not into poaching talent from other agencies, but … . but what? She's not into it but she does it anyway, she can't help herself? Like it's this weird compulsion … Only I don't say this, just think it, because the compulsion is not all that weird. The modeling biz is musical chairs.

If you want it to be, which I don't. Abigail is a horrendous cow but Cora Burke is the perfect agency for me, and so it's one thing to gripe about it all with the other girls, like dishing your teachers when you're a kid, but it's another thing to do the big public number of hopping from one agency to the next. Not me. Never happen, not unless I decide to get truly ambitious about my career. Which I can't do because, if I did, it wouldn't be me doing it. It would be this sort of Invasion-of-the-Body-Snatchers version of Fiona …

Anyway, Angela must know something about me, my circle of acquaintances, because she gets onto the subject of Brenda, but only for a second. She doesn't want to come across as a ditzy fangirl. Then she talks about her cousin's place in Aspen and a recent jaunt to Venice … I tell her I love Venice in the winter and suddenly she grabs my forearm and looks into my eyes, telling me, yes, absolutely, Venice is so exquisite then.

A moment later she's gone and this very sweet makeup girl is dabbing away at my face and one of the photographer's people is yanking on my arm. Time to get up on my new pedestal. It's higher than the last one, a promotion, I guess, and this is it, finally, all the girls are in place, Trevor and his assistant mess around with the lighting for a while, then we get into our poses and the strobes start popping, like the camera is having one bright idea after the other.

The next thing you know, we're all done.

While it was happening I was thinking, this is so great, like, the camera is just so into me, it really loves me. Or maybe not, who knows, but at the very least I am the object of its latest crush. At the very, very least, and that's a nice thought to cling to while I wait for a ladder to get around to me. Thinking about Venice the whole time, it's February, the city is flooded with this lovely cold light. And I'm warm, glowing, really, from deep inside out, wherever I am, even walking in the Sestiere di Dorsoduro, the very edge of the city, it's drizzling, the Adriatic Sea or whatever it is is looking all mean and gray and frigid, and I'm still feeling warm …

I felt warm even on the one day it snowed, for about fifteen minutes, because of this guy or, I should say, a man, very male and very dignified. Very well formed, like a statue, who came alive for the sole purpose of taking me to bed for hours on end. Days on end, really … with everything beautifully staged, every moment, a wonderful feeling, and I've been wondering ever since exactly why I didn't like it. Or it's not that I didn't like it, I did, the warm feeling and the security, but I didn't want it. I was in Venice in winter for only three weeks but, the weird thing is, it felt like forever. Really, forever, and not in a good way. I felt just so happy and energized the day I left.

When I was up on one of my pedestals, there was this girl sort of glancing at me from this other pedestal, about as tall as mine, and she was my height, a touch skinnier. Not just another pretty face, a really pretty face, I mean, interesting, with a wide forehead. Slightly pointy chin. Actually, I noticed her when I first arrived, talked to her a little bit, while everyone was milling around getting organized. Afterward, when I was changing out of that gorgeous dress, she came over and introduced herself. Elise.

So it's nice to meet you, Elise, I'm Fiona, and we talked some more, about Trevor the photographer, like, does the fringe have to be that long? I mean, we get the point, and then we talked about our schedules, so hectic, and she told me her boyfriend didn't know anything about the biz. He's a financial type, which is nice but kind of dull, and well, anyway, nice to meet you, Fiona.

"You too," I said, then she told me she had a car waiting, which is wild, right? She usually has to slog around the city in cabs, but her boyfriend was splurging on her this week. Could she drop me anywhere when the shoot wraps?

"Sure. I have an appointment uptown. Near Thirty-Seventh and Ninth."

The moment we get into the car, Elise tells the driver to raise the privacy panel, which is non-see-through, then she leans back in the seat and sighs a big sigh and looks over at me. Gives me a totally charming smile. So I kiss her.

She's, like, "I'm not really into girls," but she lets me reach under her skirt. Which is really pretty, this great floral print, I'm holding her crotch, feeling her lips get big inside her panties, and she's breathing really hard against my neck, sort of kissing me there, but not quite ... and then she says it again.

"I'm not really into girls. This is just me being nice to you."

I sit back and look at her. "Being nice to me?"

"Yeah. I mean, you were so sweet, so why not?"

She gets a call and then I do, it's Abigail, and of course I should have checked in by now, see if there's anything new, which there isn't. So Abigail reminds me of my next appointment and then she starts telling me she's been hearing good things about me, she's so glad I'm buckling down. Staying on the straight and narrow. Which is bullshit, the part about hearing good things, she probably made that up, she's calling because she wants to deliver these veiled threats about how I'd better stay on the straight and narrow. Or else. Or else what? She'll really piss me off and I'll go back to Europe or something?

I hang up and there's a moment when I don't remember what Elise was saying, I'm remembering the edge in Abigail's voice, then I say to Elise, "I was so sweet?"

"Umm, well. Not aggressive or anything. Not at all, and some of the girls are so competitive, I mean ..."

"We're all competitive."

"Yeah, but ... anyway ... I thought you were nice ..." By now she's looking out the window, looking at her nails, looking at her phone. Scrolling through her messages. Her calendar. Whatever.

Her skirt is still way up on her thighs, so I reach for her again, and suddenly, she sits up, turns on the intercom and tells the driver to drive around for a while. Which he does, and she slips off her panties and I am doing her and doing her, she is so much fun and it is so great to have this power, control this one little button and you control a soul. Not that I'm a power freak. In fact, I'm getting her to the verge and I'm not thinking, aha, total domination. I'm thinking, who's going to do me? I mean, this is sweet, but, boo-hoo-hoo, when am I going to get off?

Then I'm thinking, never mind, this truly is sweet, the girl is so pretty and wet and she smells so great ... what an unexpected treat, I'm just really, really happy, she's beginning to twitch, and my phone rings.

With my free hand, I check the number. Brenda.

Elise is right at the top of her orgasm but I let her go, I can't help it, and then Brenda's not there when I answer. Which is ever so slightly spooky, then she's calling again, to say hello, maybe her manicurist didn't show up or something, and I'm asking her how she is and of course she says she's great, because even if she's upset about something she's not all that aware of it. It's like the weather, like, maybe you think it's a gloomy day but as far as the day itself is concerned it's just fine. Anyway, I can tell how Brenda feels, whatever she says, and today what she says is true. She actually is feeling great. So that's great.

Ringing off, I slip my phone in my bag and reach for Elise. She raises a leg, to block me, saying, "What?"

"This is just me being nice to you. I mean, we got interrupted and I thought we should finish."

"I finished by myself." Which could have been snotty, but wasn't. She was really nice about it, smiling at me in this understanding way, like, we all lead such busy lives, multi-tasking from morning to night, who hasn't had to step in and take over right in the middle of getting off? Such a sweet attitude. I leaned over and kissed her on the cheek.

She kissed me back, on the lips, and we got back into it, lots of tongue action, then she said, "Oh my god, what time is it? I had another booking, oh god, where are my panties..."

Which she found and slipped into with this elegant sort of porpoise-y motion, and then she was scrabbling in her bag and finding her card and giving it to me and exiting the limo with her bag and her book and her phone and everything else and saying, all breathless and happy, "Just tell the driver where you want to go. Let's stay in touch, I mean it, really, really mean it, I really do, good-bye."

My general impression was that she really did mean it. But maybe only the way you really, really mean things right after you've orgasmed and the world feels like it was designed with you expressly in mind.

So I'm back on the old roller-coaster, hitting the heights with Elise, then down in the depths, really deep ones, a bunch of unbelievably boring appointments, waiting around for hours so one set of eyes after another could glaze over at the very sight of me. Next, I'm rushing back to the agency so Abigail can bore me some more, telling me I should have showed up a couple of days ago, there is a reason for paperwork, it's not something to ignore, then she puts me in this cubicle and gives me a copy of my new contract. Which is just my old contract, as far as I can tell. Maybe I should show it to my lawyer. Except that I don't have a lawyer. And don't feel like getting one. So this is Fiona the Ditz, going through the motions, on the assumption that the Cora Burke Agency is a reputable outfit, never had any serious complaints, where do I sign?

Here, obviously, at the end, where it says "Signature." Pretty sure I got that right. When I bring the contract over to Abigail, she's on the phone, getting all frantic, waving her free hand around, meaning, I guess, that she wants me to wait until she's done with this call. Which I do, and about ten minutes later she's telling me that really I have to make an appointment with Fred Galimberti, who is going to help me get my book organized.

Now she's saying, "Let's coordinate," and rooting around in her computer, some sort of online calendar. Which Abigail hasn't exactly mastered, there's all this muttering and lip pursing and hair twirling, then she tells me to show her my calendar. Which I do, and after she leaves out the other stuff and concentrates on the hair twirling she manages to figure out that both Fred and I are free the day after tomorrow at four-thirty. Great. An hour with my book. Total tedium, even if it's nothing but pictures of me.

I take the elevator down from the agency with this magnificent babe who is also a friend of mine. Her name is Alison McBride and she's six foot-one. Not only that, she always wears heels, really high, even during the day. Slim as she is, she's big. But I've always thought of her as fragile in some funny way, with a neck like a swan. I'd call her Ms. Swan, except that her legs are even more amazing than her neck, so legs plus neck equals my secret name for Alison—Mademoiselle Giraffe.

Out on the street, she's telling me about this shoot in Mexico, somewhere on the Pacific coast. This place I've never heard of. Can't quite catch the name. San Something-or-other, right? Allesandra's is right around the corner, on Seventh Avenue, so we go there and get a table far, far away from the UV rays streaming in through the windows. The waitress wanders over. She's kind of nice looking, but she has an attitude. She's so tired of all these models coming in here all the time, never ordering anything but coffee. As if models coming in all the time wasn't the whole point of Allesandra's.

Anyway, we order double espressos, with one brioche. Which we'll split. Then Alison goes on about the shoot in Mexico, these pink beaches, well, not really pink, but late in the day, the sand sort of gets this pinkish glow, it's magical, so the photographer would wait around all afternoon and try to get everything done in this, like, half-hour time frame, it was crazy, but exciting. But not half as exciting as the security situation.

"Security situation?"

"Right, there was a revolution or a drug war or something going on, so the ad agency sent down this whole bunch of personnel. Guys with radios and these kind of military vests. Not to mention guns. Nothing ever happened, except for one night, near the end, when we heard all this shooting. Like, machine guns or something. The security guys got all excited, with their radios and all, but it was OK."

"Alison. What? Machine guns in the middle of the night and it was OK? I'd be out of my mind. Jumping on the next flight out."

Alison just shrugged. There weren't any next flights out. The nearest airport was a hundred kilometers away. So they finished the shoot, then everything was loaded into the vans and they took off. No problem. I'm amazed. This big, gentle, gorgeous thing looks fragile, but I'm realizing she's not fragile at all.

I tell her what I'm up to, not all the boring cattle calls, of course, but the one highlight in my immediate future, a shoot for Basha Edwards. She asks me where and I tell her, "We're doing it on Thirty-Fifth Street. This super-great studio. Supposedly."

Alison tells me it really is a great facility, she's done a few shoots there, they even have this fitness center, with a sauna and so on, in case you want to take a moment out and get toned up or relax or whatever, which nobody ever does, but, anyway … it's great … and then she asks me about Brenda. Everyone always asks me about Brenda. Naturally enough. And so, because Alison is my friend, I relay the latest news.

"Someone is saying he's going to kill her."

"What?"

"It's this guy, Sergei. Sergei Propokoff. He says he's going to kill Brenda. Have her killed. I don't know ... I'm just so ... "

"Oh, Fiona." Alison puts a hand on my arm. "I'm so sorry. This is terrible. What's his name again?"

"Sergei Propokoff. He's a gangster or something."

"Gangster?"

"Yeah. That's the impression I'm getting. Things are, you know, really vague, but, on the other hand, what kind of person threatens to kill people?"

Alison is, like, right, I see what you mean, saying she thinks maybe she's heard of this Sergei person. Then she tells me a story that lights up all my panic-synapses.

It happened a couple of years ago, maybe three ... or maybe that's just when Alison first heard the story, but, anyway, there was this party on one of those big rent-a-boats that spend the night circling Manhattan while everybody on board gets wasted, and, this one time, things got out of hand ... people were chuga-lugging vodka and this person who might possibly be Sergei, who supposedly also was doing uppers, got really pissed at this girl. He wanted her to blow him right there on deck, in front of every-body, and she wouldn't, he was grabbing her by the hair, dragging her around on her knees, she was crying, trying to fight him off, and so finally he said, OK, that's enough, and put her in one of the life boats ... then he had the life boat lowered into the water ... the idea was to tow her along for a while, teach her a lesson, but ... at some point, the party-goers realized that the life boat was missing. So was the girl. They turned around to look for her but she was gone. Never seen again. End of story.

I just stare at Alison. Finally, I'm, like, "What? Are you kidding me?"

"It's what I heard."

"Was this on the news?"

"Not sure. Maybe. I never saw anything. I guess it must be something I heard."

I stare at her some more, trying to come up with some way of thinking about this. Some bearable take on it. Because I cannot let this story just sit there, zapping my brain to the point where I can think only one thought, that my life is basically over, which it will be if this Sergei What's-His-Name goes on another rampage and something like this happens to Brenda.

I say, "This is horrible." Which is pretty lame but also true. Because this is truly horrible.

Alison frowns, upset that she upset me. She's trying to think of something to say. So am I, and eventually I tell her it sounds to me like an urban legend. You know, one of these stories that gets repeated over and over and everyone loves to tell it but it's essentially not true. Which is a theory, not brilliant, maybe, but it gives me something to glom onto. As opposed to watching myself free falling into total terror.

OK. Great. That's settled, sort of, and Alison has an appointment uptown. It's time to go. We get up and hug and it is really nice to be surrounded for a second by this big, lovely personage. Then I'm all alone, out on Seventh Avenue, looking for a cab and wondering what the fuck Sergei is doing. At this very moment. And getting pissed off that I would be wondering such a thing. Because why does someone like Sergei even exist?

After dinner with Bennett, we were standing outside the restaurant, me thinking, OK, time to go, I've had enough of my shithead ex to last me for another three years. But he was holding onto me by the elbow, saying, "What should I tell my friend the district attorney about you?"

"Tell him I'm this hot babe who will make his life worth living. If he helps me out."

"Seriously, Fiona. Should I tell him you're a model?"

"Sure. Guys like to meet models."

"True. But sometimes they get the wrong idea."

"That's so sweet, Bennett. Worrying about guys getting the wrong idea about me."

He smiled and winked and strode off into the night. God, that wink of his irritates me.

Now I am sitting across a table from Assistant District Attorney Fletcher Marks and realizing that he never gets the wrong idea about women. He doesn't bother. There is a wedding band on his ring finger, meaning, probably, that he has a wonderful wife and three wonderful kids. But that isn't the main point. The main point is that here is a guy completely into his work. So I'm listening but I'm also wondering what that's like. I mean, I'm good at modeling, love all those eyes on me, but what I'm mainly into is having certain feelings.

And avoiding certain others, like, total exasperation. I mean, OK, I know he's got to establish some ground rules for this conversation, which is off the record, yes, of course, understood, and he'd be a lot more comfortable talking hypotheticals, I get that too, so, right, it's a big concession even to listen to me name certain names, like Sergei Propokoff, for example. And Brenda Rawlings. But I did name them, with his permission. I did agree that this conversation is completely confidential, nothing said here is to be repeated anywhere. Ever. So now what? Because, come on, I'm thinking to myself, is it really all that necessary to go back over the fucking ground rules a second time?

We're in this Thai place on Baxter Street, which Fletcher had
said was OK. Not terrible. Sounds perfect, I said, and he gave me
this lopsided smile.

Now bowls of slightly murky-looking soup arrive and he's saying, "Well, I can say this, we do know of Mr. Propokoff."

Fletcher pauses and looks at me. I get this look on my face
somewhere between eager and impatient, the message being,
OK, great, but there's got to be more. Fletcher stalls, asking me if
the threatening phone calls are on-going.

I take a spoonful of soup. Coriander. Also ginger? Not bad.
Actually, it's terrific. Fiona's latest culinary discovery.

Fletcher keeps watching me, waiting for an answer to his perfectly reasonable question. So I say, "Sergei is kind of obsessive.
But there's been nothing today. Or yesterday."

Which is true. Technically. Of course, there have been no calls
from Sergei for a while. It's been all quiet on the Russian front,
not something I want to mention because I don't want Fletcher
to decide there's no problem.

He purses his lips. Then he says, "Harassment of this kind is
not a surprise, I suppose. We know Mr. Propokoff to be unsavory.
But, frankly, he is not a primary object of our attention."

"But you've heard things."

"We've heard things. Everybody hears things. But, and again I
want to be as frank as possible with you, what we hear does not
bring this individual up to the mark as a major offender."

"So what is he? Sort of a petty criminal?"

Fletcher smiles. "We don't know quite what he is. In recent
years, Russian oligarchs have been settling in New York and, for
the most part, behaving themselves. Mr. Propokoff is one of them.
As far as we know."

"As far as you know?"

Fletcher smiles again, slightly annoyed this time.

"Yes, as far as we know. We don't have all that clear a picture of his resources, but we know that he is interested chiefly in real estate. There have been hints of other activities. On-line gambling, various kinds of cyber-crime. And it has to be said, additionally, that he is making an effort to become respectable."

"Respectable?"

"Socially—ah, what shall I say? Negotiable. Socially negotiable, meaning that he has been associating himself quite actively with prominent charities ... cultural institutions ... there have been a series of rather substantial donations. Substantial and highly-publicized."

"Right. I mean, I sort of got that from Brenda's people. So that's the idea, that Sergei has been making a big splash with his money?'

"Right."

"So, OK." I take another spoonful of soup. "OK, so before I was hoping you'd decide Sergei was this major problem, but now, from what you're saying, maybe this is good. Sergei is trying to go straight ... I mean, look. He's always wanting to take Brenda to these high-profile places. Like the ballet. The Modern. He craves the spotlight. Far more than Brenda, and she's a supermodel. So maybe he had these violent tendencies, but he's leaving all that behind. Joining the ranks of respectable citizens."

Fletcher sees what I want, desperately, and he'd like to provide it. But he can't.

"Look, Ms. Mays. Fiona. There's a general trend with these people, true enough. They go from shady to legit. From violent to law-abiding. But a general trend doesn't tell us anything about individuals. A certain individual's people might have come over on the Mayflower. This individual might have gone to Choate and Harvard and keep horses in Millbrook. Fine, but there is nothing to guarantee that he won't kill his wife. Or his girlfriend. By the same token, there is nothing to say that a dubious character like Propokoff is going to kill anybody. Or have anybody killed. By the way, what set him off?"

Good question, but I'm slightly distracted by my heaping plate of something unrecognizable. I get the rice part, but what is this other stuff? Bits of green and yellow and more or less beige ... Fletcher is halfway through his whatever-it-is ... working away at it ... I take a bite ... more coriander ... I put down my fork.

"What set him off? This was the big mystery. Brenda doesn't like to talk about it but finally she did, the other night, and the problem, it turns out, is that Brenda saw Sergei with this person she didn't know. A business associate or something. But a member of the criminal classes, I guess, because she wasn't supposed to see them together and she did and now he's threatening to have her killed."

Fletcher frowns. Then, "Forgive me. But this is nonsense. Total nonsense. Maybe he wants her dead. Maybe he doesn't. Whatever he wants, it isn't because of this."

"But that's when the threats began. Right after that."

Fletcher winces. "I'm not disputing that. All I'm saying is that Propokoff isn't going to go off like Rumpelstiltskin just because this girl saw him with someone she doesn't know."

"OK, so if that isn't it, maybe this whole death threat business is also just so much bullshit."

"Fiona. You know that doesn't follow. He might have some other motive. Or not."

"What about charging him with assault?"

Fletcher gives me this tired look. Like, do I really have to explain that criminal charges require something a little more substantial than he-said-she-said?

So I say, "All right, I guess that's that."

Fletcher is nodding now, his eyebrows raised. Looking down at the table. With his empty plate and greasy silverware and his cup of tea. Bits of rice here and there. He's going over the pros and cons of something or other.

Finally, he looks up and says, "We always know a lot more than we can prove. We know for example—and, by the way, I want to remind you here of our agreement. All this has to be completely confidential."

I look into his eyes and nod. Then I say, "Yes. I understand. Completely confidential."

He trusts me, I can tell, which is only right, I would never say anything to anyone about any of this, so he goes on, "We have informants. Triangulating from the bits and pieces we get from those quarters, we know that what we have here is a matter of dishonor among thieves. Propokoff has more to fear from his associates than from us. I can't really say any more than that, the substance of which has already appeared in the press. The *Times* ran an investigative series about half a year ago, mostly speculative, in our view, though it has to be said that they, too, have their sources. In any case, there is nothing on which we can move at this point. We can't go after him on rumors alone and of course he can't be indicted simply for being a nasty customer. Which we know him to be, so, uh … a word to the wise, Fiona, be careful. That's really all I can say."

He digs into his wallet, takes out a business card, turns it over and writes something. Then he pushes it across the table, between the dirty dishes, saying, "If there's anything else, anything definite, get back to me. That's my cell number on the back."

I take the card, slip it into the front pocket of my jeans. He pays, we get up, shake hands, and I'm telling him I hope all his informants are wrong about Sergei. That they're just being melodramatic.

He gives me another weary smile and buzzes off. So do I, thinking, let's just hope everyone is being melodramatic. Because, OK, you tie the heroine to the railroad tracks, par for the course, it's what the audience expects, lots of cutting back and forth between the oncoming freight train and the heroine who is squirming like—umm, like someone tied to the railroad tracks. Perfectly natural, except you have to work it out so her faithful dog, this super-smart collie who rescued her from the raging torrent when she was a baby and raised her as one of her own, arrives at the very last moment and manages to untie her. Right before the freight train comes roaring by. And everything's fine, because what was the problem, anyway? Everyone was just being melodramatic.

I'm alone in the conference room at the agency, waiting for Fred the media resource coordinator to show up, and I wasn't kidding when I said my book bores me. I've seen these pictures a million times and the thrill is gone, believe me. The only way I get it back is when I take new pictures. Or maybe I should think of something else to do with my life.

Fred arrives with coffee. Two mugs, one of which he sets down on the big oval conference table. The other he hangs onto, walking back and forth, looking at my photos, which he scattered all over the table. I like watching him move. He's my height, maybe an inch taller. Handsome in his white polo shirt and chinos. John Lobb loafers. Meaning, he comes across as corporate-on-casual-Friday. Not a fashion-world type.

After a while, he points at a picture of me in a torn T-shirt and a straw hat. Shorts with the legs rolled up. I'm turning my face away, looking back at the camera sideways.

"You sure you want to keep this one? Makes you look like Daffy Duck after a hard night on the town."

"Daffy Duck? I don't even know what that means."

"You were trying for sultry but it came out goofy."

"Are you kidding me? Goofy?"

"Just around the edges."

"I think you picked the wrong word. But I sort of see what you mean. So. Let's say we leave that one out. What about this?"

"This is hot. Perfect." It's me in heels, a long luscious leg stepping through the slit in a long luscious dress. Black silk, of course. For a nano-second or so, I'm dumbstruck. What a babe! Fred is gay but he agrees. Or he agrees because he's gay. Who knows? All this stuff about gender and orientation is kind of tangled and no one ever unravels it because who cares?

I mean, I do, in a way, and I love it when a writer like Proust or someone gets wrapped up in the subtleties of it all, but when you're out there, in the bright lights, what matters is the take on your image. Not the whys and the wherefores, just the take, which is instantaneous, and then it's on to the next image and the next and the next and I'm thinking about the Mind of Fletcher Marks, this huge repository of things he knows and other things he believes, none of which he can do anything about.

What a waste of my time that was ... like, sometimes you thread your way through a labyrinth of bullshit to set up a meeting and nothing comes of it but at least you meet somebody cute. Someone it's fun to think about. Not that Fletcher isn't cute, it's just that I can't see myself getting off on the memory of this seriously professional guy telling me, essentially, that my theory of urban legends is wrong. Sergei really does do terrible stuff. Sergei is dangerous.

Meanwhile, Fred and I are making one snap decision after the next, because that's what you have to do with images. Otherwise, you outsmart yourself. Pretty soon we're done, that wasn't bad, and Fred is saying, "I'll look it all over tomorrow, but I think that's pretty much it. For the still photos."

"Abigail isn't thinking of scheduling me for new pictures?"

A quick frown from Fred. "Don't think so. No. But, um, these are oldies but goldies and no one has seen them for a while. Because you dropped out for some strange reason that maybe you'll explain to me one of these days. The only new thing is getting some of these pix on the agency website, but don't worry, Tom the tech guy will take care of it."

Like I was going to worry about me and the web. No way, not my department, I don't even have a computer, it's already too much that I have to check my phone all day to see if I've got any new appointments. I mean, OK, let's keep up with the new technology but please, please, please do not try to explain it to me. Which Fred looks like he's about to do, so I say, let's go to Brainwave. Get a Margarita or something.

On our way out the door, we run into Abigail. She's on her cell phone with somebody at one of the magazines. Nabbing Fred by the arm, holding on, sort of hauling him around in this big, distracted circle, she keeps yapping about layouts and synergy and deadlines. As Fred sails by, he raises his eyebrows. Abigail gets off the phone and asks him how it went.

"Great," he says. "Really great. You should be proud, Abigail. Fiona is one of your major discoveries."

In fact, Abigail nixed me the first time she saw me, which Fred knows. He also knows how Abigail will react to this compliment, her face going rigid with all sorts of fucked-up feelings. Then breaking out in a great big fashion-world smile.

A cab down to Second Avenue and Third, into the world of dim bulbs and bright chatter. Happy Hour at Brainwave, this place with no décor. Tons of bottles behind the bar, all sparkly of course, but the tables are just plain unpainted wood and the chairs are really cheesy, these canvas-back things. Director's chairs.

The music is techno-whatever, like some nerd's idea of turning traffic sounds into art. So un-brilliant, which must be why Fred and I like this place. It's a relief from the fashion biz, where you have to pretend all the time that you're being swept off your feet, completely knocked out, by this or that sign of absolute genius.

Fred sips his Margarita, puts it down and stares at it for a while. Then he leans over and says, right into my ear, "Abigail is such a cow."

I ought to tell him that's also my word for her, but I'm too busy flashing back on myself in the mirror, especially this one image, my ass at a certain angle, and the small of my back, and wondering who invented mirrors in the first place. I mean, if you hadn't ever seen yourself in one you'd never know what you were missing, so what was the inspiration? It's not like, oh, I'm so tired of walking all day, let's invent the wheel. Or reinvent it, the way Brenda reinvents glam every time she appears in the latest bright idea from some designer, because glam is timeless, think Taj Mahal, but also it has to be timely, which is why we have designers, not to mention bright ideas. Don't want to get left in the dust with all the dumb ideas, even if they're sort of timeless, too, which may not make much sense, but so what? This is just me, my racing thoughts taking me wherever.

Which some people find really unpleasant, their racing thoughts, but not me, I actually like mine a lot. Because they always take me away from me and back to Brenda, who is probably doing what right now? At this very moment? Flipping through a magazine, her hair sort of hiding the side of her face … or she's going out tonight, so she's poking around in her vast inventory of lingerie, more or less trying to make a decision, with

Rosalie standing by, to ease her on to the next stage in the amazing process ... because, let's face it, whatever's going on, no matter how frantic or glamorous, there's always this slight feeling of suspended animation, like the world is standing by, waiting to see the very latest version of Brenda ...

Waking up, I realize it's only Tuesday, groan, then I remember my first go-see isn't until ten-thirty, so I go back to sleep and dream about this snowy landscape, except that *snowy landscape* doesn't really say it. It's really a dream about light, this totally luminous universe, and I wake up remembering a conversation I had in Greece, at a bar in Piraeus. It's at the top of this flight of wooden stairs, all creaky and nostalgic, like you're climbing up to another era, and then there's a great view of the harbor. I was sitting all alone, drinking a glass of retsina, which is basically undrinkable but, you know, when in Greece do as the Grecians do, and then this tall guy in a safari jacket asked if he could join me. Sure, why not, so he sits down and orders Ouzo. The local rotgut.

His name is Vasily Yeseyev and it turns out that he's on his way to a monastery on Mt. Athos, which evidently is this ultra-holy peninsula sticking into the Aegean Sea. Vasily is not a monk or anything, he's just going for a retreat. You pick olives eighteen hours a day and don't talk to anyone, which sounds like a pretty limited existence, to put it mildly, so I ask him how long he's planning to be there. That depends, he says, on the strength of his vocation. Which is not for him to determine. So I'm sitting there, wondering if I really want to pursue this topic, talk about god with a very serious Russian, when he notices the book I've got with me. This beaten-up paperback. *A Hero of Our Time* by

Mikhail Lermontov. Vasily asks me what I think of Grigory Alex-
androvich Pechorin. The hero.

"Well," I say. "He's a little stuck-up."

"Stuck-up?"

"You know, stuck on himself. Self-absorbed."

Vasily smiles and asks me what is my favorite scene in the
story. I tell him it's the whole section when Pechorin is traveling through this mountainous region, all covered with snow, the
mountains practically blocking out the sky, which is also white,
and just this one little speck moving across it. A man on a horse.

Vasily gets a touch professorial at this point, telling me that
literary historians would file this image under the heading of
Byronism. Byronic melancholy at a heroic scale. And they are not
incorrect, according to Vasily. But it's much larger than that. It's
archetypal, an image of the hero damned by his own heroism.
The tragic flaw of true self-sufficiency.

I'm impressed but with a few reservations, I guess, because I
say, "Couldn't it be that the hero is just checking out the beauty
of the place? Seeing if he measures up to it?"

Vasily smiles again and asks me what I do for a living. I tell
him I'm a fashion model, as if he didn't know, couldn't possibly guess, and then he asks me where I'll be going after I leave
Greece. I tell him I really don't know, and I really didn't, I was just
a random factor in those days. Or a girl at the mercy of random
factors. Anyway, that was one of the more interesting conversa-
tions I had during my hiatus, and I guess it was the inspiration for
my dream about the all-enveloping light. Which I wouldn't mind
having again, so I get deep inside my bed clothes and fall asleep
and then, about a minute later, I get a call from one of Pam the
personal manager's endless supply of girls.

She sounds like she's about twelve, and she's going on and on,
telling me way too much about Brenda's schedule for tomorrow,

an interview on NBC, taping at eight-thirty, some program I've never heard of, then brunch at the National Academy for the Arts, then an afternoon tea for some charity at the French Consulate, then ...

It was like this lesson she'd learned, and she was very nervous about reciting it. Also, very proud to be connected in her low-level way to all this high-level stuff. So I wasn't impatient. I mean, I was but I was nice about it, waiting for her to get to the point, which was that Brenda had this really huge favor to ask of me, do I know this designer, Alysha Bata?

"No. Never heard of her."

"Well, uh, she's fairly new and Brenda really loves her, so, uh ..." It's not all that complicated but it takes the girl about half an hour to explain that Alysha is working on her next show and of course Brenda doesn't do runways anymore but she's making an exception for Alysha, she just loves her stuff so, so much, and so Brenda is going to appear right at the end, all alone, the grand finale, but, um ...

The thing is, Alysha isn't sure which dress she wants Brenda to wear, there are about three possibilities and not one of them is exactly ready and the show is tomorrow evening and um ... uh ... what it comes down to is that Brenda said she'd spend the afternoon at the Alysha Bata studio while Alysha's people finish up the dresses and Brenda gets fitted, and, well, um—

"Brenda is afraid of getting bored while this Alysha person gets her thing together. So she wants me to hang out with her. Is that about it?"

"Um, yeah ... also ... do you happen to remember which movie you told her she might like? The other evening? She can't remember ..."

"Yeah. *Batman and Robin*. With George Clooney." The caped crusader lite.

"And you told her you have an old DVD of it?"

"I did. I also said I haven't seen it for a while so I'm not really sure I have it any more."

Now the assistant gets all hesitant, on the verge of giggly. "So, um … if you could … er…"

"OK, I'm getting the picture. Brenda wants me to ransack my place, dig up my *Batman and Robin* DVD, bring it to Sixty-Third Street, and then go over to the studio with her."

"Right, and … um—"

"Why don't they just get it from Netflix?"

"Oh. Well. Um—"

"Never mind. I'll do it."

So now the girl is sort of squealing with relief, telling me how happy Brenda is going to be, how Alysha's assistant said she could watch the movie on one of their big computers and so—

"So you're going to send a car over here, right? "

"Right."

"What tine?"

"Uh, quarter to three? Because Brenda said she'd be at Alysha's place by three …"

"And Pam's thinking she ought to be a little late?"

"Uh—"

"Terrific. So I'll expect the car at three." I hang up, thinking it must seem weird, me volunteering for this dopey chore. It must seem weird even if the world's most gorgeous supermodel is saying she wants to see me. Like I don't have anything else to do with my life. Which I don't. I'm going to be busy until about two but I've been checking in with Abigail by phone, just like I'm supposed to, and there's nothing after that. So I'll be free. Of course, something might pop up, probably will, and so, to head that off, I call Abigail again, tell her I have to go bungee jumping at two-thirty this afternoon and—

"What!"

"Bungee jumping, Abigail, you tie this cord to your ankle and—"

"I know what bungee jumping is, Fiona. I am simply trying to convey to you that, my god—"

"Don't worry Abigail, I'm kidding. I haven't gone bungee jumping since about two years ago, when I tried it for the first time, and it was this amazing rush, like the first time I, um—anyway, I jumped off a bridge and there was this speed boat going by and I kind of bashed heads with this very tall guy who was—"

"Fiona!"

"Yes, Abigail?"

"Why do you waste my time with this nonsense, I don't have—"

"I was just trying to feel you out, Abigail, see if you really care."

"Oh, for—" For Christ's sake is what she meant to say, but she hung up on me before she could get it out, leaving me with this kind of triumphant feeling, all fizzy but not like Pellegrino, which sort of explodes all over your lips and your tongue … more like that other brand people always ask for … Lurisia or something … the subtler fizziness …

Anyway, I got through my appointments with no lasting damage to my self-esteem. In fact, there was this one casting director right at the end who started slobbering all over me, trying to get me to go out with him until his boyfriend and immediate superior came by, saying, don't mind Heinrich, he sort of lives in his head. I'm the one with the eye and we'd love you for this. Meaning, a shoot for a Neiman-Marcus catalog. So that was nice, and moments later I was back in my apartment, putting my Pilates ball through its paces, getting all hot and sort of semi-bothered.

Then I was taking a shower and donning the outfit. Jeans and a lime-green T-shirt and this super-sleek jacket by Michael Kors, black linen, just to remind this Alysha Bata person of which league she's trying to play in. My buzzer buzzes and I find a very distinguished-looking guy in shirtsleeves and sunglasses waiting for me on the sidewalk, with a silver Lexus to take me up to Brenda's place.

He's new so he introduces himself but I don't catch his name, and then he asks if he may call me Fiona, he learned my name from one of Miss Rawlings's assistants, and I say, of course, and we talk about what a beautiful day it is, light traffic, the city is so nice in September, a lot of people still out of town ... he keeps looking at me in the rearview mirror but not catching my eye, exactly, because of his sunglasses.

When we get to Brenda's house, he double-parks, and Brenda appears in a few minutes, dazzling in this dark blue summer dress by Max Mara, V-neck with a shape like it's an edition of one, custom-made for the person who just happens to be wearing it. She's being escorted by an assistant with a look on her face like, oh my god, this is so unbelievable, I don't know if I'm going to be able to live up to the sheer honor of it all.

The assistant opens the door for Brenda, who goes from standing to sitting in one curvy motion, you can't quite see how anyone could be that graceful, then the door closes and the car takes off. I'm leaning back in the seat, breathing out, then there's this huge screech and I'm banging my forehead against the front seat.

A grubby gray car has just cut us off, our driver is frozen at the wheel, and I see a guy in black pants and a black T-shirt get out of the passenger seat of the car that's blocking us. Our driver starts to open his door and my first impulse is to do the same, get out and charge the guy, screaming, like I'm this martial arts master, which I'm not, so what the fuck next?

What the fuck next is that the black T-shirt guy is kicking our driver's door shut and now he's trying to open the back door on the street side, where Brenda is and she's screaming but the driver has locked all the doors, great move, so the T-shirt guy keeps yanking at the back door handle, Brenda has turned away, she's all curled up in my arms, not screaming any more, and I see Mike the security guy racing around the back end of the Lexus.

Black T-shirt sees him, too, suddenly he's this blur, like a cartoon creature, vanishing into the gray car, which takes off before he gets his door shut, and now Mike is at our driver's window, rotating his hand, meaning, lower it. But the driver decides to get out and I'm sitting there watching them talk while a whole platoon of girls rushes out to get Brenda, take her back to the house.

After a while, the driver wanders off, like he wants to smoke a cigarette, but he doesn't, and Mike comes over to my window, makes the same rotating motion. So I lower the window and he sort of slouches and looks in, saying, "You OK, Fiona?"

"Sure. What was that?"

Mike shrugs. "I may have seen that car before. Not sure. This time I got the plate number."

"Meaning the car probably won't be back."

"Probably not." Mike is now resting his forearms on the window frame, squinting up the street toward Park, no doubt thinking all these professional-grade security thoughts. While he's still looking away, I touch one of his arms, letting my hand rest there for a moment. Several moments. Because this is one of the ways I figure people out, touching them, getting the physical vibe. It always works, except with Brenda. We touch all the time, hugging, kissing, and she is still this mystery. The ultimate mystery, as far as I'm concerned.

Mike is the opposite, totally readable. The strong male, and not just because of his obvious muscles, but also—what? Strength of character in the masculine mode? Absolutely, but I'm not feeling anything sexual. Not that he's not sexy. He is, in this boring, buzz-cut kind of way. So if I'm not feeling it, even a little bit, he's a real disciplinarian, keeping the hormones on ice while he's on the job.

Just to tease him, I say, "You've been working for Brenda for about three years now, Mike, and you've never hit on me. How come?"

He looks at me and smiles. This amuses him. "I don't know, Fiona." Looking away for a second. Then he looks back, saying, "I do know. Of course I do. It's because I'm a bigamist."

"A bigamist?"

This is such a curveball, I guess I'm gawking and now he's really amused. Giving me this look of fake sincerity.

"Yeah. I have one family in New Jersey, the other on Long Island, so if I make it with you I'd be doubly unfaithful. Can't hack it. The guilt would be too much."

I laugh and he straightens up, giving the window frame a slap. "OK, Fiona. You'd better go wait in the house. Let Brenda take a little time and then you can get the show back on the road. Like this never happened."

Which is how it turned out, especially the part about the show, because Alysha Bata and everyone at her studio were so happy to have Brenda there, they put so much effort into appreciating her, being the audience for this major star. The amazing thing is that Brenda watched *Batman and Robin* from start to finish. With lots of interruptions, of course, because there was so much work to be done and she looked so fabulous in Alysha's gowns, which are super-elegant, sort of early Dior meets late Vivienne Westwood and not anywhere near as weird as that sounds.

Fitting took forever, with everyone wasting all this emotional energy, afraid that Brenda was about to lose her patience any second now. Which would never happen in a million years, of course, they didn't get that Brenda is not your run-of-the-mill superstar, and then they rehearsed her runway turn a few times, with this stunning music, a sort of electro-pop version of that song from *Turandot* people always play. *Nessun Dorma*.

It was so beautiful everyone was practically crying and I was thinking, poor Batman and Robin, you two could swoop down right in the middle of this huge flood of female emotion and no one would even see you.

By the time everything was wound down and packed up, it wasn't much past nine but Brenda snoozed a bit in the car, on the way back to Sixty-Third Street, with her head back and her mouth slightly open. Not snoring, exactly, just this faint whistling in her nose. And so glamorous because, come on, it was her nose.

Pam was waiting at the front door, smiling at Brenda and pretty much ignoring me. So I was pretty much ignoring her, as Rosalie came downstairs to get Brenda, take her back upstairs, get her ready for dinner. At which point, Brenda turned and looked at me with these lovely sleepy eyes and asked me if I had dinner plans … she's staying in tonight, maybe I'd like to join her … meaning Pam had to acknowledge my existence, saying, well, we'll have to check. See if Brenda is already booked for dinner, like, some major star of stage or screen is about to show up on the doorstep any moment now.

Such bullshit, obviously, and Pam knew that I knew it was bullshit, but it was also obvious that the Fiona presence was getting on her nerves. So she asked me if I could just wait here for a moment, in the foyer, someone will let me know as soon as possible. Meaning fifteen or twenty minutes from now, me standing around like a job applicant, for god's sake, because Brenda is not only the world's most beautiful woman, she is also this vast bureaucracy. A girl wrapped in red tape.

Which I don't even see when I'm alone with her, she acts like whatever she does in the course of a day is just what she wants to, every last thing on her schedule, and it's all fun. Because every effort—and I mean every effort—is made to make sure that everything goes smoothly for the lovely and truly adorable Brenda Rawlings.

So what can I say, people who have people are the luckiest people in the world. But Brenda doesn't get this. She's always mildly surprised when she notices her people doing things for her. It's like her beauty is this faraway land where she lives all alone and sometimes people visit to make sure everything is the way it's supposed to be. Meaning, Rosalie is going to find her something casual and also dazzling to wear for dinner and in a little while she is going to reappear, sheer Brenda, the same as she always is.

Down in the foyer, I spent about half an hour looking at this print of some sort of flower, an ancient daffodil, I guess, and really lovely, like this prim girl with no eyes for her own attractiveness, except it made me sad, I kept remembering what this dealer told me once, that people buy these old books and rip them apart, sell the prints one by one, so no more book, no idea where the images came from. It's sort of like grave robbers, fucking up the archeological site before the archeologists get there, so, adios, insight into the human past. It's all about ROI, according to the dealer, which I didn't get, so he said, return on investment. When it comes to beauty, return on investment is king.

After a while Susanna or whoever came down and led me up to the small dining room on the third floor, giving me this running commentary on where we were going, take a right here, a left, three steps down, watch your step. Like I'd never been in Brenda's house before. What a dope. Anyway, she finally left me alone and I was standing at the window, looking out at the dusk descending on Sixty-Third Street. So ritzy and well-swept. Behind me, I heard all this coming and going.

Turning around, I saw a young maid in a uniform fussing with the silverware on a small dining table. Another maid came in with an open bottle of red wine, which she placed very carefully on a silver coaster, both of them ignoring me with that sweet self-consciousness which says, we're on our best behavior, not even dreaming for a moment of attracting the slightest bit of attention to ourselves.

They left and Andrej the major domo or whatever he is appeared, in his weirdly worn-out black suit. Then, a moment later, Brenda, in this charcoal gray jacket, Bottega Veneta, over a sky-blue T-shirt. Nicely faded jeans with sandals by Marc Jacobs … I think, not sure … anyway, we hugged and sat down at the table and Andrej served us these fluffy salads with walnuts. Then Chilean sea bass with a sherry cream sauce, which Brenda loves, with Andrej refilling my glass after just about every sip.

And, I figured, disapproving of having to pour a red, this scrumptious Barolo, with fish, but what could he do? At some point in the misty past I told Brenda or somebody that I like red wine with everything, and this had turned into an iron-clad law. At dinner at Brenda's I am always given red wine. Thank god.

Brenda was talking about her interview this morning, how nice the interviewer was, then the French consulate, what a beautiful building, and I was thinking about that scene in *From Russia with Love* where James Bond figures out that there's something fucked-up about the villain, who has not yet bared his fangs, because he orders red wine with fish, meaning, OK, there's a right way and a wrong way, and this guy is all wrong.

Except that the right way is the way you like it, as far as I'm concerned, and that's what I like, red wine, except when I want something bubbly and if that's what I want I'll even have it with red meat. Not that I eat red meat all that much. So James Bond has a right to have his doubts about me, and there is another reason.

Which is that I'm never really crazy about him no matter who plays the part. I usually watch the actresses, like Daniela What's-Her-Name who is Tatiana What's-Her-Face in *From Russia with Love*, except that it's less about her face and more about her body. So lush, like she's lying on a bed and she's the bed itself, you want to sink into all that warmth, sort of a strange image, I agree, but this is just me, letting my thoughts take me here and there. Waiting for them to take me back to Brenda.

Who seems a little distracted, telling Andrej to bring another bottle of Barolo and I say, no, we've had enough, meaning I've had enough, most of the bottle, because Brenda, as usual, is hardly drinking a thing. So she smiles up at Andrej and he goes away and comes back a minute later with a plateful of bite-size fruit tarts, followed by Rosalie with coffee and cream and sugar on a huge silver tray.

I ask Brenda when her interview is going to air. She thinks for a moment. Maybe tomorrow? Or already … Sylvia the publicist would know … we both eat one fruit tart each, drink coffee, talk about Cooper's ligaments, Brenda wondering if they really stretch if you don't wear a bra, and then it's time to wander down the hall and watch a movie. Or not watch it. Either way, the next stage in the leisurely plan. Which got sidetracked the moment Brenda dropped her next bombshell.

We were heading for the living room when she got a call on her cell from Pam, who was still in her office downstairs, hanging on to the bitter end of another fourteen-hour day. Brenda stayed in the hallway to talk and I went on ahead, getting steam-rollered, practically, by yet another assistant-assistant, a pretty girl in an MIT sweatshirt with a look of total panic on her face. She knew she should stop and apologize, but she just couldn't. She had to deal with whatever world-shattering crisis was scaring her shitless.

I hung around in the living room for a while, looking at this book of Edward Steichen photographs, so refined and nonchalant, like, I'm Edward Steichen and this happens to be how I see things … and you don't? What a shame.

Then Brenda appeared, saying, "She can't find the right DVD."

"Which one?"

"I don't know. It's this one with Hugh Grant."

"Terrif."

"You don't like him?" Slightly fretful, so I took her hand as I sat down on the sofa with her, saying, "I love him, sweetie. Can't get enough."

She smiled and then this odd shadow zipped across her face. I tilted my head and looked into her eyes, meaning, what's up? I kept staring. Come on, babe. Don't hold out.

Looking away, she said, "I didn't tell you everything about Sergei."

"Oh?"

"He hit me."

My blood froze. I hadn't expected this. On the other hand, of course I had.

"Any marks?"

"No. I don't know. It wasn't my face. On the side of my head. Then he sort of knocked me down. Threw me. Against some furniture."

"Any marks from that?"

Brenda pulled down her jeans to show me her left thigh. A faint yellowish blotch near her hip.

"He was really sorry."

"He said he was sorry, Brenda? They always say that."

"I know. But he was. Really sorry." She was huddled into herself, her knees together, looking down at the floor.

Really sorry. Yeah, right. Really thrilled is more like it, but of course this is what I don't say. Instead I say, "So. This happened right after you saw him with that guy."

She looks at me and then stares across the room. Silent, holding her breath. I hug her but she doesn't hug me back. I kiss the side of her head. Her lovely chestnut hair.

The girl in the MIT sweatshirt reappears, all relieved, explaining that the Hugh Grant DVD was slipped into the wrong case. *Going the Distance*. With Drew Barrymore, a nice image, if you think about it. Anyway, the right DVD has been located, the world is back on its axis.

The movie begins and we don't talk, we watch Hugh Grant dithering from one scene to the next, like no turn in the plot is going to be too terrible if he just keeps on dithering. Brenda sits close to me, leaning against my shoulder, until the movie is over and she's sleepy and it's time for me to help her get to bed.

Which I did, sort of, waiting in the bedroom doorway while Rosalie turned out the light on the night stand. Gazing at Brenda's face, dim but all aglow in the light from the hallway. When I watch her falling asleep, I get this all's-right-with-the-world feeling. It's a feeling I like to have. Meaning, I can't really live without it.

Except that I am living without it, feeling like I'm sinking into some weird, dark place. There's this horrible thing lurking out there in the dark, because that's his medium, the darkness, like music is Beethoven's medium, only this music is really spooky, I can't really hear it. Like I can't see the horrible thing. So I keep telling Brenda, don't worry. I'll take care of it. I'll protect you. Sure I will. But on the other hand, honestly, what else can I say?

Which was the question I was still asking myself an hour later, washed up and moisturized and snuggled up in this great summer-weight comforter I found at Bloomingdale's the other day ... sort of lemony beige ... and I was drifting off, remembering this wallpaper from when I was a little kid, these bright yellow flowers, then leaving Brenda's place, my hand on the doorknob, and Pam sticking her head out of her office, inviting me in.

We sat and Pam started fiddling with a set of keys, saying, "The men in the car, this morning... that was quite an adventure, Fiona."

I said, "Yes. It was. I keep thinking I should have jumped out and wrestled the guy to the ground."

Pam smiled this understanding little smile, saying, "It's a good thing you didn't. According to Mike's report, the car belongs to some fly-by-night rental place upstate. No luck in tracking down the person who rented it."

"So what's his idea?"

"He thinks it was probably paparazzi assuming that Brenda was in the Lexus. Trying to get a shot of our girl."

"But, um, Pam. The guy didn't have a camera."

"Maybe he was a reporter."

Yeah, maybe, an ace reporter in a black T-shirt, with a look on his face like the feral dog in that Buñuel movie I can never remember the name of.

Pam asked me if I thought Sergei was behind the incident and I said, "Possibly. Sure. Why not? I mean, yes, it's obviously a possibility."

Pam got this big, serious frown on her face and nodded, not because she agreed with me, just to show that she really was serious about all this. Then she looked at me for a while, deciding if she should say anything else. Which she did, telling me, "In light of everything that's going on, Fiona, you might like to know there has been a general agreement to sequester Brenda in a safe place."

"This place isn't safe?"

Pam chewed a lip, looking indecisive, not her usual look, saying, "It is. But we're opting for an excess of caution."

"What about work?"

"Brenda's plate isn't terribly full at the moment. Before all this blew up, we'd been descheduling her a bit. Giving her a rest. We'll just take that a step further."

I nodded. Sort of like, good move, Pam. Very judicious.

Wandering over to Fifth and then in the cab, zipping south alongside the park, I kept telling myself Pam was right, shutting things down. Or this was Ronnie the lawyer's idea. Because, OK, Sergei isn't calling anymore but what does that mean? Given that silence is maybe more sinister than a steady stream of homicidal voice mails. Or maybe not, who knows? So Brenda Xavier Rawlings Inc. has decided that its one and only asset is going to have to disappear and wait it out. Her career can stand it. A mysterious disappearance might even help. Cut down on the risk of overexposure … of course, hiding out really isn't any kind of a solution. So maybe the logic of that is, OK, if hiding out isn't the solution, maybe there isn't any problem. Great. Let's go with that for the time being.

Brenda hiding out is no solution to the Sergei problem but it's dreamy, here in this undisclosed location, which happens to be a huge house behind a huge hedge in Southampton. Brenda's house is two minutes away, behind another huge hedge, and of course everyone, including Sergei, knows where that is. So the thinking was, OK, she could fly to Palm Springs or Fiji or the dark side of the moon, but she wouldn't be any safer there than she is here. In the house of these people, business acquaintances of some kind, who are in Palm Springs or Fiji, who knows, but it's a pretty shrewd plan and everybody is pretty relaxed.

Of course, it's hard not to feel relaxed when you're surrounded by three different alarm systems and enough staff to run one of those boutique hotels they have downtown. I showed up at Brenda's hideout about an hour ago, feeling very much the responsible young adult, having finished taping this ad with a director who looked like he was about fifteen years old. And also the flaky genius type, so he postponed the shoot about a dozen times, fucking up my schedule with all these empty stretches of wasted time. Which I loved. Anyway, when it finally happened there were three of us in front of a green screen, just laughing and dancing and prancing and out of our minds with happiness to be sporting these fresh new styles for spring. It was fun, and I'm still thinking about this one babe with big pouty lips while a man in a dark suit ushers me into a three-story atrium which turns out to be the living room.

I look around, trying to get a take on this house and not getting anywhere ... the place feels like a huge, walk-in monument to stuff that doesn't go together. There's all this rough brick ... the fire place, a couple of walls ... then there're these other walls, sheer glass held in place by industrial looking metal. Like the metal is straining, twenty-four hours a day, because, if it doesn't, the whole house is going to collapse. The furniture is a weird mix of antiques and Ikea. With a big orange overstuffed armchair, sitting in the middle of the room and looking like a prop in some kind of comedy.

At this point Pam appears, skirt suit, clipboard, and all, saying, "Well. Fiona. It's nice that you could come out and spend some time with Brenda."

I smile. We sit down in these huge bamboo chairs in front of the fireplace and Pam smiles back, saying, "Actually, there hasn't been a peep from Sergei for some time now … still … going forward …"

I say, "Maybe he's lying low. Planning a surprise attack."

Pam frowns, gives a quick shake of her head. Meaning, let's not go off on any wild tangents, Fiona.

"Of course," she says, "We *do* take Sergei seriously. Otherwise …" She pauses and makes a big, sweeping gesture at the entire room. The whole setup, meaning, that's why we're out here. Because we take Sergei seriously. Then she's telling me this is not the first time Brenda has received a death threat.

"Every celebrity gets them, on a fairly regular basis. As I'm sure you're aware. But usually they come from unknown people. Nobodies, if that's not too harsh. And there's a steady stream of money-requests, which is sad, although this sort of thing can become quite aggressive. We now have an individual in Orlando saying that he has a signed contract committing Brenda to an ad campaign for a department store down there plus personal appearances at Disney World plus, I don't know, a plethora of other nonsense. Ronnie will quash that. Then there are the men who send Brenda marriage proposals. One of them included a financial statement, to show that he wasn't after her money."

"So what's he after? Long walks on the beach?"

"True love, I suppose. He said he's in his eighties, so maybe he thinks Brenda is going to jump at the chance to inherit his supposed millions in the not too distant future. Or possibly he likes the idea of Brenda Xavier Rawlings pushing his wheel chair."

"Maybe. But some guys in their eighties are pretty spry."

Pam is on the verge of saying I should know, but she doesn't. That would be too much like friendly teasing and Pam has no intention of being friends. She wants to maintain professional distance. To use one of her phrases, and now she's saying, "We're confident that we can handle anything that comes along, though of course much depends on a realistic risk assessment and the better part of valor, I think you'll agree, is to assume that this Sergei Propokoff matter has the potential to become major."

To be*come* major? I'm thinking, it's already major, has been major ever since the creep hit Brenda, and here it comes, the image of Brenda hurt ... crying ... I keep trying to evade it but how can I? Here it is and it fucks up my breathing. Tears start to form. Because of this rage I really don't want to feel. So I make a big point of breathing deeply. Blink my eyes. It's my ritual for getting back to more or less normal, and I'm asking myself if Pam noticed.

Silly question.

Pam has been consulting her clipboard. Going over a checklist or something. Looking up, she says, "Brenda is still upstairs. Head of the stairs, first bedroom to the right. Would you like to see her?"

Another silly question.

The door is half-open. I knock, gently, and Brenda says, "Come in"

She's sitting up, leaning against two or three huge pillows and wearing satin pajamas. Which are apricot, except they're also silvery gray. A luscious color. I sit down on the edge of the bed. We kiss and talk about what she's been doing, which is, essentially, nothing, and that's soothing. Like this place, which is huge and ugly and trying too hard but feels really cozy. Because Brenda feels safe here. She feels safe, I feel safe.

I tell her I'm going to be hanging out in the living room, we'll meet up later on, no hurry, and eventually I see her walking downstairs, dazzling in these old, perfectly fitting jeans and a clingy beige sweater, V-neck, under a beaten-up old blazer. The outfit is basically no-name but it might as well be Balenciaga. Prada. Chanel. Whatever, she's dazzling in the harsh morning light. In bed, her hair was sort of mussed. Now it's this lush, absolutely gorgeous tangle. Do-it-yourself and so inspired, she should get rid of her hairdressers, her stylists, the whole useless crew.

We sit near the fireplace, not saying anything, there's no need. A maid in a maid's outfit, not just a white apron but this little white cap, is bringing us cups of coffee. We don't really want any coffee right now, but the cups are pretty. The Royal Albert pattern, which matches absolutely nothing else in this house. But so what, everything's great, total peace and quiet, except for this dumb beep-beep-beep.

When the owners took off, they left their eleven-year-old kid, which is pretty understandable, considering that he's a knobbly-kneed geek with an addiction to video games. He just sits there on one of the sofas, beep-beep-beep, making a point of not looking at Brenda. Like, yeah, sure, she's beautiful, who cares? Actually, I can't blame him. A kid like that, he knows what Brenda means, even if he doesn't know he knows, and he knows he'll never be able to deal with it.

To get away from the beep-beep-beep, I take Brenda out through these gigantic French doors, onto the terrace. More bricks, only these are the size of Kleenex boxes. Onward but not upward, and pretty soon we're wandering around in the grass. It's late afternoon, the sunlight is gorgeous. It didn't rain in the city, but it must've rained here, the bottoms of my jeans are all wet and my feet are starting to slosh around in my sandals. Everything is so green and bright. Even the shadows.

Brenda is meandering back toward the house. I catch up with her right when her phone begins ringing. She takes it out of her blazer pocket. Looks at the screen and then she looks at me, like she just saw Dracula crossed with Dr. Caligari.

"Who is it?"

She doesn't tell me but I know it's Sergei and, shit, why didn't she turn off her phone, like everyone kept reminding her, and now it's ringing and she's half-crouching, not screaming but looking like she would if she weren't too scared, so I try to put my arms around her, which I can't because I'm so freaked. Sort of frozen in place. We're both having this girly meltdown, like, whimpering and just staring at each other.

Helpless.

It's pathetic, and by the time I snap out of it, it's too late. But of course it isn't. I find Sergei's number and ring back.

"Yes?" The guy has a deep voice, which he is trying to make even deeper.

"Sergei?"

"Who is this?"

"This is Fiona. I'm a friend of Brenda's."

"Put Brenda on telephone."

I tell him she's away, so of course he asks me where is Brenda, and I say, "That's classified, Sergei, but—"

"Classified?"

"Yeah, Sergei, classified, meaning none of your fucking business." I was still being very girly, but in a completely-in-control kind of way. The power of the pussy.

"My fucking business?" Now his voice is ultra-deep. The Russian bear getting up on his hind legs.

"Look, Sergei—"

"Who are you?"

"A friend of Brenda's."

"You are close friend?"

"Very close. We're in the same business."

Brenda is drifting away. Curling up in the big orange armchair.

"What business?" Sergei is asking. "Porn business?"

"Very funny, Sergei. You're quite the comedian."

There is this pause, while Sergei tries to come up with something. What he comes up with is really brilliant. Original. He asks me for a date.

"Umm. Maybe. Let me think." I'm riffling through my brain a mile a minute and I actually get an idea.

"There's this launch."

"Launch? What is launch?"

"A party. A really big party, Sergei. To launch this new scent, Opaline. You know Marta Marakova?"

"Yes, of course I know. Marta is beautiful model."

"And you know a scent is, like, perfume, right?"

"Of course I know."

"Well, it's her scent, and—"

Sergei interrupts, saying, "Marta is very beautiful so scent must be very beautiful also." Another sign of his comedic genius.

Anyway, I'm telling him the launch is next Thursday night, at the Armory on Lexington, maybe he'd like to take me.

"Yes, I take you. Tell me details. But not now. Call me later. I pick you up in limo."

I say, "A limo? Gee, Sergei, I'm impressed." But he was already gone. Figuring, no doubt, that I am girl and girl is always impressed by big limo.

.2.

Sergei may not know this, but there are girls and then there are girls. We're impressed by all sorts of things. Like, for example, I'm, impressed by my tendency to get off in bed. It's part of my skill-set, as Tom the techno-nerd at the agency would say.

Of course, there is getting off and then there's getting off. There's umm, ummm, umm, stretch like a cat, every part of me is purring, I'm lolling around in the sex object's arms, and the message of my body language is, yes, great, let's do it again sometime. Then there's, oh my god, it's this scary wet fire, I'm burning up, I'm drowning, I'm turning myself inside out, I really, truly didn't remember it could be like this. But I do remember. And I know where to find it. Even better, it knows where to find me. Which it did, yesterday, just as I was leaving Brenda in her undisclosed location.

I was all, like, OK, sweetie, relax, listen to your trainer. Listen to Rosalie. Listen to Pam and your nutritionist, who is working on something really scrumptious. For lunch. Avocado what-d'you-call-it. I'll be fine. Which she doesn't believe, and I'm not totally convinced either, because, what? A date with Sergei? I must be out of my mind, so I'm telling Brenda, really, I'll be fine. I really will.

She was holding onto both my elbows, I didn't want to pull away but suddenly there's this text message from Bill Hollander. The best fuck on the planet.

GET BACK TO ME.

So I do. HANG ON

To which Bill replies, OK, and I kiss Brenda on the face and hug her and now I'm in one of Brenda's cars, being driven to the Jitney, and there's another message from Bill. U ON YR WAY???

YES HAD 2 SAY G-BY 2 B

FUCK B

To which I reply, U WISH!

JST GET OVR HERE. Bill is getting antsy.

I am getting damp, so I text him the awful truth. IM 2 HRS FRM NY OK?

2 HRS? GOING

Then about ten seconds later, GOING

I'm, like, DON'T GO IM COMING RLLY COMING HA HA

Now it's eleven at night, I'm completely comed out, and Bill is sleeping, squishing his face into the pillow, like he doesn't care what happens to his collagen or his elasticity or anything. Which he doesn't. He has the kind of good looks that don't depend on looking good.

Usually, afterwards, we lie on our backs and talk. He never asks me what it's like to be a model. I never ask him what it's like to run an art gallery. Because why would I? The only world dumber than the fashion world is the art world, though most people think it's the other way around. Anyway, we talk about the movies. Sometimes we go to a movie. Bill's place, which is where we hook up, is on Hudson, right around the corner from the Film Forum. We like the obvious stuff. Hitchcock. Howard Hawks revivals. And when we talk about the movies we're total amateurs. Like, who's hot and who's not. Take Jennifer Lopez.

Bill is a Jennifer Lopez fan. Rabid. Which is a bit of a puzzler, given Jennifer's huge butt. Because Bill is not into butts. Before I

took off for Europe, we had sex a million times, and not once did
he do me in the butt. He never even sticks his finger up there. So
the first time he started going on and on about Jennifer Lopez, I
was, like, what? I don't get it. Jennifer Big-Ass? And he says it's
not about her ass. It's her face. She has a great face.

"OK, she has a great face. But she was never beautiful. Not till
she had all that work done"

"Not beautiful? She was always beautiful. Beautiful enough to
do that hair thing. Years ago"

"Hair thing? You mean L'Oréal? How would you know that?"

"Hey. I'm a fan. I know stuff like that. Also, she's a great actress."

"Yeah. Right. How can you be a great actress in the dumb
movies she does?"

"She was great in *Out of Sight*. With George Clooney."

"Any girl would be great with George Clooney. The Wicked
Witch of the West would be great with George Clooney. But,
seriously, Bill, you can't be serious. That movie is prehistoric. I
was about three when that movie came out."

"Try again, babe. You are not that young."

"But I am young. Really. Otherwise, why would you be so hot
for me? You're practically a pedophile."

Bill laughed. A confident laugh. A manly laugh, if that doesn't
sound too dopey. Because Bill is not a pedophile. He likes grown-
up women. If anything, I'm a little unripe for him. But I know
how to do the grown-up-woman thing between the sheets, if not
elsewhere, so Bill really likes me. Which is nice, because I really
like him. Not just his personality. Also his splendid dick. Which
would be getting hard about now if he happened to be awake.

Or maybe it is getting hard, dreaming of Jennifer Lopez, but
what good does that do me, he's so totally asleep, lying on his
stomach, snoring this worn-out snore. Poor baby. The gallery biz
is wearing him down.

So I snuggle up to his manly bod, and the next thing I know I'm asleep too. I mean, the next thing I know it's nearly nine in the morning and Bill is nuzzling my neck, grabbing me with one hand and with the other hand he's scrabbling around in the drawer of the night table, trying to get a condom without actually stopping to look for it, and his cock is so hard, I want it so much, and I love that I want it so much, it's so great to want things you can actually get, but not this very minute, sad to say, because I have to hurry home.

Get myself scrubbed down and spiffed up for a go-see on Forty-Fifth Street. Some more ad people. A girl has to pay the rent. Also, a girl has to get laid now and then, and it's nice if getting laid doesn't get mixed up with paying the rent. Which is why Bill is such a good deal. We fuck for fuck's sake. It's like art for art's sake, only different.

The trouble with being photographed all the time is that you have to deal with photographers. Which can be so not fun, except that I've been pretty lucky. Until today. Abigail changed her mind about new pictures for my look-book, so here I am, getting ready to pose for this guy named Andy Giles. I'm wearing a dress by Elie Vettori, all sparkly and see-through, and the stylist, this nice woman, is fussing with my hair.

Just fussing and fussing, turning it into a fright wig, kind of silly, but, OK, no prob, and I'm noticing that she has absolutely no makeup on. Really beautiful skin and no makeup, like she's quietly voting for truth in packaging in the midst of all this fashion-world magic. She gets done with my face, which is now this doll mask with big red lips and big patches of red on my cheeks. The photographer's assistant does a bunch of light-meter readings, and we're off. Except that we're only about a minute into the shoot when it is obvious that things are not working out between me and Andy Giles.

He wants to catch me in motion. Leaping. But not like those Philippe Halsman things, where you see Marilyn Monroe or somebody jumping straight up in the air. Andy wants me to leap forward. Like a gazelle, I guess, but I could be wrong. I mean, he's not giving me much of a hint, just saying, over and over, "Keep it extended. I need to see full extension." Whatever that means, in this exasperated tone of voice. Just over and over.

Finally, I decide it's time to stop and stare at him. Like, what the fuck?

So Andy starts fooling around with his camera, taking the back off, getting a different one from his assistant, this fat kid who is acting embarrassed. Then Andy is asking for meter readings, screwing around with the umbrellas on the strobe lights. Basically giving himself lots of time to get really, really steamed. Meanwhile, the stylist is off in a corner, making believe she's all alone in the world, nothing but a Blackberry to keep her company.

Eventually, when all the inanimate objects are just so, Andy turns to me and says, "Balletic, Fiona. What I need is balletic."

I don't know what to say. It would have been better if he had done the bad-boy photographer thing and whipped out his dick. So I could tell him to fuck himself with it. How can he fuck himself with balletic?

By now, he's frozen in place, glaring at me, so I say, "Look. Andy. You've been asking me to jump, so I've been jumping. Like mad. And it's been great. I look great. I can feel it. So. Andy. Tell me. What is your major malfunction?"

Andy puts a look of fear and loathing on his face. Tilts his head to one side, gives a big, angry sigh. Time to call Abigail.

Which I do, telling her it's not going all that well with Andy. He tries to grab my phone, and I turn on him with this look that really does the trick. He backs off, holding up his hands, like, OK, don't hurt me, and when I get back to Abigail, she is asking me to put him on.

Andy takes my phone, very meekly but still pretty nasty, and goes and sits in a distant corner of his loft. After about half an hour, he comes back and says Abigail thinks we ought to do some head shots.

Great. Let's do it.

Meaning, the stylist has to get rid of the porcelain-doll look, which she does in record time, and then she slows down, holding herself back, doing just enough to bring my face into focus, pure Fiona, and guess what, this turned out to be one of Abigail's brilliant ideas, because the head shots look really good. Really great.

Andy Giles is a great photographer, not that wild horses could ever drag me back to his studio. No chance, not even if I really believed that Andy is a great photographer and not just an OK photographer who once upon a time happened to be holding the camera when the camera decided, yes, I love Fiona. I really, truly love her, I always have and I always will. Which is bullshit, of course, the camera is such a liar.

The amazing Marta Marakova is holding me, kissing my cheek, I'm closing my eyes, inhaling, and I realize that her new perfume is total genius. Opaline is the naked girl scent, but not exactly. It's the naked girl scent all dressed up for a gala event. Like Marta, who is kissing my other cheek. I open my eyes and she's still holding onto me, arm's length, so tall and so happy that I'm seeing her so perfectly decked out in this flouncy gown, all satin and sequins. It's Naeem Khan ... I think ... anyway, I'm getting that slightly spooky, melty feeling I always get with Brenda. Not that Marta is the new Brenda. It's just the occasion. And Marta's vibe, which is genuinely nice. Because that's what counts, the vibe plus the look. Plus her scent, which is, like, soaking into me, and then a huge wave of other people are saying hello, and I'm swept away.

But where is Sergei?

As far he's concerned, I seem to be a case of out-of-sight-out-of-mind, which is OK, except that it's not vice versa. I keep thinking about him, what he said to Brenda, what he did to her, and I can't handle it. Sergei the pig.

The pig with no need to know where I live, which is why I had him pick me up at Bottino, on Tenth Avenue. So there I was, sipping prosecco, when in came this alien presence. A creature from another planet, who is telling me that he's Viktor. Sergei's driver. He's tall and thin, with dark hair, slicked back, and this startling face. Pasty with huge features, just what the camera's looking for, except he has this weird gaze. Way too intense, like, is this guy going to break the lens without even trying?

I followed him out to the street, then I was perched inside the limo, and Sergei started needling him on the way up Sixth. "Viktor is educated man. Tell her how much you are educated, Viktor."

Viktor was reluctant, but finally he said he had a PhD in electrical engineering or something. He was the head of his department at some university with a name I don't catch in some city whose name I also don't catch. But I was impressed.

Sergei said, "Viktor is very educated man. Now he drive limo. He drive for me." Which I had actually figured out for myself, Sergei, you ridiculous jerk. Speaking of which, where the fuck are you now?

The minute I got through the door of the Armory, I looked back and he'd vanished into thin air, leaving me at the mercy of Charles Bartram, a trustee of the Met and a gatekeeper at the Brook Club. A total snob who doesn't really like to talk to anyone. Except girls like me. I'm telling him, yes, I was away for a while, just taking a break. Rethinking things. He's giving me a not-so-subtle leer, meaning, time to move on and, great, there's Alison, Mademoiselle Giraffe, clawing her way through a wall of living flesh. We meet up at one of the bars, where this cute, very short Hispanic guy in a waiter's jacket is gazing up at Alison, with a look of total adoration on his face.

"Miss? Miss? May I give you something?"

She's not paying attention, a couple of other girls materialized, so it's all kissy, giggle, oh my god, for about five minutes, and the Hispanic guy is starting to get a lot of static because he's ignoring everyone else, trying desperately to get Alison's attention. I can hardly blame him. She looks so great, in this tight green sheath by Marquesa with her hair, all this fabulous auburn, all just piled up on her head. And seven-inch heels. At least.

Finally, we get some champagne and find a couple of chairs in a corner. Everybody is yakking away like mad, it's one big dull roar and now the music is getting cranked up. So I'm nearly screaming all this stuff about my date with Sergei, the oligarch from hell, and what the A.D.A. told me about his charitable donations and Russians in New York and how nobody can do anything about anything. All these unauthorized disclosures, which are no problem, because no one can hear me. Alison can barely hear me. But she gets a take on the subject, I guess, because she leans forward and says, in my ear, "Where is he?"

I shrug. She leans forward again, saying, "This doesn't seem like a real date. Like, he's not your type."

I laugh. "Not my type? Sergei isn't anybody's type. Believe me."

"I believe you." Her lips are so close and she's saying it again, "I believe you, Fiona, but guys like that can be interesting."

"Interesting?"

"If you look at them the right way."

"The right way? There's, um, like, a right way?"

She sits back and nods, with a certain look on her face, sort of … I don't know … this gorgeous sphinx with some sort of secret. Then she leans in again and says, "Maybe I should take him off your hands."

This strikes me as a terrific idea. And I love her breath in my ear, so I say, "Really? You'd do that?"

"Just for tonight. Sort of babysit him. Leave you free for a while."

"Great." The problem, of course, is to find the elusive Sergei. And to convince myself that it's all right to hand him off to Alison. The whole idea was to keep him in my sights, get to know the beast.

But, fuck it, I can't stand to be anywhere near him, so I say, "Let's fan out, the first one to spot him brings him back to the bar. We'll meet up there."

"But how am I supposed to spot him?"

"Oh, right. Well, he's this obnoxious blob, loud voice, always spouting some line of bullshit and—"

"Sounds like I can't miss him."

"If in doubt, just ask. Are you Sergei the total creep who threatened to kill Brenda?"

Alison smiles and plunges into the crowd. I plunge in in the opposite direction, getting nowhere fast when I hear my name.

"Fiona. Over here, babe."

I turn around and here he is again, my one truly awful ex, Bennett Ross, who is gripping the upper arm of this prime piece of jailbait. Not tall and modely. More short and curvy. Massive cleavage, and when she says, hi, I'm Celine, I catch a glittery glimpse of something. A tongue stud.

Bennett is telling Celine I'm this world-class model, really major career, and I'm going to get him a date with Brenda.

"Brenda who?"

"Brenda who?" Bennett gives me this look, like, can you believe the sheer ignorance? Then he looks back at Celine, repeating himself in that really delightful way of his.

"Brenda who? Come on, Celine, are you kidding me? Just Brenda Xavier Rawlings. Supermodel. That's who."

Celine gets really pissed. "What the fuck, this is what you tell me? In front of her? That she's going to get you a date with a supermodel?"

Bennett shrugs, complete twerp that he is, like, you should be happy to go out with a guy who's going to be going out with Brenda Rawlings. So I give him a sarcastic kiss on the cheek and it's back into the swirling mass of humanity. Only, it's not really swirling. People have gotten territorial. And then I feel a hand on my elbow.

Turning around, I'm looking at Viktor. He's saying something and after a while I realize he's asking me why I let Sergei get so drunk, and I'm, like, me? Are you kidding? If he's drunk he can take full credit for his achievement. He did it all on his own.

Viktor nods. Then his eyes go into this long-distance stare and says, "People don't like it."

I shrug, thinking, what is Sergei's driver doing in here? Assuming that he is just Sergei's driver. Which evidently he isn't. Anyway, I'm looking around, saying, "People seem to be putting up with it pretty well."

Not that I really know. Given that I've hardly seen Sergei all evening. On the other hand, I haven't noticed any major crises, Sergei carried out on a stretcher or anything like that. Viktor is standing absolutely still, his lips pressed together, giving me his Chauffeur-from-Outer-Space look, and I'm thinking, the people he means are not the ones I'm talking about. Not the people at the party, who might actually find Sergei amusing. The drunken philanthropist.

Viktor fades. Ages later I break into a clearing, and there's Sergei and I understand what Viktor was getting at. Because Sergei has an empty champagne glass in one hand, waving it around, making these choppy gestures with the other. Very emphatic and obviously blotto. When he sees me he gets this slightly demented grin on his face, saying, "Good. I am looking for you."

Then he holds his choppy-gesture hand out toward me, like a ringmaster, saying, "My date. Very beautiful. Not as beautiful as Brenda but very beautiful."

"Brenda?" This question comes from a man in a gray pin-striped suit, about the only male not in evening clothes.

"Yes," says Sergei. "Very important supermodel."

"Brenda Rawlings?" says the man in the suit. I nod and he keeps looking at me. Staring, actually, which could be a little off but isn't, he seems kind of sweet.

Sergei makes his ringmaster gesture in the man's direction, saying, "Very important executive in advertising industry. I introduce you."

We introduce ourselves, and of course I don't catch his name. Which he realizes, so he gives me his card.

Sergei is beaming, leaning back on his heels. "You see. I help your career."

The man smiles at me, I smile back, and then he is looking at me in this amazingly tender way. He obviously wants me and doesn't know what to do about it. So, lucky for him, Alison shows up, someone he knows. They say hello and kiss, he slips away, and I introduce her to Sergei. Which makes him very happy. He's practically licking his chops as she leads him away toward the bar. She's about twice as tall as Sergei, but he's five or six times as wide, so I'm watching them bulldoze their way through the crowd and thinking, if this were a picture in a book for kids it would be so cute. Mr. Hippo and Mademoiselle Giraffe.

The next morning I was hanging out in bed, half-asleep, when I got a call from Brenda. It's so wonderful now, when she calls, so calm and dreamy, Brenda the way she always was. Not that she thinks Sergei has backed off. It's more that she was really impressed when I took the call from the guy and went out with him, actually consorted with the Big Bad Wolf, and now she thinks of me as a combination Little Red Riding Hood and Wonder Woman, not to mention Joan of Arc.

Like my sword is going to go snicker-snack and I'll show up on Sixty-Third Street holding Sergei's head by the hair. Which would make sense if Sergei had any hair and Brenda liked her drama drizzled with blood. She doesn't like drama of any kind, unless it fades on a kiss, so now she's acting like life pre-Sergei is just around the corner, meaning, I'm going to get out there and take care of things. And spare her the details.

Which is what I have to do, given that Brenda's people have assumed a defensive posture—another phrase courtesy of Mike the security guy. Of course, I have absolutely no plan, the whole situation is so ridiculous, but it is so nice that Brenda and I are in sync, not even mentioning Sergei or any other problem ... so nice to feel that there aren't any problems, nothing I can't handle, which is bullshit, but, anyway, Brenda hangs up and I'm all relaxed now, drifting back into this lovely morning snooze.

When I woke up half an hour later, I gave Alison a call. She said she was getting ready for a shoot, she'll call me back when it's over, which left me with the image of her in a dressing room, essentially naked. In heels. Her hair up. So hot, even though it probably wasn't like that at all. No doubt she was all dressed and made up, sort of gift-wrapped, because that's what fashion is. This fancy packaging that someone like Alison doesn't really need.

A couple of hours later she gets back to me, knowing what I want to hear, so she starts right in, telling me Sergei is this drunken clown, kind of funny but also really pathetic.

I ask her if he's head-over-heels with her now.

"Um, well … actually … yeah. He is. He's been calling since seven-thirty this morning."

"He wants to take you out."

"He wants to take me to Moscow."

"Oh my god."

"I told him I'm busy."

"Anything about Brenda?"

"Actually, yes. Last night, he took me to the Bemelmans Bar, then we went to his place and he was really drunk by then, practically collapsing, so I brought him a chair. He more or less fell on the floor trying to sit down, but then he was sitting there, sort of snoring … really gross … so I asked him about Brenda. Do you know Brenda Rawlings? He's hiccupping and snorting and he finally says he knows her. He's going to kill her."

"Just like that?"

"Just like that. Like, he's basically unconscious … but …"

"But?"

"Well, it's like he doesn't know what he's saying but, on the other hand, he does know. And he means it. He's a terrible person, Fiona. You get that vibe from him. Of course, he was on his best behavior at the launch-party the other night. Aside from drinking too much and nearly passing out. But people were ignoring it. So he wouldn't have to be officially ostracized. Because, if that happens, all these contributions to all sorts of things would dry up. I mean, I know how it works but I was actually surprised at all the people coming over, being nice to him. Sergei must be unloading really huge wads of cash on every upscale charity in New York. So, OK, fine, but he's still not presentable. Meaning, I don't get how Brenda could go out with him. I really don't. And I don't want you to go out with him anymore, Fiona. He's the violent type. He obviously wasn't going to show that side at the party, but he didn't have to. It's just obvious."

"OK. He's really not charming. Also, he's a stone cold psychopath. So you're going to go out with him again?"

"I can handle him."

"You can handle him?"

"There are these signs, Fiona. As psychopaths go, he's kind of special. I can handle him."

"And I can't?"

"Fiona. Darling. Just stay away. Leave Sergei to me."

Which sounds like a great idea, Alison takes care of the Sergei problem and I'm off the hook. So I say, "OK, babe. Just be careful."

"Tell that to Sergei. Not that it would help. He's not going to know what hit him."

Alison hangs up and I get busy getting ready to get busy, busy, busy, lots of go-sees all afternoon, which is good, it'll keep me from wondering if Alison is going to be able to handle Sergei, I mean, she's tough, but what if he really is a psychopath and not just a drunken buffoon? Either way, he's the one who smacked Brenda, and so now I'm always seeing her on the floor, the guy standing over her. What kept him from killing her right then? What's going to keep me from killing the nasty creep the next time I see him? My girly nature? This question keeps popping up and I don't want to face it, so I'm hoping that Pam and company have finally shaped up and gotten this truly horrible situation under control.

Because that's one thing Sergei has accomplished. I used to love my racing thoughts, but now, thanks to him, I'm in this nightmare loop, my thoughts and I are having real problems, we're estranged, thinking about a trial separation, because, no matter how far my thoughts roam, no matter how fast, they always head back to that image, Brenda hurt and helpless. Crying. Which she never does. Except now she cries all the time, in my thoughts, even when I keep myself from thinking them.

So that's the downside of busy, busy, busy. It's a lot of work, work, work and it doesn't really cure you of your racing thoughts. Just puts them on the back burner, all the better to simmer like mad, twenty-four-seven, as Pam would say. The other downside is that busy, busy, busy gets in the way of dolce far niente, which is Italian for fucking off. My favorite activity. Except for fucking. Should I call Bill? Ummm, no, not now … maybe over the weekend … because now I have just enough time to pop over to Bergdorf's, where I get Crème de la Mer.

A super product, absolutely love it, though I have to admit that it's when I'm buying this fabulous goo that I get all weak and weepy and feeling sorry for myself, that I don't have anyone to apply it all over me, every nook and cranny, head to toe. Boo-hoo-hoo, if you know what I mean. Though applying it all over me all by myself is not such a bad option. I mean, a girl can always use a bracing dose of good old self-reliance.

So now I am outside of Bergdorf's, wondering if I should grab a cab to my first gig, which would be standard operating procedure, or should I hoof it, given that there will be no room for the gym in today's hectic schedule. I'm still dithering when my phone rings. It's Mike.

"Hi, Fiona."

"Hi, Mike."

"You ready for this?"

"For what?"

"The real reason."

"The real reason? Can't wait."

"Herpes."

"That's the real reason?"

"Right. I'm this very moral guy and I can't hit on you if I've got herpes."

I don't know what to say, realizing that Mike isn't the boring, readable person I thought he was. He's turning into yet another mystery. But not a scary one, which is nice.

He's asking me if I get the logic of what he's saying and I tell him, "Yes. I do. And this certainly is very moral of you, Mike. I appreciate it. Except if you're not hitting on me because of herpes and you're this very moral guy, it's pretty obvious it's not just me you're not hitting on. You're not hitting on anybody. In general."

"That's very astute, Fiona."

"So that's it. You're not hitting on anyone?"

Right."

"Not even your wives?"

"Who said I'm married?"

"OK, Mike. You obviously live in a very strange world, where the basic realities are like silly putty or something."

"Or something. You got that right. Ever hear of nasty putty?"

"No, but I think I know what you mean."

"I think you probably don't, Fiona. But that's OK. Be careful, right?"

"Right, Mike. I will."

Meaning, no, I won't, because why would I make a big point of being careful unless I felt scared all the time and that is not what

I want to feel. Anything but that, so … what to do, what to do? Get to my first go-see. And the next and the next and the next. And call Jillian Wright, to set up an appointment for the end of the day.

Because here's the big theory. Truth is beauty, beauty is skin-deep, and so the truth isn't going to push me into the spooky abyss, it's going to be like beauty, skin-deep and relaxing, as long as a highly trained professional is giving me one of those amazing exfoliating massages that are the specialty of the house at Jillian Wright.

Bill and I usually agree on which movie to see but the other night he had to drag me to the Film Forum, for this Nick Nolte flick about Viet Nam, not my thing, and drugs, not my thing, and the basic assumption that the world is a terrible place where nothing is what it seems and forget about ever feeling safe for even a moment, also not my thing, though it's sort of turning into my thing. My basic assumption. Thanks to Sergei.

There was this one terrific scene where Nick Nolte says to Tuesday Weld, "Your husband said I was a psychopath. What do you think? Do you think I'm a psychopath?" And I don't remember what Tuesday Weld said, just how she was getting all gooey inside because of the proximity of the young Nick Nolte, who is not exactly my thing but I could certainly get her point. I mean, the young Nick Nolte was hot. Anyway, he seemed to be implying that being a psychopath was this role you could play. Or not, depending on the circumstances, and I liked that idea. No personality trait is a totally done deal, no matter how terrible, it depends on the circumstances. So there is always hope, and then I was in Bill's bed, a place of total certainty, it is always so great.

It begins almost casually, like this is no big deal, same old-same old, but there is always something slightly unexpected and then it begins to build and it just builds and builds and builds. Time beyond time until time kicks back in and, what can I say, Bill did the job once again. Not that it's a job for him, more like a passion. Which is interesting, a passion for passion. I have that too. Anyway, it never gets old, just how ideally we fit together, body and soul, so slippery and sweet, meaning, it's always brand-new and I am always surprised to realize just how great I feel afterward. Because it's something you can't keep in memory, not entirely, so there is nothing to do except do it, get to that perfect point. Which we did. Especially the second time, which was just so unbelievably great that I decided to leave right after, why let anything fuck up the afterglow?

Of course Bill wanted me to stay, he even dug up this super-expensive single-malt Scotch and got me to take a sip, but I told him I had an very early cattle call, which was true but not the reason I was leaving. It was all about the afterglow, not the cattle call, which turned out to be a waste of time but so what, I was still feeling so great, sort of languorous and energized all at once. It was such a lovely, sort of orangey day, in the middle of which I zipped back to my apartment to rinse off and look for this grapefruit I vaguely remembered. And now cannot find anywhere in my not all that overcrowded fridge. Maybe it ran away from home, I mean, I did neglect it for quite a while. Anyway, I am now drip-drying, standing in front of my mirror and touching my nipples to see how they look hard … not that I don't know … and I'm wondering, is this weird? Because there's this idea that it's men who like to look, women are more into feelings, but why not be into both? The image and the emotion … my phone rings and this time it's Brenda.

She's bored. Not that she says that. Brenda never complains. But I can tell from her voice, which gets all wispy when she

realizes there's a blank spot in her schedule and she has no idea
of what to do next. She's asking me when I'm coming back out to
see her, and I'm saying, honey, sweetheart, I'd love to come today
but I'd get in so late and I have to be in town tomorrow and ...
Brenda sighs, then she says, why don't you skip the Jitney? Take
the helicopter.

Because this is the new development. Brenda commutes
between Southampton and Manhattan by helicopter. Sometimes twice a day. And sometimes she just sits in that big house
behind the tall hedge and gets bored with her trainer. Her nutritionist. The dermatologist-slash-make-up artist who is now in
residence. Meanwhile Brenda Xavier Rawlings Incorporated
keeps humming along, leveraging her image. Enhancing the
brand.

Brenda is telling me helicopters leave from West Thirtieth
Street all the time, why not come out for a few hours? It's a really
short flight, not really fun, but it would be so nice to see me ...
she keeps talking and I'm listening and of course I'm getting that
sweet, Jell-O-y feeling in my stomach ... I see in the mirror my
chest is all flushed.

So I say, yes, of course, darling. But I can't come until later and
I really should get back to town this evening. And who is going to
arrange it? Also, who is going to pay for this outrageous waste of
money? But I don't say this last part out loud. No one ever talks
to Brenda about money.

She's saying, Pam will take care of it, so I ring off and call Sergei. Reconnaissance in the Russian sector. He answers and starts
clearing his throat. This goes on for about fifteen minutes, then he
sort of gurgles, "Who is this?"

I tell him and by now he's got his normal voice back, bellowing, "I am glad you introduce me to Alison. We are having date."

"Really? That's wonderful Sergei. But I'm jealous."

"I understand. Alison is very beautiful girl. More beautiful than you. Also, very big girl. She will be trouble for you if you are not nice."

"What are you saying, Sergei? I shouldn't go out with you? Alison might beat me up?"

"I think Alison is very strong girl." Meaning, if you have strength, you use it to hurt people.

"She's strong all right, Sergei—"

"Alison is smart girl. But smart girl doesn't know everything."

"Right. So. Where are you taking me?"

"Brighton Beach. Very expensive night club. Romanov's. More expensive than Manhattan."

"Sounds pretty expensive."

"Yes. Is very expensive."

"So. Sergei, you're going to spend lots of money on me?"

"Yes. I spend lot of money. You are very expensive."

"If you only knew, Sergei."

"What?" He's shouting. "What you are saying? What? What? What this is?"

I hang up, because how can I explain to Sergei what this is? If he really wants to take me to Brighton Beach, he'll have Viktor call me. Arrange to pick me up at Bottino. So now I have to call Pam, act like it would be perfectly natural for her to arrange a quick helicopter hop to and from the Hamptons. Only to be expected. Given that that's what Brenda wants. Her wish is everybody else's command. Not that she makes all that many wishes. Mostly she just does the stuff her people put on her calendar.

The helicopter ride really wasn't fun, basically tons of noise trying to scramble my brains. But Breda's hideout was weirdly quiet. Hardly anyone around. I found her beside the indoor pool, all alone and stretched out on an old deck chair, with the creaky wood and the faded cushions. In a fuchsia two-piece by Badgley

Mischka. Before she noticed me I stood there for a minute realizing that her face has been upstaging her body for a couple of years now. Her miraculous face in the high-end ads. Like, that's enough, we can't even deal with the rest.

So times have changed because, when she was on the runway, people would look and look and look at all of her, the complete Brenda, just looking through the clothes. Looking at the way she moved. Or gape, pretending that they weren't. Brenda in motion, so beautiful, everyone would be ashamed. Ashamed to be gaping. Ashamed to be who they were, their ordinary selves, in a world where she was the standard. Is the standard, whether she's striding the earth or lying absolutely still, like she was in the pool house, water reflections bouncing off the ceiling, rippling all over her body.

I lay down beside her in the pool room, on another deck chair. We talked about this and that. Our usual topic. Then Brenda made another stunning revelation and I'm back at my place, still stunned, lying here on my bed, not even undressed, thinking, what am I going to do with this? Brenda isn't supposed to make stunning revelations. She's the stunning revelation. That's how it always was and so I don't want to think about this new thing. I just want to keep thinking the way people think I think when they look at me and say, oh, she must be a model, long legs, which is nice, but obviously short on brain power. Not much going on upstairs.

When Sergei and I get to Romanov's, a couple of nights later, I think, oh my god, this place has got to be ultra-pricey. Otherwise, how are they ever going to get back all the capital they sank into the maître d.'s uniform, which is sort of a generalissimo outfit crossed with a flight suit in shiny black nylon. On the shoulders, golden tassel things, really huge, with sequins on the lapels and more gold in the seams of the flight suit.

Then it begins to look like the big-ticket item was all the blue neon, which runs along every corner of every wall and every possible edge of anything … balconies, stairways, you name it. Then there are all the gilded surfaces. And the mirrors. And the gilded mirrors and the red shag carpeting. Just the thing for women in high heels, with their silk dresses and fur stoles, which function as these hairy showcases for some really vast boob acreage. All of it heavily powdered.

And I am seeing these boobs in intimate detail because one female after another is stopping by our table to lean way over and plant a big red lip imprint on every male face she can find. Sergei and his pals love it. It makes them feel sexy. Or maybe it makes them feel they don't really have to be sexy. All they have to be is rich. And male. Anyway, they're chortling and chuckling and babbling away in Russian. We've been here about fifteen minutes and they're already buzzed on vodka.

Some of these Brighton Beach babes are gorgeous, others would be gorgeous if they lost fifty pounds and went a little easier on the hard stuff. And the lipstick. But way too much booze and lipstick is not their only problem. They also have way too much pancake, way too much mascara, and the dresses are so tight across their asses you can't help noticing that a lot of them are wearing girdles. Mostly the older ones but some of the younger ones, too. Amazing. It's like time travel.

Back to the fifties, I guess, except the music is some really irritating Italian disco stuff from the Eighties, and then it stops and these guys in Cossack outfits pop up at our table and begin this hysterical strumming on some sort of Russian guitar-thing … sort of triangular … and then a team in red jackets comes by with this huge object ... a vase made of ice. The red jackets give a sort of heave-ho and drop the vase in the middle of our table and then they jam a huge bouquet of lilies into the cavity. The next thing, all this food starts arriving. Sergei is immediately stuffing his face with one hand, swilling vodka with the other, but not for long because a couple of women are dragging him out of his seat, onto the dance floor.

A huge orchestra has appeared on a revolving stage and the music is, like, the theme from Star Wars with Latin accents. A little strange. The women think so too. So they're standing around, considering their options. Then one of them gets the bright idea of trying to waltz with Sergei. This doesn't work, so another one gives it a shot. Another no-go and then another and another and finally they end up spinning him this way and that, sort of laughing and bringing him more vodka in the crystal goblets they have here. Only they're not crystal. I checked, with a fork. No ring, just a clunk, so I guess glassware was not a major budget item. Also, the vodka isn't exactly primo. I take a sip or two and it's pretty rough. Like rubbing alcohol cut with Drano.

Just kidding, but, seriously, I can't get a take on this place, all the money and the cheesiness, the noise and the people of various kinds, lots of Americans mixed in with the Russians, and some Europeans, too, looking dazed and also amused, like, we traveled all this way and this is what we found ... it's really exotic, but, well ... the stage is revolving again and now there's this floor show, a Rod Stewart look-alike singing in Russian and surrounded by a troupe of showgirls who look like they just stepped off the plane from Vegas.

Except for their headdresses, these gigantic Bird-of-Paradise extravaganzas, they're basically naked. Which is nice. All these gorgeous legs and lovely strong backs and perky tits and perfect, adorable asses. All the more perfect and adorable because the girls are up on high heels like chopsticks. So I'm sitting there, transfixed, because what else is there for me to do?

The girls on the other side of my table are either smooching with their dates, these semi-elderly guys in super-expensive sports jackets, or their dates are like Sergei, leaving them all alone while they dance the drunken tango with person or persons unknown. So there is this small patch of wallflowers, sitting and talking among themselves. In Russian. Young girls, very Manhattanish, very calm and elegant, not at all like the local babes with their powdered boobs, which are starting to get kind of streaky.

Everything is getting kind of streaky. There's a general build-up of sweatiness, given all the vodka and the ever-increasing decibels and the light show getting into high gear, with waiters running back and forth serving way too much food and customers going nuts on the dance floor and up on the revolving stage the performers have turned into Cossacks, only there are a lot more of them now and they're leaping and shouting and banging away at their instruments more hysterically than ever. Nothing to do but wait for Sergei to stagger back to his seat. And get on with this brilliant idea I came up with a couple of days ago, which I am thinking of as Plan A.

But first I have to deal with this large, middle-aged woman in a sequined gown who is making a big deal of sitting down in the chair beside me, adjusting her stole, arching her back, arranging her tiny little purse on her knees just so. She's wearing no makeup except for wild patches of lavender on her upper eyelids, and now she's tilting her head back, looking at me through these weird little slits. Very judgmental. "You would be good wife for Sergei. Very young, very beautiful."

"Is that how he likes his punching bags? Young and beautiful?"

Blank stare. Can't tell if she's offended or just doesn't get the concept of punching bags. Or the problem with girls as punching bags.

Shifting into Nancy Drew mode, I say, "Tell me about Sergei."

"Sergei is very rich man."

"Really?"

"Yes. Sergei is important businessman. Many important contacts."

"Contacts?"

"Yes. With Russian ministry personnel. Also, American capitalists."

"Gee," I say. "It sounds like Sergei has it pretty much covered."

The woman decides it's time to give me another gimlet-eyed once-over, so I give her a great big All-American smile and ask her how Sergei makes his money.

With this impatient little shake of her head, she says, "Sergei is important businessman."

"Yeah, right, but what's his game? Oil? Guns? Tell me all about it. Hey, I've got it. Sergei is into human trafficking. The reason I ask, people at my agency are always warning us about that, watch out for the guys offering these super great jobs in faraway places. So. Is that it? Human trafficking?"

At this, she stalks off and I'm trying to explain to this waiter who is very nice but not exactly conversant in English that I want him to bring me some caviar, which he gets, but also Melba toast, which he doesn't get. After he leaves, the woman in the sequined gown comes back and plunks herself down beside me, saying, "You are too tall for Sergei. Like boy who plays football."

"You mean soccer?"

Another blank stare.

"Anyway," I said. "I'm not too tall. Sergei's too short. Like a dwarf hippo."

"Dwarf?"

"You know, like, pygmy."

I don't think she understands any of it—hippo or dwarf or pygmy—but she thinks she does. In other words, she gets the "pig" in pygmy and figures that was my insult. To call Sergei a pig.

"You are not cultured girl," she says, very huffily, pursing her lips and tossing her head with this big show of cultural refinement. Suddenly, there's a man standing behind her, kneading her shoulders with both hands. She looks up at him, with this look of sappy gratitude. He leans down, whispers something in her ear, and she gets up with great dignity and sashays into the crowd.

The man sits down beside me, telling me his name is Sergei, so I say, what a coincidence blah-blah-blah, and pretty soon he is letting me know that his Porsche is parked just outside. Whispering from behind his hand, like he's slipping me the key to the secret code.

Would I like to go someplace quieter?

The guy is tall, dark, and handsome, literally, and very spiffily dressed. Blue blazer and gray flannel slacks. With a white shirt and an ascot, of all things. Back to the fifties again. He is fluent in English, with a not-exactly-Russian accent, and his hand is resting on my thigh. His lips are on my ear, telling me he lives in Manhattan, a couple of minutes over the bridge ...

I'm tempted and he knows it. What he doesn't know is that Plan A trumps everything, even my throbbing pussy. Even my demented fantasy of finding a quiet stall in the ladies room and getting it on with him there. As if there were any quiet stalls in the ladies room at Romanov's... as if I would ever get it on with this tall, dark, and handsome stranger under any circumstances, given that he really, truly is a stranger and my safe-sex policy is really, truly in force.

By now his hand is in my crotch, he's going to start fooling around with my panties any second ... I'm wondering if he realizes how wet I am ... and then, for the first time ever, I am glad to see the original Sergei, lurching up and practically sitting down on the other Sergei before he can get out of the way.

The original Sergei starts bellowing for vodka. The other Sergei, ever the gentleman, touches my face wistfully with his crotch-grabbing hand and vanishes forever. So I look over at the original Sergei. He has stopped bellowing. He is pouring himself shots and toasting "most beautiful woman in world."

Meaning Brenda, I guess, and now Sergei is looking in all his pockets, saying, "Telephone ... where is telephone ... most beautiful woman—" Huge belch and then, "Most beautiful woman is expecting telephone call—"

Suddenly he's slumping in his chair, his forehead on the table. He's not even snoring. So I take Fletcher Marks's business card out of my purse and slip it into the pocket of Sergei's jacket. Because that is Plan A. The idea being that whoever puts Sergei to bed will find the card, show it to Viktor, and Viktor will ask himself what it's doing there. Wonder if maybe Sergei has been talking to the wrong people.

As hard as I try to get along with my racing thoughts, I'd get along a lot better if they didn't have a mind of their own. I mean, OK, I can keep them away from the image of Brenda lying there hurt but then, while I'm busy with that, her latest revelation sneaks in, the one I mentioned. And really, truly can't handle. It's about Sergei's real motive. Why he wants to kill her.

Brenda was walking me out of the pool house, through the atrium, out to the big circular driveway ... a car was waiting and so I was leaning in close to kiss her good-bye when she pulled back, saying, "You know that man I saw with Sergei?"

"Yes."

"I don't think that was it."

"It?"

"Why he, you know ... got upset with me."

"Oh?"

"Umm. No, I mean … he's very sensitive, and …"

"Sensitive? Really?"

"Really, because he cares a lot about his performance, and, er, um …"

Sergei's performance was not a subject I really wanted to delve into but I had to, even if it meant the driver had to wait and wait … and wait … even if I missed one helicopter and then another … I had to, standing there with Brenda on the snow-white gravel, dusk falling, quite the scenic setting for a stunning revelation. Which I have really not wanted to think about ever since I heard it.

It's too stunning. Or yucky. Anyway, Brenda didn't give me the whole thing, just bits and pieces I had to put together, something to do while I hung around at the Southampton heliport looking at stuff in little wooden frames, underneath these scratchy sheets of plastic. Waiting for the last flight to take off.

It had all occurred to me before, sort of, but only sort of, because it was way too awful to contemplate. Brenda and Sergei, their big night of romance. The mere thought of him alone with her was too creepy for words, but that goes for all of Brenda's escorts and walkers and whatever, quite the unappetizing crew, so, anyway … she was saying they were up in her bedroom and, er, um … she kind of stalled there and I had to fight the urge to tell her, that's OK, never mind, if this is making you uncomfortable … but I didn't do that, I put on this big act, staying all calm and reassuring and getting her to explain how Sergei managed to penetrate the boudoir, something very few people on the face of the earth have ever accomplished, as far as I know.

Brenda wasn't all that clear on the subject, telling me something about this really special champagne, how Sergei talked his way into her house with it after one of their big nights on the town. There's this girl, still on duty, Sergei gets her to put the champagne in the fridge, then he and Brenda go to the living room. By now, it's really late, Brenda should be getting her nine or ten hours of beauty sleep. But she isn't, she's sitting around with Sergei, and this supposedly on-duty girl turns out to be a pretty lame excuse for a chaperone. If that's what she was supposed to be. I mean, Pam was really not on the case this time.

After a while, Sergei tells the girl to go get the champagne. But, big mistake, instead of bringing it to the living room she takes it up to Brenda's bedroom. Some mistake, right? Anyway, Sergei convinces Brenda they might as well drink it up there and so up they go. Sergei is already pretty wasted but he's got a plan and he's carrying it out, getting Brenda to sit with him on this sofa, offering her some champagne.

Which she doesn't want, but I can just hear him, telling her how great it is, best champagne in world, this is special occasion, have some, why not? World's most beautiful woman must drink world's greatest champagne and so, Brenda being her super-nice self, has a few sips, and of course he won't shut up, he keeps badgering her, most beautiful woman, world's greatest champagne, blah-blah-blah, so she has a little more and then a little more and he actually gets her a bit tipsy. After a while, she has to go pee.

Things have been going downhill, and when Brenda gets back from the bathroom, it turns out that things have jumped off a cliff. Because Sergei is standing there, totally naked, his arms out to the side, babbling something in Russian. With this maniacal grin on his face, the Pillsbury Dough Boy in nightmare mode, which really cannot be a pretty sight … really not … he's half-hard … his dick is just this little nothing, Brenda's actual words, but the problem is not Sergei's dick.

The real, major, call-in-the-Marines problem is Brenda's reaction. Because, from what she tells me, there is no reaction. She is not disappointed. She is not outraged, a pussy scorned. Don't I excite you? How dare you insult me with this lame excuse for a hard-on? Brenda is so zonked she couldn't care less.

So here is this guy, he's been dreaming for weeks about his shot at most beautiful woman in world—he's going to slip it in and voilà, this is the great Sergei Propokoff, deep inside the magic circle. Major-league acceptance. At last. But the moment has arrived and he not only can't take his shot, most beautiful woman in world hardly seems to notice.

This is the second time he hits her, but he doesn't throw her around. Wouldn't want to wake up Brenda's security people. Just one slap to the side of the head, and then he tells her he's sorry. Sorry, sorry, sorry, he spends an hour telling her how sorry he is and even now she's saying she believes him, Sergei was really so sorry for what he did, which is pure Brenda, given that he called her up the next day and told her he's going to kill her. Which she also believed and of course she has no idea why he would want to do such a thing.

It's pretty extreme, I admit, but logical, I mean, he shows her the essence of his manhood, it's limp and the limpness doesn't even register. It's like he doesn't exist. So now Brenda can't exist. He has to kill her.

That's how I figure it, from limp dick to death warrant. So here I am in Sergei's limo, we're pulling away from Romanov's, I'm looking at the same limp dick, and he's making it clear that I'd better care. Not that he's all that articulate. He's growling and slobbering, so drunk he's about to puke, but he's getting the message across. Limpness is the issue, one that should concern me deeply. Because Sergei wants a blow job.

We zip along the Belt Parkway for a while, Sergei comatose, mostly, with me gazing out at the harbor. Gateway to the world but with the curtain drawn. A cloudy night, I guess, and then the

What-d'you-call-it Expressway, just poking along, Viktor opting for life in the slow lane. Like, here we are in limbo, what's the hurry? Next he opts for the Manhattan Bridge, which would not have been my choice. Given that the other choice was the Brooklyn Bridge, still gorgeous after all these years. Then, rattle, bang, we're on the lower level of the Manhattan, another lousy option. All that grungy gray light.

Next, we're cruising up Lexington Avenue and I'm thinking, OK, at least Plan A is in motion. A long shot, needless to say, and maybe not even that. Because after I slipped the business card into Sergei's pocket I looked up and noticed one of the elegant girls across the table. The others were chatting away but this one was staring right at me. Keeping her face blank, like, I saw what you did.

Eventually, Sergei returns to the land of the living. Not only that, he's trying to grab my head and shove it into his lap. I pull away and bring my right foot up, plant it on his chest, push him back. But not that far back. He weighs a ton. Now he's coming at me again, so I reach out and grab him by the chin.

"Listen, Sergei. You don't want a blow job from me. I've got herpes."

"Herpes … herpes are big joke."

"OK, you simple-minded creep. I've got AIDS."

"AIDS. Bullshit …" And he passes out again, his dick just lying there. Completely shriveled. Ugh. I mean, pussies are gorgeous even if they're not all juicy and hot, but a dick has to be hard if it wants to qualify as a thing of beauty. Hard or at least getting there. Otherwise, it's mundane at best.

I look around. We're standing at the light at Forty-Fifth and Park, so I tap on the privacy panel. I hear this crackling sort of microphone sound, so I say, "Look, Viktor. Head downtown, then west on Twenty-Sixth. I'll get out when we hit Seventh Avenue. Either side is fine."

All I hear is the door locks clicking shut and Sergei is shouting, "You think you do not satisfy me?"

I say, "Gosh, Sergei, I haven't really given the matter much thought."

So he repeats himself, louder and louder, and, strangely enough, this seems to help. I figure out what he means, which is something along the lines of, hey, guess what, we're going to have sex. And you don't have any choice in the matter.

To emphasize the point, he slaps at my head. I duck but he manages to clip me. Just barely. I kick at him, catching his knee, which, instead of feeling, he passes out again. I bang on the privacy panel for about five minutes, getting no response from Viktor, who has decided to take the limo on a leisurely tour of Park Avenue South and selected side streets.

So. I'm a prisoner, basically, and this is rape. I mean, I'm being coerced but, on the other hand, I have to take the initiative. That or serve a life sentence in the back of this limo, because the situation is pretty clear. I'm not getting out of here until Sergei gets off. So I rummage around in my purse and find this tube of lubricant I always carry.

I'm squirting some onto my hand when Sergei wakes up. He's impressed by the lube. I'm grabbing his dick and he's telling me I am smart girl. Very efficient. Too bad his dick isn't. We're driving around in these random zigs and zags and it takes me about an hour of pulling on Sergei's dick and working his balls and the spot behind his balls to get him more or less hard, then it takes another hour and the entire tube of lubricant to jerk him off.

He makes quite the occasion out of his orgasm, bellowing and flopping around like a walrus getting tazed. So now I'm wiping off my hand on his jacket, telling Viktor there's no need to take me way out of his way, Twenty-Third and Seventh will be perfect. But Viktor is feeling chivalrous. He wants to do more. He wants to show me how grateful he is that mission impossible is accomplished and the night is finally winding down. So he's insisting he can't let me out at a corner. He has to take me right to my building.

We have some back and forth, until I give in and tell him a lie, that my place is on Seventh between Twenty-Fifth and Twenty-Sixth. When we get to the block and we're passing this doorman building, I say, "Here it is. Thanks."

Viktor unlocks the doors and I'm out of the car, into the building, in about five seconds. Behind the desk there's a black woman in a rent-a-cop jacket. I stand at the desk, my back to the street, and ask her to tell me if the limo has left.

"Nope. He just standing there."

"Can I go around the corner for a minute, to the elevators?"

"Sure."

So I'm hanging out in this strange building, getting slightly panicky, when the woman calls out to me.

"He took off."

I come around the corner, thank her, and she says, "No offense, Sugarpuss, but maybe you ought to vet your boyfriends a little better."

"You think?"

"Yeah. Due diligence, know what I'm saying?"

I'm smiling at her. Because this is very good advice and this is a very nice woman. I'm just across the desk, but she gives me a wave like I'm already far away.

"Night, honey."

"Good-night," I tell her. "And, really, thanks."

More work, work, work, I'm just running, running, running all over the place, feeling great, all psyched up and congratulating myself on getting to the gym again last night. This cute trainer showed me a new move involving an eighteen-inch platform and my glistening abs, and now it's afternoon and there's nothing. Nothing at all. Which is sheer exasperation. I mean, come on, career, you're supposed to keep me so busy it would never occur to me to think about anything else. Meaning, anything unpleasant, like slobbery drunks, slug-like sex parts. That sort of thing. So I set out in search of something pleasant and here I am, falling in love again. I can't help it.

The love object is this pair of dark maroon flats in the shoe department at Barney's, they are so elegant … not like I really need these shoes … as if that is ever the point … so … what to do? What to do? I'm standing in front of the foot mirror, blissing out on the new look for my totally sexy feet, when I feel a very soft touch in the small of my back. Turning around, I see it's this old girlfriend of mine. So we're hugging and laughing and sort of deliberately not kissing, and she's saying, "I know it's late but have you had lunch? I've got a reservation at Adour."

I tell her, no, I forgot about lunch, I was obsessing about these shoes … which I decide not to buy, and of course they're heart-broken … just kidding … so this ex of mine calls ahead from the taxi and tells them about me and a few minutes later we've been seated and we're ordering good-girl appetizers, vegetable things instead of sweetbreads or any of the other truly yummy possibilities. Then this wild-sounding soufflé, with truffles and a bunch of spices I never heard of. Our waiter says "Très bien" and marches off, this very serious French guy who acts like he's conducting research on idiotic American girls.

We let the wine steward tell us exactly which Burgundy we want, considering which entrée we ordered, then he goes away and for a minute we just look at each other. Her name is Maisie and her joke was to call me Maysie, a lover's version of my last name ... like we were so compatible because we were basically the same person, and sometimes it did feel that way when we were in bed but, really, we're completely different. Except for height. We're both five-ten. The perfect height for a model. When I met her, she was being repped by Elite, one of those girls who isn't exactly pretty, almost homely, actually, but in this really adorable way ... big ears, big forehead ... a face the casting agents call interesting or, if they're selling hard, they'll say she's fresh or original. Or real. Like straight-ahead beauty is unreal.

Anyway, I loved her looks and everything else about her and we were so happy together but we didn't live happily ever after because she wanted to be somebody's wife. You get better invitations if you're somebody's wife, provided he's properly connected.

After the wine steward showed up and went through his song and dance with the burgundy, we clinked our glasses and talked about my brilliant career, then my self-imposed exile in Europe, about which I provided a few juicy details. Then we switched over to Maisie's calendar, which is pretty impressive, because the guy she married is not only well placed but also rich and now she's doing tons of committee work, meaning she attends all these dinners and parties and charity balls she obviously loves and loves dressing up for ... so I'm sitting there sipping the scrumptious vino and gazing at Maisie, this charming young matron, totally Upper East Side.

Which is what she is and what she wants to be, no question, but I also see her as this lovely animal, full of exotic energy ... all these strange, pretty gestures of hers ... which I had forgotten and she has never even known about … her hands, the way they move, and her neck, the lovely tendons …

Pretty soon we're talking about the weather and clothes and then I bring up the subject of Brenda, not telling her about the Sergei problem, just how great it is to be around her and Maisie thinks I'm name-dropping. Which I never do. She's upset, this is not the old Fiona. But of course she doesn't say anything and I keep talking, Brenda this, Brenda that, and Maisie begins to get it, how I'm sharing with her something deeply personal, not showing off or being statusy. After a while she says, "So Brenda Rawlings is what? The meaning of life?"

She's sort of teasing me, like, wow, you really are mad about the girl. I smile, meaning yes, I am, absolutely, and she says, "Are you sleeping with her?"

This gives me a jolt and I realize that there has been some heavy-duty naiveté in charge of my innermost thoughts because I am telling the truth when I say, "No, and I never even think about that. Which is strange maybe but it's more like … I don't know … it's like she's just there…"

Which is pretty meaningless, but Maisie knows what I mean. Because, actually, how could I make love to Brenda? It'd be like making love to one of the basic realities … a wild idea and, later, when I was thinking about running into Maisie, I asked myself whose wild idea it was, hers or mine?

Of course it was mine, technically speaking, because Maisie didn't actually say anything about making it with reality. On the other hand, we're still on the same wave length, totally, and everyone has that fantasy, whether they know it or not. Without it, you'd lose interest in everything. Like, reality isn't really into me all that much, I can't even imagine us hooking up. So why go on living? Just forget it. Which nobody does, whatever they tell you. As long as you can feel anything, you feel like there's hope.

Abigail. I get so tired of her little games. Every time she calls me over, she's always sitting there and I have to stand. Sometimes I feel like shoving aside some of the junk on her incredibly junked-up desk and taking a seat, but I never do. It's not that she's the boss. She's the flunky, working for all us beautiful girls. Which is what she has to do because she herself is no longer beautiful. Which is also, let's face it, what makes her indispensable. Without her I'm sunk.

So she's not really a flunky, I admit, even though she has all these status issues. Meaning I have to stand while she sits, only this time she's standing too. She's all upset. She's got something serious to say. This is what I'm supposed to get from the way she's fiddling with this ballpoint pen and pursing her lips and sort of scowling and not looking me in the eye.

It turns out that Abigail has issues with my attitude. I'm rude. Really? Because I called her a no-neck, overweight moron with only one talent, which is to waste my time and piss me off? Just kidding. All I did was sigh and roll my eyes the last time she kept badgering me about my yes. Is that a definite yes? Really definite? Abigail's brain seems to be dominated by this idea. The definite yes. I've given her a million definite yeses since I went back to work.

But, well, OK, she's got this brain thing about the definite yes, let's go with it, no prob, except that I did get a little impatient with her the other day. So I guess it was obvious even over the phone that I was rolling my eyes, but is that any reason to stir up these dense clouds of bullshit on the subject of team spirit, good interpersonal relations, mutual respect?

After a couple of very deep breaths I finally say, "Great. Mutual respect. What about you, making me go through this dumb routine about the definite yes? Every time. What kind of respect is that?"

"You're not the only girl I handle, Fiona. I am constantly coordinating a number of very tight schedules. I expect a definite yes from all my girls."

I put my hands on my hips. My confrontational pose. "First of all, I knew you were going to say that. Second, ever since I went back to work, I have not fucked up in any way, shape, or form. I have never shown up wasted for a go-see or called you at three in the morning telling you I'm planning to be hung over the next day. So I think it's about time you started to give me a little credit for just saying yes and meaning it."

By the time I finish, I'm screaming except that actually I'm whispering, almost hissing, because I don't want anyone else to realize that Abigail and I are having a fight. She looks around, to see if anyone does realize, then stalks off toward the conference room where I looked at my pictures with Fred. When I get there, she's standing on the far side of the long oval table. I grab a chair and sit down across from her. This big assertive gesture, which doesn't seem to make any impression.

In a very low voice, like we were still out in the main office, Abigail says, "This isn't really about getting to appointments on time. It is, in part, of course, but there is a larger issue. And it's time we faced it."

"Really?"

"Yes, Fiona. Really. It's a question of commitment. There's a feeling at the agency that, um, you're not entirely committed to your career—"

"Not entirely committed?" I was sitting there staring at her now, like her face was a dart board.

"Not entirely, Fiona. There was that rather extensive period of time that you took off and then some of us here … even some of the other girls, I think, were wondering what your investment in this job actually is. Meaning that—"

"Meaning that what? That it's any of their business? Because this is just one big happy family? We're all in it together? I've heard this from you before, Abigail, despite the obvious fact that this biz is a snake pit. Which you ought to know, better than anybody."

Abigail looks away, really angry, and sighs a big sigh. Then she plasters a look of genuine concern on her face and looks back at me. "With your attitude, Fiona …"

"With my attitude. I mean, fuck my attitude—"

"Fiona—"

"OK, all right … all right… but I'm steamed and how can you blame me? Because what has my attitude got to do with it? Aside from the fact that it's terrific? The minute I get in front of the camera my attitude is exactly what it's supposed to be. Happy girl next door. Handsome boy next door. Vamp—"

"Oh, Fiona." Abigail is smiling at me now. Sort of arrogant. "You can't do vamp."

"I can do vamp. I can do under-aged mistress. I can do jaded European. Strung-out waif. Horsey bitch. Junior executive. Hamptons hottie. I can do anything. Which is why you like being my booker."

"Fiona, I'm not saying you aren't extremely talented. You are. But there is reason for concern. There's a question of fitting in here at the agency. We actually are a kind of family and…"

I groaned. "We're a family and … and, and, and … and what, for god's sake?"

Abigail crosses her arms over her chest and sort of hunches her shoulders, staring down at me. Like I'm some little kid who is misbehaving very badly.

I just keep staring back at her. Then I stand up, telling her, "This is total bullshit."

"Bullshit, Fiona?" Abigail's voice is all soothing and reproachful. "Is this the language you want to be using in the workplace?"

I laugh, saying, "Yeah. In the workplace. Where else? I mean, let's get real here, Abigail. Let's dispense with the total madness."

Abigail looks down and slowly shakes her head and then looks up at me and I'm startled. Her gaze is so soft. And, oh my god, so loving.

I'm freaked. So is Abigail. Saying she'll be right back, she runs out, and I'm thinking, that can't be it. Really can't. Abigail has been married to the same guy for a hundred years. I've seen them at the office, they're like this hopelessly married couple, so hopelessly married they're way beyond sex. With each other or anyone else. So … what is it?

Maybe Abigail sees me as her wayward daughter. The wayward daughter she never had. Which would be a disaster, given my complete lack of talent in the surrogate daughter department.

Abigail comes back and stands there in her arms-across-the-chest pose, gazing at me, really hard, and it looks like she's lost that loving feeling.

I sit in my chair, look down at the table. Look up at her. Really drawing it out … After a while, I say, "Abigail. I'm sorry. Really sorry."

"So this is an apology?"

"This is the fashion world. Right? So it's all about image, meaning, you can have this image of me apologizing to you and even if you know it's, like, totally insincere, you can hang onto it. Gloat over it. Because images are also real. Right? I mean, what other reality is there, if you get right down to it. So, yes. It's an apology. And that's a definite yes."

Abigail smiles and I shrug, and now we both smile. Abigail says there's been a lot of interest in me. Ian Vrdolyak, do I remember

him? Do I? No photographer was ever hotter for me, but not as
a bod, as an image … which is great, career-wise … and now Ian
wants to work with me again … there are other nibbles … some
solid interest from *Elle* and from Marc Jacobs, who is getting his
next show together … he's been hinting that he wants to cast me
in the swimwear segment … so I'm thinking this entire heart-to-
heart extravaganza has been sheer kabuki. A shadow play about
nothing.

Then, as I'm leaving the conference room, Abigail says, "Oh.
Fiona. There's just one more thing."

I turn around and hold my breath. Abigail gives this creepy
smile, saying, "Several of the media directors have been going over
their numbers. Leading, in certain quarters, to a reassessment of
priorities. Whatever that may mean"—another smile—"and so, to
keep you in play, I've had to go along with a ten-per cent reduc-
tion of your fee … in certain cases… it's probably temporary…"

All the way down in the elevator, I keep my mind blank. As if
that's going to help. Hitting the street, I think, what a total crock.
Like, I'm supposed to sympathize with poor Abigail, victim of
the nasty ad agencies. She probably came up with the idea of
cutting my fee all by herself, to get on their good side. For when
she goes to the mat for some other girl. Meaning the shadow play
wasn't about nothing, it was about putting me on the defensive,
softening me up for the news about the fee. Abigail really is a
horrendous cow.

I'm standing at the corner of Thirty-Fifth and Broadway, fum-
ing, and this off-duty cabby pulls up. He wants to get one last
fare for the day. Or maybe he just wants to ogle me … not that I
blame him. I wave the cab away and decide to call the ad-agency
guy who gave me his card at the Armory affair. If I can find his
card, figuring, it's about time I go behind Abigail's back.

I'm walking east on my street, got to get some half-and-half, and I get a text message. I can't read the screen, the sunset is blasting in at exactly the wrong angle, but I'm feeling all this jittery energy and I'm hoping it's Bill. I get into the shade of one of those U-Haul trucks and, yes, it is Bill.

U FREE?

I text back, TOTALLY LIBERATED

HA HA. WANT TO MEET???

YES!!! BOTTINO?

LETS CUT TO THE CHASE

YR PLACE?

8PM?

YES SHE SD YES YES YES

GREAT

Getting back to my place with the half-and-half, I figure I have an hour or maybe less to make myself into the world's most delectable piece of girl-meat. Not that Bill thinks of me that way, it's more that I am so incredibly horny that that's how I'm beginning to think of myself. Must be all this unresolved stuff, bringing with it the need for distraction and with sex, at least, the distraction is total. Already, just knowing that very soon I am going to come, really hard, is enough to turn everything else into a bunch of minor details.

Except, as I'm checking my pits, deciding I don't have to shave, I notice there's a fresh text message. It's Bill.

GOT TO BAIL. BIZNIZ. SO VRY SRRY

ME TOO

SO VRY VRY SRRY

DON'T OVERDO IT I MGHT THNK YR FUCKING
SMBDY ELSE
NO WAY THR IS NOBDY ELSE
AWW BILL HOW SWEET MAKE TONS OF $$$
THANKS

And now I am screwed. Because I'm not getting screwed,
which I desperately need, it's like this weird hunger, so what, for
god's sake, now? Hit the bars? Crawl into bed and get myself off
about twenty times?

Then, major brainstorm, I'll go over to the gym, which I love,
all these machines just aching to make me look great, except
that the whole experience always has this slightly spooky edge.
Especially in the locker room, which always feels like it's bracing
for an Invasion of the Body Haters. Actually, I'm exaggerating,
the really grotesque ones are pretty rare. But, still, I have these
apprehensions. Because the idea of women hating their bodies
gets me all exasperated and creeped out. Meaning, every time
I go to the gym I hope and pray that I won't come out of the
shower, feeling energized, and have to rub elbows with a living
skeleton.

This time it was just the opposite. The girl across from my
locker was ultra-tall and almost fat. Not fat, more muscular,
like—what? Steroids? Anyway, she was a splendid spectacle and
when she caught me looking it would have been awkward except
that she gave me this smile that said, no, I'm not gay but I'm cool
and you can look as much as you want. I smiled back, of course,
but I'm not all that sure what my smile was saying.

Ideally, it would have said I'm bi and sort of a sex fiend and
you are amazing and you don't actually have to be gay or even bi
to get it on with a girl like me, all you have to do is lie back and let
me show you a few things. Which probably wasn't the message of
my smile. It probably said something fairly lame like, no, I'm not

going to come on to you, I am well behaved, at least in the locker room, and, by the way, you are just incredible.

Heading for the snack bar, I realized that the monumental woman was reminding me of Alison, who is of course slim and willowy, not super-plus-sized, but, anyway, Alison was now on my mind. So I left a voice mail on her cell, right in the middle of replenishing my fluids with this blueberry glop, and she called back in about fifteen seconds.

"Hi, Fiona. Sweetie. I've been thinking I should call you. To thank you."

"For Sergei?"

"Bingo. He's a fucking gold mine."

"Not a vicious psychopath who gets off on battering women?"

"That too. But I've got him on a short leash."

"Literally?"

"Almost. The other night he was slobbering over one of my shoes. And I didn't even have to tell him to do it."

"Yuck. I mean, way to go, babe. Another conquest."

"Yeah. He's totally tamed. When he wants to give me something, he has to get down on his knees, and that's pretty much where he stays for the rest of the evening."

"Really?"

"Well … pretty much. I mean, he staggers around to get himself a drink. Then he thinks it's time for sex. Then he realizes he can't get it up—"

"He's too drunk."

"Right, so I recommend another drink and then I tell him how disgusting he is, I was really looking forward to some beautiful sex, so now he's completely hopeless, back down on his knees, apologizing, and I tell him I'm not all that interested in his pathetic apologies, so he promises me more stuff, and I tell him I'll think about it. Because I'm not even sure I can accept anything from such a pathetic piece of shit. Of course, it's a fine line …"

"A fine line?"

"Yeah, because he's always about to flip, go from pathetic to berserk. Misogyny in action. So I have to keep the focus on him. On how inferior he is to gorgeous, untouchable me. So the way it works is, the closer he gets to gorgeous, untouchable me, the more he obsesses about himself, what a fat, limp, disgusting piece of nothing he is."

"Meaning you practically shove your snatch in his face."

"Bingo again. Gosh, Fiona, I know you're a nice kid and all, but you might have a future in this line of work."

"So, what is it, garter belt—"

"Garter belt, no panties, nine-inch heels. Louboutins. Sometimes the pumps, sometimes the boots. And one of those bras that turn your tits into torpedoes."

"Does he ever say anything more about Brenda?"

"No, but here's the thing. He doesn't have to. Because Sergei is not exactly complicated. If a girl is at all girly, he'll abuse her. If the girl is nasty and mean and abusive, he'll take it—"

"And like it."

"Yeah. He likes it … or, mmm … I don't know … it's not like he likes it, it's more like it's real to him. Life is tough, and you're not really living unless you're pissing on someone. Or someone is pissing on you—"

"You're pissing on Sergei?"

"Umm, no, not … uh, well, not—"

"Not really or not yet?"

"Not at all, Fiona. It's all psychological. I don't even have to hit him."

"You just give him your shoe to lick."

"Right. And guess what he's going to give me."

"What?"

"This ring I saw at Bulgari the other day. A huge emerald in a diamond setting. One-hundred and fifteen thou, and I'm worth it. I mean, emeralds look so great on me."

Which is so true, no doubt, even if I've never seen Alison in emeralds. It's just that she's so tawny. So tawny and tall. Mademoiselle Giraffe with a scattering of emeralds, what a concept, provided she's not all mean and dominant and practically naked but wrapped in pinkish tulle … sort of pinkish orange … or, better yet, see-through silk … and then the silk falls away, revealing all this golden skin … so luscious with these hot green accents … her hard-earned emeralds.

We say good-bye and I'd be getting all worked up and sort of wistful at the thought of Alison's body except that it makes more sense to take something else from this conversation. A lesson in how to be tough, which isn't exactly wasted on me. I mean, what Alison said is right, I do understand this shit. Intuitively.

Pam the personal manager has been getting a bit business-like with me, saying, maybe next time I come out to the Hamptons why don't I hitch a ride with somebody. Because what? They're getting cost-conscious all of a sudden? Like Brenda couldn't just buy a helicopter if she wanted to? Not that she would ever want to … as far as she's concerned, she has everything. It would never occur to her to buy anything, not even a chocolate croissant from Sant Ambroeus, which she loves. Every morning, a chocolate croissant and orange juice just show up in her bedroom.

The point is, there's been a shift. Which I couldn't help noticing the last time I visited the Hamptons hideaway and asked Pam if there have been any recent problems with Sergei. She was, like, Sergei? What Sergei? What problems? Brenda Xavier Rawlings Incorporated doesn't have problems, never has problems. You must be hallucinating. Not that she actually said that, it was more like, why am I talking to you, anyway? You're not part of this organization.

I felt like saying, OK, Sergei is no problem, so why is Brenda still hiding out out here? But that would have given Pam another opportunity to stonewall, one of her great pleasures in life, and, in fact, Brenda wasn't there. She was on a shoot somewhere in Florida, which, I admit, did make it a little odd that I flew out this morning. It's just that, last night, Brenda asked me to come, so I did, and now she was gone. Typical Brenda. Typical me, I was in no mood to justify anything to anyone, especially Pam, with her clipboard and her menagerie of wireless gizmos. So I decided to wander around in this slapped-together house, see what I could see, and am I ever glad that I did.

Right off the living room is a solarium and then another solarium, which may be a greenhouse, given all the cacti, then this sort of sunken patio ... next, a library or something, with a bunch of empty shelves made of metal ... empty shelves everywhere ... and the entire house is all ups and downs, with these quirky turns and rooms that are tall and narrow and then wide and squat and not really rooms, just corridors pretending to be rooms. Or the other way around ... but, anyway, lots of glass, meaning lots of light ...

Which made it bearable and kind of poignant, you got the impression that here was a house desperate to be featured in some magazine. Not *Architectural Digest*, one of the newer ones. *Wallpaper* or *Details*, which I only know about because Fred loves architecture and we look at these mags online sometimes, when he's supposed to be working. He doesn't really like the fashion biz, which he calls the beauty jungle, and I guess he'd leave it if he didn't see himself as Tarzan in a place crawling with all these other Tarzans, most of them super-cute.

I never really knew where I was in this house, though I did get the general impression that I was climbing higher and higher, then I was scrambling up this metal ladder and, all of a sudden, I was on a wide porch, way above everything. There were two big beds with metal frames and these screened-in windows. It was so wonderful, sort of déjà vu, reminding me of the sleeping porch in the house where I spent my summers when I was a kid, after my horrible parents went off and left me with my grandmother.

Of course, that porch was different. The leaves came right up to the screens and all night long all the insects would sing away like mad, which was so soothing even though it was this terrible racket if you decided to stop falling asleep and pay attention. Here, on this porch in the Hamptons, no leaves, just sky over water and a lot of glare. And silence.

And no books.

On the sleeping porch at my grandmother's place, there was a wooden chest covered with this flimsy old fabric, cotton, I guess, with a tiny flower pattern, and it was filled with Oz books, Nancy Drew books, the Bobbsey Twins. *The Wind in the Willows.* My grandmother's books, from when she was little. I would swim and ride horses and run around from morning to night, which I don't know how I did all that, because what I remember mostly was reading. I was a total bookworm and my favorites were the Oz books.

In one of them, there is this boy, Tip, who was born a girl and then Mombi the witch turned her into a boy and then she was turned back into a girl by Glinda the Good, and I always wondered if something like that had happened to me. Not really, of course, but when the boy-girl thing started I was confused. I must have been about ten or eleven, and I was always wondering, I have this girl-body but what am I? Really? Because there were all sorts of feelings, all tangled up, and then I decided they were just my feelings, and maybe I was all over the map, girl-boy-feeling-wise, but so what?

A pretty mature attitude for a kid that age, but there is something else, which I didn't get until that afternoon, nodding off on one of the beds in Brenda's hideaway and realizing something kind of obvious, like, reality versus fantasy and why I went to Europe for a whole year ... because real life in New York was getting to be too real ... not that I'm against reality, not really, because reality, fantasy, whatever, it's all just this story you tell yourself, wanting to know what's going to happen next, and you can switch back and forth, doing realism for a while, until that gets old, then back to childhood, a spell of fantasy, all the neat maps of the Land of Oz and so on ... so I loved it when I was wandering around in Europe, I'd get a new map of the new place I was in, spread it out on the bed, really getting into it ...

It wasn't just that the new map was so totally fascinating, it made me feel safe, like here, in this house, where Brenda is safe, even if she's in Florida because Florida is like one of those funny places on the edge of the Oz map. The Oz characters might go there, for the sake of the story, but they always come back safe and sound. So I guess I was thinking, no sweat, Alison is taking care of the Sergei problem, wrapping him around her little finger. Or shoving one of her Louboutin boots all the way up his ass. Down his throat? Which sounds pretty hardcore, I know, but let's not be too judgmental. I mean, Alison is this stunning presence, like the Statue of Liberty or something, deep down inside a force for the good. So look at it this way, Brenda hasn't heard from nasty old Sergei for weeks. And not only that but, who knows, maybe Plan A is also working, meaning Sergei's sinister confederates found

Fletcher's business card, figured he was ratting them out, and now they were waiting for the perfect moment to dump him in the East River. Or something.

So I was feeling free to get into the Oz mood, just drifting in that landscape ...having all these story-feelings, the loose ends tied up, because what is the point of loose ends unless they get tied up and you get that great feeling of THE END, with everything perfect again and all calm and safe and even a little sad ... but basically perfect ... except that, here I am, back from the Hamptons, approaching my building on Twenty-Eighth Street and there is Sergei's limo at the curb, just waiting.

The ogre's house on wheels.

I'm crossing the street toward the limo, the back window is coming down, and there is the ogre's face. What else? But it's a real shock, this big blob of grinning idiocy, and for a second I feel like I'm having another meltdown. Sheer panic, which I cannot afford under the circumstances, so I go around to the curb side and yank on the door handle. Which would have fallen pretty flat if the door was locked, but it wasn't, so I hop in.

Without being invited, so Sergei is all offended by this move, like, I am important person from Moscow, this is not refined behavior. Quite the presto-chango, from grinning idiot to pompous idiot. Really fast, considering that Sergei is semi-brain dead, thanks to all the booze he's been swilling. The inside of the limo smells like a back room where a whole troupe of drunks has been sleeping it off.

Trying not to breathe too deeply, I ask him, "What's up, big guy? Smack any girls around lately?"

He doesn't hear me, his phone is ringing. This is obvious to me and also to Viktor, because the privacy panel is down, but it does not seem to be all that obvious to Sergei what he ought to do about it. He sits there for about three rings, then he starts digging away in his jacket pockets. Eventually, it's Eureka, I have found it, except that the phone he finds is not the one that's ringing. He has two, evidently, and by the time he finds the second one he's missed the call.

Now I'm saying, "You missed it, Sergei. Why don't you at least check, see who it was? That's what most people would do. In case, you were wondering."

But I'm not getting through. After staring at the second phone for a while, he holds it up and says, "This is smart phone. Other phone is stupid but this phone is very smart."

"Gee, Sergei. I'm impressed. A smart phone. Maybe it could lend you a few IQ points."

As usual, my zinger gets no reaction. Not that it missed its target, which is huge. It's more that the target is anesthetized by booze. Can't feel a thing. Can only repeat itself.

"This is smart phone. You know how smart is this phone? It tells me about money."

"Oooh. That is smart. How much, Sergei? How much money is your phone telling you about?"

He gives me this condescending look. Plus a condescending snort. "How much? I tell you how much. Five billions of dollars. Five and a half billions. This is lot of money, no?"

"Yes, indeed. Beaucoup dinero—"

"What?"

Before I can say anything, Viktor has swung around in his seat, giving Sergei this stare. Like, Herman Munster plus Godzilla, this laser beam of rage just drilling into Sergei's skull.

Only Sergei doesn't notice. He's sort of shoving the phone in my face, saying, "Is lot of money, no?"

"It certainly is, Sergei, so tell me why you carry your smart phone around with you. Sounds like you ought to keep it in a safety deposit box."

Now he isn't condescending. He's indignant, drawing himself up, so he can look down at me. Only he isn't tall enough.

"No," he says. "How do I get text message if phone is in safety deposit box? You are stupid girl. I keep phone in apartment."

"OK, Sergei. That makes sense. Where else would you keep it? Right?"

"That is right." Smirking. Then looking terrified because Viktor has gotten out of the driver's seat and now he's opening the back door on Sergei's side, reaching in, snatching the phone away from him. Muttering something in Russian, which scares Sergei even more. He looks like he's about to cry.

Time to change the subject, so I put my hand on his shoulder and lean my face into his. "When are you going to take me back to Brighton Beach?"

"Ach. Brighton Beach." He's practically snorting in disgust. "I do not go to Brooklyn. I am Manhattan person."

I can't help it, I laugh, and he raises his hand. "You want me to teach you to be nice girl?"

I scramble back against the doors, saying, "Watch it, Sergei. I don't want to have to beat the living shit out of you."

Now he laughs, but it's forced. Should he let me talk to him like this or not? In front, Viktor is giving every sign of freaking out that you can give if you're determined to stay cool and not move a muscle. Like this ice statue about to shatter into a million smithereens.

I lean forward again, and this time I slap Sergei's face. Not hard. Soft and dainty, like a girl. He collapses into his seat. Out cold, the knockout punch delivered, of course, by the booze.

Viktor heaves himself around again, to see if what just happened is what he thinks just happened, which it is, so he turns back around and now he is looking at me in the rearview mirror, telling me that Sergei wants a date. But not with me. With Brenda.

"This is a terrible idea, Viktor."

"Yes. Terrible idea." A long pause. Then, "This is what Sergei wants."

I'm thinking back to the launch party, what Viktor said then, and I say, "OK. This is what Sergei wants. Is this what people want?"

"People?" Viktor is pretending he doesn't know what I mean.

"Yes, Viktor. People. The ones who worry about Sergei getting drunk in public. Making death threats. It's all high-profile stuff …"

"High-profile?"

"Yeah, you know, high-profile, as in headline-grabbing. The wrong kind of publicity. And what's up with the smart phone, anyway?"

Another pause, this one so long that I finally say, "Come on, Viktor. Don't play dumb. A smart guy like you—"

"I am not smart guy."

"Tell me, Viktor. Who's the smart guy? Sergei?"

I hear him laugh, just barely, then he puts on his best Welcome-to-the-castle-the-master-is-waiting-for-you voice and says, "Sergei wants date with Brenda. Where is she?"

"She vanished, poof, on a magic carpet ride. No one can reach her."

"Poof?"

"Yeah. Poof. It means one thing in England, and another in America. In America it means, forget it, Sergei isn't going to get within ten-thousand miles of Brenda. If he wants a date, tell him I'm available. Can't wait to see him. Tell him to give me a call."

"Yes? Really? I tell him this?"

"Tell him, Viktor, that … um, no … actually … tell him this … tell him I'm going to get Brenda to come back to the city tomorrow. Then I'll get him a date with her. OK? Tell him it's a done deal, she'll be waiting for him in a private room at Naxos, Tenth Avenue, between Nineteenth and Twentieth. Seven-thirty sharp. Don't use her name, ask for me. Then you'll be taking her and Sergei to a gallery opening at 545 East Twenty-Sixth, so he doesn't want to show up too early, doesn't want to show up too late, the idea is to show up at just the right moment. Brenda always does, so this is important."

At this point, Sergei is coming out of it, more or less, and then he suddenly snaps into focus. Remembering that I slapped him.

"Why you do this? I am gentleman."

"Right. I forgot. OK, Sergei, you're a gentleman, so if I get Brenda to go with you to an opening at the Wallenberg-Bruno Gallery behave yourself?"

"Allen Wallenberg is good friend of mine."

"Great. So you'll behave and if you don't Allen's security people will throw you out on your butt."

"They don't touch me. If they touch me, I kill them."

"Ah. Right. You'll kill them. I wanted to talk to you about that. When you say you're going to kill somebody, what do you mean? Exactly? Do you mean that you are actually, like, going to kill them?"

"If they touch me—"

"OK, OK. You drunken creep. If they touch you you'll kill them. Great. So." I lean back and watch him nodding off. Truly a drunken creep. The one who smacked Brenda. The enemy I have to stay close to. The enemy who was now turning back into this soggy blur and might be harmless but probably isn't. Meaning, I need a strategy. It's just that it's hard to come up with one of those when your enemy has a brain like a rag soaked with vodka.

One stray spark and it's brain flambé, blue flames and god knows what weird mayhem.

I put my hand on Viktor's shoulder, to see if he'll flinch, which he doesn't, and I say, "Seven-thirty sharp."

He nods. I get out. Sergei tips over on his side. I close the door and the limo takes off. It is a beautiful evening, all quiet and full of itself, if that makes any sense. If not, so what? It's still a beautiful evening.

I decided to wander over to Bottino and be the girl in the corner, sipping her lonely glass of prosecco. Hoping somebody cute will hit on me. Not because I want to hook up, just to put something nice between me and the image of Sergei, this pointless thing that is flopping around like a drunken fish out of water, creating this really yucky nuisance.

The morning after came and went, leaving me feeling a little wobbly because I did kind of splurge on the prosecco. Having sworn that I'd have only one. Another broken resolution. But I got through a fairly grueling round of go-sees without any major mishaps and I'm feeling like quite the productive member of society, standing here at Eighth Avenue and Twenty-Seventh wondering where all the cabs are … it's nowhere near the end of the shift, so what is this, the beginning of some sci-fi thriller? The aliens have landed and New York cabs are their idea of the perfect sex object and … god, this is tedious, I'm about to be late for this one last go-see … and now my phone is ringing.

It's the number of this person I don't know, a woman, every week or so she calls, asking if I remember her. So I say no and she says she thinks I do remember her, and I say, OK, who are you?

And then she fades. It's creepy, so this time I take the call and a second later press END. To hell with it.

So then I see this cab, I'm waving my arm, and, I cannot believe this, another call. I'm about to do the on-off number again when I see that it's Bennett, my shithead ex. Wondering why I haven't gotten him a date with Brenda. Before he can say anything else, I tell him I'm on it.

"You're on it?"

"Yes, Bennett. I'm on it."

Silence. He's trying to think of some snappy remark about me being on it. On some drug, maybe, or going down on some girl.

"So. Bennett. I give you an opening like that and your mind goes blank?"

"Goes blank? What blank? What the fuck are you talking about, Fiona?"

"Never mind, Bennett. Just relax. It's like I told you. I'm on it."

"Don't tell me she's out of town."

Actually, Bennett, she is out of town."

"Actually, Fiona, you're full of shit. Where out of town is she?"

"Ummm … Morocco. Or Tangiers. Or maybe Tangiers is in Morocco, I don't really know. But she's basically unreachable."

"Basically?"

"That's about the size of it, Bennett. Basically. Unreachable, that is."

"For how long?"

"Oh. A month."

Bennett gives this big, exasperated groan and hangs up, and I'm thinking, my improvisation on the theme of Brenda in Morocco was not all that inspired. On the other hand, Bennett has no way of knowing where Brenda is and, anyway, Brenda is this mythical creature, so anything you say about her whereabouts is just as believable as anything else you might say.

An opening at the Wallenberg-Bruno Gallery is of course a big deal, but not as big a deal as the private opening, the night before. And then, a night before that—in other words, tonight—there is this opening, an occasion for Allen Wallenberg and Neil Bruno to get together with three hundred of their closest friends. I hate crowds, because who doesn't, but I have to admit that everyone is making a big effort to be civilized. And I look super great in this clingy nude chiffon cocktail dress by Bibhu Mohapatra.

So it's fun to be caught up in a mass of bright-eyed humanity, like I'm in a school of sardines in a glitzy ocean. Except sardines turn all together in that amazing way and the guests at this opening are going every which way at once. The sardines have lost their collective mind, meaning, it's already noisy and borderline sweaty and the waiters with their trays of canapés look like they're reciting mantras they learned in anger management school.

So why am I here? As I tried to explain to Sergei when he picked me up at Naxos, it's because of what we Americans call bait and switch. Like, he showed up expecting to find Brenda, the great love of his life, and, surprise, it's me. Your date for the evening, you drunken oaf. Of course he was totally enraged and sputtering. Because he had so much to say. But all he got out was one simple thought. "You are big problem."

"No, Sergei, you're the big problem." Which Plan A, with the business card, was supposed to solve. But didn't. So there I was, on another date with Sergei the Horrible, trying to figure out how to launch Plan B. Which involves his smart phone, all that money he mentioned. Because I've been figuring, there's got to be something I can do with that … not sure exactly what …

Meanwhile, Sergei was tilting his head in this truly peculiar way, eyeing me with one eye as he returns to his original point. "You are big problem."

"Come on, Sergei. I'm the best thing that ever happened to you." Putting my hand on his knee, which seemed to give him the impression that I was this strange being from Bizarro Planet where gender roles are reversed. On his planet, men touch women. When they're not hitting them. So he gave my hand this squeamish glance and then looked up at me, saying, "I tell people about you. Very beautiful girl. But big problem."

"Gee, Sergei, if I'm such a big problem, what's the solution?"

At this he snorted and Viktor put the limo in gear. By the time we reached the gallery, just a few blocks away, Sergei had had one or two refreshing naps. Meaning, he was full of vim and vigor when Viktor came round to open the door for him. Approaching the two-ton doors of the Wallenberg-Bruno Gallery, Sergei was sort of strutting, oligarch on parade, and of course he grabbed the wrong door. But Viktor was there to open the right one for him and then a bunch of people piled in right after Sergei, so, by the time I got inside, I realized I'd lost him.

Just like at the Armory, which is making me feel a little incompetent. Or, brilliant insight, maybe I don't actually like being around Sergei all that much. Anyway, I'm about to launch a one-girl search party when I notice Cora Burke on the far side of the gallery. A very rare sighting. Abigail and the other bookers say she practically lives in her office at the agency. You leave things outside her door. And now here she is, looking fabulous from the neck up, which is all I can see. Her face like a hawk, with a helmet of chestnut-colored hair and around her neck this golden choker, so huge and clunky only she could get away with it, just sailing along, taller than everyone else in the maddening crowd.

I know the original is "madding crowd," but this crowd has already gone from slightly annoying to really maddening. Then Cora looks over in my direction and smiles, right at me, but I'm not really sure I'm the target of this super-rare sign of her approval. I mean, she's so far away, she could have been smiling at anybody. Or everybody. Just to let it be known, Cora Burke considers this a marvelous event.

So I'm standing there, getting jostled, when I see Sergei milling around with this bunch of beefy guys in evening clothes. And he is one of their own, because he's, like, beyond beefy, so they're slapping him on the back, lots of big hugs. Colleagues, I guess, and it's weird, how seedy these guys look, even though they're obviously rich. Manicures and these beautifully tailored suits. Three-hundred-dollar haircuts. And for those who don't need haircuts anymore a couple of rugs that look like they cost more than a used Jaguar.. Then I'm feeling this clunky touch on my shoulder, the hand, it turns out, of Brandon Something-or-Other. One of Bill's backers and another guy with more money than taste.

We're doing the hello-nice-to-see-you business when I notice out of the corner of my eye that a couple of Sergei's seedy-slash-elegant friends are whisking him away, acting like they've bagged one of the bigger fishes in the big New York pond. Brandon is droning on about this Philip Taaffe canvas he saw at Bill Hollander's gallery, truly impressive, though perhaps he's talking out of school, not sure Bill wants everyone to know, quite yet, it's just that blah-blah-blah … anyway, Brandon knows I'll keep it under my hat.

All this time, he's been looking over my shoulder and now he's mouthing hello to someone behind me and inching away, not a moment too soon, because I really was getting ready to tell him that I couldn't give a fuck less about Philip Taaffe or any other artists, as long as Bill keeps raking in the dough … so I'm standing there, thinking, how can art, which is so great, be so boring when certain people begin talking about it, and I see that a tight little circle has formed around my buffoon of a date.

Only, he's not coming across as all that buffoonish, leaning back on his heels, tilting his chin up, hitting his audience over the head with all these heavy statements on the subject of asset allocation and the art market's long-term price trends and other fun topics. Stuff they already know, obviously, but they're acting like it's a privilege to hear it straight from the ogre's mouth.

Meaning Sergei is not just into oversized donations to charity. He also buys art, big time, because the attention he's being paid is the kind you pay a major player. So much for my fantasy of Sergei the drunken super nova, burning out and leaving Brenda in peace. At this high-end event, he turns out to be an impressive presence.

I'm the expendable item, the girl Sergei happened to bring along this evening. So this is Fiona the Unattached, drifting along on the surge of people, about forty-five percent of which I know. In other words, vaguely recognize, and when they recognize me I go through the hello-nice-to-see-you thing with them ... pleasant but kind of pointless, and then I see Bill, the man with the splendid cock, and this would be sheer joy except that he's with a gorgeous older woman.

I can't believe it. She is tall, like a statue, with this vast sweep of silver hair and lovely high cheekbones and now she's looking over at me, I must have been staring at her, too, and she's got this elegant look on her face. Like the kindly lioness, interested and amused and not even bothering to act all imperious. She's got imperiousness built into her, from the legs up. Very impressive.

And smart. When Bill brings her over, she sees in about half a second that there's something between him and me, and so, the moment introductions are over and done with, she lets this other super-elegant babe borrow her for a moment, and I'm saying, "Who is she, exactly? I didn't quite ..."

"Imogen Rittenhauer. She had all these houses all over the place, London, Aspen, which she would do up with total pizzazz—"

"Pizzazz?"

"Yeah, it's her word. An antique, I suppose, except that people are saying it now. The ones who live in her stratosphere. Anyway, her houses started getting written up all over the place and then she started redoing her friends' houses, just as a favor, and, ah, you see where this is going … her hobby turned into a business, and she hooked up with this designer, Alberto Something-or-Other. In a few months, they're going to open their flagship shop."

"And it's going to be in SoHo, right? Next door to Chanel. Or maybe Hugo Boss."

Bill shrugged.

"Then it's on to Palm Beach. Paris. Poughkeepsie."

"Well, yes. That's the general idea. Pretty soon you're going to be seeing ads for Imogen's shops on TV."

"Except I don't watch TV."

"But you were watching Imogen. Think I didn't see that?"

Bill is smiling now, so I say, "What do you want me to do? She's splendid. I'm jealous."

"Don't be."

I give him a smirk of the yeah-right variety, and he says, "All right, feel jealous. I mean, she did ask me to marry her."

"Great. When's the happy day?"

Bill smiles again, he is so good looking, and puts a sort of fatherly hand on my shoulder, or maybe a brotherly hand, how would I know? Then he's gone and I'm left to observe Sergei from a distance, delivering a load of bullshit on who knows what additional topic.

This is so strange, Sergei as a normal jerk. What is going on? Thinking back to the lecture I got from Fletcher Marks, Sociology for Dummies, I'm telling myself, maybe Sergei really is becoming a respectable member of decent society. Not an attractive member of decent society, and maybe the society isn't all that decent, but still ... Sergei seems to be finding a niche somewhere in a world where people don't kill people just because they look at you and don't see much of anything, like you're not even there.

I'm drifting off, all alone in a crowd, when these girls spot me and sort of descend, like a flock of tropical birds, all different colors and so adorable, fluttering and making little noises. They're friends of Alison's, babbling about bookings and shoots and people at the opening, some really uggy dress this woman is wearing, and great shoes and this new eye shadow and other modely stuff. Then I'm plucked out of the group by the ad-agency guy I met at the Armory event. The one who gave me his card, which I haven't been able to find.

Kind of a problem when I was thinking of going behind Abigail's back ... and not such a bad problem to have, because do I really want to screw up my relationship with the Cora Burke Agency? Maybe I can get them to put me with another booker ... as if ... given that Abigail has been doing a pretty good job for me ... it's just that she is so ... I don't know. . . anyway, this time the ad-agency guy is dressed like everyone else, in evening clothes, and he introduces himself.

Jon Ackerman. And this is his wife, Andrea, who is attractive and gracious and showing this kind of iron determination not to actually, like, look at me. Ackerman is saying, "So, you're a friend of Sergei Propokoff?" Trying to be casual, as if this is going to hide the obvious fact that there is this nice feeling between us. He reminds me of something nice from a when I was a kid.

I say, "A friend of Sergei's? I wouldn't go that far. It's not like he has this brilliant talent for friendship."

Ackerman smiles and starts telling me about his company's new approach to fashion marketing. I try to act business-like, too, asking semi-bright questions and making sure not to ignore Mrs. Ackerman, including her in the conversation, even though she'd stab herself in the eye with her mascara brush before she said anything directly to my face.

Now he's asking if I have agency representation and I am right in the middle of saying, well, as a matter of fact, that is up in the air, when his wife turns and tells him it's time to say goodnight to the So-and-Sos, they're leaving early for Greenwich. So Ackerman gives me another business card, right before his wife grabs him by the arm and nearly yanks him off his feet. They vanish into the heaving mass of art-lovers and here is Bill again and again he's all alone. Which is nice.

"You know Ackerman?"

"Sort of. Not really."

"He is the proud possessor of the most boring collection of paintings on the East Coast."

"I guess he bought a lot from you, Bill." Then I give him a blank look and say, "Just kidding."

Which he knows. What he doesn't know is who brought me and he can't keep from asking, so I look around and don't see Sergei. Then I do.

He has snagged a fresh flute of champagne and now he isn't just tilting back on his heels a bit. He's doing this Leaning Tower of Pisa impersonation, which is slightly frightening. His fans, of course, are taking no notice. They're too busy hanging on every word, none of which is audible at this distance. All you can hear is this pompous gurgling.

When I point Sergei out to Bill, he gives me a puzzled look. "You're here with him?"

"Yes, Bill. I am. Why?"

"He looks like one half of a comedy team. The unfunny half."

I nod, meaning, yeah, he is definitely not amusing … even though he's a hopeless clown … I mean, a well-respected member of this upscale demographic, and I'm thinking, someone should do a study of how much money it takes to buy the kind of respect Sergei has been getting all evening. Then I hear this sudden panicky roar. Sergei is actually tipping over backwards and all these people are leaping into action, struggling with the sheer bulk of the phenomenon, trying to keep it upright.

Bill is grinning at me. "You're really here with this guy? He's your date?"

"Yeah."

"Really? What's the point?"

"I'm conducting surveillance."

"What?"

"Trying to get a take on him."

"Why?"

"He, um … he told Brenda he was going to kill her and—"

"What the fuck Fiona, are you serious?"

"Well, he did tell her—"

"I know, but what I mean—"

"Is it real? I don't know. At this point I really don't know."

"But there's a possibility?"

"Uhh …"

"This is not what you should be doing, Fiona. This is something for the police."

"I need to know if he's really homicidal. A psycho killer. Or maybe he's just a run-of-the-mill knuckle dragger, one of these guys who can't handle women."

"But you're going to handle him?"

"Sure. Why not? Anyway …"

"Anyway ..." Bill is looking down, shaking his head. Then he looks sideways at me. "It's all about Brenda. I get that. But, to be frank, this is either pointless or too dangerous. So knock it off, Fiona."

"I can't."

"Why not?"

"Because it's ... because you're right, Bill, it is all about Brenda. So, um ..."

"So, um, what, Fiona? Finish your sentences, because, I have to say, I have no idea what you're talking about."

"Neither do I. Not exactly. All I know is ... I have to do something about Sergei."

Bill shrugs and says, "OK, Fiona. I truly don't get it but, in any case ... it would be nice for you and Imogen to get to know each other."

"Yes. That would be great." Really great, like, Imogen and I could get together over banana daiquiris and compare notes on Bill's performance. Now he's putting his hand on my shoulder again and actually squeezing it this time, in this totally friendly, unsexy way, and I'm letting myself think what I really didn't want to think the first time he touched me like that. Namely, this is not good. Because Bill is always sexy, absolutely, all of the time. I was supposed to be able to count on that. Like the things that happen when I feel Bill's touch. Which are happening, even now, in spite of the big-brother attitude ... these purely physiological responses of mine, so sweet and of course so sad under the circumstances, except I'm not letting myself feel that. I'm suspending all feelings on that particular subject.

◊

Never, never, ever am I late for a gig, only this time I was and now I've been exiled to the corridor outside the studio while this bitch in jodhpurs and ballet slippers decides if the photographer should forgive me. Actually, the photographer has forgiven me, I could see it on his face while the bitch was bawling me out. He's David Summers, a very nice guy and very good. He did some of the pictures in my book, including the one of me in the black silk dress showing all that leg.

So, come on, David, come on, come on, come on, explain to the bitch that this shoot will not work without me, I will look so great in the outfits I'm supposed to wear, I just need to dash into make-up and let a gifted virtuoso or two get to work on disguising the fact that I stayed up until three o'clock in the morning.

After the opening at Wallenberg-Bruno, I climbed into the back seat with Sergei and explained to Viktor that time's up, got to get home. So off we went and, all of a sudden, Sergei started bellowing. Something in Russian, which must have meant stop, stop, stop, for god's sake. Because that's what Viktor did, at the corner of Ninth and Twenty-First. Just in time for Sergei to stagger out, puke up a storm, and climb back in, wiping his face with the sleeve of his evening jacket.

"Much better," he said, starting to grope me. I smacked his hands away, not all that impressive a feat, for the usual reason. Champagne had done a real number on Sergei's eye-hand coordination. Not to mention his basic cognitive functions. When we got to Fourteenth Street, he thought we were at Twenty-Third, and he told Viktor to head for that European fast-food place between Seventh and Eighth.

"Excellent French fries," he said, not once but many times. "Better than American. In America, French fries are with ketchup. Very bad. In Europe are with mayonnaise. Is excellent with mayonnaise."

"Gee, Sergei," I said. "That is so fascinating. A fascinating tidbit from a seasoned international traveler."

At that, Viktor smirked, more or less admitting how fed up he was. In general and tonight in particular. Because he knew what he wasn't supposed to do, namely, take me home, but he had no idea what he was supposed to do instead. Just drive around all night, lost in the urban labyrinth? Sergei hadn't bothered to say, because Sergei was in no condition.

So Viktor inched the limo along that last block of Fourteenth Street, over the cobblestones, out toward the West Side Highway … the windows of the high-end shops lit up like cafés … and streaming around the limo the crowds of pretty people, the boys and girls like sexy shadows in the raking light and the glamorous noise. Another lovely night in the metropolis … and suddenly I had a brilliant inspiration.

"Viktor." I was leaning forward. "I want to take Sergei to this place I know on Twenty-Second Street. Between Eight and Ninth. It's called Up."

No argument from Viktor, and pretty soon I was standing at the velvet rope, Sergei by my side, explaining to a Chelsea muscle boy that my date was a famous Russian businessman who was totally ready for new experiences. The muscle boy knitted his brows. Then he frowned. Then he let us in, and the next thing I knew this lovely, over-amplified alto had slammed me against the wall. I was hearing the last notes of "All the Way," belted out by a red-headed drag queen in a gold lamé dress. Talk about an hour-glass figure, this one required at least half a dozen throw pillows.

By the time Sergei and I were seated, the next singer was on stage, draping herself over the guy at the electronic keyboard, and she really looked like a girl. A tall, slim, utterly beautiful girl in—what else?—a gold lamé dress. It was like someone had waved a magic wand and the previous singer had returned with a new body, a new face, and an actual sex change. Then she began to sing and you knew there had been no sex change. She was a boy, deep down, a boy who loved being a girl.

She sang "So in Love," one of my grandmother's favorites, she adored Cole Porter, and I considered the song for my ringtone before I decided against fancy ringtones. Anyway, I also adored Cole Porter, even though I was just a little kid in those days, but I got his songs, even the funny ones—not that I got all the jokes. But I got the basically crazed desperation of the fabulous Cole Porter, which this singer was obviously feeling.

Now it was "Night and Day," and I began to think, this is not exactly fair, because what is all this deep feeling doing in the same room with Sergei? The drunken slug who is nodding off and giving all the cute waiters something to snicker at.

The last time I was at Up, a few months before my hiatus, the décor was cowboy-slash-biker, with lots of branding irons and silver chains and what not. Now they're trying for an Arabian Nights look. I guess. I mean, there are gauzy swags of fabric all over the place and Oriental rugs, obviously cheapo, and these curved swords—what-d'you-call-'em, scimitars—suspended from the ceiling. The lighting is from spots, oh-so-cleverly hidden and sending these hot beams of various colors here and there. It looks pretty random, except when a beam is aimed at a scimitar and its sparkles are all lit up.

By now, the beautiful singer is long gone, replaced by I don't know what, sort of Neo-Disco-Revival, blasting over the speakers, quite the transition, and so loud that the snide waiter-boys don't even ask Sergei if he wants another vodka on the rocks. They just keep bringing them, he keeps drinking them, and they take one twenty-dollar bill after another from the wet stack on the table in front of the night's best customer. Of course, I can't always tell the difference between the waiters and the other customers, they all look young and great and obsessed with looking great.

The vibe is narcissistic, to say the least, all these guys playing the alone-in-a-crowd game, not really acknowledging the existence of another human being unless he's more or less a mirror image. I'm not in the game, meaning invisible, meaning my idea that I'm kind of boyish is beginning to look like a stretch. At Up I am definitely, ugh, a girl. Third grade all over again.

Sergei's phone rings. He doesn't hear it but I do, so I dig it out of his jacket pocket and hold it up in front of his face. He sort of squints at it and then he gets this big scowl on his face. "Stupid phone," he says. "I need smart phone."

I lean close to his ear and say, "You need your smart phone?" He nods, so I ask, "What do you need it for, Sergei?"

After staring at me for about a minute, he shakes his head.

"You don't need it?"

More head shaking. Like if he shakes it hard enough I'll disappear.

"So, tell me, Sergei, where is it? Where is your smart phone?"

At this point in the process of getting hammered, he doesn't really know, so he starts rummaging around in his pockets, can't find it, gets freaked and frustrated and turns to me. His scowl is now a Loony Tunes version of the Mask of Tragedy. "Is in apartment."

Then he tries to look blank, which comes across as scared shitless. Like he's waiting for this super-smart phone to descend from the sky and ask him how he could be so dumb. You're not supposed to talk about me to unauthorized people, you fucking idiot. So Sergei starts to bluster, waving his arms around like a panicky penguin, trying to fix his mistake, which was to mention the smart phone in the first place.

Which he keeps doing, telling me his stupid phone is really his smart phone, is not in apartment, is here, in pocket, over and over, and he shuts up only when a drag queen in a shimmery green dress sits in his lap, leaning back and kicking her feet up in the air. Her pumps, of course, are shimmery red.

"I'm Cherise," she says, "and I want you to be having a *good* time." Chucking him under the chin, she leans into his face, asking him what's happening. "You having a good time, honey?"

Sergei grins and Cherise orders a bottle of Veuve Clicquot. But, oh my god, before it arrives, Cherise is leading him back to the VIP room, this obvious den of iniquity where the lights are dim and the music is all nostalgic and soft. Dionne Warwick, "Show me the way . . ."

Cherise disappears and her replacement is this very tall person sporting six-inch wedges and a Carmen Miranda headdress on top. Modified but still pretty wild. The skirt is tropical chorus-girl, bustle in back, open in front to showcase a pair of pink panties. A fluorescent hotspot in the general gloom. Above that, another hotspot, this tight yellow halter. The face is more like a painting than a face, big blotches of pink lipstick and green eye shadow, tons and tons of blush. Hands on hips, this amazing vision bends a little at the waist and croons, "Hi, Serggy. I'm Laverne."

Sergei looks up at her, baffled. Laverne snaps her fingers and the Veuve Clicquot appears, in a silver cooler complete with a linen napkin. Laverne watches with immense patience, meaning, total scorn, while a team of waiters fusses with the cooler, trying to arrange it in one of those tripod things. When they are at long last done, Laverne raises her arms in a big, triumphant V and yells, "Let the revels begin."

Of course, the revels are on a pay-as-you-go basis, so I start digging around in Sergei's pockets to find some more cash. This is a total bummer, given that he is too fat for his clothes and most of his pockets are twisted around, so you have to straighten them out before you can get into them. Plus, you have to actually feel Sergei's body, and that is not fun.

I find Sergei's dumb phone, an empty money clip, a Rolex watch—what is this doing here, he's already got one on his wrist—and a wallet, also with no money. So I keep digging, and eventually I find a wad of fifties in Sergei's hip pocket, much to the delight of Laverne and the bouncer-types who are hanging around in the darkness.

The champagne is popped, Laverne gets to work on Sergei's good time, and I sit there looking at my other discovery, a ring of keys. Hmmm. With these I could get into Sergei's apartment, find the smart phone. With the five and a half billion. Supposedly. But, whatever, it's bound to be interesting. So I have to hold onto the whole ring, have another set made, get the originals back to Sergei the next time I see him. Except … oh, shit … I'm taking a close squint and one key is that special brand … Medeco … the kind they won't duplicate. Bummer. So I stuff the whole ring back into Sergei's pants and realize no one brought me a champagne glass. So now I have to get a waiter to bring me one. This happens, eventually, but it's like being in a convent and trying to get a date with a nun. Not that that would be entirely out of the question, it just takes a bit of doing.

Two bottles of champagne later, Laverne is straddling Sergei's legs, with her yellow halter in his face, then her lips are right next to his ear. Like she's about to whisper, but no such luck. Laverne likes to yell, and now she's yelling, "Serggy, Serggy, Serggy, are you ready for it? Can you handle it?"

Sergei is barely conscious, but he notices, more or less, when Laverne zips open her halter and lets her tits hang out. Or, actually, that's not quite right, because they are big and full and they are not hanging, they're standing up like tits on a department store mannequin, meaning they've been recently installed, real works of art, and now Sergei is pawing at them with both hands.

Laverne is leaning back, her eyes closed, Sergei keeps fumbling away and she's making these demented, mm, mm, mmmmm sounds … theater of the thoroughly unbelievable orgasm … then she stands up and removes her panties. Which must have been some kind of tear-away item, because suddenly this huge cock is pointing right at Sergei's face. Not erect but not completely soft, sort of horizontal with an elegant curve, like the scimitars featured out front. Only not so sparkly. More a creamy amber, and Laverne is saying, "Touch it, Serggy. Go on, honey. Give it a feel."

Sergei is falling into a coma, so Laverne tilts her pelvis, touching his cheek with the tip of her cock. No response, so she gives him a few more pokes, the cheeks, the nose, his lips. All at once, he snaps out of it and everyone, because everyone is really, really watching, sees his eyes go wide and they laugh and Sergei stands up and takes a swing at Laverne.

He misses with his fist but not with his hippo-esque bulk, meaning they go down in a heap and this guy, one of the bouncers, picks Sergei up and starts punching him in the stomach. Pretty extreme behavior, given that this bouncer is not like the others, a pumped-up pretty boy. He's freakish, muscles all bulgy and weird, like they were made out of Play-Doh by some untalented kid, and of course he has all this steroidal rage.

So.

Sergei is getting pummeled and I'm thinking, maybe this is the solution to the Sergei problem, coming here was a great idea, then one of the other bouncers manages to get the rageaholic's attention, signaling him to lay off. Which he does. Sergei is on his knees, doing his best to puke. Two more muscle types appear and haul him off toward the exit, and the one who got the rageaholic to cease and desist just looks at me, really disgusted, and raises his hand. Like he's the rageaholic now and I'm the one who ruined his little paradise. Boo-hoo-hoo. So now he has to smack me.

I clench my fist and cock it, trying not to be completely girly. Not that I could have had any impact, the guy outweighs me by a hundred and fifty pounds, but in that instant—the image of my fist—he hesitates. Then he gives a snort, grabbing me by the arm and dragging me to my feet. Shaking his head, saying, "You bring a guy like that in here? I got a better idea. Why don't you get the fuck out."

So that was my late-night adventure and then I was late for the shoot and now, oh my god, David Summers, the nice photographer, is inviting me in. The bitch in ballet slippers is at the far end of the studio, going over some voucher books or something. Making a big, huffy point of ignoring me. So all is not forgiven but, on the other hand, it's too late to replace me and so I am all done up in record time, make-up and hair, and then I'm being sewn into this really fabulous dress by Joseph Altuzarra, I'm hot and fresh and it is really working with the other girls ... we're supposed to be leaning all over each other like these geometric puppets ... they are so cute.

Which is so inspiring, and even though this is supposed to be an ensemble effort I know I am coming across as the star, maybe because David is focusing on me, or maybe he isn't, maybe I'm just grateful to him. Whatever, I'm sizzling and then it's over and I am toweling the sweat off my armpits and smiling at this other girl who is also nicely sweaty and a light bulb goes on.

Tom the tech guy at the agency.

You can't duplicate Medeco keys but of course you can, if you know how, and Tom is the type who would. So that's the way to go because I've been thinking, keys like that may not even come with the apartment, even in an ultra-high-end building where someone like Sergei would want to live. So it looks like he's overdoing the security, meaning, it would be definitely worth the trouble to break in. Plan B is beginning to take shape. In other words, it's going from non-existent to just barely non-non-existent. Meaning Plan B is embryonic at best, more like ectoplasmic, but I swear to myself I'll work on it, and my next thought is Laverne. What happened to her? A big mystery because, as far as I know, she completely vanished when Sergei fell on her. No sign of Laverne after that moment, and now I'm thinking, forget Plan B, let's have something like Sergei fall on Sergei.

Great idea, but you have to work out the logic, meaning, if anything is going to have the Sergei effect on Sergei, it's going to have to be even creepier than Sergei himself. Which is about as implausible as it gets, think of an asteroid in one of those movies Bill and I would never see, it's hurtling toward earth and the only hope for humanity is another asteroid coming along and demolishing the first one. Fat chance, right?

.3.

Unlike Abigail, the ad-agency guy offers me a chair. He even comes around from behind his desk and holds it for me, quite the gentleman, and I am quite the lady, sitting up straight and crossing my ladylike legs and giving him a ladylike smile and just generally behaving like someone who knows how to behave.

"I'm glad I was able to make time for you, Fiona. I'm glad, also, that you were available on such short notice." And he actually does seem kind of glad.

So I say, "Well, Mr. Ackerman—"

He interrupts, just like he's supposed to, saying, "Please. Jon." With this slightly tense smile.

I smile back, not at all tense. "Well. Jon. The thing is, for me, everything is on short notice. Name of the game. Nature of the beast."

"Yes," he says, getting all sober and managerial. "Yes. I understand. And there are certain inefficiencies in that situation that we would like to iron out. Telescope the procedure, which, ironically enough, would entail adding new functionalities. In-house ..."

Yeah, great, in-house, outsourced, streamlined, blah, blah, blah, I'm listening and I'm getting it but I am also getting a bit impatient because this is not as brilliant as Jon seems to think. Strip away the fluff and it's the old cut-out-the middleman gag, meaning, Ackerman & Thatcher is going to hire a few bookers so a girl can go from the ad agency to the client without having to take a detour through a modeling agency. Except, for a model, a modeling agency is not a detour. It's her one foothold in day-to-day reality that actually seems real. Most of the time. Real and fully staffed.

Also, Jon is telling me about their time horizon, which seems to be way out there somewhere, in the misty future, like, nothing is all that imminent. So what is this? As if I didn't know. This isn't about stealing me away from the Cora Burke Agency, it's about Jon wanting to have me on the other side of his desk, giving me the look he gave me the first time we met. Such a tender look, I like being here, feeling so wanted.

Except that wanting me is making Jon a little uneasy, he's drifting now, more or less repeating himself ... a new organizational concept ... reconfiguring the image-flow ... so I ask if there is going to be someone like Fred, to go over my book with me? Jon doesn't quite get the question. I give him Fred's title, media resource coordinator, and a bit of a job description and he's, like, er, ah, um, yes, I'm sure we'll have that covered. You could always talk to Samantha Lewis, who is in charge of, er, um, structuring the new initiative.

But of course I have zero desire to talk to Samantha Lewis, so I just smile, thinking, what makes Ackerman & Thatcher think they're going to be able to hire bookers with any clout? They might end up with a bunch of amateurs who can't get their foot in door one. Then there's the question of Ackerman & Thatcher's clients. Do they actually have any? I mean, any that are any good?

On the other hand, I am pretty much irrational and ... . you know that rock group Rage Against the Machine? Well, I'm always feeling this insane rage against the Abigail ... and, anyway, this is probably never going to happen. So I say, "Your approach sounds very innovative, Jon."

He agrees, looking down at his desk with oodles of false modesty. Looking up, he says, "We are still in the early, trial stages of this project, Fiona, but I think I'm in a position to say that we would like to include you, going forward."

Going forward. Right. So Jon has joined the ever expanding ranks of the movers and shakers and highly competent professionals capable of this one thought—going forward.

I say, "That's good to hear."

He nods and stares at me. He's all blank now, meaning that if I want him to give me that yearning look again it's up to me. Like everything else. So I smooth my prim linen dress over my breasts and my thighs and then I give him the kind of smile that says, being here is so nice, maybe we have some sort of future together. Personal, not professional.

Standing up, he comes around and stands behind my chair. Kisses me on the top of my head. Puts his hands on my shoulders. I bring them down to my breasts, wondering what he'll do next, and, no big shock, he doesn't do anything. Just holds onto me, sort of like a statue. A shy statue. Because Jon has lots of yearnings but even more inhibitions.

Which makes him pretty much beside the point, from my point of view, except that he has this strange power to remind me of something that meant so much to me a long time ago … and still does, so I stand up and we kiss.

So sweet, and he feels really good in my arms … I hold him harder, feeling his cock getting hard … but when I reach down for it he backs off … actually goes and sits at his desk. And puts this look on his face, all sober and serious but panicky around the edges.

This is going nowhere, which would be fine except that I want to keep feeling this thing he reminds me of … something so tender … so I can't let his panic carry the day … got to appeal to his finer feelings, meaning, Fiona the Exhibitionist needs to take another turn. I stand, bend my knees way down to gather my skirt up around my waist, and the next thing he knows he's staring at my gorgeous legs and my gorgeous hips and my gorgeous snatch just barely hidden by this mini-micro-thong.

Turning around, I give him a squint at my perfect ass, and when I turn back around I see him getting up, he's coming toward me, and then … really strange … he's on his knees in front of me, his face buried in my crotch, hugging my ass … kind of frozen, not doing anything sexy.

After about fifteen seconds of that, I kneel down and he lets go. I lift him up and we hug again. Then I lean back, holding his shoulders, giving him my very level, very intense stare. He waits for me to say something. But I don't. I keep looking into his eyes, which are getting wobbly. After a while, he clears his throat and says, "You are a very unusual girl, Fiona."

I lean in and kiss him on the cheek, saying, "Not really, Jon. Most girls are pretty much the same. Deep down. But let's stay in touch. It's just so nice being with you." A lame exit line, after that performance of mine, but, on the other hand, it *had* been so nice.

A few days later, I was standing at a light on Madison, wondering, first, do I have time to pop into Jil Sander and look around and, second, why did I say that thing about girls being all the same deep down? Of course, people always say things like that, just to sound jaded, like Catherine the Great saying cocks are all the same. And she should know, having worked her way through the whole Russian army. Right? So fair's fair, meaning all the mean things we say about men we have to say about women too. Except I'm flipping through scads of stuff, not finding any must-haves and thinking it really isn't true, pussies are so much more individualistic than cocks, which are just this slightly simple-minded matter of thickness and length.

Not that slightly simple-minded creates any real problems … the problem, I guess, is me, when I'm in this mood, going back and forth, round and round in this drifty circle, obsessing about the anatomical options, so it's great when my cell phone rings, pulls me back to the moment. Except, it's Bennett my shithead ex. Which is not so great.

"What the fuck do you want?"

"I want to hear from you, Fiona. I want to hear that you have kept your side of the bargain and set me up with the beautiful Brenda."

"Oh. Right. Your date with Brenda. Uh—"

"Uh, uh, uh, guess what you're going to tell me? You're going to tell me the same thing you told me the last time, Brenda is out of town."

"Uh—"

"Out of town, right? For how long, Fiona? Never mind. I know you're on it. How do I know? You said so. And I know I can depend on your word. Because if I can't, you're fucked."

"Fucked?"

"Totally fucked, Fiona."

"Oooh. Totally fucked. Sounds scrumptious. Think you can manage it?"

"You know me, Fiona. I can definitely manage it."

I was asking him exactly how he was going to manage it, fuck me totally, did he buy himself a new dildo? But he hung up too fast. Bummer.

I stow my phone and stand there for a minute, thinking how much I love those old movies where there's a calendar and the pages start curling and falling away, one after the other, autumn leaves, time is passing in this big, glamorous blur, with maybe the image of a train zooming through it all. Only, in my case, it's not a train, it's cabs, one after another, until it's just this one cab, the basic cab, which is basically never there when you need it, and of course the calendar as far as I'm concerned is the one on my phone, I'm always pawing through my bag to see if I have it.

Which of course I do, I have to, my career is buzzing along and this morning it really sparkled, everything all noisy and crazed in this really nice way, with a couple of go-sees and a really hot shoot, an editorial spread in *Elle* featuring sportswear by Justin Schloss. All that booked by Abigail and now I am on my way to meet some Ackerman & Thatcher clients. Which I didn't expect to happen so soon. Someone in that office is a lot more decisive than Jon Ackerman.

Anyway, I am about to be officially in breach of contract, so it's a good thing I'm so busy, busy, busy because busy, busy means blank, blank, blank, life as a mindless pawn in the hands of meaningless forces. Then they drop you, the hands of the meaningless forces, because the workday is done and you're just standing on the sidewalk somewhere on the West Side of Manhattan, loaded down with all your stuff.

So now what?

It's too early for dinner but not for margaritas, so I grab another cab to my place, drop the whole heap of stuff on my bed, and go back down in search of yet another cab. I'm hoping to find Fred at Brainwave, and, no big surprise, I do.

He's on the far side of the room with this guy, almost as cute as him, even better dressed, and I'm wondering, how much career-babble or real-estate babble am I going to have to listen to now? But I get to their table and Fred is the sole proprietor. The cute guy has vanished.

I sit down and Fred nods. But no smile. He's pissed and possibly hurt. Not to mention frustrated. So I order two Margaritas and wait. The Margaritas come, I drink about half of mine and

I'm still waiting for Fred to explain the Case of the Elusive Cutie Pie. But, nothing, nada, just gloomy silence, meaning it's time for me to tell him about the time, when I was fourteen and I got this really popular girl to make out with me. The idea was, we weren't queer, we were just practice kissing, for when we did it with boys. Only I was completely into it, and she got a little scared. Like, if she's doing this, maybe she's queer for real.

Fred looks up at me, still upset but amused, so I tell him I'm thinking about all this because the waitress reminds me of that girl, not true, but, anyway, I go on, saying the really popular girl wasn't just a little scared, she was a lot scared, and the next time I saw her, she was with this really hot boy, and she was nice to me and everything, but then she started whispering in the boy's ear and he started to sort of, like, laugh, like she was telling him what a lesbo perv I was, but the thing of it, actually, was this. I had given the guy a blow job a few nights before, and—

Suddenly Fred grins. "This is such bullshit, Fiona. Such unbelievable bullshit. I mean, I appreciate what you're trying to do—"

"No, really, it's really true, and my point is that—"

"That you're just so fucking empathetic. Because many years ago, when you were a kid, your heart was broken, sob, because you didn't know which heartthrob you wanted the most and you couldn't have either one. Lesbo perv."

I shrug. "Don't forget the blow job."

"How could I? I should have said, cocksucking lesbo perv."

Now I grin. But he doesn't grin back, he's giving me this look, this lovely, naked look right into my eyes, and I'm stunned because, OK, we've always gotten along really well at the agency, hanging out at Brainwave, but suddenly, oh my god, there's this chemistry. Between me and Fred. I'm not only stunned but also feeling the wild, tingly surge that means this is really real. So I'm saying, "More booze?"

By now Fred is standing, gripping my elbow, meaning, let's go. And saying, "Sure. More booze. At my place. On West Twelfth."

So I'm, like, "Great. Anything we should get?"

"Umm. Yeah. Triple sec. And we probably need more tequila."

"What about limes? Salt? Maybe some glasses."

Fred is rushing me now, but very sweetly. We hike to Astor Wines, get a bunch of stuff, and then we take a cab to his block … I love that stretch of West Twelfth Street, between Fifth and Sixth … up to his apartment, which is low-keyed and really brilliant. With exactly the right number of these beautifully placed pieces of furniture. Fifties Moderne, but so understated you have to look twice to see that these things are in any style whatsoever. At first glance, they just look like the essence of whatever—table, chair, sofa.

He goes into the kitchen area, and I watch him mixing drinks… he is so handsome … then he brings the drinks to the low table in front of the sofa. We sit and sip away, talking about the people at the agency and bars and books Fred wonders if he'll ever get around to reading, like *War and Peace*, and I'm thinking I'll ask him what books he read as a kid … if he knows about the map of the Land of Make-Believe, which was on the wall in my grandmother's summer house … in the stairway leading up to the sleeping porch … but I don't ask him that … I just watch these shadows flickering on the wall, leaf shadows, and time is getting a little out of focus.

It's not that things were all blurry when I was with Fred, not at all, I can remember everything with this terrific clarity, how he said he'd probably never read Tolstoy, given the hectic pace of contemporary life … putting the phrase in quotation marks, the way he said it, and then deciding we needed more drinks.

So I was watching him, again, his back turned, in the kitchen area, and this time I got up and stood behind him. I touched him on the shoulder and he didn't react, so I reached around and felt the front of his pants. He was hard and still not reacting. Just finishing up the drinks. We clinked our glasses, drank down our drinks, and looked at each other. Then he smiled. Faintly.

I led him into the bedroom and we got undressed. Here was a guy who worked out but not too much. A slim, shapely bod. Impressive cock. I said, "Are you really up for this?"

Silly question.

The next thing I knew we were hugging, then he kissed me on the throat and we were in bed, just flowing into position. Getting in sync and staying there. Such luscious motion, it felt so good to be so welcoming to all that hot energy … that lovely power …

Afterward, he held me tight for a long time, and from that moment on we were close. Amazingly close, which I have never understood, not that I have to or anything. But, still, what happened in that ultra-sweet moment? It wasn't male bonding, because I'm a girl, and it wasn't boy and girl fall in love, because he's gay. He loves men. But he likes me. Liked fucking me. For sure. I mean, talk about a truth that is pretty much self-evident. Anyway, that one time made him my friend. Really close, I feel I can trust him.

For one thing, he can think on his feet. Or whatever position he happens to be in, and he is super-competent. I should know. Sometimes you weigh up the evidence, come to a conclusion. So-and-So seems pretty competent. It's a judgment call. But when I say Fred is super-competent, it's not just a judgment call. I really, really know.

Something pretty special today, lunch at the Union Square Café, with this young woman known only as Irina. Very posh in a Chanel suit and a string of pearls. With eyebrows that look like they've been plucked out and rewoven and pasted back on, but never mind, she's nicely done up. We're surrounded by a full-capacity crowd, half of them these underdressed out-of-town-ers who probably found out about the fabulous, four-star Union Square Café by going online. So I am wondering what I am doing here. As if I didn't know.

The day before yesterday, I was leaving a shoot booked by Ackerman's office, just basking in the afterglow of the good reaction I got, when my phone rings, and this person asks me, like she always does, if I remember her. I say, not yet, who are you? Before, she would always get coy at this point and ring off but this time around something has changed. She's telling me we should meet.

So now we have met and I do remember her. She is one of the elegant babes who sat across from me at Romanov's, on my second date with Sergei. And I get it. This is the girl who saw me planting the business card on Sergei, thinking she caught me steal-ing. So this is not a girly get-together. It's a shakedown, as I found out when we were seated and got through the stuff about tap water or sparkling and I finally had a chance to ask her what this is about. She got this sly look on her face and said, "Perhaps you could help me. I don't like to tell anybody what you did, but ..."

But she will tell somebody, even though it never happened, if I don't give her a certain consideration in this matter. This is her phrase, a certain consideration in this matter.

So I say, "How much?"

This startles her, which she tries to hide, and then she tells me Sergei is very famous for carrying a thousand dollars in cash wherever he goes.

I say, "A thousand? Exactly?"

She leans back in her chair and closes her eyes. Gives a severe little shake of her head, like, how can you question one of the sacred truths of our time? Of all times?

Opening her eyes, she says, very sternly, "He carries one thousand dollars. Always. In cash."

"So your share is half of that?"

A very faint, very definite nod. Yes. Exactly.

"And you think I'm going to fork that over to you. Today."

"Fork over?"

"Tell you what, Irina. I'll do it. Of course, I'll have to pop round
the corner, find an ATM."

Which I do, because it's nice to be dealing with a nuisance I
can buy off for not all that much money, and when I get back
with the dough Irina is digging into a dozen and a half oysters and
washing them down with a half-bottle of champagne. Rosé. Bil-
lecart-Salmon Brut, which is eighty dollars, according to a quick
squint at the wine list.

The waiter, this jittery individual with precision trimmed
stubble, is standing there, eyeing me, like, where have *you* been?
And he doesn't exactly melt when I order a watercress salad and
no drink to start. But Irina is his kind of gal, every time she orders
he beams like mad, he can't help it, every choice is just such sheer
genius, he's speechless. Having polished off the oysters, Irina is on
to the main course, a grilled shell steak, medium rare, and a 2005
Barbaresco Angelo Gaja, at a hundred and twenty dollars a half
bottle.

I have a tuna burger and a gin and tonic and more or less listen
to Irina babble away in this snooty voice about her very estab-
lished family in Romania, which is where she's from, and her
very fine education in the most prestigious university in Russia,
the Sholokhov Moscow State University for Humanities, where
she studied art history with the finest professors. Now she is a
consultant to many important collectors. Premiere individuals. In
other words, mooks who wouldn't know an art consultant from
a masseuse.

Irina is halfway through her steak, chewing away, totally focused, when my phone rings. Suddenly, she's frozen, staring at me with this really offended look on her face. How rude! So I take the call and it's Abigail, can I move things around, be up at 575 Seventh Avenue by two-thirty? I check my calendar ... sure, no problem, and Abigail rings off without even waiting for a definite yes.

The whole time, Irina keeps staring at me, not moving a muscle but obviously just itching to get back to her steak. Which she does the second I hang up and then, about five seconds later, my phone rings again and Irina has to crank herself up a second time for the whole frozen-in-outrage number.

Not only that, but our waiter is now terribly upset, he let me get away with the first call but, really, this is too much, there's a rule ... he's coming over to give me a hard time, but something about my face gets him to back off. Because the call is from Mike and I'm panicked.

But not for long. He's telling me he thinks it's time for him to come clean about the real reason he never hits on me. He's not human.

"Uh, what?"

"You know, Fiona, not human. I'm a cyborg. Or a replicant. They never exactly told me, but—"

"They?"

"This super-classified bio-engineering outfit attached to Special Forces. They designed quite a few of us. We were supposed to be the spearhead of this new robowar doctrine."

"Doctrine?"

"Yeah, that's what they have in the war business. Doctrines."

"So what went wrong?"

"I hit on this girl."

"Was she human?"

"Very bright question, Fiona. Heart of the issue. I'm impressed. Yes. She was human."

"And this was not part of the doctrine? Hitting on humans?"

Mike gave this quick laugh. Slightly bitter. "No. You got that right. Definitely not part of the doctrine."

"So you figure I'm human and—"

"And I've learned my lesson."

"A tough lesson."

"Well …" His voice had a shrug in it. "I thought you might like to know the real reason."

"I appreciate it, Mike."

"No sweat."

I put my phone away, Irina gives me this look of demented reproach, and then she goes back to her steak, completely obsessed, eating away with no time out to tell me about her personal background, her hopes and dreams … her next scam …

For dessert, I have coffee and Irina is not sure what she wants. All the desserts are ten dollars, so, no guidance there. But her eyes light up when she sees that there's a dessert wine, a 1945 Vouvray Moelleux, going for seventy dollars a glass. She has one of those. Having skipped dessert, she has another. Then she pats the sticky residue from her lips and says, "We must now arrive at the satisfactory conclusion."

I ask for the check, which is a lot for lunch but a small price to pay for tying up a loose end. Not a very important loose end, but neatness counts. Of course, it also helps to get your priorities straight, and suddenly I have this terrible moment of total clarity about the major loose end, which has been nagging me day in, day out, semi-consciously, the loose end all the other loose ends are connected to, namely, Sergei's smart phone. With all the money on it. Which he never should have said anything about, he is such a moron, but, then, so are you, Fiona.

This is what I'm saying to myself as Irina pats her lips again and then gets out a lipstick and mirror, starts working away. With great precision, like she's this traditional craftsperson painting a pattern on one of those Russian dolls. Except that she's Romanian and, well, um, OK, who the fuck cares, the point is, what on earth is wrong with you, Fiona, you're letting the whole smartphone thing slide, you have to deal with it.

Meaning, get your mitts on the thing. Meaning, get into Sergei's apartment. Meaning, find out from Tom the tech guy how to duplicate Medeco keys. And don't think about the Godzilla look Viktor gave Sergei in the limo, that time he took the smart phone away. Concentrate on Sergei, the drunken idiot, just play it out like it's this ridiculous game. Which is what it is, as long as Viktor doesn't turn that look on me. Which I don't think he will. I think he's got a soft spot for me.

Irina finishes her lips and then studies them for about five minutes in her mirror. Meanwhile, the waiter buzzes off with my credit card and I remove one of those bank envelopes from my purse, slide it across the table. Irina puts her mirror away and looks inside the envelope, counting the twenty-five twenty-dollar bills really fast. Then she raises her eyebrows, giving the money a smug little smile.

Next, she looks up at me. Perfectly blank. Like, do I know you?

Not really, bitch, because, this time I took the easy way out, which I can easily afford. But if you ever come after me again, I'll be really, really nice, get you to fall for me, and when we're in bed I'll shove a tennis racquet up your ass. Which end of the tennis racquet will depend on the mood I'm in that day.

The next booking Abigail gets for me is brilliant, this late-afternoon shoot for Rollo Rodriquez, who is the current definition of a rising star. Beyond hip. His specialty is the instant classic, meaning he is the kind of rip-off artist who gives rip-off artists a good name. Like, he makes all these shameless references to early Balmain and Valentino and so on and so forth, I mean, their greatest early stuff, but Rollo's take is always so fresh. Don't know how he does it, but, anyway, I loved his things at the fitting yesterday, and this shoot is going to be very high-concept. As Abigail tells me about twenty times.

The concept is to forget about posing, the girls are going to be walking a runway, only it won't be a runway show. It'll just be a fashion shoot but a lot more exciting. So I'm thinking, first, hasn't this been done before? Second, if it's a fake runway show because there isn't any audience, well, why not get a fake audience, and then it would be a real runway show? But, whatever, I get there and I'm immediately stoked.

It's this space way west in the Fifties, a ceiling full of lights of every variety but so high up they hardly make a dent in the general darkness. Meaning, you see things sort of highlighted here and there, racks of clothes and scads of people and the noise, the music, which is not yet blasting, and guys yelling and the murmur of the girls and everyone else, the photographer and his people and Rollo and his people and the agency gofers and a few press people and all the other people who do hair and wardrobe and lighting and the music and the food, which the girls never touch. Not even the crudités. Of course, everybody drinks the coffee, so there's that smell and the smell of make-up and girls, which I love, the not-so-subtle smell of girls all anxious and revved up.

The director, this really sweet guy, Ira Smith, lots of frizzy hair, is telling us what to do with the music, we're models, not dancers, so don't walk *with* the beat. Walk *through* the beat. Like we're on the runway in Milan, really feel it, believe it, do it, like there is this audience of glitterati in attendance, watching your every move. So pump it up, ladies. Which has never been a problem for me. I am always on. Projecting like mad. In other words, totally faking it. Unless I'm reading or lying around thinking about stuff. Or having sex. Oh, and when I'm with Brenda, I'm not on then, that's not me playing a part, it's just me, being with her, absolutely real.

Not that coming across as hot in the public eye isn't totally real, and pretty soon I'm doing it, god, I look so great I can practically see it, Fiona getting to the end of the runway, giving the nonexistent audience the arrogant stare, right over their heads, and then turning back, walking out of their lives. But slowly, slightly slower than the other girls, to provide a long, lingering look at this amazing walk of mine. The sheer, fluid heat of my total hotness.

I do this twice in two different outfits, improving quite a bit the second time, which is not Fiona the Dope unloading a crock of self-affirming bullshit. This is something I just know, like, for example, a tennis player knows when she serves up an ace, and, besides, Ira is babbling. Or stuttering, I guess, but, anyway, he's telling me to the best of his ability that it's really working and the other girls, when I come off the runway the second time, have this sweet, quiet look they get when somebody is nailing it, no question, you can't be bitchy about it, it's just too good.

The first outfit was a gray suit for daytime, very fitted, with a cinched waist. Next was a slinky red evening gown, strapless and backless, practically down to my ass, and now I'll be wearing this sky blue bikini. It's a little strange, putting the sportswear after the evening wear, but maybe Rollo isn't into the logic of the clock. More the logic of the bod, show more and more of it as we go along. Which makes total sense, as far as I'm concerned.

So this makeup girl is giving me blue eye shadow to go with my blue bikini, when my phone rings. Not supposed to happen.

My bag isn't even supposed to be within hearing distance, there was this security bin set up at the back of the studio … so, what now? The makeup girl is pausing, like, make up your mind. Which I do, diving for my purse and I miss the call. Checking, I see it's from Pam and so I call back, holding up a forefinger as nicely as I can to tell the makeup girl to just fucking wait, and Pam answers, saying, "Have you heard from Brenda?"

What? Pam is calling me and this is what she's asking? I'm baffled. Sort of amused. Then slightly freaked. "Uh, no. I haven't. I talked to her last night but, um—"

Pam hangs up on me, basically, so I let the makeup proceed, and when it's done I am really nice to the makeup girl, checking out the results in one of those mirrors standing around on little wheels, telling her what a great job she did, and I'm about to call Brenda when these two assistant makeup boys come by with a huge, family-size tub of clear hair gel and start slathering it all over me and the other girls.

The idea is that we're going to look like we just emerged from the sea, like that Botticelli painting, Aphrodite on the half-shell … except that she looks completely dry, this absolute babe, almost as beautiful as Brenda, and so, guess what? This is my favorite painting. Except for that Bronzino portrait in the Frick of this elegant guy who is handsome enough but not really a standout except that he's wearing these silk pantaloon things and you can see he's got this huge hard-on. Which is true inspiration, no? To make his hard-on a part of his portrait … anyway, the gel is supposed to make you think we're sopping wet, like pussies dreaming about the hard-on in the Frick …

Then the head makeup person comes by to check us out, this harpy in overalls and a yucky puke-green cardigan hanging off her like Spanish moss, and she's outraged … way too much gel … she says we look like we're covered with afterbirth, swab us down, for

Christ's sake, which about a dozen assistants are suddenly doing, giving me this vaguely delicious feeling, and I have to admit the results are an improvement, given that it's all for the sake of getting photographed. We're gleaming now, like statues with a thin film of girly sweat. Total show-stoppers, so I figure it's time to call Brenda.

No answer.

Now I'm naked, in heels, all greased up and shimmering and a wardrobe lady is handing me these two strips of blue cloth that are not going to make me all that much less naked, which is great, my ass really is so spectacular. My ass and my legs ... my rippling back ... and so I'm waiting to go on, the music is *I Got a Feeling*, the Black-eyed Peas, it's getting me hot, and then I have an idea.

Only it's not an idea, it's this demented obsession. I have to call Sergei. I dash back to where I hope my purse is still hanging, because what if someone swiped it, but they didn't, so I dig around and find my phone and call and Viktor answers.

"Is Sergei there?"

"Sergei is traveling."

"Have you seen Brenda lately?"

"Brenda?"

"Yes, Viktor. Brenda. Is she with Sergei?"

"Sergei is not interested in Brenda."

"No? Not interested? Look, Viktor, this is such obvious bullshit that you're scaring me. Just tell me, yes or no, is Brenda with Sergei?"

"Sergei is not interested in Brenda."

End of conversation, so once again I call Pam, who is completely locked down, putting nothing into her voice, obviously out of her mind with fear, telling me there's still no sign of Brenda.

So I run back to the runway, I'm up, I go on, I'm doing great, because the nakeder I am the better I do, I'm just that kind of girl … and, so, down to the end of the runway, stop, stare, hand on hip, turn, back up the runway, my whole body telling me I'm this stunning presence, this sizzling image, if I were watching I'd be falling in love with everything about me, total focus, but not total, I guess, because I feel this sudden wobble and then I fall on my ass.

Actually, falling on my ass would have been not so bad. What happened, my feet slid out from under me and I fell, slap, right on my back. There was this moment of total blank-out, then I'm seeing all the lights and beams way up above me, the faraway ceiling, I'm on my feet, back into my walk, and when it's over, there is Ira, not exactly biting his nails, more like chewing his fingertips.

An assistant director comes up to me and starts flipping through these papers on a clipboard, telling me we can do a do-over, later on … possibly … the music is still blasting, the next girl is on her way back up the runway and, oh my god, what am I doing, Brenda is missing, and suddenly I'm running in search of my purse, grabbing it, maybe I'm naked by now, who knows, because I had to lose the bikini somewhere along the way, I've got to get dressed, so where the fuck is the locker with my clothes?

This guy who works on the lights or something is pointing way over there and staring at my crotch, but not like it's a thrill. Like he's wondering what I'm doing with all this hair. Not that much, actually, I mean, hardly any, I knew I'd be wearing a bikini so I trimmed pretty drastically but maybe all he knows about girls is what he gets from porn and now he thinks all pussies are supposed to be bald. Which is so dumb, cunt hair is so lovely, and anyway who wants to look like a porn star, one of those hairless robots exchanging bodily fluids on camera?

Or, sure, go ahead, look like that, do that, do whatever you want, why should I care, I'm into my clothes, out to the street, no cab, then there's a cab, in fact, two cabs, the second one is acing out the first, so, terrific, let's go with this one, step on it, come on, come on, step on it, step on it, step on it, and now I'm ringing Brenda's bell, thinking, how fucking dumb *am* I, letting Plan B just sit there and gather dust, like Sergei is no longer a threat?

Pam opens the door, which is strange. Usually, she maintains this very strict pecking order, like, you get the impression that she's about to ask one of her assistants to ask one of the assistant-assistants to stir the cream in her coffee. So this door-opening performance of hers is way out of character, a sign, maybe, that she truly is freaked. Of course, she's putting on this big act of being totally calm, inviting me into her office and telling me Brenda is with a Mr. Bennett Ross. He is escorting her to a private viewing, some show at the Morgan Library, and afterward there will be a dinner at the 21 Club. It's a charity event, for the Association of American Museums or something.

I'm about to ask her what happened, why she didn't know where Brenda was, because how weird is that? Pam always knows where Brenda is, even in her sleep she knows, right? But Pam is not inviting me into her confidence, she's not even looking at me. She's looking through me with this really blank look on her face. Really blank and really bitter.

I am not about to find out what happened, that's pretty obvious, so I thank her for the information and leave. Feeling completely steamed. Bennett the stupid prick or should I say, my world-class dickhead ex, has fucked up the best gig I ever had. And, just in case I was bothering to wonder if maybe he hadn't fucked it up beyond all hope of repair, I'm going down Park in a cab when the assistant director calls to let me know that the shoot has wrapped. Too bad about my fall, they'll work with what they have. Meaning, arrivederci, unreliable jerk. It was really great getting to know what a fuck-up you are.

Major bummer and, needless to say, Abigail left me a ton of hysterical voice mails. What on earth do you think you are doing, Fiona, for Christ's sake, are you out of your mind, I can't believe it, this is too unbelievable, you are thoroughly screwing yourself six ways from Sunday, how could you betray all the trust Cora Burke placed in you, Cora and I, never mind the example it sets for the other girls, what about your responsibility to yourself?

When I show up at the agency a few days later, she doesn't put it like that. She says she is deeply concerned. She says I have issues. She says, "When you were starting out, Fiona, I had every hope that you could be major. But I never sensed any real commitment to professionalism. Modeling is work, it's discipline, it's commitment. People need to know they can rely on you."

I furrow my brow. "This is what they need to know?"

"Yes, Fiona. I shouldn't have to be telling you this."

"OK. But isn't it enough for them to know that I'm hot?"

Once upon a time, Abigail looked at me like I was her wayward daughter. Now she's looking at me like I'm the daughter who escaped from an institution for the criminally insane. Like, the horror, the horror. Meaning, her expression is really priceless.

But I keep a straight face, saying, "Is there anything lined up for me?"

Abigail looks down at her desk, starts screwing around with some papers. And she keeps screwing around, not looking up, just muttering away to herself. Eventually, she gives me a couple of go-sees tomorrow. And the next day. And, oh, right, here's another one the day after that.

On my way out, I dig up Tom the tech guy, the one most likely to succeed in explaining to idiot me how to duplicate Medeco keys. The crucial step, if Plan B is ever going to get off the ground. Of course, Plan B would be a lot more streamlined if I had just swiped Sergei's key ring that night at Up. He was so blotto at the time he'd never have realized it was me. On the other hand, he might've and that would not be good. Don't want guys in plain clothes showing up at my place, asking if they could have a word with me. So, I'm telling myself, be glad you played it safe, plodding along, one dumb step after another.

When I finally find Tom he is deep in the middle of all kinds of complicated stuff with about three computers, which means I am seriously interrupting him with this request of mine. But he's nice about it. Actually, he seems kind of interested, saying he'll look into it and get back to me.

Downstairs at Allesandra's I run into some girls I know from the agency, they're telling me about this shoot in these islands near Vancouver, all foggy and gorgeous ... like the perfect girl, but I don't say that. I get an espresso and when the Cora Burke girls buzz off I check in with Ackerman's office, finding out they've gotten me even more stuff in the near future, all of which looks a lot more promising than anything I'm getting from Abigail.

So, great, time to fuck off for a day. I call Maisie, my favorite ex, to see if she wants to go shopping or something. She does but some people are coming over to her place in about forty-five minutes, some massive gala is in the early planning stages, evidently, and Maisie is weirdly nervous about it. And really into her own nervousness. Like, the thrill of performance anxiety, which she never had with me. So maybe this new life of hers is even sexier than sex, what do I know? Anyway, I decide to see some art, which is always relaxing, because who gets all worked up about art? Unless, of course, you're dealing the stuff.

I drop by the Whitney, take a spin through the galleries, and then I'm sitting downstairs, at the café, picking at one of their salads. Which are more or less inedible, meaning, good for the figure. And I'm reading this brochure about the show on the first floor, all this incredible architecture that never got built. The look is Rockefeller Center if Rockefeller Center had been designed by the wonderful people who brought you the pyramids of Egypt.

Then there's this voice. "Had enough art?"

I turn around, knowing who it is. My shithead ex. "What the hell are you doing here, Bennett? Are you my new stalker?"

"Not sure I like your tone of voice."

"No? Really? Tell me why I should care. I mean, I look at a bunch of dumb installation pieces and now I have to look at you? Why not fuck off, Bennett?"

"Now I'm sure I don't like your tone of voice. Mind if I sit down?"

I just glare at him. So he sits down and I keep glaring at him, which is pretty lame, no doubt, but what is there to say? Aside from the obvious.

"How did a jerk like you manage to pull off that brilliant stunt with Brenda?"

This was what he is hoping to hear and of course I wouldn't have asked except, let's face it, I really want to know. He leans back, elbows up, hands behind his head. That typical masculine pose, like, I'm on top of the world and couldn't be more sure of myself. Also, I'm really enjoying this big, arrogant grin I'm plastering all over my face, because I know how much it pisses you off.

"So, Bennett. How did you manage it?"

"Well, Fiona, as you may know ... or perhaps you don't ... at any rate, I am becoming fairly prominent in the Manhattan donor community—"

"Yeah, yeah. I know. You bought your way into the Morgan Library benefit. What I don't get is how you got someone like

Brenda to go along with you. Not that there is anyone else like Brenda."

Suddenly he leans forward and smirks and says, "That Sylvia Miller is quite the lean, mean—"

"Sylvia? Brenda's publicist? Get real. She's a total nothing. Pam runs the entire show—"

"Excuse me? Pam?" Bennett is doing this big, I'm-shocked-that-you-could-be-so-naïve number, his eyebrows half-way up across his scalp. His bald scalp with the slightly phony tan. And the sarcasm just keeps coming. "Pam? Really? Runs everything? Are you sure?"

Then he shifts gears, going into this very considerate, I-am-talking-to-a-idiot mode. "Pam looks after Brenda's pedicures. Maybe her magazine subscriptions. Whatever. But the powerhouse is Sylvia, because she's the connection to the outside world. Brenda lives in a bubble, as quite possibly you may have noticed, and she dies if the connection isn't precisely right. It has to be tended—"

"Bennett. Cut the bullshit. Brenda is major. The media comes to her. The day after your date or whatever it was, I was with her, it was late, *W* was trying to get through all that day, trying to snag Brenda for something Pam doesn't want her to do. Anyway, it was after ten at night and they were still trying. They're always trying, all the media. Fashion, entertainment, the straight news. Sylvia and her people are just traffic cops. Pam is in charge, which you would know if—"

"Which I would know if? If what? If the world were the happy little playground our little friend Fiona thinks it is?" Bennett goes back to his annoying grin, saying, "OK. If Pam is in charge, how come she didn't know I had taken Brenda to the Morgan Library thing? Which was, incidentally, my idea. I proposed it to Sylvia and she—"

"How the fuck do you know Sylvia?"

Bennett gives this dramatic shrug. Plus he furrows his brow. Thinking it over, the arrogant dope. Then he says, "Gee, I don't quite remember how I got to know Sylvia. The point is, Fiona, I know people. Get what I'm saying? What I'm saying is that I didn't have to wait around for you to make good on your promise. Keep your side of the bargain. Not that I didn't give you more than enough time ..."

The truth is that I never had any intention of keeping my side of the bargain. With Bennett? A bargain with Bennett is like a pledge to a fake charity. Sure, why not, put me down for a hundred grand. Now leave me alone. Strictly speaking, of course, I was in the wrong, I did break my promise, so I return to the previous subject. Sylvia Miller the publicist. Shaking my head in sheer wonderment, I say, "This makes no sense at all, Bennett. I don't even know what this Sylvia Miller looks like."

"She's quite attractive, Fiona."

"Right. Bennett Ross finds her attractive, meaning what? Botox lips and her tits are, oh, mm, uh, let's hazard a guess. Forty-six double D?"

"Now you're being childish, babe."

"True. I am."

"Because, as you may have figured out by now, my idea of a beautiful woman doesn't have much to do with forty-six double D. It has more to do with Brenda Rawlings."

"Speaking of whom, how was your date?"

"It was fine."

"Fine?"

"Yeah, fine. Though it has to be said that Brenda is a little boring. Just to be frank with you."

"Frank with me?"

"Yes, Fiona. Frank with you. This is total frankness. And I feel it is incumbent upon me to add that I don't see what you see in her. She is, admittedly, a great-looking woman. Fabulous looks, which are no less fabulous in person than in the pages of a magazine. But, beyond that, I don't get it. What's the big attraction?"

"It's not about Brenda's looks."

"No? Really? This is quite a remarkable thing for you to say, Fiona, given that Brenda's looks are about the only thing—never mind. The point is that you are not making a whole lot of sense."

"It's not about making sense."

Bennett gets up, brushes the crumbs from his pants. Which there aren't any, it's just that he likes to brush away the crumbs whether or not they exist. Then he shoots his cuffs, with the ultra-ritzy cuff links. Messes around with his tie. A whole performance, which he makes you watch every time, what an irritating twerp. When he's done, he gives me his patented empty smile and says, "It's not about making sense? I'm afraid you lost me there, Fiona."

"I'll bet." I get up, telling him I'll walk him out of the museum. Because I am not about to let go of the Sylvia Miller mystery. It is really bothering me, so I say, "This is all a little weird. I mean, the Brenda thing—"

"The Brenda thing?"

We're upstairs by now, in the museum lobby, and at least two batches of museum-goers are milling around, ignoring their guides and squishing Bennett and me together. This is not what we want. Bennett steps back, a bit too decisively, just about knocking this one very frail woman on her ass. Then he stands there, hands on hips, waiting for me to explain.

"You know, Bennett. The Brenda thing. The BXR machine. Brenda Rawlings Incorporated. It's not that big, so this theory of yours, about the right hand, how it doesn't always know which one the left hand is doing—I mean—you know what I mean—it doesn't exactly figure."

Bennett purses his lips. Looks down and scratches an eyebrow. Looks up and really starts to annoy me all over again, with this pompous, here-comes-the-final-summation voice. "The size of the organization is not the crucial factor. The crucial factor is the configuration of power."

I let my face go blank, saying, "Gee, Bennett, this is just such a dazzling concept I'm not sure I'm going to be able to handle it."

He smiles. A semi-nice smile. "OK. I grant you. It's not that complicated. Not in general, but it sometimes becomes very complicated when you drill down to specifics. Because it's about organizational karate. It's about palace intrigue." He pauses, tries to hold back and then just can't, letting go with this zinger, "You might understand it a little better if you lived in a palace."

"And you do? You live in a palace?"

"I have access, babe. It's pretty much the same thing."

I laugh a yeah-right sort of laugh.

Bennett smiles again. A semi-nasty smile. "At least I don't live in a hole in the wall on West Twenty-Eighth Street. But, then, you haven't seen my new place, have you, babe? Let's not talk about the five bedrooms and the view of the Park. Let's talk about the wired environment. State-of-the-art technology, everything from the security system to the multi-screen media center. Not to mention the two-thousand-dollar coffee maker."

"You sound like a sales brochure."

"And you? What do you sound like? Babe? You sound like Little Girl Lost, a runway has-been who wouldn't have a life if she didn't have her hooks into this year's supermodel. Who happens to be such an airhead she has no idea when she's being conned. I mean, come on, Fiona. All this stuff about Brenda. How it's not about making sense. You got that right. It's about bamboozling the airhead."

"Brenda's an airhead?"

Bennett nods.

"And I'm a has-been?"

Another nod, then, "It's your choice, babe."

I'm about to ask him what that is supposed to mean, when he gives me that irritating wink of his. So I knee him in the balls.

The thrill of victory and the agony of remorse. In other words, the big betrayal is working out well. Abigail is still booking me steadily and I have just finished another shoot for an Ackerman & Thatcher client. More catalog work, dull but low pressure and the money is OK. Getting people to look at me is a good alternative to looking into the abyss, so it's nice that I have all this stuff to do. Work, gym, sleep … it's all great, especially sleep, so I am fairly annoyed at six-thirty in the morning when I hear my phone … which I didn't know where it was, so I had to track it down, under some stuff on the kitchen counter, missing the call, of course, so I rang back and it was Mike the security guy, asking if I've noticed any unusual occurrences since the last one. The time that car cut us off. I say no and why are you asking?

"Well. There was something about ten minutes ago. A home invasion thing."

"What? What are you talking about, Mike?"

"One of the girls was showing up early to go over some things with Pam and this guy pushed right in behind her—"

"Oh, god."

"Simon was on duty, you don't know him, a very competent guy. So the home invader is screwed before he begins. Ends up on the floor, zipped up tight. Plastic restraints. Boot in the face? Really?"

"No, Fiona, not really. Figure of speech. Except for the plastic restraints. Anyway, the cops came, we're pressing charges."

"So who is he?"

"Mystery man. No idea."

"Any connection to Sergei?"

"No idea."

"God, Mike. This is spooky. But thanks for telling me."

"No sweat."

"What can I do?"

"Nothing. Keep Brenda calm. When you see her."

"Does she know about this?"

"No. I'm just saying …"

"No, yes, I mean … I mean, right. You're right. I will."

"Good. And I apologize for calling so early but it just happened and I wanted to let you know before I forget."

"In other words, before Pam tells you who's in the loop and who isn't."

A soft laugh from Mike.

So I say, "Thanks again."

"No sweat."

I hang up, thinking, OK, no sweat. No blood, no sweat, no tears, except for the ones that are running down my face, and now my bed feels all clammy and cold. Because I'm so scared. Or not scared, just so frustrated and pissed off I can't stand it. Why does this shit keep happening around Brenda? And why do I always have to be figuring out what to do about it? Because maybe I don't have to but I feel like I do, and it's beginning to feel like this is all I'm ever going to be feeling … aside from pissed off and frustrated.

The solution to which would be Bill, if he weren't getting married. Sob. Because, it turns out Bill is a man of honor. I know because I called him a while ago and before I could even start hinting he told me he's planning to be faithful to Imogen. Already, which is sweet, I suppose, and after I got off the phone I realized I should have asked him if he'd been faithful to me.

Silly question.

Our thing was totally casual, which is what made it so great and why I miss it so much. It's like there had been this service, flights to the moon, not to mention the stars and beyond, Bill took me higher than anyone ever did, and then one day you get this notice. We're shutting it down. Sorry for any inconvenience this may cause to our valued customers. Right, like, something irreplaceable goes out of my life and my only option is to go from feeling pissed off and frustrated to feeling frustrated and really sad ... thinking about this box of condoms I brought over to Bill's place the last time we slept together ...

I mean, there they are, only a couple of them used up, and now the rest are going to lie there forever, in the drawer beside Bill's bed, feeling useless ... because, one, Bill probably sleeps with Imogen at her place, wherever that is, she doesn't seem like the downtown loft type, and, two, they probably don't even use condoms, given her age and no doubt they've gotten all checked out and so nothing gets between Bill and his new love except her lubricant ... oh god, I *am* jealous, I wish I could have had that with Bill, no safe-sex worries, just Bill, free-flowing ... so it really is sad, in this way that isn't the least bit sentimental. No nostalgia, no wistfulness, none of that sweet, self-pitying pain that is, if you're honest about it, pleasure dressed up in a gloomy outfit. What I'm feeling now is true, burning sadness.

When I was a kid, about ten, I guess, there was this older girl one summer, sort of a hulking creature who went around challenging people to arm wrestle. Even boys, and she beat some of them, too, and so once, for a joke, these kids said, hey, Fiona, why don't you arm wrestle with Cecily? Like I had these toothpick arms and this was the most ridiculous thing in the world. So I said, sure, and of course she beat me but I held out for a long time, refusing to give in and surprising everyone. Myself included, a little bit.

Anyway, I was standing around on Seventh Avenue, thinking of Cecily, having fought my lousy mood to a draw, right to the last gasp of an unbelievably boring day in the fashion biz. Then the mood won, I couldn't hold out any longer, and the next thing, I got a call from someone named Ralph Something-or-Other who tells me I gave him my comp card a while back, he can't quite remember where, but there's this party tonight, a bunch of important agency people and production people and all these hot photographers are going to be there, in this penthouse, this incredibly cool place, and, uh, wait a minute …

He's going to give me the address, and while he pretends to look for it I can practically hear the casting couch squeaking away in the background, squeak, squeak, squeak, so I say, Ralph, thanks so much for thinking of me but I'm busy tonight, have to help a friend pick out a new goldfish, ending the call and then standing there for a while, just looking at the light on the buildings. It was so beautiful, unlike the buildings themselves … one of those days in the city when the shadows are so crisp. The air is so clear. And the point of it all is so elusive, sort of teasing you. Like, did you ever consider the possibility that there isn't any point?

To which I can honestly say, no, I never did consider that, because it seems to me that if there were no point, really, none whatsoever, there would have to be some point to that and then some point to *that*, and, uh . . . you could spend your whole life getting to the bottom of it, which you never would, so it stands to reason that … um … why bother? So I walked down the Avenue for a few blocks, watching the shadows get darker and maybe a little blurrier, then I got in touch with Fred and it turns out that we are both a little tired of Brainwave. The no-look look. So Fred said we should meet at Bungalow 9, this place on West Nineteenth Street. Which, when I get there, I'm slightly overwhelmed.

It's totally tricked-out, South Beach in Chelsea, with a forest of mini-palm trees and these big murals on the walls that look like stills from *Miami Vice*. Fred's favorite TV show of all time, so I tease him about Don Johnson. Is he really your major culture hero? And he says, yes, of course, how could you even ask? By now we are sinking into these armchairs, over-the-top garish, and ordering Margaritas that are not Margaritas. There's this addition of watermelon, which we decide to try.

A big mistake.

The next round is real Margaritas and so that's one problem solved. But there is still the Sergei problem. Which I would like to discuss with Fred. But discussing it with Fred is not so easy because, I suddenly realize, I don't want to lay it all out for him. I mean, I do, but maybe it's not such a great idea to name names. So I say I have this major dilemma but I'm going to give it to him like it's a hypothetical. He says, OK, and I tell him there's this very famous person, very prominent, image-wise, and this guy who is, um, smitten with her and she acts like he doesn't exist and this upsets him—

"Upsets him?"

"Yes."

"How upset? I hate you, I never want to see you again or I hate you, I'm going to do everything I can to fuck up your life? Or I hate you, you have to die?"

"The latter. You have to die."

"Hmm. OK."

"So. OK. I have this plan—"

"A plan?"

"Yeah. Plan B. Plan A didn't work—"

"So—"

"So I'm going to get into the guy's apartment—"

"Fiona." Fred is sitting up now, his hands on his knees, looking down at the floor. "First, this sounds like a really terrible plan, whatever it is. Second, even if it's a good plan, which it isn't, I'm not sure you should be—"

"I know. I shouldn't be telling you. That's why I'm keeping it hypothetical."

Fred looks over at me with a funny expression on his face. Sympathetic but also very stern. "This is about Brenda Rawlings, right?"

"How do you know about Brenda?"

"You mean, how do I know about you and Brenda?"

"OK. Me and Brenda. How do you know?"

"I know you. So I know about that." Which didn't really explain anything, but now Fred is saying, "What's up with you and Brenda? Are you, like …"

"Fucking her? No. We're just good friends. So, being her friend, I have to figure out some way to deal with this terrible guy."

"Because he's going to kill Brenda."

"Right. Maybe. I don't know. Actually, her people have pretty much stopped worrying about the guy, but there was this incident at Brenda's place, early yesterday morning—"

"Incident?"

"Somebody tried to push his way in."

"But not this guy. Right?"

"Right. On the other hand, he might be behind it, and so … um … anyway, that's not the point."

"Not the point?"

"Uh—"

"What's the point?"

"The point is, uh ..." Here I start to sound sort of inarticulate because the point is the spookiness, how it's been lurking around every corner in my universe, got to get rid of it, but of course Fred wouldn't understand that. He's way too level-headed. So I hem and haw some more and then I say, "OK. The point is to get into this person's apartment and, well, there's this thing I have to find—"

"This thing? Which you have to find after you break into his apartment?"

"Not break in. Get in. With his keys. I mean, duplicates—"

"So this is why you wanted Tom to tell you about Medeco keys."

"Oh. He mentioned that? OK. Anyway, I have to get in, get this thing—"

"Great. But, look. Fiona. Don't tell me what this thing is, because it sounds like this is the sort of madness I should avoid like the plague. Which is what I'm going to do, so let me say it again. This is a terrible plan. Drop it. Because, all right, let's think the unthinkable and say this person actually does harm Brenda in some way. Which I am sensing even you do not think is all that likely. But, erring on the side of caution, let's go ahead and assume the possibility. And then leave it to the professionals. The cops. Brenda's security people. In other words, get real. You care very deeply for Brenda and I respect that but lots of people care for lots of people very deeply and they don't screw around with the kind of people that make death threats. They don't commit felonies, like breaking and entering. It's like you're the Lone Ranger. You have to take care of it all by yourself."

"There's always Tonto."

"Fuck Tonto, Fiona."

"Just so I don't have to fuck Sergei."

"That's the guy's name? Sergei?"

"Yes."

"Great. Don't tell me his last name. The point is, fine, you think you can handle this Sergei character. But if you can handle him, how much of a threat can he be? I'm not trying to be a jerk but—"

"Look. Fred." I'm leaning forward, about to put my hand on his knee. Which I don't, I just say, "Look, I know you're not being a jerk and, as a matter of fact, I know you're basically right. But, basically, this is up to me. Because there really isn't anything to leave up to the professionals—"

"So what's the problem?"

"The problem is that Sergei is this horrible thing in Brenda's world. And he just can't be there. It's not right—"

"So you have to make it right?"

"Right. I mean, yes, that's it. Exactly, because there has been this big cloud hanging over me ever since I got back to New York and I get that I have lots of other stuff to worry about, like, for example, my dazzling career, and a lot of the time I am completely into that. And other stuff. Shopping and, um . . ."

Fred is about to say something, I know it, tease me about being such a sex fiend, but I keep babbling away, saying, "The problem is that I have no idea what I'm doing ninety percent of the time, because of this thing hanging over my head, soaking into everything, which I have to deal with because nothing means what it's supposed to mean unless I straighten it out."

Now Fred nods, very faintly but definitely. He gets it. The basic logic, which is, it's not up to me but it *is* up to me. And I am going to do something about it. Which worries him, given that I am not the most rational person he has ever met, and I am feeling so touched that he's so worried, asking me if Sergei is really all that nasty.

I tell him, "Yes. Really. Sergei is nastiness on steroids. His steroids are on steroids. But, on the other hand, let's give credit where credit is due, he is not immune to the finer things. Money.

Booze. Glamor. So it was a big thrill for this creep to be one of Brenda's escorts."

"How did he swing that?"

"You'll have to ask Brenda. Or Pam the personal manager. It's Pam's little secret, which I will not get out of her in a million years. Anyway, can you imagine this? Brenda, the world's most gorgeous woman, sailing through these high-end events, like she always does, half-asleep and all dreamy, only now she's being shadowed by this creature who makes Lon Chaney as the Hunchback of Notre Dame look like Cary Grant—"

"Love the movie references, Fiona."

"Yeah. Me too."

"So you're a cinephile?"

"God, Fred. That is such an old-fashioned word. I had this teacher once who used to say that. Cinephile. Also cinephobe. Which is what he was. It sounded totally out of it even then."

"I never said I wasn't out of it."

I smile, thinking Fred is about as out of it as the next hot club, the one that hasn't even opened yet.

He's smiling back at me, saying, "I'm a little surprised about this cinephilia of yours, Fiona. I saw you more as a dancing girl. A music fan. You know. A slave to the rhythm."

I'm about to ask him which rhythm he has in mind, but I don't. I just shake my head, telling him I'm not really up on music. And I hate the stuff they play at fashion shoots. Yuck. All this Eighties stuff, and they don't even draw the line at *Eye of the Tiger*. The lamest song ever. But it gets people pumped, so … whatever works, I guess, and Fred asks me what I think they ought to play.

"Well, if it has to be Eighties, how about those Robert Palmer songs? Which would make sense, given that he had all these tranced-out models in his videos."

"*Addicted to Love*."

"And the other one, with rows and rows of models, in the last row they're doing this group hump."

"*Simply Irresistible.*"

"Fred. I'm so impressed. You know all this shit."

He laughs. "I know all sorts of shit. Except, for a long time I didn't get the lyrics of *Addicted to Love*. I thought it was 'a dickhead in love.'"

"Sounds like my ex. Except he was never in love. Maybe with himself. But probably not. He has bad taste but not that bad."

"I can't believe he has bad taste if he got involved with you."

"Fred. That's so sweet." Sort of teasing him, but only sort of. "Anyway, the big question is, if I have such great taste what was I doing with him?"

"Maybe—"

"Maybe he was great in bed? That's what you were going to say, right?"

Fred nods. "Yeah. Of course."

I shake my head, realizing I hardly remember what Bennett was like in bed. That was the one place our paths hardly ever crossed ... what a waste of time, hooking up with a guy I never hooked up with ...

Snapping out of it, I polish off my latest Margarita and say, "That thing about a dickhead in love? Getting the lyrics wrong? It reminds me of 'Tequila Mockingbird.' Which is my name for *To Kill a Mockingbird*. Not that I didn't get the real title. 'Tequila Mockingbird' wasn't my mistake, I just made it up. I thought it was so original. And it was original, in the sense that I came up with it all on my own. Then I found out that every other out-of-town restaurant with one of those big, floppy menus features a drink called Tequila Mockingbird. It's like sex when you're a kid, you're with somebody great and you're really inspired and you come up with something new. Some great, sexy move and you think, wow, I'm a creative genius, no one has ever done this before, sex will never be the same again. I have changed the course of human history, and then you're making out a while later with somebody else and they do the same move on you. It's really hot, sweet, lovely, but also kind of a bummer because you realize that your great inspiration is common knowledge. People have been doing it since forever."

Fred is about to say there is nothing new under the sun but he doesn't, because why bother? Anyway, if you're going to say something like that, why not say, nothing new under the moon? Or nothing East of the Sun, West of the Moon ... the Watermelon moon ... not to mention the Zigzag Railroad ... because I am getting a little tipsy, here in the glare of the *Miami Vice* mural ...

Given that we have been ordering round after round all this time and, actually, I am not that much of a drinker, and no drugs whatsoever, still an absolute rule, despite all the shit that's gone down ... but Fred is very quick and reliable and now he is folding me into this taxi, like one of those six-foot rulers, only I'm only five-ten, and he smiles and hugs me as best he can, because I'm just a bunch of sharp angles ... all elbows and knees ... awkward and woozy ... and saying goodnight ... and thanks ... and then I'm off, into the night ... everything sort of grainy now ... grainy and blurry ... one glammed-up movie still after the next ...

Jon Ackerman keeps calling me, why don't you stop by, there are some options we really ought to look at. Yeah, right, like, are we going to do it on his desk or figure out some way that involves a chair? There's always the floor, but not really, not with him, he's beginning to come across as so finicky. Every time he calls, it takes him about half an hour to get to the point of even hinting at sex. Before that, he overdoes the compliments, like he's hearing all these good things about me, the new initiative seems to be working out, better than we dared hope, blah, blah, blah. Then the insinuating remarks, how we really ought to get together, pick up where we left off ... but nothing definite, so I decide to show up at his office one slow afternoon and, much to his secretary's surprise, he is able to see me immediately.

We talk about some of the shoots his people booked me on, the possibility of better money, which he calls a carefully monitored escalation of my compensation, then he tells me one more time that he is very pleased with the feedback he's getting about me. I tell him that's really terrific, I'm so happy to hear it, and then I get up and walk around behind his chair and reach over his shoulder and start massaging his cock through his pants.

Also, I'm nuzzling his ear and telling him to tell his secretary to hold his calls, which he does, even though it's beginning to look like the office-quickie scenario is not going to be unfolding. I mean, he's squirming and practically gasping for breath. Wondering what has he gotten himself into?

What he's gotten himself into is an afternoon with Fiona at the Carlyle or possibly the Pierre, I leave it up to him and head for the door. Having made it clear that it has to be the afternoon after next, because that's the only open time in the schedule of the gorgeous and constantly in-demand girl he is now wishing, maybe, he had never met.

Jon opted for the Pierre, three-thirty-ish on the designated afternoon, and I got to the suite about an hour early. It's on the eleventh floor, this big bland space full of amenities I didn't want to hear about. So I told the bellhop to leave my bag on the rack and buzz off, though I was nicer about it than that, over-tipping him and all. Then I spent a few minutes gazing out the window at the Park. Beautiful but boring, which you wouldn't say about a beautiful person. Even if the person were boring, their beauty wouldn't be. It would be a thrill.

I put some towels on the floor in front of the bathroom-door mirror and did some naked yoga. Then some naked Pilates. Then, at the risk of turning into Irina, I ordered a dozen oysters and bottle of Pol Roger. When the bell rang, I grabbed a robe, this summer-weight wool thing, that was hanging on the other side of the door. My nipples were hard for some reason, just popping out, and the waiter was this young Eastern European guy who seemed to be pretty blasé about seeing the likes of me in the middle of the afternoon. Because, I think, he actually was blasé, which struck me as admirable.

I slurped down the oysters and drank about half the champagne, then took off the robe and got into bed ... sort of snoozing, but not really, because I was up and out of bed the moment I heard Jon's knock. He came in without a word, all embarrassed to see that I was already naked, and wanting to take a shower right away. And wanting me to get in there with him, so, OK, I did, and he started washing me all over, after which he washed himself and then rinsed us both off with the hand-held gizmo. In the shower, he focused quite a bit on my butt but in bed he went straight for my tits. Licking, sucking, squeezing. A little inept, maybe, but sweet. Next, he lay there for a while and hugged me, like what he really wanted was just me to be close to him, hugging him back, at which point I realized if I didn't turn into a take-charge kind of girl I was going to turn into the totally frustrated kind.

So I got him to stretch out on his back and started caressing his dick, kissing his neck and his chest, his nipples, which gave him this shock, like my tongue was zapping him with electric currents, and after a while he was hard enough to slip on a condom. So I straddled him and got him inside me ... not all that forceful a presence, if you know what I mean, so I had to ride him with extreme delicacy, showing his cock how to get hard, harder, hard-est … the pussy as teaching device …

Not that he didn't know how to fuck. He just didn't know how to fuck me. Or any girl under circumstances like these, being too worried about professional ethics or his wife or whatever. Or all of the above, especially the elusive whatever, which seemed to give him this edginess about sex that he was feeling, probably always felt, even under the best of circumstances. Like now, when he's doing it with this ultra-hot babe, namely, me.

After a while, he came and I didn't and we lay around some more, kissing and touching, with me thinking, it's so nice that he got off and wondering, also, why should I care? Except that I did, it was so sweet afterward, letting myself feel that thing he reminded me of, something sad from when I thought sad things were the sweetest of all. Which I don't any more, though Jon obviously does. From the way he was going in for all this close-up gazing into my eyes, I could tell he was getting super-gloomy and sort of sappy realizing that we were probably never going to do this again.

Jon left before I did, leaving me with the thought that I will def-initely be getting more bookings through Ackerman & Thatcher. Because things were nice right up to the last moment, our good-bye kiss was actually almost sexy, and, anyway, even if he decides he hates me for creating this complication in his life, he's not going to want to piss me off. I might decide to play the part of the woman scorned, the mistreated mistress running to the mistreated wife for sympathy. Not really, I would never, ever do that, but so what? Because, nice, edgy man that he is, Jon will never stop wor-rying about it, and maybe, to fend off the risk of complete disaster, he'll make me the star of this new initiative of his.

Assuming that his new initiative doesn't tank. Because it's not all that great an idea, running a modeling agency out of an advertising agency. It's OK now but the odds of success long-term aren't even even money but fuck it, the odds on anything else in my life aren't much better. That's why I don't play the odds. I go for broke. Or I fold. Go read a book. Or get myself off, at those moments when I feel like playing it safe, rigging the odds totally in my favor.

Brenda asked me to come over to her place last night, so I was happy and just the slightest bit apprehensive, wondering if the Fortress had come in for any more attacks. Evidently not, Brenda was so calm and sweet from the very first moment. We decided not to watch a movie, we were going to look around in her closet, find something for her to wear to this luncheon the next day. It was going to be at some foundation in Chelsea, a haven for stray artists or something, and Brenda is on the committee for their big annual fundraiser. Like she cares about art. Or committee work. Anyway, they want to do a Fashion Evening and Brenda is the star, natch, so there has to be a luncheon ahead of time. And Brenda has to look just right, not too uptown, not too downtown … casual but utterly glam.

Quite the wardrobe puzzler, so we were looking and looking, trying all these various combos on her, all of which looked great but not exactly right. But we kept at it, because it was so much fun, playing dress up, and then my phone rang.

It was Sergei, for god's sake, so I looked at Brenda and shrugged, meaning, I have to take this. So, being the nicest person in the world, she wandered off, started looking through this other closet, full of shoes, and it turns out to be Viktor, asking where Brenda is. I'm baffled. Because why assume that of course I know and, even if I did, why would I tell?

Before I can ask, Sergei is on the line, saying, "Tell me where is Brenda. I am worried."

By now I've gotten a bit of a grip on myself and I say, "Hi Sergei. You sound drunk." Because he does, utterly sloshed.

Silence, so I say, "Look, Sergei, why are you so concerned about Brenda? I thought you wanted to kill her."

He makes this weird little sound. Then he laughs, lots of phony scorn, meaning, what are you talking about? Where did you get that stupid idea? I am about to tell him to get real, I got the idea from him, when he says, "Brenda wants to kill me."

"Brenda wants to kill you?"

"Yes. She wants to kill me."

"Sergei, this is so dumb. Are you talking on your dumb phone? Why don't you call me back on your smart phone, maybe sound a bit brighter?"

More silence, then, after about five minutes, he says, "You want I call Brenda?"

"No, Sergei. Don't call Brenda. Don't call me. Don't call anybody. Except, on second thought, why don't you call the Russian consulate? Ask them to send you back to Russia, put you in one of those psych wards they have there. Give you a psychiatric evaluation. See if you're competent to stand trial."

"Trial? Trial? For what I stand trial?"

"Oh, I don't know, Sergei. Just for being yourself. Who knows? Get a good lawyer, maybe you could beat the rap."

Silence again, and I got this image of him trying to work out the new brainteaser. Not a pretty picture so I hung up and saw that Brenda had vanished. I found her downstairs, in the living room, sitting on her boat-sized couch and looking at an issue of *Vogue*. Probably last month's, which has her on the cover. I sat down and almost asked her what she thought of the spread on her. She'd been styled as a Fifties movie goddess and I hardly recognized her. Because the idea of Brenda is *now*, now being this vast place including the foreseeable future, meaning, I don't really like the new retro pictures.

But Brenda never wants to talk about images of herself, she was reading a piece on moisturizers, so I didn't ask her what she thought. Instead, I made a much worse mistake. A humongous faux pas. For which I blame a Thirties movie goddess, namely, Carol Lombard, in *My Man Godfrey*, where she says, "Isn't it strange the way you think of something and then it makes you think of something else?" It's strange, all right, and even stranger if you blurt out something the other something made you think of. For which I can't blame anyone but myself, obviously, as much as I'd like to. Anyway, Sergei had just called and that had gotten me to wondering if he had anything to do with the home-invasion thing the other night. So I asked Brenda if Mike and his people had come up with any theories.

Immediately she got all distant and—what? Sort of prim or something, like I'd never seen her act before. Because before, anything even vaguely reminiscent of Sergei would make her nervous and she would look to me, like I was going to help her. Or we were in it together, and I'd comfort her. But I couldn't do that now, she was suddenly so far away from me, like she was connecting me with that security incident. Connecting me with Sergei, so I was making the problem worse by even mentioning stuff like this.

I wanted to talk to her about it, reassure her, but just then Pam walked in with a guy in gray flannel slacks and this suede jacket that made you stop and stare. So creamy and supple, like it was alive. A creepy thought, I admit, and all the creepier because the guy was like some famous person you don't recognize in the wax museum, except totally hyper, one of these corporate types who wants you to think of him as a catalyst, the guy who makes things happen. So he's got a tan and a boatload of sincere, appreciative looks to get on his face. Everything is always "interesting" and "remarkable," according to guys like this, and this one made a big production number of saying how it was such "a remarkable privilege to meet Brenda Xavier Rawlings in the flesh."

Which it was, no question, for him or anybody else. So he offered these heartfelt apologies for intruding at this late hour and said how it really was so gratifying to be getting together with her for the first time in her truly impressive digs. Then he went a little too quickly into some bullshit about licensing, a detail in one of Brenda's tons of contracts that needed ironing out, a matter of real urgency, so important to get her personal input, et cetera, et cetera, all this legal stuff that sounded like it was super high-level and confidential, the kind of thing that Brenda never has to listen to.

Because why should she, this would normally be a job for Ronnie the dickhead lawyer and his team of pompous flunkies but a legal glitch had popped up and Brenda's personal OK was required. This very evening. Otherwise, some leaning tower of corporate bullshit would just topple and fall, total disaster, meaning time was of the essence, needless to say, and so this corporate jerk had appeared in Brenda's living room way, way after business hours.

He didn't look at me when we were introduced and now it was like I wasn't there, as far as he was concerned. But Pam was getting all nervous and jittery and pretty soon she had her hand on my shoulder, pressuring me in the direction of the door. Like I was this object you could push in a certain direction and I'd just go there. Which I did, because it had gotten pretty obvious that I didn't belong in the room right at that moment.

So I left, noticing that the corporate type didn't even notice what Pam was doing. Which was OK, but Brenda didn't notice, either, and that hurt. Because Brenda always notices me. That's part of who I am, that she always notices me, so even if I'm not there it feels in some strange way like she's talking to me, listening to me. But now it was like I didn't even exist for her.

So this is me, a lost soul floating in outer darkness. Frozen to the bone, the moral of the story being that body and soul don't have to be on totally intimate terms, because, frozen soul to the contrary, my bod is getting good reactions at work. Not that misery is having no effect. I've been moping along with that glum zombie look you see on so many of the girls, especially the beginners, like, OK, I'm beautiful but so what? Or, fuck off, because, sure, you appreciate my beauty but that gives you zero leverage. Unless you're the camera, which maybe got a little bored with the old Fiona, always so up and energetic and unbelievably hot.

Or maybe not. How should I know? As long as I keep showing up and keep my bad attitude on a tight leash, everything keeps humming along. Fiona the Cog in the vast machinery of seduction. Which doesn't feel all that vast when you're jammed into an elevator with a bunch of girls, all of them just as cute as you are, all of them hungry—or, forget hungry, more like famished, ravenous, for the chance to wait around for forty-five minutes for a go-see which amounts to, oh, hi, didn't I see you last week at that Revlon audition? Lancôme? ... no and no, a thousand times no, but it doesn't matter, the guy has never seen me before but he thinks he possibly has ... it's the small-world syndrome, meaning claustrophobia is right up there among the fashion biz's leading occupational hazards.

Claustrophobia and Scopophobia, fear of being looked at, I looked it up on one of the other girl's iPads, and of course I'm kidding. I have no fear of being looked at, it's just that the admiring glances are bouncing off me, bouncing off and hitting the ground with a dull thud, meaning work is feeling more than ever like work. To which I am buckling down like a good little zombie, and late in the day I got this great gig. A spot in Jill Lepore's show in a few weeks. So I popped down to Orchard Street, figuring I would reward myself with a double portion of the dreamy olive oil gelato they have at Laboratorio.

I'm in the middle of ordering when I get a call. It's Fred. Juggling phone and money and gelato and then my change, I say, hi, what's up, and he cuts to the chase, telling me he knew I was flaky but not completely insane, what the hell do I think I'm doing, getting bookings from Ackerman & Thatcher?

"So the whole fashion world is buzzing?"

"No. The whole fashion world is not buzzing. Not about you, Fiona. But this friend of mine at Ackerman noticed your name on a booking sheet and thought, that's kind of weird."

"It is kind of weird."

"He's not going to say anything but, come on, what are you doing?"

"I don't know, Fred. I never really do. I guess I'm just a child of impulse."

"You're a girl with a screw loose, Fiona. I mean, you know what I think of Abigail, but…"

"Yeah. I know. But, look, maybe it's time for me to quit again. Go on hiatus."

"Hiatus? What are you? A television show? *Fiona Fucks Up?*"

"Right. Exactly. *Fiona Fucks Up.* Let's pitch it to one of the cable networks."

"Fiona—"

"Or I'll just take off and you'll come with me. It'll be fun, landing in some exotic place, hanging out on the beach, and when night falls—"

"We go our separate ways."

"Yeah. Pretty much. Anyway—"

"That would be fun. Of course, you're overlooking something, Fiona, the obvious fact that I need a job. So do you."

"I do."

"So maybe you should rethink things."

"Maybe I should."

Fred rings off and I'm standing out on the sidewalk, gobbling gelato, thinking, OK, let's rethink things, but, come to think of it, I don't feel like thinking. I'm more in the mood for fucking off. But how? No idea. Then, light bulb, and I am heading up Eighth Avenue in a cab, to Lincoln Center, way off the beaten track. For me, anyway, because I'm going to the opera, which I never do. But now I am because of something Fred told me awhile back. You show up a couple of hours early, stand in line, and you get a ticket.

Maybe, and of course I'm pretty late, but, as it happens, I do get a ticket. And the show is starting fairly soon, so I stand around in the lobby, thinking, OK, everybody is acting all excited, happy to be there, but maybe this isn't the hottest ticket ever. I mean, I only had to wait in line for about five minutes, so what is this?

Silly question.

It's plastered all over the lobby. *Pelléas et Mélisande* by Claude Debussy. No idea what I'm in for, and way into the first act, I'm still clueless. Of course, I can read about the plot in the program, all this weepy, mysterious love in the deep, dark past, and then the girl marries one brother and falls in love with the other, lots of pointless jealousy, then she loses her wedding ring, meaning, another bunch of pointless problems, a bunch of conflicts, a bunch of resolutions, and there you have it. The dynamics of sibling rivalry, the bumpy road to love, happily ever after, fine, I get it, but the music is beyond me. Lovely, but way beyond me, so drifty, all these currents I can't quite catch. So I concentrate on the stage sets, which are so great.

Of course, this is yet another sign of my idiocy, according to the guy who starts chatting me up during the first intermission. He's nice looking in a spiffy gray linen suit, with a lime green tie, the perfect visual accent, but he is not coming on to me. He just needs someone to talk to, the stage sets are doing this terrible number on his head, because the music is abstract, the costumes, the acting, the voices, it's all so abstract but the sets are so terribly overdone, all that fussy detail. It's like painting an abstract painting and, right in the middle of it, sticking on a snapshot of somebody's face.

Which would be a pretty bad idea, no doubt, so I'm nice, not saying anything, even though I love all the fussy detail in the sets, they remind me of the pictures in this book of fairy tales my grandmother had. Which I would look at all day. But later, when I was back in my seat, not really listening to the music, sort of swimming around in it, I was thinking I really ought to feel more sympathy for the man in the lime green tie. He was upset because he wanted things to be a certain way, all the way through, and they weren't. Something was off. Which is pretty much my big complaint. Something is off. I know what it is, I have a plan, but I keep not doing anything about it.

And just to remind me, this special something keeps getting in touch. Meaning, Sergei, who called me during the second intermission. Which I had kind of expected, weirdly enough, given that I'm not one of these people who say, I was thinking of So-and-so and then they called. This never happens to me. Except that I'd been thinking of Sergei, a minute before, half a minute, literally, and now he was calling. So I took the call, saying, "Hi," and he said, "I have good news. For Brenda. Albanian friend has new job for her."

"Brenda doesn't need a new job, Sergei."

"New job in Abu Dhabi. Working for very rich man."

"What? The Sheik of Araby? Brenda's going to join the harem?"

Sergei laughed. An unbelievably nasty laugh. I thought hyena and realized that not all hyenas are the same. Some are psychopaths.

"I tell Albanian friend to make appointment with Brenda."

"Oh, for—"

But he was gone and now I'm wondering why I didn't shut off my phone, like you're supposed to. I mean, these opera lovers are serious. If Sergei's call had interrupted a major aria, they might have strangled me. I'd have ended up dead, like everyone else in the opera. A great way to deal with inconveniences. But only in an opera. Right?

People talk about the feeling that something is missing from their lives but they don't know what it is. I know exactly what's missing from my life. Because it hardly seems like a life if I don't hear from Brenda, and then I do.

I'm stunned, the tears are welling up, what a relief, I do exist. Because Brenda is acting like there was never anything wrong between us, so I'm thinking, maybe the guy in the suede jacket was some sort of hallucination … ridiculous, needless to say, but maybe not, maybe nothing did go wrong between me and Brenda, how should I know? All I know is that I'm in a daze, flopping back onto my king-size bed and feeling so happy and realizing I also feel wet, which is weird because I can't even imagine sex with Brenda, it's just that I love her so much and I'm so happy to be talking to her about nothing in particular.

Like, for example, the lunch at that foundation in Chelsea, she could hardly leave afterwards, there were so many paparazzi outside ... it was supposed to be secret of course but, anyway, who cares, she's going to donate a huge bunch of money as well as her time and her heartbreakingly gorgeous presence, which I tell her is so sweet ... you are so sweet, darling ... darling, darling, darling ...

We hung up and then, when I went over to her place that night, the cabbie could hardly get onto her block, it was all flashers and squad cars and this van practically blocking the entire street ... people running back and forth, lights just chopping at things, like some brainwashing technique, these patterns of red and blue, over and over, so harsh, and the police radio, every other word snap, crackle, and pop, the entire ensemble trying to get you to believe that nothing was happening anywhere except here. And not only that but what was happening here was living proof that daily life had fallen apart. Could no longer get it together. Wasn't up to the task. The center cannot hold and so on and so forth.

If that was the message, I was buying it, completely, figuring, here it was, at last, a real crisis, oh god, oh god, oh god, like, I went nuts over the fake one, fucked up the Rollo Rodriguez shoot ... and that was bad enough ... so what is a real crisis going to do? I was trying like mad to get past the uniforms, telling everyone I was a member of Miss Rawlings's staff, not making much progress. And of course not getting any answers to my questions. Like, what the fuck is going on?

After a few cops told me members of the press had to wait on the other side of the street, my cooperation would really be appreciated, and a few more asked me if I could prove I was a member of the immediate family, I decided, OK, there is a better way and I have to do it. I have to call Pam, which I didn't want to, but I did, telling whoever answered, it's Fiona, please, please send someone to get me.

After a while one of the assistants—a handsome girl in a bathrobe, for god's sake—came out and grabbed me and explained to a couple of dozen more cops that, yes, I really was a member of Miss Rawlings's staff and Miss Rawlings was expecting me. Not all that swiftly I realized this meant that Brenda was OK. So. What the fuck was going on?

The lobby of her house was jammed with blue uniforms of various kinds, and there was a jurisdictional dispute going on. One set of uniforms was New York City cops and the other was from the ASPCA and, actually, it wasn't that both groups were claiming the case. It was the other way around, no one wanted any part of it, because there wasn't any case, there was hardly even an incident, just a bunch of paperwork to be done, and the group that got tagged as primary on the scene would have to write up a lot more than the group that managed to weasel out.

This is what I got from standing around and listening for a while, everyone trying to sound like a lawyer, all the bullshit about timely response and interagency cooperation and relevant expertise and what not. It was kind of fascinating, and then Mel What's-His-Name, this ex-FBI guy on Brenda's security staff tried to mediate and got ignored, which made me feel bad. I wanted him to succeed, sort of make himself indispensable under these unexpected circumstances, but what I really wanted to do was go up and see Brenda.

Which was next to impossible for a while, all her people going in circles, asking me to wait, a moment or two, things are so crazy, blah-blah-blah in this hysterical I'm-in-charge-here tone of voice, meaning no one was in charge, and when I finally got upstairs, there was Brenda, on the floor playing with these three gigantic dogs.

Russian Wolfhounds. Gifts from Sergei.

What happened, the wolfhounds showed up at her door a few hours ago, this kid hands their leashes over to this other kid, one of Pam's assistants, who is too shocked to tell him, uh, no thanks. We didn't order any wolfhounds. So, according to the girl in the bathrobe, who shows up to watch Brenda and her new pals, they were suddenly all over the place, not trying to hurt anybody, just running up and down the stairs, knocking over furniture and lamps and generally getting to know their new environment.

The creatures are so elegant, everyone agrees, and of course unmanageable. The smallest one weighs as much as the biggest girl on Brenda's staff, so there was an extended period of girly screaming and yelping until someone got the really dippy idea of calling the ASPCA. Which zipped right over and calmed two of the dogs down quite a bit, then started an investigation into any possible acts of cruelty against the canine subjects, while the third dog was on the fifth floor, backing one of the girls into a corner, poking away at her crotch with his long and very distinguished nose and she flipped—because, yipes, interspecies rape—and so she called 911. I arrived a little after that.

They're great dogs. Rolling around on the Aubusson carpet, begging Brenda to pet their stomachs, they get that she is some-one special. Much more special than Andrej the major domo, who is getting no attention whatsoever, even though he's stand-ing by with a plateful of raw filet mignon.

I ask Brenda if she's going to keep the creatures. "No. I can't keep anything Sergei gives me. And they wouldn't work here."

Meaning, in her house, and she's right. Their new home is unsuitable. They need a newer home, and suddenly I've got just the thing. The perfect solution. So now I have to make a phone call, see if my bright idea is as bright as I think it is.

After a while, I buzz off, giving everyone a quick kiss, including the wolfhounds. And when I wake up the next morning, all energized for some reason, I realize it has gotten to the point where I don't remember which gigs were booked by Abigail and which were booked by Ackerman & Thatcher. Then, a day later, uh-oh, Abigail calls me in and makes me wait for about half an hour, while she talks to somebody on the beach in Belize or somewhere. Then she puts down the phone and just looks at me.

After a while I ask her what's up.

She sighs and says, "Our contracts are quite clear. Quite explicit. Quite fair. And quite standard. So you do not need a sophisticated grasp of legal matters to understand what is perhaps the most important clause in the contracts that all the girls at the agency are required to sign. And are usually quite willing to sign. Quite eager, as a matter of fact."

She stops, picks up a pencil, looks at it, pops it into an empty coffee cup, and I'm thinking, she's been rehearsing this speech for a while. For the past few days, probably.

"The basic concept is exclusivity. If you are represented by us you are not represented by anyone else. Not by Ackerman & Thatcher, for example. Which is not even a modeling agency, Fiona, so I have not the slightest idea what you think you are doing and I do not want to hear from you what you think you are doing. I called you in today to let you know that you are suspended. Until you are informed otherwise, the Cora Burke Agency is not representing you. This suspension is not permanent but it very well could become permanent."

All through this she has been looking over my shoulder, making her voice icy and maybe a little too loud, to cut through the buzz of the office. So other people could hear what she's saying, I guess, making an example of me, but nobody is paying much attention. And I'm wondering, how did she find out? Also, why did it take her this long?

Now Abigail looks at me and gives this sharp little nod. Like, dismissed. Then she gets up and goes toward the filing cabinets in the back of the office. And I'm off to my next appointment, which, actually, I think she probably booked. And of course I'm slightly freaked by this career setback, which was inevitable, no doubt, because what was I thinking?

I guess I have this happy-go-lucky self-destructive streak, but never mind. At least this gives me something to brood about instead of having paranoid fits about something that happened when I was leaving Brenda's house a couple of nights after the attack of the giant wolfhounds. We watched this silly movie, Scarlett Johansson and somebody, already I can't remember. Anyway, Brenda and I mostly just flipped through an issue of *W* and then Andrej the major-domo appeared, with two small bowls of chocolate dipped strawberries, carrying them on a silver tray like they were the rarest liqueur in the world. Then he came back, and that's what he had, two crystal glasses of the rarest liqueur in the world. Chartreuse from 1890. Supposedly.

It was incredibly delicious, a single sip and you could feel about a million things going on all at once, like sex with someone who is completely there, and I also felt something else, not at all like sex ... this strange delicacy, like the liqueur was just a ghost of its former self. Which makes sense, I guess, if it really was from 1890. According to Andrej, some executive at one of the big ad agencies bought it at auction last week and sent it right over to

Brenda. Usually, Andrej is sphinxlike, never a word, but this was such a thrill for him, he had to explain. How this stunning example of Old-World excellence ended up here, in New York, on the ragged edge of the civilized world. Like Andrej himself. Anyway, Brenda actually finished her glass, which she never does.

So that was nice and then things took a turn for the strange after Andrej left the room and Brenda stood up, looking down at her breasts, saying she's afraid her period is making them more swollen than usual. I'm trying to be reassuring, natch, but it isn't working. Suddenly she's taking off her sweater and her blouse and her bra and standing there in front of me ... my god, I know how beautiful she is but I don't always feel it, even when I'm looking at her. I mean, who has the energy to feel all that all the time, no one, not even me, and now I have no idea what I'm feeling.

I'm practically fainting and now she wants me to feel her breasts, actually, feel how heavy they are, like she has no idea what she's asking ... and no idea about the magic of photography, how it can make anything look like anything. Not really, but, come on, so I'm saying ... darling ... sweetheart, don't worry, it's only for a few days and if you have a shoot before then, it'll be all right. Really, the photographer ... the photographer's people ... all your people, that nice new person you were telling me about ... Bettina? ... anyway, no one is going to let this turn into a real problem ... you are always so gorgeous ...

An assistant comes in with two glasses of Pellegrino or something or other on a tray, her eyes lowered but not at all surprised. Maybe Brenda gets undressed like this all the time. Because why not? She's this major presence, so it would be sort of like a statue getting undressed ... or a landscape ... somewhere spectacular, and it's not even the beautiful features of the place. It's the light that flows through you. And the scale, which doesn't make any sense to compare to a human being, I understand that, but so what? I was touching her breasts, like she wanted me to, I mean, who wouldn't touch a beautiful landscape if the landscape wanted you to … and of course her breasts feel as perfect as they look … because how would you expect Nature to feel?

Absolutely natural and way beyond my reach, even though I am now cupping a breast in each hand and Brenda is saying, see? See? But I can hardly see, I'm just saying, Brenda … darling, really … don't worry … and I can feel her getting a little calmer, which is all that matters. Brenda getting back to that calm place at the center of my universe … meaning this wasn't sexual, not at all …

Except that everything is. No kidding, right? Who doesn't know that … and now I'm sitting down and she's putting her sweater back on and something occurs to me for the first time, like, I've been this little kid who can't bear to understand anything. Because it's pretty obvious that when Sergei smacked Brenda that was also sexual. He got off on it. Or maybe he got off when he begged her to forgive him, creeping around on the floor, humiliating himself like that.

Only I've never believed that happened. Not that Brenda is lying, of course he groveled and said he was sorry, but of course he wasn't. Sergei is too nasty to apologize for anything. Also, there's a practical angle, because if Sergei started apologizing there'd be no end to it, he'd have no time for anything else, I mean, people like Sergei ought to spend their whole lives apologizing for everything. Not for stuff they didn't do, but, the thing is, you can't be sure what people like Sergei do or don't do. I mean, his nastiness has this, like, ripple effect and it gets into every nook and cranny. You begin to feel the sheer awfulness of it every place you go.

◊

Of which I had lots—lots of places to go, lots and lots, and lots of people to see. And I went there, I saw them, every single one of them, but nothing clicked. Just nothing. All day long, and when it was over, the sun was an angry red ball sinking slowly in the west and I figured it was time for something instead of nothing, so I took a cab to a tapas place on Ninth Avenue, Taberna Vivar, and ordered this coconut-shrimp thing to go. Now I'm sitting up in bed, pigging out, guzzling vino, and flashing back for the millionth time to the thing that happened after Brenda showed me her breasts.

It was fairly late when I left her house, but the street is well lit, so right away I noticed this guy hanging around on the other side, not a major red flag, because paparazzi are always sauntering by, kind of semi-loitering, hoping to get a shot of Brenda Rawlings Superstar, and of course they can't loiter too much because Mike or one of his stand-ins will come out, remind them about the personal-privacy statutes and maybe rough them up a little bit.

I've seen it happen, like, the loiterer is a little stubborn and Mike will sort of fake-trip and grab onto the guy, throw him off balance, maybe get a knee or an elbow in there somewhere, and of course the guy squawks, threatens to sue, call the cops, contact the media, and Mike stays very cool, apologizing, maybe brushing the guy off, not violently or anything, but in a way that makes it pretty clear who has the muscle and who is a useless parasite who really ought to keep his distance. Not that Brenda's people complain when there's a nice picture of her in the tabloids. But, according to Mike, you have to fuck with the paparazzi on a regular basis if you want them to take you seriously. Meaning, take Brenda seriously.

Not that I couldn't have figured that out for myself, but, anyway, the person hanging around this time seemed a little different. For one thing, he was focused on me, staring at me as I crossed the street in his direction. Not that I could see his eyes, he was wearing sunglasses, but still ... I kept walking toward him, he was backing up, then he whipped out this camera and started snapping away ... still wearing the sunglasses ... by now I was almost on top of the guy, snatching at his camera, which he didn't expect. Stepping back, he stumbled and fell, just about, which was my cue to keep on coming and then he stopped. Holding his ground.

So I stopped, no idea what I was doing, saying, "What do you want?"

Brilliant question.

He sort of smirked and snapped some more pictures, and I was yelling, "You want pictures?" Pulling my blouse out of my jeans, like I was going to show him my tits. Which seemed to freak him, a few people were wandering by, more or less watching, pretending they weren't, so I kept going, my whole torso exposed, about to flip myself out of my bra, and now the guy was panicking, turning and prancing off toward Park Avenue, these funny stiff-legged strides, trying to keep from breaking into a run.

I stayed right on his heels, telling him what a stupid fuck he was, what was he afraid of, why not let me take a squint at the pictures he's taking, maybe I'd like one for my boyfriend. When we got to the Avenue, he scampered around the corner, heading downtown, and I stood there, wondering, what on earth is this? I am not paparazzi bait, not unless I'm at some upper-echelon affair and hanging out with Brenda or some major donor, so this has to have something to do with Sergei. Because what else could it be?

I'm walking back along Brenda's block, then down Fifth, and to keep myself from asking the Sergei question over and over, I switched my thoughts to the woman who played Mélisande in the opera, so beautiful in her white costume, all gauzy and abstract, like that guy in the lobby said. Meaning, generalized. I guess. Not so much a gown as the designer's big idea of a gown, just floating around this beautiful girl ... or woman, really, such a strong voice for such a slim person ...

And the mother, Geneviève ... my fave, actually, her voice mellower than Mélisande's and her body ... so solid and calm she seemed kind of weightless ... I loved watching her as she watched things getting out of hand ... which reminds me, what should I do? Call Fletcher Marks, family man-slash-district attorney, tell him about the fake paparazzo?

Maybe, but now that I think about it, I know I'm not about to do that. I'm probably not even going to tell Mike the security guy, have him give me this deadpan look and tell me that impersonating a paparazzo does not rate as a major felony. Then give me another reason why he never hits on me, like, he's not really there, he's one of those what-d'you-call-'ems ... holograms ... you go in for the kiss and all you get is thin air.

It's the next day and I'm sitting at a table at Allesandra's, all alone, except for the semi-grouchy waitress, who is coming toward me, and I snap out of it.

Another café au lait?

Sure, why not, I order and my phone rings. It's Tom the techno-nerd. Finally getting back to me about duping Medeco keys. First you take a picture of the key, then print the picture on sticky-back paper, which you stick to a piece of plastic, an old credit card or something. Then you cut out the key with your Exacto knife, and Voilà. Open Sesame.

I'm, like, "Really? Sounds weird. But thank you, Tom, so much."

My next call, about thirty seconds later, is from Alison. About my perfect solution to the surplus wolfhound problem, which was, I told Brenda she ought to give the dogs to Alison, which she did, and Alison is thrilled that Brenda would think of her and also she loves these new creatures and I love that she loves them, because I never give a girl advice about her look, I would just never do that, it's like violating some basic principle about what a look is, your image in the eyes of others, which is, for all practical purposes, who you are—your responsibility, entirely, and none of my business—but I could not resist the idea of these beautiful tall dogs with beautiful tall Alison.

She is a notch below supermodel at this point, so she can afford to have someone nice and reliable take care of them when they're not out with her, just stunning everyone who lays eyes on them in the company of their new mistress. Who is also Sergei's mistress, in the sense that he's her slave, and now I'm sitting there, slurping my café au lait with girlish delicacy and listening to her tell me how she walked out of the bedroom in heels and the rest of her worship-me-you-worthless-scum outfit, plus the three dogs yanking on their leashes, and Sergei lost it.

He was already on his knees and he totally collapsed, sobbing and snorting, his ass in the air, with the dogs licking him and Alison trying to get a take on this fairly bizarre turn of events. What it was, she thought, was that Sergei wanted to give Brenda these wolfhounds, who happened to be Russian, so the great love of his life would possess the best possible version of him. Which is crazy, no doubt about it, but it's not about being sane, it's about Sergei's feelings for Brenda. So, he sees best possible version of him in the company of Alison—the girl who pees on him, which she hadn't actually told me they'd gotten to that point but she's given me enough hints—and this is too much. This is crushing, it wipes him out. Him and his world. A pretty good theory of Sergei, I had to admit.

Which I told Alison, how smart she is, like, this mad scientist, she figures out how to shrink an entire world to the size of a golf ball. Then she squishes it beneath her foot. A mad scientist in stiletto heels. Only, I didn't tell her that part, only about how smart she is, and she said, not really, she just thinks like a girl.

So that's great and not only that, because Abigail may have suspended me but my calendar is full to overflowing, in fact I'm on the verge of not leaving enough time to get to my next go-see, way east on Forty-Eighth Street, so I dig out a twenty dollar bill and leave it under my coffee cup, about a three-hundred percent tip, but what the hell, I'm in a hurry, not walking but running on air and thinking things are really looking up, the semi-grouchy waitress went so far as to smile at me once or twice.

And my cab driver is nice but a little unfocused. By the time I get to the building on Forty-Eighth Street I actually am late and much to my amazement the moment I'm getting into the elevator and losing contact with the outside world, Bill calls, saying, why don't you come over, bring some prosecco or something … and that's sweet, he remembers what I drink … so I say, sure. See you at about nine this evening.

When I show up, he doesn't kiss me, just takes the prosecco and opens it. Pours it for us, and we sit down at his dining room table. Clink our glasses. Bill's loft is very, very large and very, very empty, hardly any art, with the light from the street pressing right up against the windows. All the times I was here before, I thought it was sort of theatrical, like a minimalist stage set. Now it just feels like Bill made a good investment.

He pours me a second glass, saying, "Guess who stopped by the gallery the other day."

"I don't know. What's-His-Name, the director of MoMA."

Bill shook his head.

"OK. Let me see. The Ghost of Christmas Past?"

"Good guess but no."

"Umm … uhh … Batman? The mayor? Oh, I know. Otherwise you wouldn't be telling me. It was Sergei."

"Right."

"Sergei? Really?"

"Yes."

"Really?"

"Yes, and he was with your friend Alison."

"Right. They're an item."

"I'll bet. But she's nice. Not just for a model, but as a person. A very nice person."

"She is. But tell me about Sergei. Your shrewd impressions."

"OK, Fiona, I remember what you told me about this guy at that opening awhile back. And, knowing you, I know that in your mind he has spent the past few months morphing into this major menace, the Russian gangster-maniac who is stalking the world's most beautiful supermodel. It's like some movie, only it isn't. Not really. And don't be fooled by the comic accent. It's Russian but he isn't. I mean he is, but, for all practical purposes, he's just a certain type of guy. A typical operator. A thug in a business suit. Lots of people like that in New York. I deal with them all the time."

"I don't."

"I know, which is why I think you ought to give up this girl-vigilante stuff."

I'm about to explain why I can't possibly do that when his phone rings and he goes to the far end of the loft. Which is business-like, I guess, except that the acoustics are weird, I can hear that he's talking to someone about a very expensive painting.

He comes back and I ask him what's up. He says, "I've got this other dealer over a barrel, not a pretty picture, so let's not talk about it."

"Oh, let's," I said. "Because it was win-win, right? That's what you would always say. You and the client, win-win, happy-happy, so what's the deal?"

"OK, if you really want to know. It's about this big Richter, one of the abstract ones, I just made a shitload of money and I don't really have the other guy over a barrel. The deal went through because I let him cover his ugly ass. So, right again, Fiona, it was win-win."

"Wow, that's great. Check out the big business brain on Bill."

Being slightly sarcastic because I don't know how I feel about all this buying and selling of supposedly creative efforts like paintings, for example. It seems kind of crass. On the other hand, if that's crass what do you call it when somebody tries to sell images of herself to the highest bidder? Which is what I do every day of the week. Not that I'm creative, but, um ... I don't know ... this image-trafficking thing is another one of those issues I haven't worked out to my total satisfaction. So I ask about Imogen Rittenhauer's new design business, how's it doing?

Bill smiles. "There were a few kinks. But everything's on track."

"So I guess you've lots of fresh walls to fill up with art."

Bill smiles again and I say, "You should marry a motel chain. Even more walls."

He stands up, lifts me out of my chair. Kisses me. I kiss him back and lead him into the bedroom. After we get undressed and into bed, we kiss some more and then he's touching my cunt ... mmm, so brilliant ... then I stop him and lean away, looking into his eyes, saying, "This is it, right? Sort of like Claude Rains and Humphrey Bogart in *Casablanca*. But in reverse. We're celebrating the end of a beautiful friendship"

He nods and kisses me and starts putting on a condom, me trying to help and getting in the way, but I can't help it, not just because I'm in a hurry, I have this dopey desire to be helpful and

Bill is nice about it and then that's done and we start making love and it is so super-sad I can't let myself even begin to feel that. What I feel is totally at home in Bill's arms, with him inside me, and after a long, lovely time I realize I'm being carried away on this massive, utterly wavy wave, so huge and so intimate and intricate and wrapping itself totally around Bill's orgasm, oh my god, I am getting to the multi-orgasmic place, melting into this dreamy flesh state, like a cloud, which isn't really a place, it's too infinite and time decides it's time for a hiatus, so it feels like this is just what I am, my orgasm, timelessly, and the feeling is going to go on and on and on like this forever and ever and after.

.4.

Which the feeling sort of did, even after the space-time continuum got back in gear and I was sitting in this reception area with a girl and a bunch of ficus trees, realizing that I shouldn't have to be waiting this long for an appointment that probably is going to be a waste of time and is definitely going to put me behind the chronological eight-ball for the rest of the day. But it was all right, I was still so mellow, happy to be listening to the other girl prattling away about an article she read somewhere, how the unconscious mind, which is basically the brain, is this amazing factory working around the clock, producing all these decisions and attitudes and a lot more, I guess, that we don't even know about. So we think we're in charge but we aren't. We're just puppets and the brain is pulling the strings.

Which, um, well, OK, but if that's the case, why am I now having such a tough time figuring out what to do for lunch? Shouldn't the brain be settling the matter? Of course, my brain may be the indecisive kind or maybe it really wants me to be standing here, at the corner of Broadway and Thirty-Ninth, thinking about the girl with all the brain info, how young she was and how amazingly pale. Albino, almost, with such light blue eyes I kept thinking I was going to be able to look right through them. Into her soul, I guess, which might have been a little boring ... a mean thought, true, but she looked like she was about sixteen and already convinced that everything she said was totally fascinating. On the other hand, who doesn't think that?

Anyway, I am popping into this too-hopelessly-hip diner on Tenth Avenue and ordering an avocado-and-mango salad, no oil, just rice vinegar and lemon juice, plus coffee. Then I turn my phone back on, hoping that no one called and found out that I've been breaking rule one, which is, never turn your phone off. And of course there are a bunch of missed calls. Mike and Sergei, hmm, and also one from Angela Auerbach, that booker from Alliance. With the frumpy sweater and the lovely breasts. Double hmm. I call Mike first and he says, "I'm gay."

"You're gay?"

"Yeah. That's the reason I don't hit on you."

"OK. Except that's not much of a reason ... I mean ..."

"I get what you're saying Fiona and, in fact, I figured you like that. But for me, there are not so many options. I am strictly gay."

"OK."

"Thought you'd like to know. Also, I'm getting from Pam's girls that Brenda is really glad you've been coming by again."

"What about Pam? Is Pam really glad?"

"Sure. Really glad. Maybe not about that, but ..."

I laugh and Mike says, "OK, Fiona. Just thought you should know. Morale is good."

"Great. And it's so sweet of you to let me know, Mike."

"No sweat."

That's nice and so I call Angela, the booker from Alliance, who tells me what I had already figured out. Or not me but the neurons working away in the vast subterranean workshop of the brain. Which is that people are beginning to wonder about me a little bit. None of the Cora Burke girls ever get suspended, so what happened? I tell her about my connection with Ackerman & Thatcher, which kind of surprises her. Ackerman & Thatcher has not exactly impressed the pants off the fashion world, even though they're doing OK for me, so Angela wishes me luck, saying we should definitely stay in touch. In case something comes up in the near future. Like her brain is telling my brain something about the near future I would just as soon not know.

And now for something else I would just as soon not know anything about, namely, why Sergei called me. I ring him and he answers, asking me why I'm calling.

"I'm calling because you called. I'm calling you back. Get it?"

"Get what? I get what?"

"Not much, Sergei. Really. But, actually, now that I've got you on the line, how about you and me getting together the night after next?"

"Night after next?"

"Yes, Sergei. Night after next. Not a difficult concept."

"No … uh, er …" It sounds like he's pondering it and deciding, actually, no, as a concept it really isn't all that difficult.

"How about it, Sergei?" I'm feeling reckless and also fairly sensible, like, take the battle to the enemy. Otherwise, there's no battle, things keep sliding in the wrong direction. Or the enemy regroups and we're all screwed, so I keep pushing him, how a-fucking-bout it, you moron.

Finally, he says, "OK. I see you Thursday night at eight o'clock."

Now it's the big night and I'm strangely excited, thinking, maybe this is my real career, dealing with Sergei, the unforeseen factor that ruined my life. Lots to think about, starting with what to wear, what to wear? Maybe a Hazmat suit. Or maybe this really great dress they gave me after a shoot a while back, Roberto Torretta, which is going to give me a bunch of options in the how-much-cleavage-to-show department.

Quite a bit, needless to say, now that I'm leaning over the desk in
Sergei's lobby, getting the doorman to try one more time. It's shocking, really, the simplicity of what works. Provided it works, the way
cleavage always does. Even if you're a demure B-cup, like me.

Sergei finally answers and he's not expecting me. The doorman looks up at me and shrugs.

"Tell him I'm his big surprise."

He does and Sergei decides he likes surprises. So I'm on my
way up, totally psyched. Plan B is back in gear.

When I get to Sergei's place, he says, "I am not expecting girl
tonight."

"You would be if you had any memory, Sergei."

"I have good memory." All the while doing shots of Stoli.

"No you don't. Your memory is pretty much gone. Haven't
noticed? That's understandable. But, hey, Sergei, never mind.
Why don't you show me where you keep your smart phone?"

He comes toward me, sort of stiff-legged, like, it walks! The
monster walks!

"What smart phone?"

"The one with all the money on it, Sergei. You know, you told
me about it in the limo that time."

"That time? What time?" He is still coming at me and I'm
backing up, bumping into furniture, glancing around for blunt
instruments.

"I say nothing about smart phone."

"OK, Sergei, here's another idea. Let's go to some nice quiet
spot and you can tell me your sad story. Like, exactly which childhood traumas turned you into such a nasty creep."

All this talk about phones has got him thinking, he starts looking through his pockets, jacket, pants, back to the jacket. When
he eventually finds his dumb phone, which I recognize, he calls
Viktor, tells him to bring the car around.

Then he pours vodka for two. I don't drink mine, just hand it to him when he's done with his, and he tosses it back. So he's pretty shaky, getting through the lobby, into the limo. Where he sits without saying a word, his chin on his chest. Staring at nothing. Or, another possibility, he's staring at a big, sparkly heap of broken dreams, how would I know?

Viktor is taking us slowly down Park and when we get to Sixty-Third, Brenda's street, Sergei tells him to turn right. Viktor acts like he's suddenly deaf, can't hear a word, and keeps heading south on Park. Sergei starts jabbering at him in Russian and then he's sort of snarling, and I'm not understanding a word except for "Brenda" but I'm getting the gist. Like, I am boss, I tell you turn onto street of most beautiful woman in world and you disobey me? What you think you are doing, turn around immediately or I have special friends of mine send you to Siberia, feed you to wolves. But Viktor keeps going. Sergei's wolves do not seem to be terrifying him all that much this evening.

We are now in the Fifties and Sergei is so pissed he can no longer speak or snarl or even mutter to himself under his breath. In fact, he's so mad he's not even breathing, just sitting and glaring at the back of Viktor's head and turning purple, which means that what we need now is some sort of distraction. So I unbutton another button and snuggle up to Sergei the Furious, touching him as little as possible, which is quite a feat. But. Anyway. I'm doing it, more or less, and suddenly I feel this object in his jacket pocket. I pull it out.

It's a gun.

Absolutely no idea of what to do next, so I hold it up and wave it around, saying, "Sergei. I'm shocked. But tell me. Is this your smart gun or your stupid gun?"

Looking over, he gives it a sour look. Or maybe the sour look is for me. By now, we've gotten almost to the end of Park Avenue, and I'm asking, "Ever hit anything with this?"

Sergei says, "Is most accurate gun in world."

"Not what I asked you. I'll try again. Ever hit anything with this?"

"Very expensive gun."

"Really? How much?"

"Very expensive. Official gun of FSB. Is called Drotik. Very good to pierce body armor."

"It pierces body armor? OK, Sergei, here's the deal. I won't wear any next time. Save you some trouble."

"You are stupid girl."

"Yeah. I know. Stupid but curious. I mean, did you ever kill anyone with this gun, Sergei?"

"I am not killer. I kill only Brenda."

"You know what, Sergei? Kill me instead. Get it out of your system."

"Out of system? What system?"

"What system? You know, I've got to hand it to you, Sergei, you have a knack for the brilliant question. The question that everybody else is trying to ask but only you are brilliant enough to actually, like, you know … ask. Maybe it's because you have such a brilliant command of the English language."

"I speak very good English."

"That's what I'm trying to tell you, Sergei. Only your English is so shitty you don't get what I'm saying."

Sergei grabs the gun, puts it back in his pocket. "You are very stupid girl, Fiona."

Wow, he remembers my name. I'm flattered, saying, "Yeah. You already told me that. So why don't you show me your smart phone?"

"Stupid girl. You should shut up."

"Yeah. I know. I should. But I'm this total chatterbox. Can't stop yakking. So. If I'm so stupid, show me your smart phone. Maybe it'll rub off on me."

"Rub off? What is rub off?"

"I'd explain but—never mind. Just show me your smart phone. Show me the five and a half billion dollars."

Sergei leans back and squints at me, like, who is this idiot? Why am I talking to her? "Eleven billion dollars. Not five and a half billion dollars. Eleven billions."

"Ah. Well. That's great, Sergei. Since I talked to you last, you doubled your money. You must be quite the investor."

"Investor? What investor? I am venture capitalist."

"Even better. So show me. Show me the eleven billion dollars."

We are now on Park Avenue South, drifting along, heading for a yellow light at Twenty-Seventh Street. Viktor could get through it but he doesn't, cruising to a stop before the light turns red. Sergei snorts in disgust, but the whole point, I guess, is that we're on a drive to nowhere and Viktor sees no reason to hurry. Sergei, of course, doesn't see it that way. He's suddenly this bundle of demented energy, opening the door on his side and—you know how writers say that someone is surprisingly nimble for such a fat man?

Well, Sergei is surprisingly clumsy, even if you take his excess baggage into consideration. I mean, the guy is a total tub and he looks even tubbier than the last time I saw him, but he manages to wriggle between a couple of parked cars, onto the sidewalk, and now he's heading north, holding his gun down alongside his leg. Like—what? He's going to march all the way back to Sixty-Third Street and storm the barricades? Of course Viktor swings into action, jumping out and stalking after Sergei. And, silly me, I do the same. Don't want to miss out on anything, right? So I jump out, coming down wrong on my right foot and banging into a parked car. Then I'm catching up to Sergei and I guess he hears me, the girly clatter of heels on concrete, because he suddenly stops, turns, presses the gun barrel to my forehead.

Which feels weird.

It would feel even weirder, of course, if Viktor weren't there, frozen in place. I mean, Sergei isn't going to do anything totally crazy in front of his babysitter, right? And there are a few other people standing around, trying to decide whether or not to get involved. They seem to be leaning toward, no, let's not, or maybe they're just dazed with fear. Whatever. It's time to spin the situation, so I tell Sergei to put the gun away. "That girl over there is calling 911."

"911? I shit on 911."

"You shit on 911. OK. But how does that work? Sounds kind of conceptual."

Sergei laughs, a quick little bark, and takes the gun away from my forehead. "You are fun girl, Fiona."

Stepping back, he holds the gun up to his eyes, frowning, giving it a judicious once-over. Then he stretches both arms in the air, a big smile on his face. To reassure the remaining by-standers.

"Is big joke," he bellows. "Gun is not even loaded." Which I never really did find out the truth of.

Fast forward and here he is, Sergei the Magnificent, lying on his back. Dead to the world and completely naked. Ugh. Before I actually saw him naked, I figured he'd be the Pillsbury Dough Boy. Wrong! He's the Michelin Man, but not the one you see in the ads. More the Michelin Man in a parallel universe where he leads a dissolute life and those rolls of his have lost their rubbery firmness and gotten all soft and saggy and weird.

So I'm looking at him, thinking, good grief, the things we do for Plan B. Even a half-baked Plan B like mine, which did not, as originally conceived, include a visit to Sergei's apartment with Sergei himself on the premises. But after the incident with the gun I figured, OK, can't let the evening go to waste. So I stood there on the sidewalk, my hip cocked, giving Sergei the look that to an idiot like him means only one thing. In a matter of nano-seconds he was asking me back up to his place.

First off, he waddled over to the sideboard and poured himself a few more shots of Stoli. Like, he's been out of the house for what? Forty-five minutes? Time to replenish. Then he told me to get undressed. Which I did. Got to get him to think he's in charge. Because the gun thing is obviously this twisted sex thing, meaning his twisted sex thing is sheer theater. Or just bad theater. Has Sergei ever actually fucked anyone? His idea of sex is barking instructions at females. Or getting them to pee on him. So, yawn, it's all about power.

Except that the power was slipping through his fingers. To put it mildly. He was pouring himself another drink and missing his glass, splashing vodka all over the sideboard, leering and tilting this way and that, so I said, "Come on, Sergei. Your turn. You get undressed."

He laughed. Like, stupid girl. I do not take orders from stupid girl. So I told him it looked like he was scared, what are you hiding, why not just take off your clothes? Got to do that if we're going to have sex. This subtle logic was the clincher, I guess, because he started scrabbling at his jacket, his shirt … after about half an hour, he managed to take off his tie. And his shoes, big accomplishment, after which he took a few more swigs of firewater and turned and started glaring at me. Like, what? Like it pissed him off that I was so naked and I looked so good?

I walked over to him, still wearing my heels, and stood there with my hands on my hips. This shamed him into taking off the rest of his clothes, because what else would a stud like Sergei do under the circumstances? But wouldn't you know it, by the time he got undressed I was no longer the highest item on his agenda. He had the panicky look of a lush running low, so I was about to get him a great big glass of jolly old Mr. Vodka when suddenly there was this young girl, standing in the doorway to the living room. Watching us.

I'd made sure to leave the front door unlocked, in case I had to leave all of a sudden, and evidently the doorman recognized the girl, sent her right up. She was wearing a school girl's outfit, for god's sake. Plaid skirt, gray blazer. The moment Sergei noticed her, he changed. Walking toward the sideboard, he was all feral now, the cat who noticed the wounded mouse. Pouring himself another shot, he said, "This is Kristina. Kristina is very nice girl. Very well-behaved girl."

Kristina was watching Sergei like she was cringing but, actually, she was frozen, wanting to come over to him but she couldn't move, then she did and when she got near enough he took one giant step and hit her in the face. Really hard. She didn't try to avoid it and afterward she just stood there, sort of moping, watching his dick get hard.

I guess this is what she was watching, because it's what I was watching, completely pissed off. Because it was, like, violence against women as Viagra. Not that Sergei's little nothing of a dick was turning into this eye-popping spectacle. It got half-hard, then began to droop and Kristina turned and walked out of the apartment. Totally dejected, like Sergei's dick was dismissing her. She hadn't done her job, which was what? To look so hurt that Sergei would get this raging hard-on? I wanted to go after the girl but, one, I was naked and, two, I had to find Sergei's smart phone. Because that was the whole point. Consummate Plan B.

By now, Sergei was stumbling around like some uncoordinated kid trying to walk on stilts, so I thought of zipping in, tripping him up … but before I made my move, he was sprawled on his back. Lights out. Time to go gather up Sergei's clothes, go through his pockets … OK, here are the keys … now where is a camera? Got to find a camera, take pictures of the keys. Then I realized the pressure must be getting to me. Or maybe I'm not the clearest of thinkers. Because why did I need keys to get into Sergei's apartment? I already was in Sergei's apartment, he was out cold, so come on, Fiona, just look for the fucking smart phone.

This is what I did, for about forty-five minutes. I looked in drawers, closets, a stray brief case, filing cabinets, everywhere I could think of. No smart phone. Plenty of cameras, but no smart phone. So I kept looking, the dirty clothes hamper, double ugh, the linen closet, all the cabinets in the kitchen, the pantry, this was so fucking boring … but I carried on …

Going back to the living room, I rifled the sideboard for the second time, and then I heard a timid little noise and turned around and there was Kristina again. She must have been wandering around in the hallway, fretting about the man in her life, wondering what she could do to help.

Sergei was still comatose, so here we are, Kristina and me, contemplating the decline and fall of the Michelin Man's evil twin. One of the nastiest creatures who ever lived. Not that Kristina sees him that way. Not that I really know what she's seeing, but she obviously has a pretty fucked up take on reality. Because it's beginning to look like he's the center of her universe. So why—whimper, whimper—is the center of her universe lying there like a bag of garbage the garbage guys forgot?

I grab her by the arm and drag her into the kitchen, telling her to stay there, and go off in search of a robe. Why I should cover up I don't know, I mean, this is the first time in my life I've been naked in front of someone who doesn't even notice. Anyway, a woman's robe is hanging on the back of Sergei's bathroom door,

Tisseron, because this is what Sergei would call "best bathrobe in world" and it's nothing but the best for Sergei. If the right person told him Wal-Mart is "best department store in world," he'd do all his shopping at Wal-Mart.

I put the robe on and go back to the kitchen. Not really knowing what to do about Kristina. I would give her some milk and cookies except that I have searched this apartment top to bottom and I know that the only food in the fridge is a huge tin of Almas Beluga. "Best caviar in world." To go with the pepper-flavored vodka I saw in the freezer. Kristina tells me it's all right, she's not hungry, maybe she ought to go. I tell her there's no hurry, relax, and, um, let me ask you something, how did you meet Sergei?

Her eyes go blank, like she's looking at something she can't bear to see. Then she says, "I'm so worried about him."

She has some kind of accent, ever so faint, and I have this odd thought, like, come on, Kristina, you are so close to turning into a typical American girl. Lose the accent, go all the way, get the great American girl attitude, one part superficiality, two parts self-esteem. With a dash of sheer silliness. Not that there are not American girls beaten down even harder than Kristina.

Anyway, I tell her Sergei will be fine, he just needs to rest a little. Then I take her by the arm again, over to the front door, and kiss her on the cheek. The next moment she's leaning up against my chest, sort of huddling in my arms. So terrified she hardly seems to be there. Then she isn't, she's gone, and, OK, time to focus.

No smart phone, so I am trying to psych myself up to swipe Sergei's keys. Come back at an opportune moment, have another look for the phone … of course, I'd have to get past the doorman, not a major problem, but who knows how dilapidated Sergei's brain really is at this point, so … what if he figures out where his keys went and snitches on me to the police … or sends his shadowy minions to track me down … meaning, much as I hate to admit it, I'm scared to swipe the keys. Got to take pictures, like Fred's nerdy friend Tom said, so he can make me some dupes. Maybe the phone'll be back in its hiding place by then. It better be, because that maybe is the only thing keeping Plan B alive.

I go to the cabinet in Sergei's office where I saw a bunch of cameras, grab one, and now I'm trying to figure out how it works. Hmmm. Considering that I'm getting photographed all the time, I ought to know about cameras. On the other hand, why should I? Like, oh, you ride around in cars? You should know how to fix the engine. But of course I don't. I don't even know about buttons. A button falls off, that's fucking *it*. Send it to the seamstress.

By now I've looked at a bunch of cameras and they're all too complicated for Fiona, poster girl for girly ineptitude. Finally, there is this really simple one, I press a button pretty much at random and, great, it's ready to go. So I get Sergei's key ring from the sideboard, take the Medeco key off the ring, place it flat on the coffee table and take its picture. I can't figure out how to check the result, see how it turned out, so I take some more. Then it occurs to me, maybe none of them are any good, so I go through the same routine with this other camera for lamebrains I found. And, what the fuck, another camera. Something is bound to turn out.

The next step, according to Tom, is to remove the flashcards, pop them into my purse. I have no idea what that means, so I pop two of the cameras into my purse. No room for the third, which has this huge lens. But it also has this dippy strap. Plastic with a panoramic shot of Miami Beach at sunset from somewhere way out in the ocean. So. Time to get dressed, make my getaway … and what happens next is right out of the trailer for one of those ultra-creepy movies I never see. Bill also hates them, ones where the whole point is the blood and the guts and the sudden screaming shock.

I've got my panties on and both hands are behind me, high on my back, I'm hooking myself into my bra when I feel this slight motion somewhere and I look up and there's Sergei, still naked, with a huge butcher knife in his hand. I shriek and freeze, in this awkward pose.

Then I rush him, not because I'm brave, I'm truly terrified, and I swerve at the last moment. He hacks at me, and of course he misses—by a mile, actually, I have these cat-woman reflexes, but, shit, I feel a major twinge in my back. From when I slammed against that car. So I'm immobilized for about five seconds, long enough for Sergei to get some traction and take another shot at me. Which also would have missed, except that he trips and falls, giving himself the crucial burst of speed. I feel this horrendous pain in my right forearm and there's all this blood welling up out of the gash.

I grab a towel from the rack beside the sink and wrap it around the wound, watching Sergei crawling across the floor on all fours, not realizing he scored a hit on me. Still watching him, I find my bra, get into it, with the towel falling off, so I get another, wrap my arm again, slip into my dress, jam my feet into my shoes, then I go into the bathroom, unwind the towel and rinse off, which is a bit pointless, I'm still bleeding profusely, meaning I have to find another towel, wrap it really tight, and now I'm grabbing my purse, slinging the third camera over my shoulder, figuring I'm about to have a problem.

Because Sergei may be out of it, completely wasted, but, face it, he's going to get to the phone, call the doorman. Who is just hanging up his phone when I get to the lobby. This is not the one who saw me go up with Sergei. That one is off-duty and his replacement is this older guy who obviously doesn't have a very good attitude toward gorgeous young girls. Or girls in general. Or maybe he just hates humanity, the squinty-eyed old creep, and he starts yelling at me when he sees me walking past.

"Miss, miss. Just a moment. Security. Just a moment."

Like, what, I'm going to stop and show him my papers? I flash him a smile and keep walking, which, when he sees this, means that total chaos is breaking out. He's got to do something, save the day, so he comes around the counter, all worked up, not yelling any more, just sort of twitching. When he gets near me, I cross my legs and bend over. Looking helpless and desperate, like I've really got to pee. In fact, I tell him I really have to pee, where's the ladies room?

He stops, this old guy in a gray uniform, no way he's going to discuss the subject of peeing with a member of the female sex, except he has a job to do, so he comes at me again. I go back into my oh-my-god-I've-got-to-pee pose, holding up my hand this time, glaring at him, like, what do you want me to do? Pee right here in the lobby? This slows him down, then his phone rings again, so he runs back to his desk and I run out to the sidewalk, the camera on the strap flopping around like crazy and it's after midnight but there's a cab and I catch it and the camera bangs against the cab as I'm getting in, oh shit, have I completely scrambled the pixels? But at least I'm safe and sound and beyond the reach of all the terrible ogres.

When I got back to my place, the bleeding had pretty much stopped, so I went out to the all-night drugstore over on Sixth Avenue, got a bunch of cotton and gauze and tape, and made myself this bandage which wasn't too ridiculous, considering that I had only one free hand to work with. This morning, the gaping wound was still gaping, so I swabbed it in alcohol, which I should have done last night, but, anyway, ouch.

Now I'm off to see the wizard or whoever is going to turn me into the magical creature I am supposed to be on this next shoot, for L'Idée Bleu, I love their stuff and things are going pretty well, no one is paying any attention to my bandage, not the hardworking professionals and certainly not the not-so-hardworking professionals, the ones with clipboards and two or three iPhones each. In fact, no one even noticed that I am one of the walking wounded, except for this one wardrobe girl, who grabbed my arm, took a quick squint at the gauze and the seeping blood and got this look of profound wisdom on her face, like she understood everything, down to the very last detail, and told me I'd live. And to consider myself lucky it's sportswear today, just get into this blazer, don't take it off if anyone is looking. A practical approach to life's little nightmares.

Which made me a touch envious, I don't have a practical approach to anything these days, though I did remember to lug Sergei's cameras along with me this morning. So later on I could pop up to the agency and hand them over to Tom the tech guy. In the meantime, I look fabulous in this blazer with these short shorts and heels. Then the photographer, a guy in a three-piece suit, decides it's time to have a tantrum.

Nobody can quite get his problem. Despite the lawyer's getup, he doesn't seem to be all that verbal, so there's a lot of sputtering and groaning to get through, and I'm feeling this throbbing in my arm. But so what, I'm standing around with the other girls, watching the guy in the three-piece suit wallowing in all the attention everyone is lavishing on him, wondering where my thoughts are going to take me next. Then I hear my phone ringing.

I go over to the rack where my street clothes are hanging and see a missed call from Maisie. Which I don't return right away because the photographer is now under control, the shoot is on and so am I, all eyes are just soaking me up, and I'm deciding the man in the suit, Robin de Noyer, is a genius. Because, what can I say, he's getting me, I can tell without even seeing the pictures, which is strange but true, and what Robin is getting about me is my energy. All this juicy, fluid energy.

Which I am still feeling when I get back to Maisie. She says she just felt like calling, no particular reason ... just thinking of me ... then she says she has to go to Los Angeles with Jake, her husband, so, um, it'll be all this boring lawyer stuff but she's hoping to get to the beach, and, um, anyway ...

"Have fun."

She laughs, very softly. "OK."

"No, really. L.A. can be fun."

"Really?"

"No, not really, sweetie, but sometimes a girl has to pretend."

Maisie laughs again, kind of breathy and sad, as we're hanging up, and I realize we're missing each other and not going to do anything about it. A nicely bittersweet thought, now that the shoot is over and I'm thinking, my god, I was so hot, so totally hot. I could feel it and feel what the camera was feeling, this where-do-I-leave-off-and-you-begin sort of thing, perfect unity, I'm right on the brink, and then it's a wrap. The big let-down, meaning, no payoff. The same old story, if you know what I mean, though it feels a little weird, wondering if the camera is ever going to get over its crush on me and fall head over heels in love. Care enough about me to really get me off.

Which is a slightly creepy fantasy, I guess. Like, getting photographed is like having bad sex with—what? The camera? Your image? Anyway, that fantasy doesn't take me down as far as this other one I've been having and not admitting it, because it is more than creepy, it's sort of scary and dank, the idea that, OK, that was a great shoot. Despite the letdown I was hot, like old times. But what if this Dorian Grey thing is going on? The new pictures are going to be terrific, everybody is going to love them, but the dark side of Robin de Noyer has this other set of pix and they're different. They're seeping blood, just like my wound is starting to do. Again.

So I'm rushing home and then I realize I have to give Sergei's cameras to Tom at the agency, who doesn't quite remember what they're for, which I remind him of and he seems really happy. Like, now he is going to have this hands-on experience with yet another minor detail in the great big puzzle of how the world works. Of course, I was slightly apprehensive about running into Abigail, but she must have been taking one of her late, late lunches or indulging some secret vice, shooting herself up with anti-cellulite cream or something, so that was a relief.

When I got home I put on a new bandage and tried to get a grip. Meaning, one, convince myself that I'm nuts, photographs don't seep blood, and, two, convince myself that I'm not really nuts, I won't be obsessing about this non-stop forever. Because I really am beginning to feel slightly nuts, flashing back all the time to the image of Sergei lying there on his back, like something that got washed up on the shore, a sign of ecological disaster, my entire universe gone past the tipping point, way too big a problem for me to deal with …

I guess my brain must have done quite a number on my inner self when I was asleep, because I woke up in a great mood, not a care in the world, except that I had to run out and get more first-aid supplies at the drugstore. But, no problem, there was plenty of time, and so now I'm all scrubbed and silky smooth and taped up and out the door, the sun is shining, the bluebirds of happiness are just fluttering around my head, chirping away so hysterically I can hardly hear my phone ringing. I answer and suddenly it's the end of the road, finito, I have been officially booted out of the fashion biz.

The call is from Ackerman's office, this woman's voice, fairly nasty and rushed, like she's forcing herself to tackle the unpleasant stuff early in the day, telling me, "Mr. Ackerman has decided that, for the time being, Ackerman & Thatcher will not be pursuing any further bookings in reference to you." Which is really dumb, I've been doing so well for them. Maybe they're the bumbling amateurs I always thought they'd be. Or there are other factors in play, shit I will never know, like Ackerman's wife suspects something or he's doing some other girl who knows about me and hates me. Except why would he tell some girl he's fucking that he also fucked me? And how likely is it that Jon found another girl to feel about him the way I did?

Anyway, my life as a fashion model has come to a screeching halt. It was bad enough getting suspended by Cora Burke, creating all this buzz, Fiona the Disloyal. Now I'll be Fiona the Totally Unemployable and it's time to review my options. I could always throw myself on the mercy of strangers. A little more realistically, I could sit in my apartment and stare at the wall. A real possibility. I mean, I've accumulated some money from all the work I've been doing. On the other hand, it isn't that much, and, anyway, a girl needs a job. A career. Otherwise, you're just this female item on display in the metropolitan meat market, hoping that some guy decides to pick you up and take you home to mother.

I've been wandering down the block, toward Eighth Avenue, for no particular reason, so I turn around, wander back and while I'm in front of my building looking for my keys my phone rings. It's Fred, saying a magazine in Brazil wants to license this picture of me they found on the Cora Burke website, which has been happening a fair amount lately, so that's terrific. Of course, there might be a few problems, given that I've been suspended. So I'm asking what my pictures are still doing online.

Fred laughs, saying, "Don't worry about it, gorgeous. The pictures stay, for the time being, and—"

"And, um, how am I going to get paid?"

"That's something else you don't have to worry about. There are workarounds. For the time being."

"I'm asking about money because Ackerman & Thatcher just dropped me."

Long pause, while Fred gets his voice under control, I guess, because he sounds really nice when he comes back, saying, "I suppose it was only a matter of time."

"Sort of a ticking clock, huh?"

"A ticking clock?"

"Yeah, there was a guy from one of the ad agencies at this shoot a while back and he kept saying narrative, story, flow, you have to build to the big payoff. So there has to be a ticking clock in every image."

I can see Fred shaking his head, saying, "That is so dumb. There's no narrative at a fashion shoot. Every shot is supposed to be the big payoff. One right after the other."

Like multiple orgasms, I'm thinking, but I don't say that, just, "Yes, that's it. Right on the nose. You should be a photographer, Fred."

"Right. And get up close and personal with flaky females every day of my life."

"You'd love it."

He laughs again and rings off and I stand there in the bright sunlight thinking, there are all these ticking clocks. When will Abigail find out? Of course, we know that, but when will Ackerman's wife find out for sure? When will Mike the security guy reveal the real reason he never hits on me? When will I discover the true meaning of life? Meaning, my life, in particular . . . oh, and when will Sergei kill Brenda? Except that clock gave up the ghost long ago, just ran down, stopped ticking …

And that would be great except for one thing, which has been staring at me for quite a while now, something really obvious that I've been ignoring. Studiously ignoring, I believe the phrase is. It's like you're at a party and you can tell this troll has been staring, staring, staring at you all night, but you don't want to look over. Don't want to acknowledge his existence. Then you do and he's just as awful as you thought, except worse, like this obvious fact that I've been refusing all this time to look in the face.

Which is that Sergei was never really Brenda's problem. Sergei was always my problem, right from the moment Brenda told me he hit her. Because nothing like that was ever supposed to happen. It was supposed to be unimaginable, and I really never did imagine anything like that. Not in Brenda's world. That was the whole idea of Brenda's world, which is also my world, and when Sergei hit her he bent it totally out of shape and that's why it's my problem. Because I'm the only one who gets what Sergei did. The sheer enormity of it, which not even Brenda gets.

Because that's not the point of Brenda. Brenda doesn't get things. Brenda just is, meaning, I'm the only one who knows what has to be done. Which is what? Keep believing in Plan B? OK, I can do that. Because anything you think up you can believe in. No matter how ridiculous it is. It's a matter of will power. Like getting yourself to go to the gym, which I've been doing a lot and what can I say? I'm more perfect than ever, except maybe my arms are getting a little too muscly. On the other hand, maybe that's the way to go.

I mean, forget about the Popeye motto, I Yam What I Yam, meaning I've got to be me, the one and only Fiona Mays, though

it might be better, at this point, to be Popeye himself, muscle-
bound with a couple of tattoos and a really simple diet. Spinach
and Olive Oyl, what could be yummier? Definitely an option to
consider, a thought to soak up all the brain-static as I head for
the gym, to work on my already scrumptious inner thighs. The
adductor muscles, according to my new trainer. Who is hot and a
possibility, I mean, why not?

Except that he is always explaining the anatomical details of
this or that move, running his finger along the muscle in question,
not quite touching my skin, like this is supposed to be some kind
of naughty thrill. Or maybe that's not it, maybe it's more like my
body is this slightly weird object, he can't quite bring himself to
touch it. I actually don't know what to think, about this or anything else. For example, I was thinking of myself as an ex-model
but, guess what, in a couple of days there's going to be this one
last gig.

I mean, Ackerman & Thatcher just drummed me out of the ranks
but it must have been too late to replace me, so here I am. In the
desert. The wide open spaces. With an unusual problem, unusual
for me, which is, I can't sleep. I've been telling myself the culprit
is this bunk in this trailer, because bunks in trailers are uncomfortable and basically impossible to sleep in, right? But it's not
that, this is a luxury vehicle and everything is spiffy and comfortable, including this bunk, which is huge, so what's to blame?

Lots of suspects, of course, there always are if you're looking
for them. Which I'm usually not, my world was so wonderful, I
even liked the snake-pit part. So, Sergei aside, I never bothered to
blame people for things. Even if they're obviously guilty, because

I was too busy being Professional Fiona, superstar of the future ... Fiona the Hot Number ... not to mention, Fiona the Mastermind of Plan B ... and now ... I'm lying here in the dark, all pissed off and horny, and I don't even feel like getting myself off. Because why should I be so horny, given that I got laid about fifteen minutes ago?

Silly question.

I'm horny because I didn't come, despite my best efforts. The amazing swivel-hips got quite the workout, so I have that lazy, after the gym feeling, which is nice but fading fast because what I'm really feeling is slightly puzzled because why did I let this dick rub me raw for no reason whatsoever? It was just hump, hump, hump and while that was going on I was rooting for the guy, I really was, which, if you think about it, means it was my fault I didn't come, sitting it out on the sidelines like that. And that was strange. I'm usually so into it, and not just usually but always, right from the very first time, so very long ago ... in the lovely sweat-soaked past.

Anyway, the guy attached to the most recent dick is the photographer on this shoot. Which features the latest from Alain Bertrand-Leshkov, a great designer, so why would he hook up with this crew? And I mean, what a crew ... in addition to the photographer and a couple of assistants there is a production designer and a guy running around with a roll of tape calling himself the head gaffer. Or gaffer-in-chief or something. And a storyboard girl, completely pointless, no one pays her any attention at all, poor kid, they're too busy making everything up as they go along. Then they make it up again, not that that does any good.

The problem is, they think they're making a movie. Like it wouldn't be enough for these people to do a fashion shoot and do it right. So we're *on location*, a phrase they just love, and OK, I'll give them that, it's standard lingo for when you go out of town.

But there's also all this talk about dressing the set, which makes no sense whatsoever. Either you're on location or you're working on a set, and this set idea is really silly, considering we're in this big, flat patch of nothing in the middle of Texas, some kind of animal preserve, burnt-out grass in every direction, as far as the eye can see, and then a bunch of guys get in a pickup and drive out to the horizon and plant this fake tree, which is supposed to make you think we're in Africa, and that's what they call dressing the set.

I couldn't believe it the first time I saw it, and then I had to keep seeing it, over and over, because the photographer and the production designer are constantly having these impromptu conferences and deciding that we need another tree. Then the trees need to be moved around. Unbelievable, really, but the animals are great. Especially this one giraffe who came over to our jeep yesterday and stood there, just looking at us, then she bent her neck down and rubbed these huge lips on my face ... not a kiss, exactly, but so sweet, and I was wondering how these creatures fuck, it must be quite an accomplishment.

Then I was up on a platform, smelling this smell of dust and sun, not to mention elephant shit, piss, and sweat, resting my elbow on an elephant tusk, which wasn't all that big for a tusk, I guess, but huge for a dick, meaning I was already feeling weird about sex, because this was not a comparison I would have made at any other time in my life, between dead bone and a throbbing dick.

But the show must go on, so I was creeped out on the inside but great for the camera, dazzling, in fact, with my chin up and my shoulders back, in a black satin extravaganza by the brilliant Alain B.-L. Then it was on to the zebra and one of Alain's extravaganzas in red satin. The zebra was so nice, bored out of his skull, no doubt, but then so was I, watching the photographer running around, making these hysterical gestures, then huddling with the production designer and the makeup people and practically everyone else … the drivers, the on-location accountant.

Finally he says to the world at large, "Crazy me, but I have an idea and I think it could work. It's going to be a really fun effect. Somewhat tricky, people, so let's really focus, and I think you'll see that it's just a matter of timing." I've been leaning on the zebra, watching, and now he gallops over, saying, "Fiona. You're going to like it. Love it. Really love it." Which of course I don't.

The gown I'm wearing is not a standard model, it's this special version with a long train, and the idea is for one of the photographer's assistants to hold it up and stretch it out behind me, then let go right when the shutter snaps, so this cloud of bright red fabric is floating all around me. Terrific, let's do it.

The trouble is that the assistant never lets it go at just the right moment. Or you could say the photographer never presses the button at just the right moment. Either way, he's flipping out and loving every minute of it, really thriving on his own dysfunction, so … but … anyway … what am I going to do? Storm off the set? So I'm communing with the zebra, caressing his bristly coat and wondering, what would it be like to get it on with a beast like this?

Now it's three in the morning and I don't even have a zebra to fantasize about, I'm deep in the heart of nowhere, pacing the floor of this trailer, which really is huge and luxurious and I know I should feel privileged, but I don't, I feel touchy and sore and for something to do I stop and look out a window every now and then and of course there's nothing to see, not even one of those fake trees, it's a cloudy night, like the air turned into this fuzzy gray stuffing, and the only thing to think about is how I'm having all these useless thoughts. Like, the moment I got undressed tonight the photographer started fixating on the scar Sergei gave me, which should have told me, right there, not to expect too much.

In fact, it did tell me but I wasn't listening, so now what? I've been so jumpy from the first moment of this shoot, I'm surprised the zebra didn't pick up on it and run screaming into the distance. Maybe he was waiting for me to do it first. So, anyway, we stood around, me sort of draping myself all over him, waiting and waiting and waiting for the photographer to get things in gear. Then I was grinding away like mad, a little while ago, trying to get this same guy to get it over with. Like, what? Like this was the courteous thing to do? The professional thing?

Maybe I'm turning into a grown-up, setting up permanent residence on the near side of the rainbow and feeling way too much sympathy with all the bad-sex girls, the babes who bond over stories of twisted love and total frustration. And all the sour, sarcastic people who infest the big city, burrowing into the nooks and crannies of Manhattan like maggots on meat.

Speaking of meat, my pussy doesn't even feel like flesh to me now. It's more like this rubbery thing that just happens to be there. Fucking is the furthest thing from its mind, like sex is just these anatomical parts doing what they do because of the way they're built. No other reason. So what on earth is going on? I've never felt like this before, not once, ever since I was really, really little, too young to know what fucking is. But completely alive to my pussy, as I remember. So that was me then. Who am I now? Who have I become? *What* have I become? And how could I possibly know, given that I am now the sort of person who asks cornball questions like, what the hell have I become?

On the flight back to New York it was obvious what I had become, just a number, but a pampered one, because I was in business class, part of the deal, on these full-flat seats. So, OK, a glass of champagne right after take-off and a slightly woozy nap followed by dinner, this chicken thing with deviled eggs, kind of shockingly delish, then more champagne and a longer snooze, all wrapped up in blankets and pestered now and then by the flight attendant, this spectacular combination of cute boy and babe in her late thirties. June, according to her name tag, with these brilliant tan cheekbones. I was so hot for her, in this long-distance way, I mean, she was being totally professional the whole time and I was still bummed out by my night of passion in the luxury trailer. So whenever she dealt with me she was, like, inflight-robot, but lovely to look at and definitely something to think about when I was all tucked in, feeling the airliner vibrations.

I tried to hang onto her image, I really did, while I was standing around at JFK, listening to that carrousel thing clanking away and waiting for my luggage to show up ... and having all sorts of fun thoughts about fun things, like, for example, clients who would tell Abigail they've been looking at me online, they need to see me, like, half an hour ago, in the flesh, and when I get there, fifteen minutes later, they make me wait in the reception area for an hour or two. Not to mention the ones who say that payment will be forthcoming but there has been a restructuring or an outsourcing or something, maybe an apocalypse, and there is going to be a slight delay ...

And lest we forget, what about dimwitted cab drivers and idiots in the street who bump into your book, like it's not big enough to see, for god's sake, and practically knock it out of your hands. All this petty stuff is flooding back, along with the really spooky and terrifying stuff ... Sergei doing his Jack the Ripper number ... unauthorized people barging into Brenda's place ...

and then there's the clerk who sees you holding out your hand for your change and he puts it on the counter, yelling, Next ... and then all my bitchy competitors ... I mean, former competitors ...

Oh, and what about the guys who stare at your tits... and guys who, if they got you into bed, would come in about a minute, you know this just by looking at them and they know it, too, and they know that you know, but they're thinking, hey, I pulled down a seven-figure bonus last year, so what's the problem? OK, right, let's say there's no problem, because, come on, we're all adults, supposedly, and we know how the game is played, but of course there *is* a problem, an endless parade of boring bullshit. And I'm beginning to figure it out, what I've become, the kind of person who bores the hell out of you complaining about life-as-usual, the endless parade of boring bullshit.

Because that was never me, not when I was seeing Brenda all the time and had a career and nothing threw me, it was all good or better than good, more like fabulous, because I loved the energy zapping through my world, the glam and the crazy beauty of it. No matter how fucked-up it got, it would bounce right off me, I didn't even notice the bad stuff, it all felt just really and truly real and fascinating and now I'm thinking, now what? A week in bed, totally pissed at the utter idiocy of everything? That was one option, which I have pretty much glommed onto, reading Jean Rhys part of the time but mostly lying around in a semi-coma ... losing all this muscle tone.

Not that slouching over to Alessandra's is beyond me, and so now I'm looking at this huge slice of apricot tart, not even fin-ishing my espresso, obsessing about this casting director from a while back, who asked me if I'd ever thought of getting new caps on my teeth. The stupid bitch, I don't have caps, the reason it looks like I do is my teeth are so great.

Right in the middle of my fantasy about asking the stupid bitch if she ever thought of getting a chin implant, look a little less like Elmer Fudd, I get a call from Brenda, and I'm coming out of this daze, wondering why haven't I been in touch? Because that's the real mystery, not what have I become, but where have I been ... drifting out of Brenda's orbit ... and drifting back now, hearing her say she's going to Paris for ten days and wanted to say hi before she went.

Which is fine. I've been missing Brenda so much I didn't even realize it, it was just this lousy mood that got mixed up with other things. On the other hand, I'm not sure I'm up to her company at this point, it's enough to hear her voice, which is beginning to melt the lousiness away, all the snotty remarks I wish I had made to whoever and all the bitterness and the boredom and the clammy feeling I've been feeling ever since that interlude with the photographer. Brenda's voice is dissolving me, a weird thought, true, but I've been expecting it to happen.

Because what was going on underneath all those prickly feelings I was having, I was turning into one of those see-through girls with no presence. No edge. Which I don't need, now that I have no career, no reason to stand out, I'm just blending in, it's like camouflage, you can't tell me apart from the dappled glade where I'm not even hiding. I'm just there, body and soul, and it's like I'm not. No one can see me and I feel safe. Once again. Totally safe and all alone and I've got no complaints, not about that or anything else. And it feels so nice, to be back in bed, all tangled up in the sheets, like they know they've wrapped themselves around me, they're sort of picking me up very gently and carrying me away, to the Land of Nod.

Awake around a quarter after seven in the morning, and it seems brighter than usual in my apartment. Like I'm still on the plane and we're way above the clouds, June hasn't pulled down the window shade, which she comes by and does without asking, and I fall back asleep, it's dark now but really it isn't. So I'm not even blending in anymore, the light is shining right through me and I'm fading, sailing into this lovely, weightless feeling. Which is going to last only so long and even if I stay in bed all day I know that sooner or later I am going to have to face facts.

It's like I'm in this spooky house, there's this narrow corridor, it's all shadowy and I'm walking down it, slowly, slowly, slowly toward this door I have to open but I really, really, really don't want to. Meaning, that stab wound of mine healed but I didn't. I'm still tender and really scared of admitting that I am now this quivering shadow of my former self, hiding out in my place, thinking, what if Sergei had nicked one of the what-d'you-call-'em arteries in my neck and I collapsed?

So I'm lying there all night, just bleeding out, as they say in cop thrillers ... then it's dawn, the night owls are flipping off the lights in their apartments. It's like there are lights going out in my brain, quite the picture, which my mind is watching, hovering up there, looking down at my body getting colder and colder ... it's crazy, or maybe I've never thought it through, the mind-brain thing. Supposedly, you can't have one without the other. But why not?

Silly question.

You just can't, it's obvious, even to someone like me, who knows absolutely nothing about the subject. Though I do remember reading somewhere that there are more neurons in the brain than stars in the sky, which is pretty impressive, so, uh ... come on, if the brain is so brainy, why can't it spare my mind these pictures of me lying dead in a pool of my own blood?

Another silly question but who cares, I am regressing beyond the point of caring if I'm making any sense whatsoever … regressing all the way back to my mother's womb … also a pretty spooky place, as I recall … just kidding, but, really, I'll bet it was even worse than Sergei's apartment … meaning, I'd be feeling suicidal if I felt like I actually existed. Like there is this person … Fiona … I really ought to kill, let's just get it over with. As it is, there is just barely enough of me left to sink back into a deep, deep sleep, which is what I've been doing for quite a while now, except that my phone is ringing, and if my dreaminess had any backbone I'd ignore the call but of course it doesn't and so I don't. I take the call and it's Angela Auerbach, the booker from Alliance, who gets in touch every time I get the boot.

So that was what got me out of bed, Angela asking me to a cocktail party at her house on East Seventieth Street. My drifty state of mind, which has been making me unfit for human company, also kept me from coming up with a way to weasel out of it, so here I am. Helpless but not miserable, in Angela's garden, which is so cozy … it's dusk, all soft and warm … no fireflies, of course, but it feels like there ought to be a ton of them sailing around, in between the white paper lanterns.

People are strolling by, with nice looks on their faces, and I'm kind of frozen, like a mannequin behind glass, basically blank and dressed up in not-so-basic black, this sleeveless number by Giambattista Valli … suddenly there is the sound of honking from the street, very angry and barely audible, like Angela's house is a filter, filtering out ninety-five per cent of life's little annoyances … and all the big ones … and now Angela herself is making her way through the other guests, looking terrific in a gray silk suit and a creamy silk blouse, with a string of ultra-creamy pearls.

She has a smile like someone who used to be a brilliant athlete, just radiating this toned-up confidence. When she gets to me she gives me a kiss, asking what I've been up to.

"Not much. I guess you heard ..."

"I did. And of course my ears perked right up." She turns and I follow her to the bar at the back of the garden, where she asks for a gin and tonic. This is a relaxed atmosphere, to put it mildly, but in the bartender's mind it's the bar-tending Olympics and he's going for the gold, slapping Angela's drink together with this wild mix of precision and reckless abandon.

When he's done, he hands it to her with a big winner's smile and she takes it without even looking at him. Which seems kind of callous but, um ... anyway, she tastes her gin and tonic and approves, still without a glance at the bartender, saying, "My first thought was that you wanted to take a breather, then ..."

"Then you heard I was thrown out on my ear."

"For the second time."

I give her a lame grin and she says, "Sometimes it takes a girl a while to find the right representation."

Angela touches me on the elbow and we walk over to a cluster of guests she thinks it would be nice for me to meet. And it is, I mean, if this isn't nice, what does the word mean? All these good clothes topped off by good haircuts, both the men and the women, everybody's voice set at exactly the right volume. These people are niceness personified. Not that the men are not feeling all these yearnings, just eating me up with their eyes. While the women check out my outfit. But you know there's zero chance of stormy weather.

This is life in the temperate zone, even the extreme emotions are on their best behavior, pulsing with life, no doubt, but all

pruned, along with the plants in Angela's garden. Strictly orna-
mental, like the things these people say, so you don't have to
think, you just say whatever you're supposed to say, to make sure
there aren't any bare spots in the general effect.

Niceness rules and Angela is playing the part of the naughty
exception, getting a little bright-eyed on gin and tonics and circling around to tell me about her husband, a television producer
and very successful. So I'm feeling slightly tense, wondering if an
angry mob of totally nice people is going to descend on Angela
and tear her limb from limb for hinting at the grubby old subject
of money. But all is calm, the ears in Angela's garden hear only
what they're supposed to hear.

Now she's saying her husband is away, hates to travel, poor
dear, and he's going to have to put up with it for weeks and weeks
… slipping me the big, fat clue of the evening, guess what, Fiona,
I'm available … next she tells me about this shoot, Melissa Patrick's spring line, how brilliant Melissa is, and suddenly the garden is being invaded by a platoon of waiters bearing trays. One
stops beside us, offering a small heap of large shrimp all glopped-
up in a golden sauce. I peer at them and Angela is peering at me,
scoping out the anatomy, part by part, saying, "You don't look as
if you need to skip this sort of thing, Fiona."

So I pick up a canapé fork and spear one of the shrimp. So
does Angela, with this slightly ruthless motion, telling me, "These
are new. Let's see …" Now she's chewing the shrimp with a quiz-
zical look on her face, like, just how delicious is this going to be,
holding the fork up the whole time, then licking her lips and saying, um, um, umm, in a very charming manner. Which would be
so seductive if I were still the old, seducible me.

Now she does a double-take, saying, "Fiona. You don't have a
drink." Holding me by the wrist, she leads me back toward the
bar. Halfway there, she gets pounced on by this almost elderly

couple, leaving me with a slim man in a very expensive jacket, beige linen, can't place the designer ... anyway, he's wearing it over a dark green polo shirt, with slacks of a slightly lighter beige. He is tall and handsome and likes to smile because his smile just lights up the garden with the flash of white teeth. Super-white teeth, bleached to the point where they're blue around the edges.

So he's talking and smiling and I space out, waking up in time to realize he's actually talking about something specific, this painting by Philip Guston he saw last night at a Sotheby's preview. I'm not all that sure who Philip Guston is, somebody big, obviously, but it doesn't matter because this man, Alan Something, doesn't care if I know this or anything else. What he cares about is the look of dopey surrender on my face, which just sort of showed up, not my choice at all.

But I know it's there. I can tell by Alan's behavior, alpha-male on an effortless roll, wowing this helpless babe and not making all that big a deal about it. The world is full of girls like me. Like the girl I have become. This very minute, anyway, because who or what I have become is pretty much up for grabs, one minute to the next.

Alan pauses in the midst of his brilliant speech on the subject of his sheer brilliance as an appraiser of oil paint or horseflesh or how the hell should I know? Anyway, he's looking over my head, scanning the garden. Then he looks down at his glass, like he's just realizing that it's empty, flashes me another smile and says he needs a refill. Can he bring me anything? No, he can't, except maybe a reminder of the way I would deal with a jerk like this in the not too distant past. I really am losing track of myself.

And it's darker now, in Angela's garden, darker and a little chilly, with servants bringing out more of these lantern-on-a-stick things and planting them in the cracks between the flagstones. Angela walks over to me, her gray suit looking all luminous. She smiles, saying, "Alan is a major collector. As I suppose he let you know."

I smile back.

"And, it ought to be noted, one of the few men in this neck of the woods whose divorce, in fact, wasn't messy."

Angela looks to the side as she says this, nodding hello at someone, then looking back to see how I'm responding to this fairly loaded bit of information. Am I on the prowl? If so, am I on the prowl for men?

I put my hand on Angela's arm, which is holding her latest drink at midriff level. And I let it rest there. Which means I haven't merely jumped the gun. I've grabbed the gun and pointed it at my head, this is so nuts. Except that it isn't. I mean, it is and it isn't, depends who you ask, the new Fiona, namely, me, or the old Fiona, my former self, who is goading me on, getting me to leave my hand on Angela's arm way too long. Giving her a squeeze. Checking out the vibe.

There isn't any. Or there is, of course there is, Angela is looking right into my eyes, and, really, she is so attractive, but I'm not feeling anything except in this totally theoretical way. The mind versus body thing has kicked in again in big-time, the brain putting the body through its usual paces and the mind just watching. Which is so weird.

Alan the major collector reappears at this point, in the middle of this conversation he's been having with himself, saying, "You know, I think I will—"

Angela interrupts, almost laughing, telling him, "Yes, Alan. You will. You'll buy it. You know you will."

He's looking at me now, to see if I'm getting the picture. How the whole world is revolving around the question of will he or won't he buy the important painting by Philip Guston. Then a flinch sort of flickers across his face, like he's been slapped for the first time in his life by the odd thought that maybe a girl like me doesn't care. Or maybe I wasn't even listening.

Angela hauls him away by the arm, telling him it's late. Doesn't he have a business to run? I wander back toward the bar, pretty much by accident, and the high-speed bartender stops in the middle of whatever he's doing, rearranging bottles in a carton or something, and gives me this big grin. "Last call?"

I smile and shake my head, booze would disintegrate me now, and then I'm saying goodnight to this couple that told me way back when the night was young, well, if you're not working as a model at this very moment, why not go back to school? Pursue your interest in literature, which they kind of thought up for me. I mean, I told them I like to read but does that mean I have to have an interest in literature? It's like, OK, I like to fuck but does that mean I have an interest in sex as a topic of scientific inquiry? The question is moot, as the lawyers say, given that I don't even remember what it's like to fuck.

I wander around a bit more, say a few more goodbyes, then I give Angela a big sexy hug … because, as I said, I still have the moves if not the feelings … which Angela is actually feeling, I can tell, even now in my numbed-out condition, and I promise to stay in touch, let her know what my plans are, career-wise, and she's hanging onto me a bit, saying it would be, well, um, nice just to know how I'm getting along. So I'm promising her I'll stay in touch, I really, really will.

Then I'm catching a cab, feeling really cold now, asking the driver to roll up his window, please, great, thank you, then I'm getting out of the cab, into my building, out of my party clothes, into my bed clothes, this T-shirt I've been wearing for about a week, and I'm burrowing in, at last, all curled up and super-snug, marveling at Angela, how she popped up right on schedule, like a character in the Land of Make-Believe, to make a point according to Make-Believe logic.

Which always makes sure that everything just does that, pops up on cue, in this case to rub my nose in the grim reality. Which is that I am now one of these girls who lives in her thoughts, not in the land of living, breathing bodies and functional brains … the land of sex and jobs and love and money … and I'd better be careful or I'll turn out like this girl Angela mentioned, who reported for the Melissa Patrick shoot about fifteen pounds underweight.

Angela was still upset, telling me about her. "It's as if she'd been trying, poor thing, to will herself into proper shape, and then her will took over. Mind over matter, with disastrous results." I acted sympathetic, which was not such a big act. Angela went on about the shoot and Melissa's new things and the season and her agency, how well they're doing, and I stood there thinking, I'd better get a job. Which is what Angela is going to be offering me in the not too distant future. Along with a chance to feel her steamy little mitts all over me.

Which would be lovely if I were still me and not the new me, a figment of my own imagination. I hardly recognize myself any more. Literally don't recognize myself, because I was naked this morning, walking past my full-length mirror, and, OK, I don't mean that I didn't know who I saw in there, but the me I saw was like this very boring, very accurate diagram of myself. If that makes any sense, and it bothered me, a lot, that it didn't. It didn't make any sense at all.

Because what sense does anything make if I look this good, this great, and don't even feel like I'm living in my own body? Which I don't, not anymore, and it's not because I'm disgusted by sex or pissed off at the world or irritated by some person with shitty manners or ugly shoes. It's because I've lost all this emotional muscle tone. I'm not feeling anything. Nada, zilch. Really, nothing. Except terrified of butcher knives. Which is bad for Plan

B. The last-ditch plan I don't think I'll be resurrecting again any-time soon, having found out what a scaredy-cat I am.

But it doesn't matter. Because my mind, if you can believe it, is getting all cosmological, sort of dissolving into the warmth that is really the light at the heart of my universe … Brenda … who is getting all mixed up with Glinda the good witch, casting her spell and making everything perfect, which it would be except for one thing. My problem.

Sergei.

I mean, the logic of Sergei, which I wouldn't even know about if I hadn't read so much Ursula Le Guin as a kid. So, OK, her stuff is fantasy, unreal, except how can it be anything but totally real, this thing my thoughts are caught up in, which is what everything is all about now—not sex or jobs or love or money but the big cosmic struggle between the heart of light and the dickhead of darkness.

OK, so the warring forces are out in the open, the scale of it is getting kind of infinite and overwhelming, meaning I need to talk things over with someone, and the only one is Fred. Because he's the only one who gets things. Except—what things? It's just stuff you feel and feel the other person understands, and that's great, but I really want to talk details, the cosmological kind, and of course details like that are awfully slippery. If that's the right word, which it obviously isn't, and I don't know which is the right one. Because I don't know how to talk about any of this and that's embarrassing. Fiona the Inarticulate.

I'm afraid I'll get together with Fred and immediately go into babbling-idiot mode. He'd be patient, help me get to the point. I know I can count on that, but I'm scared of coming across as some kind of mystical ditz. So I brooded about it all day, just brooding and brooding, and all that hesitation turned out to be totally dumb, big surprise, because when I finally decided, why not take the plunge, get in touch, wing it and see what happens, my call went straight to voice mail and that was that.

I was sitting on my bed in the dark, listening to the cars going by on Twenty-Eighth Street, sort of falling into this state of semiconsciousness, when I suddenly called Bill. Who was incredibly nice, not saying too much, thank god, just, come on over whenever you want, I'll be here.

I found him at his huge dining table, also in the dark, his face all strange in the light of a computer screen. He said, hi, but didn't look up. I came over and sat in his lap, something I'd never done before. He massaged my shoulders for a while, very impersonal and efficient, then he got up and flipped the switch on his incredibly expensive, industrial-grade track lighting and went and made some coffee in his huge kitchen area.

So we sat on these tall chairs, drinking coffee and talking ... various topics ... including that dealer who bought the super-expensive Richter painting from him . . . a guy who seems to really piss Bill off, so I asked him, "What's the problem? You hate him so much you won't even mention his name?"

Bill said, "No, I don't hate him. Charles Bystrom. If you want to know. A real jerk. But very bright—"

"So what's—"

"What's the problem? The problem is that it's not about style for him or taste or meeting the right people ... of course, he knows all the right people and they like him, in a way. Because they get that for him it's a game and he's good at it."

"But not as good as you," I said.

Bill shrugged. "No ... well, maybe ... the thing is, I don't play Charles's game, which is all about numbers and remembering

who owns what, which I do too, but with me it's more about per-
sonalities, helping people get an idea of themselves. With Charles
it's just numbers."

"So he doesn't really look at paintings."

"Well. He has to look at them. In order to recognize them. But
if you mean—"

"What I mean is, there is no aesthetic pleasure in his philosophy."

"His philosophy?"

"You know, Laurence Olivier as *Hamlet*. Adapted and directed
by Laurence Olivier. A Laurence Olivier Production with music
and catering by Laurence Olivier. Plus additional dialogue by
Laurence Olivier. We saw it at the Film Forum. Together. Remember? There are more things, Horatio, than are dreamt of in your
philosophy."

"It's funny, I never got that until now. He means—"

"Cosmology."

"Right. The big picture."

"Speaking of which, you never told me what you and Sergei
talked about when he dropped by your gallery with Alison."

"Wow, Fiona, that's quite a leap. Laurence Olivier to Sergei
What's-His-Face."

"Well, yeah. I'm a big-picture girl and that's what I do. The big
leap."

"Uh, OK … Sergei … let me see … that was a while ago … we
talked … I mean, he talked, I listened. He wanted me to know
how much he knows."

"What does he know?"

"He knows what Saatchi is doing. What Eli Broad is doing. He
thinks he knows what François Pinault is doing."

"These are names I should know?"

Bill shook his head. "No. Not at all. The point is, what Sergei knows is what you need to know if you want to believe that

you're in the know. Standard stuff. Total bullshit, all the way down, except everybody believes it, so it's real. In a way. Like any other cosmology."

"You live in a third-rate cosmos."

"And you don't?"

"No. I live in the Brenda cosmos, which is the best there is, except that it's all bent out of shape. So am I. I'm not sure I even live there anymore."

"Pay her a visit. Check it out."

I shake my head, saying, "Actually, she's called me a couple of times recently. The other day, asking me to come over, watch a movie or something. But I didn't go. It didn't feel right. Not yet."

"Not yet? What are you talking about, Fiona? You're scaring me."

I shake my head some more. "It just doesn't feel right."

"Cosmologically speaking?"

I nod and Bill gives me this look he's trying to keep blank, saying, "Come on, Fiona. Lose the cosmology. Either it doesn't make any sense or it makes too much sense, you can make it mean anything you want."

"Anything?"

"Yeah. Anything. No limits to the weirdness. I'm not kidding, I'm worried about you, Fiona. I think you've gone off the deep end. Cosmologically speaking."

"You're worried about me?"

He nods.

I say, "That's a first."

He takes a deep breath, taking the time to be very patient, and before he can come up with a comeback, I say, "It's a first and it ought to be the last. I'll be fine. As soon as I come up with a new plan."

"A new plan?"

"A new plan. Which is perfectly rational, however nuts you think I am. Just because I want to fix the universe."

Bill looks down. Then he looks up, stands up, puts his hands on his hips ... scowling at me. "I was kidding but now I'm not. I'm worried about you. You seem sort of..."

I sit there, looking back at him, this wide-eyed stare. Which is supposed to be cute, but Bill isn't buying it.

"You seem sort of flimsy, Fiona, or, um ... anyway, I'm beginning to think you shouldn't be alone. Why don't you—"

"What? Sleep on the couch?"

Bill smiles. Faintly. I get up, give him a kiss on the cheek, breathing in the scent of his skin. Then we both sit down, not knowing where to go from here. I mean, I could just leave but he genuinely is worried about me. Doesn't want to throw me out in my present condition, flapping in the cosmic breeze, so he says, "Look. Fiona. Maybe there are things I don't get. But what can I tell you?"

I look over at him. "OK. What can you tell me? Tell me how to deal with Sergei. Remember you told me once that you deal with people like that all the time. Well ..."

"I said that? Um ... all right. Here's what you do. You string him along. Tell him what he wants to hear. Maneuver him into a corner, get him to see his best interests. Then he sees that his best interests are the same as yours. Or Brenda's."

I'm about to heave a depressed sigh. But I don't bother. I just sit there, sipping coffee, thinking, this is ridiculous. Brenda and Sergei can't have the same interests. They can't even be in the same universe. It's cosmologically impossible. Like Bugs Bunny showing up in a production of *Hamlet*. Not that there was never a Bugs Bunny version of *Hamlet*. There probably was, but that only proves my point. For every creature of every kind, there is a special universe, and Sergei needs me to send him back to the one where he belongs. Which is why I need a new plan.

For Bill's sake, I change the subject, tell him about Angela Auerbach and her garden party, how I was thinking of signing with Alliance, getting back to work, which convinced him that I was rational enough to at least get home by myself. It was still early by the time I left, but all the cabs were taken, so I walked up Hudson.

It was a beautiful evening full of unfocused energy ... I thought of stopping by the tapas bar on Ninth, have a glass of vino, get inspired ... but there was no need. By the time I got there, the plan had come to me. I was going to get Brenda and Sergei together in the same room, like these two elements in the same test tube. Only this isn't a chemistry experiment, it's cosmological. The light confronts the darkness, a very big deal and easy to set up, thanks to Maisie, who is on the committee for a big charity event at the New York Public Library. Books for Illiterates or something like that.

She called me last week, all excited, telling me that Brenda had agreed to make an appearance, in fact, Brenda was going to be an honorary sponsor. Knowing how I felt about her, Maisie thought maybe I'd like to come, it would be so great to see me, bring anyone you'd like. So I said, yes, thank you, and I'm so sorry I haven't been in touch, don't be too mad at me. She was, like, well, all right, I won't be *too* mad, teasing me, and when we were hanging up I was thinking, really, she was always so adorable. Why can't I have that back? Now I'm thinking I'll call her tomorrow, tell her I'm bringing someone who's going to be making a massive contribution. At which news, Maisie will give this grateful little gasp, the kind that only major money can ever produce in a girl who has turned into an Upper East Side matron.

The next step is get in touch with Sergei, tell him about the event, what a great privilege it would be for him to attend, pledge a bunch of money and just generally behave like a member of civilized society. Which is weird, making a social call to the only person I know who has actually tried to stab me to death. But all that's on the physical plane, not the spiritual plane or the astral plane or whatever plane I'm on now. And, oddly enough, our conversation goes pretty well. He says he's looking forward to important social occasion and he actually sounds like a member of civilized society.

Which is good and now I'm thinking it through, all the permutations of Sergei and Brenda suddenly finding themselves face-to-face—kind of like the Kama Sutra, every possible position, except this is not about sex, it's these basic principles, how are they going to meet up and get entangled? Or not. Which maybe is like sex on this plane I'm now on, but I can't think about that, all I can think about is the practical details, which feel unreal. Like, when I introduce Sergei to Maisie—what? Spooky music? An explosion of bats from the belfry?

Actually things do feel pretty strange on the night of the big event, Maisie lighting up when she sees me, which is fine, it's what girls do on occasions like this, getting all hysterical and squealy when we see each other, but then she takes me by the shoulders and really kisses me.

I mean, really kisses me, like, any second now she's going to be deep-throating me with her tongue, and I'm wondering, what is this? This man who must be her husband Jake is standing right behind her, I can see he's asking himself the same question, and maybe I'm imagining things but it feels like Sergei is getting all huffy and potentially violent, thinking, this is uncultured, in my country girls are not doing this, why I have to look upon such Western decadence?

Then Maisie steps back, she's all flushed and happy looking. I introduce her to Sergei and she's very sweet in this hostessy way that puts everyone on their best behavior. Including Sergei, who is actually coming across as fairly suave. And now he sees Brenda, on the far side of the room, Astor Hall, which is basically just the entrance to the New York Public Library, beautifully done up with candelabras and potted palms. There's a mini-orchestra playing in this bouncy Lester Lanin style, Fifties foxtrot, which I wouldn't even know about except for my grandmother's record collection. She loved Lester Lanin. But not as much as Cole Porter.

Anyway, Lester Lanin is maybe too strenuous for some of the more dignified attendees. So it's perfect for Brenda. Part of her allure is that she does not do the glitzy things you expect super-models to do. She does things that make you think of old money. Not that she comes from old money. It's more that she doesn't have to prove anything. No cutting edge for Brenda Xavier Rawl-ings. No struggling to stay ahead of the curve.

Brenda just is, sort of like the New York Public Library, because, OK, books are going digital, we live in a virtual world, but here we are, beneath the marble arches of the Astor Hall, they are very solid and the marble lions are still out front. Brenda, as usual, is so beautiful it breaks your heart. So beautiful and non-virtual. So real. Sergei is mesmerized. To put it mildly.

He's frozen in place, like a figure of early man under glass in one of those natural history dioramas. Ancestral human enchanted by the luminous future. Or something like that, I mean, this is supposed to be the big cosmological experiment, the darkness interacting with the light, so I tell him he should go over and say hello. He wants to but he can't. I nag him a bit, like daring a child to jump off a cliff.

Go on, give it a shot. What can happen? Just make the leap, there's all this soft, leafy foliage, you can't possibly get hurt. But

Sergei is truly spooked by the sight of Brenda. So when another member of the donor class comes by, a friend and colleague in evening clothes way too tight for the poor guy, it's the big hello, how are you, really great, and they wander off in the direction of the bar.

Leaving me free to go over to Brenda.

Her escort, this vast improvement on Bennett Ross, is a nice-looking man named Phillip Something-or-Other, a Wall Street lawyer, I think, not sure, it doesn't matter, Brenda is at ease with him, so that's fine, and she is her usual darling self with me. Not having intersected with any of the waiters with their little trays of drinks, I too head for the bar, and on the way I see Maisie in this really intense conversation with a woman. A beautiful young woman, and Maisie's face is so wonderfully alive, her eyes wide open, almost straining, like she's trying to absorb the sheer lovely look of the other woman, and I realize I'm feeling something I really don't want to feel.

Jealousy.

Which I never, ever used to feel, not until I saw Bill with Imogen Rittenhauer, because in my simple-minded view of the world there was always Brenda and the fun of being a sex fiend and no need for jealousy because the more sex and love and affection the better. Now Brenda is here but everything else is up in the air, out of whack, that's the whole point of this evening, get things back on an even keel … restore the balance of the universe … turning around, I bump into Maisie's husband, who is scanning the scene, saying this is like a Civil War reenactment. Which is pretty bright and also true, the evening just gliding along in line with everybody's expectations. Except mine. This is my big experiment, so I'm not having any expectations. Keeping an open mind. The scientific attitude.

Jake drifts away and I'm standing there, my open mind shutting down a little bit, a panic attack can have that effect. But people keep coming up to me, people I know, people who want to know me. I must be giving off a pretty hot vibe, despite my cosmological jitters. Not to mention the detachment required by my experimental approach to the events of the evening. Speaking of which, where on the spectrum of light and dark does this next phenomenon belong?

As if I didn't know, given that the phenomenon in question is this pretty girl in a beautifully fitted dress of dark green wool and low heels who is approaching me, touching me lightly on my arm, smiling, telling me that the major donors are assembling in the Leonard Silver Special Collections Room, would I like to come along, Mr. Propokoff is already there, so I smile back and say, certainly, can you show me where I should go?

She would be happy to, and I follow her through these wide corridors, lots of dim light and the nice sound of other people's feet on the shiny terrazzo ... the buzz of the reception is a whisper now ... needless to say, I'm watching my guide's trim little butt, the demure rhythm that is so really and truly hot and I'm thinking, OK, Fiona, why all this obsessing about the darkness in a world that has such treasures in it? Then I'm telling myself, don't be so dumb, when the darkness wins, sex will be no redemption, just a distraction, so keep your eye on the ball ... in other words, the big glob of dysfunctional energy that constitutes Sergei's head.

The Leonard Silver Special Collections Room is this soundproof extravaganza of oak paneling and leather bindings, the perfect place to assemble about three dozen people with tons of money and no time to read. The murmuring is intense, and then Maisie appears at the door and gets the nod from another pretty girl in low heels. Great, everyone's here, so Maisie starts banging a fork on a champagne glass, ever so delicately, and the toasts and words of sincere appreciation begin.

Maisie gives thanks first of all to Paul Leclerc, president of the Library, to a bunch of board members and big donors, all these names ... then a wide woman in a really elaborate satin dress, burgundy, with gold buttons with bits gold braid everywhere, begins to name some more names, finally getting around to extending a sincere vote of appreciation to Maisie Lattimer ... inspired leadership, enthusiastic response, a truly worthy cause ...

It goes on and on, all of it ringing true, truly true, bong, bong, bong, like this big bell, sort of hypnotizing me. My mind goes blank. Beyond blank, into deep hibernation, and when it emerges, Sergei is giving a toast, raising his glass to Brenda, a vision in shimmery gray, standing right across from him.

"To Brenda," he says, in his ringmaster voice. "This is woman who wishes me to die. To die of love."

Sergei smiles a truly ghastly smile, gazing at Brenda, but she is unfazed, smiling in his general direction with that beautiful, unfocused smile of hers. Sergei keeps gazing at her, his face getting weirder by the second. It's, like, Creature from the Weird Lagoon, and now Brenda's escort, the lawyer, is standing in front of her, blocking Sergei's view. But Sergei is stubborn. Stepping to the side, he gets this partial view of Brenda and he says, again, "To die of love." With his glass empty now.

Queasy silence, which gets queasier when somebody calls out, "To love." Trying to improve the situation. But, guess what, it doesn't help, the embarrassment is so thick you can just about taste it.

At this point, Sergei decides to walk toward Brenda. His arms stretched out. Like he's going to give her this big hug and they're going to melt together in a gooey haze of mutual understanding and acceptance. He's eyeing her as he closes in but, from my angle, it looks like Brenda hasn't even noticed what he's doing. She's digging around in her purse and her escort is beside her, leaning in, getting all concerned. What is it, dear? Your cell phone? Your lipstick? Like this is the problem.

Brenda looks up, gives Sergei an empty stare, and goes back to her purse. Sergei stops, about five feet away, and realizes what's going on. This is a replay of the original scene, the one that launched the entire fiasco, Brenda looking at Sergei and seeing nothing. Only then it was in private. Now it's happening in public, in front of people Sergei is desperate to impress. People all too willing to be impressed by an up-and-coming oligarch, and that makes it far, far worse, because he knows what is happening. Brenda is absolutely fucking up absolutely everything he ever hoped for.

So he starts screaming at her in Russian, saying no one knows what, Americans are so terrible at languages. But it's obviously horrendous. He's growling and snarling and half-choking at the top of his lungs, his hands are just hanging there, twitching, and everyone is shocked, like statues, except that Brenda's escort has escorted her out of the room, great presence of mind, and now Sergei is turning in my direction.

He's yelling at me, like I'm the real problem. For some reason, I'm focusing on his eyebrows, which look like these wild, hairy creatures, and there is spittle at the corners of his mouth. I feel this hideous energy is coming at me, weird waves I can practically see, all loopy and slimy, and I can't do anything but stand there and try not to feel it. Which is a total failure. I feel it, all right, and it's beginning to give me this rash. And these blisters. Virtual blisters, true, but, just the same, they're really disgusting.

By now, the room is empty, except for us two, and then a batch of guards in dark blue uniforms appear and surround Sergei, calming him down. Actually, they do a good job. In no time, they're leading him away, very politely, or, who knows, maybe it takes hours of patient negotiations. I really don't know, I am so freaked I go and sit in a corner and decide after a moment's reflection that it is time for the girly relief of dissolving into tears.

Only there's no relief, I'm all alone weeping and moaning, these deep, shuddering moans, like sex sounds. Sort of. I mean, they're just as deep as sex sounds and just as shuddery, but not as ecstatic. More like completely hopeless.

The next morning, around eleven, I called Maisie and she started commiserating with me like mad, you poor thing, how terrible for you, you couldn't have known, and I kept trying to apologize and she kept saying, really, truly, there's no need. Of course, it was a rather startling outburst, she was willing to grant me that, and people were genuinely shocked but, for her part, well, it was kind of exciting. Unusual, at the very least. Stirred things up. Though it's not at all certain that Mr. Propokoff will be invited to any further events of this kind.

She was almost giggling, then she got all intense, saying, "Oh, Fiona, I feel so stupid. There is this wonderful person I wanted you to meet. A very dear friend." I knew exactly who she meant, her gorgeous young woman, and I got this sudden memory of her. Bare shoulders, her back bent ever so slightly so she could look right into Maisie's eyes, I mean, right into them, all the way, and so stylish that I couldn't remember a single thing she was wearing. Which makes no sense, given my memory for clothes. It's almost as good as my memory for bodies.

Anyway, Maisie tells me the woman's name is Helen ... I don't catch her last name, just that she was such an important person in Maisie's life, her best friend at Bryn Mawr, then she married a financial type, right before Maisie did, girlish laugh, what a coincidence ... but not really ... another girlish laugh ...

"At any rate," Maisie is saying, "Helen is single now, I know you two would really hit it off, I've got to introduce you ..." And I'm realizing, this is the woman who introduced Maisie to her sweetest, deepest yearnings, and now Maisie is offering to fix me up with her.

Which is so amazingly generous and I'd be getting wet except that I'm not, I'm like sand, and I'm faking it, getting that hot girly lilt in my voice, telling Maisie I'd really love to meet Helen, she sounds wonderful, blah, blah, blah, and it's tough, putting over these phony feelings on someone I love. It would be easier to fake an orgasm, less of a betrayal. But I keep on doing it, floating above the conversation, developing the theory that Sergei's freak-out shook something loose in Maisie, and now she's fancy free, coming up with all sorts of ideas, like, maybe we should all take a trip, spend a few months in Europe next summer.

I have no idea who or what she means by "we" and I don't want to ask, I just go along, all flirty and responsive, thinking, some girls fake it like this their whole lives, from the age of seven or so. It's heroic. Awful but heroic, and I'm exhausted by the time Maisie rings off, so I slither back into bed and more or less fall asleep. Then, when it's beginning to get dark in my apartment, I more or less wake up and call Brenda and, oh my god, I can't get through.

First there's this assistant-assistant, who is very nice because that is her function in life, to be very nice no matter what, because if she isn't she's going to hear a voice, also very nice, telling her that we really appreciate all the work you've done here at BXR but we don't feel the organization is exactly right for you, meaning, you are the wrong kind of person, why were you ever born? So it doesn't mean much if an assistant-assistant is nice.

But it does mean something, it means a lot, if an assistant, next step up the ladder, is sort of official sounding, like she's never heard of me. Then Pam gets on the line, there are icicles on her speech balloon, and I realize it's crisis time. A major freeze has set in. Brenda is not available. Well, um, uh, when … Pam said she would let me know.

So, OK, I can't get through to Brenda, and this means not only that I have not restored the balance of my universe. I have collapsed it totally, like … like what? The collapse is so total I can't even think of what to compare it to. Which is not good, the collapse of my entire universe seems to have taken my mental faculties down with it. But so, on the other hand, what?

Given the magnitude of my fuck-up, I don't even feel grief or much of anything except this weird curiosity, so I call the one person in Fortress Brenda who will probably talk to me, namely, Mike, and he answers on the third ring, saying, "Don't tell me, let me guess. Pam won't let you talk to Brenda."

"Right."

"Not now, not ever."

"I guess. So what's up?"

"The word is that Brenda is afraid of you."

"Did she say that?"

"Uh, well, it seems that Brenda is genuinely scared. We're rolling out new security protocols. Because something happened. Something happened and you were a big part of it. So now the fear is focused on you."

"Really?"

"Really."

"Really, Mike? Because I know it was a pretty strange night at the library, but, uh, um … I just don't get why Brenda … " My voice is shocking me, all scratchy and pathetic.

Mike doesn't say anything for a while, then he clears his throat and says, "OK, Fiona. What I am about to tell you is completely confidential."

"OK. I understand. It's confidential."

"Not only what I'm about to tell you but the fact that I talked to you. Because I've already told Pam about this. She can't know that I told you. Nobody can know. It's confidential. All of it."

"OK, Mike. I get it. Really. It's confidential."

"OK. As I said, Brenda is afraid of you and—"

"Afraid of me? Did she actually say that?"

"Yes, she did."

"To who?"

"To me."

"Uh—"

"Don't go all tactful on me, Fiona. You can say it. Why would Brenda be talking to me about—"

"Mike—"

"No, it's all right. Why would she? Simple answer. One of Brenda's trainers was working with her on Shaolin Martial Arts—"

"Martial arts?"

"It's a meditative discipline, Fiona. Anyway, this trainer left and, as the discipline happens to be one of my competencies, I stepped in and Brenda has been working with me for about a month now."

"And you've been having these heart-to-hearts."

Mike laughs. "Not really. Not often. It's just that she was obviously shaken by the big library bash and when I asked her how she was she said, straight out, scared."

"Scared of me."

"Scared of you. Right. I had to piece it together. It was like she was telling me about a dream, something she didn't remember all that clearly. But I kept getting the sense that, after a certain point, she wasn't particularly worried about Mr. Propokoff. Yes, he said he'd have her killed, but, no, she didn't really think he'd do it. Not after you went out with him that first time, Fiona. What kept coming through is that you were this bizarre object of faith for Brenda. She had this feeling that if, uh … she kept saying that she could always talk to you about everything and then everything would be all right."

"She had this feeling? But she doesn't anymore?"

"No. Now she feels that Propokoff is truly dangerous—"

"And I had something to do with that."

"Right."

"So she's scared to talk to me. Scared to see me. Maybe I'll bring this new Sergei back into her world."

"Right."

"Oh, Mike. This is so terrible."

"I'm sorry, Fiona."

"I know, and thanks. And thank you for telling me all this. It makes a lot of sense."

"I wish it didn't."

"Me too, Mike."

So I'm flat on my back, staring at the ceiling, thinking, why doesn't something happen? Save me the trouble of making something happen, and something does. My phone rings. It's Viktor, telling me that Sergei is very angry.

"Yeah. I got that impression."

"Very angry at you."

"As I said …"

"Sergei says you are witch. Baba Yaga."

"What!"

"Special Russian witch. You live in house with chicken legs."

"Chicken legs? This is bullshit, Viktor. Sergei has seen my legs."

"You are not understanding."

"You're fucking right, Viktor. I am not understanding a fucking word you're saying. But here's a simple thought, sort of hands across the language barrier, something even Sergei can understand. Tell him to fuck himself."

One of Viktor's long pauses, then, "Sergei is very angry. Very scared. He says you are witch."

I end the call and let out this huge yell. Then I roll myself up into a ball and rock back and forth on my bed for a while. Then I get beneath the covers. It's only about six in the evening, but I really sleep. For about twelve hours, I guess.

Hopelessness makes a good sleeping pill but not much of a tranquillizer. When I woke up I was really edgy. Spooked. Meaning my dreams must have been pretty bad and I had this strange urge to get out of my apartment, the joint was jumping with all this creepy energy. So I put on some jeans and a sweater and figured I'd wander east along Twenty-Eighth Street, find some place without too many memories attached and have some coffee.

The sun was already harsh, beaming through the half-naked branches, making everything look way too scruffy. Depressing, except that I was too unfocused to feel depressed, just slack, Rag Doll in the Big City, and I was telling myself to be extra careful crossing the street, because it's when you're all blurry that things go wrong, then they did go wrong, not because I was blurry but because the forces of darkness were really on a rampage.

There was this white van double parked right where I had to
go around it, and when I did the side door slid open and some guy
right behind me grabbed both my elbows from behind. I turned
around before he could get a firm grip, screaming at him to get
the fuck off me, and trying to kick him in the shin or the knee or
the groin, which I didn't manage to do, so he got his arm around
my throat and was dragging me into the van with me still screaming like mad, only not making much noise.

His arm was too tight, so I was, like, what? You're saying I'm
not supposed to breathe? Total rage, this spring coiling through
me, I'm writhing and thrashing around, getting nowhere, not
breathing, rage turning into panic, then there's this reversal, like
a switch being flipped, I go limp, a move of mindless brilliance
because the guy relaxes, like, oh, great, I've subdued her, and in
that moment I swing my left foot back, catch his knee, he yelps
and I'm free. But only for a second.

He grabs me again in another stranglehold and he's trying to
pivot me over his hip, I can feel it, oh my god, this is it, he's heaving me into the van, it's moving now, I'm done for, ciao, bella,
we'll never forget you, and now there's darkness and this smell,
like the lion house at the zoo or something. But no time to wonder about that, the guy is coming after me, so I scramble up to the
front, smack the driver in the back of the head. He starts yelling,
reaching behind and trying to slap at me, totally useless, giving me
this opening to duck in and yank at the wheel.

Which actually works, sending the van crashing into a parked
car, at an angle, natch, but not so tight that I can't get out on the
passenger side, which I do, with the other guy trying to get his
hands on me, but I am by now so freaked that he'd have a better
chance of grabbing a chimp in the middle of a psychotic break
with so-called reality, I am just so pissed, I know I should run
away but I hit the pavement and turn and give my pursuer a poke

in the eye. It's a bull's-eye, so to speak, he makes this little whimpering sound, and I'm back to screaming my head off.

Now both mooks are lunging at me, sort of falling all over each other trying to get through the passenger door, which I try to close, but they're in the way, so I slam it on them, really hard, and they start cursing like mad. Then they decide the better part of valor is getting the fuck out of there before somebody calls the cops. The driver backs up, there's this grinding sound as the van pops free of the wrecked car and then they take off. Tires screeching, like, we're these rough, tough guys who dominate the streets.

I stand there watching the van disappear around the corner onto Seventh Avenue, my terror turning into this hilarity, I mean, why would Sergei send such total amateurs? It's dumb, feeling sorry for people who try to hurt you, and that's not really what I'm feeling, more like, god, that was so pathetic. The only thing that could possibly be more pathetic would be if I ran into one of those creeps in a bar and he tried to pick me up. I mean, so many men are such losers. Of course, there are men who would have made a success of this little assignment. Let's not think about that.

Let's call Fletcher Marks, the district attorney who probably doesn't even remember me, which is why I didn't call before, when that other shit happened, but this is too much. Got to call Fletcher, except, what's his number? Scrolling through my phone, I find a bunch of cell numbers, all 917, no names attached. I usually remember which is which or who or whatever, but now I'm so rattled ... the first one I try turns out to be Abigail's semi-secret number.

I hang up the moment I hear her voice, thinking, that was so dumb, now my number's in her phone, but maybe she's forgotten it or won't check or who cares, not I, because I'll bet this next number I'm dialing is Fletcher's ... which it is, and I give my name to his secretary and tell her, yes, I'll hold, and I have only about two or three flashbacks before Fletcher picks up and I tell him I was just attacked by a couple of guys in front of my building, they tried to kidnap me or something—

"Fiona? Fiona Mays?"

"Yes. Fiona Mays. I'm calling you because—"

"Did you call the police?"

"Uh, um, no, I'm up in my place, I'm calling because—"

"Fiona, I'm sympathetic, of course, but this sort of thing comes to me, if at all, after a complaining witness has filed a report—"

"Yeah, OK, right. I know that, Fletcher. I guess I'm not calling to set the wheels of justice in motion or anything, I just wanted to let you know what happened, maybe ask you what you think about it."

"Think about what? I mean, what happened? Exactly."

I give him a fairly detailed scenario and he says, "Hmm." There's a pause and he says, "You think Sergei Propokoff is behind this?"

"Who else?"

"Fiona, I really couldn't say—"

"And there's been other stuff." I tell him about the car that cut in front of Brenda's Lexus, the fake paparazzi, the home-invasion … the way Sergei went from phone-stalking Brenda to giving me these bizarre calls, all this really creepy stuff … his behavior the other night at the Library, screaming at me …

Another pause and then Fletcher says, "I don't necessarily see a pattern here. It may be that … actually … actually, Fiona, we have a phrase for what you're doing with Sergei. You're turning him into the all-purpose perp. Anything goes wrong, it has to be Sergei's doing."

"But it is. It is his doing."

"Perhaps it is. But this is not obviously the case. At this point … "

"OK, Fletcher, I just—"

"Again, Fiona, I am not unsympathetic, but it doesn't fly, the idea that Sergei is the author of everything terrible that's going on in the vicinity of Brenda Rawlings. That she is such a prominent figure actually makes it more likely ... you see where I'm going with this ..."

"I do. And thank you, Fletcher. I just wanted to let you know what's been happening." Which is that Sergei really did become the author of everything terrible in the vicinity of Brenda Rawlings. And if that doesn't make sense, nothing does. Of course, I don't say this, I wait for Fletcher to say he understands. Also, that I should let him know if anything actionable comes up. Meaning, OK, this is it. Don't call me anymore.

Which I won't.

So. I'm on my own. Just me and the darkness.

Before all this happened, the darkness was not all that big a problem for me. Because even the night was never all that dark, my sleep was always so luminous, the dreams I would dream and the warmth of it. Now I'm so cold. No hot tears to ward off the chill and not even that rubbery sensation I got from bad sex in the desert. Just the cold, which I'm not even feeling. Because I really don't exist, not really, except when I have these terrible thoughts about Sergei, like, I hate Sergei, therefore I am.

Of course the weird thing about Sergei is that, yes, he is obnoxious and violent and dumb but he's also smart. Smart enough to make money, spread it around in the right places. Make his influence felt ... and smart enough to hide his smart phone where I can't seem to find it. Meaning Plan B continues to sink ever deeper into oblivion. Which has been frustrating me in this subliminal way, ever since the big cosmological experiment didn't work out, leading me to suspect that the Sergei cosmos is way more complicated than mine.

Which was simple. There was Brenda, first and last, the presence that was always present, whatever I was doing, and everything I did made sense according to its distance from Brenda, whether I was fucking Bill or fantasizing about Maisie or gazing at Mademoiselle Giraffe, the fabulous Alison, or shopping for shoes or doing yoga or getting myself off or reading Proust or just walking along, watching my thoughts race on ahead of me. Meaning, it really *was* simple. It was all about Brenda, even when it wasn't.

Not at all like Sergei's setup, which puts Brenda at the heart of the bright side and Alison at the heart of the dark side, this secret world where he indulges himself in his shameful secret, this grubby cliché, Sergei the Respectable debasing himself at the feet of a gorgeous Amazon. So, he's dividing his time between the light and the dark, except that Brenda doesn't shine her light on him. On the other hand, Alison the gorgeous Amazon does take the trouble to piss on him. She's Brenda in reverse and Sergei keeps girls like Kristina handy for those moments when the big cosmological forces are just too overwhelming for poor little Sergei and he feels the need to step into his everyday role as a run-of-the-mill shithead and smack somebody around. The way regular guys do.

That's why he felt so bad after he smacked Brenda, which I now have to admit I actually do believe he did feel. In his fucked-up way he worships Brenda. To hit her was to hurt the thing that was supposed to make him feel real. It's kind of touching if I see it like an old horror movie, the black-and-white kind, Creep from the Crypt meets *Of Mice and Men*, poor dumb creature destroys lovely creature he adores. Boo-hoo-hoo, if you know what I mean, because Sergei is not a character I can really empathize with. But

I understand him, not quite the same thing, sort of like I understand the sad guy at the other end of the bar who sends me a drink I don't want any more than I want to be the girl of all the uninspired dreams he's been having about me.

Anyway, Brenda was supposed to raise Sergei's miserable life out of the muck and give it meaning, and maybe he thinks she still will, if only he can get this nuisance—namely me—out of the picture. Hitting Brenda was a big mistake, but sending me to oblivion would be tidying up. Ridding his reality of a major glitch. So the list of Sergeis includes Sergei the Nemesis of Fiona, in other words, Sergei the drooling infant, so freaked after the Astor Hall affair that he decided that I must be a witch who was casting this terrible spell.

Which is where it gets spooky, because I am beginning to think that Sergei is an idiot-savant, cosmologically speaking, this half-conscious jerk who understood right off the bat that I was going to fuck up his universe. Twist the basic principles. Or I was the one who had already done that, even before he met me, throwing some magical dust into Brenda's eyes so she would look right through his favorite idea of himself. Like the good, strong Sergei didn't exist. Unlike the bad, weak Sergei, who definitely does exist, his eyes locking on Alison's until she stares him down, reduces him to this whimpering piece of shit.

The point is that Sergei needs both Sergeis, he's a complex guy, what the fuck, a deep Russian soul, which is great, and I might be lost in admiration for this strange phenomenon, except for one thing. Brenda has exiled me from her world and so now I'm this new me incapable of admiring anything. Remember the new me that was all transparent, hardly even there, at Angela's party? That me is obsolete. So is the me that went all cosmological and set up the experiment at the Public Library. And it's not that I hate Sergei and therefore I am now this automaton capable of just that one thought. It's more like my racing thoughts have gone into overdrive and I'm realizing I hate everything. My hatred is getting so nasty, so all-inclusive, it even hates itself. Hates itself so much that it's in the process of killing itself off with its own suicidal logic, leaving me with nothing. So the newest me, the very latest update, is this useless creature that just doesn't care.

Not about Brenda, about the way she's hurting me, not about Maisie or Bill or the wonderful world of fashion or my perfect ass, nothing, not a thing, not even my new-found powers as a witch. And it's all Sergei's fault. I lived in this perfect world and now I don't even believe it ever existed. It was never real, no matter how much I believed in it, body and soul. So, if I'm going to keep living and breathing, which I guess I am, I have to face it. I have nothing. No feelings, no future. No attitude, not even the dumbest. No hope, except for a single, white-hot shred. The hope of revenge. Sergei has to be eradicated. Liquidated, as the Russians say. It has to be like nothing like Sergei ever happened.

Fred and I are driving up Madison in this brand-new Aston-Martin coupe, which he borrowed from someone, his new love object, I think, but he's being very mysterious about that. We're heading to Sergei's and Fred still hasn't gotten with the program. Not completely.

Last night I called him, from the depths, and casually mentioned that Tom the techno-nerd at the agency had gotten around to duping Sergei's keys. The famous Medecos, which he messengered down to my place. So now I had the duplicates and it was time for the big break-in. Which, when I told Fred, he was, like, what? Are you totally insane, no way.

So I said, funny you should say that because, actually, it's all about preserving my sanity. Meaning, it has to happen. I'm going to do it, and so he just said, OK, Fiona, you really have climbed to the top of the top-ten list of crazy girls I have known but I can't let you do this all by yourself. You need a look-out.

Which is why I'm sitting here in the passenger seat of the Aston-Martin with a wine cooler in my lap, very chilly, not to mention frigid, all the ice and this bottle of champagne. Dom Pérignon, because nothing's too good for Sergei. In the back seat, there's this huge bouquet of roses, which I grab, after Fred miraculously finds a parking space around the corner from Sergei's building. Fred grabs the champagne and we head for the lobby.

The young guy behind the desk seems a little withdrawn, like, just this side of catatonic, so I'm smiling at him, very prettily, laying on the bullshit … I mean, the charm, asking if Mr. Propokoff is at home. Which he isn't, pretty much as I expected on a Friday night, so now I'm waving my keys at the guy, telling him Mr. Propokoff's assistant gave me these, Mr. Propokoff is on his way, we're going on ahead to set up this surprise party, some more of his friends will be arriving soon, so it's kind of urgent, we need to get up there now … The guy nearly snarled when he heard Sergei's name, and you know he'd love to let us up, do whatever we want in Sergei's apartment, but of course it's against the rules, so he's shaking his head … can't do that, maybe you could wait over there until Mr. Propokoff shows up. So now I'm giving him the wide-eyed look, like, I never knew what love was until I gazed into his eyes, and I'm letting my hand hang over the edge of the desk, ever so casually, with this fifty dollar bill slightly visible.

He looks up at me for a second and then down at the money, contemplating it, and I'm thinking, oh for god's sake, just take it, and finally he does. Lowering his head and waving us on, like, OK, fuck off, you don't fit anywhere in my job description.

We get to Sergei's door and of course the first dupe doesn't work. The second one doesn't work, so Fred tries the first one again and, lo and behold, it works. So he goes back down, to keep an eye out for Sergei and I go in, set the champagne on the sideboard near the door, and start rummaging through everything again. But my heart isn't in it. I know the smart phone is not in any of the places I'm looking, so … I keep looking … quite the inspired approach …

This time, I'm not bothering to be careful, stuff is getting all messed up, falling on the floor. Why do I even think the phone is here? I only know about it because Sergei was carrying it around with him that time, obviously against policy … but … maybe he's got it with him again, he is such an erratic fuck-up … how did this jerk ever put himself across as an international businessman and notable man-about-town in Manhattan and probably Moscow … not to mention Palm Beach … Fort Lee, New Jersey … Timbuktu, for all I know …

I'm still opening drawers, slamming them shut, poking around in closets. My phone, which I set on the coffee table, is ringing. It's Fred, asking me what I'm doing.

"What am I doing?" I keep pawing through things. "What I'm doing is … um … I'm fucking Tonto."

"What?"

"OK. Tonto is fucking me."

"Fiona—"

"Well, what do you want me to say? You're the one who called me the Lone Ranger."

"Fiona. Get out of there."

"Not yet. There has got to be somewhere I missed. And that's where the smart phone is hiding."

"Uh-oh."

"Uh-oh? What's up?"

Fred is now completely calm, asking, "What's he look like?"

"Like a Russian. You know ... overweight ..."

"Drop the stereotypes, Fiona. Try to be more specific. What does he look like?"

"Uhhh ..." Standing in Sergei's bedroom, wondering what to check out.

"Fiona?"

"Oh, yeah, right ... what does he look like? The thing is, I remember his dick better than his face. Want to hear about his dick?"

Now I'm scrabbling through a bunch of drawers for the second or third time.

"Fiona, for Christ's sake!"

"OK, what can I say? He's a Russian. Mr. Potato Head. Only not so cute."

"Hold on."

Which I do, and then I hear Fred's voice. "Sergei? Mr. Propokoff? There's someone on the line for you."

Which is amazing. Fearless Fred has actually gotten out of the car, walked over and handed his phone to Sergei, and I hear him barking, "Who is this?"

"Hi, Sergei. It's your friend Fiona."

"Who? Where are you?"

"Where am I? I'm in Moscow, Sergei, talking to your people."

"What people?"

"You know, Sergei, the people you worry about. The ones you're in business with. You know, dishonor among thieves? I mean, international businessmen, because you are quite the businessman, aren't you, Sergei? Child porn, human trafficking, gun running. Dope, weapons, loose nuclear material. I've been talking to Interpol about you, Sergei."

"Interpol?"

"Yeah, Sergei, I have a special friend at Interpol and he's very interested in you."

"Special friend? He is fucking you, this special friend?"

"That's it, Sergei, that's exactly what he's doing, at this very moment, which reminds me, how come you never fucked me, Sergei? Oh, I remember. You couldn't get it up."

"Get it up? I get it up." This is the one idiom he understands.

"No, Sergei, actually, you don't. And guess what? You never will. I'm a witch, remember, and so now I'm putting a spell on you, Sergei. You will never again get it up. Not once in the rest of your miserable life."

At this point he starts bellowing, but in Russian, it's the Leonard Silver Special Collections Room all over again, so I put the phone back down on the coffee table and look around at all the places I've already searched, Sergei's voice this pathetic little buzz from my phone, and suddenly I get the picture.

So I ring off and go over to this huge trophy cup sitting all alone on a table, where you'd expect a lamp to be. I tilt it toward me. Reach in. Bingo. Got it.

So. What next? Leave, obviously, but I'm standing there, thinking, I am such a stupid snob. Not looking in the trophy cup, the most obvious place, because it's all gold plate and plastic and fake mother-of-pearl, just so unbelievably cheesy I didn't even see it. Didn't acknowledge its existence. I looked at everything else but not that, which is so hopelessly dumb. This snobbery of mine, not even wanting to admit that they exist, all the ugly things in the world. Like Sergei.

Or certain buildings in New York. This money guy I was seeing before I went on hiatus explained it to me, some developers are so cheap they don't even hire an architect. So there are all these buildings that are basically just slapped together by the developer. Or the contractors. Whatever, they're lousy and of course some architect buildings are also lousy. Because the architect has bad taste, which is even worse, because no taste is one thing, a guy with no taste might possibly develop some, but bad taste is hopeless. You went to architecture school and made this big effort to develop taste and it didn't turn out all that well. Like a lot of designer clothes, to be honest, not that I really care, if I have to model them. I always figure, no matter how iffy the clothes, what comes across is me. Big fantasy, of course, but it helps. I mean, it helped, back when I was working.

So these are my racing thoughts as I'm taking a last look around and my phone rings again. I answer and Fred says, "Fiona. Get out. He's inside. There's a woman with him. I think he's smashed but she isn't. If he doesn't see you, she will. So. Fiona. Get the fuck out."

"OK, Fred." But of course I stay, and when Sergei staggers into the living room, he nearly collapses from sheer astonishment. Like, I really must be a witch, a minute ago I was in Moscow, now I'm here, oh my god. Then he pulls himself together and introduces his new girlfriend.

"Fiona, this is Tammy. Tammy, Fiona." Very formal and pompous. Like, this is proof that he's not some limp dick, he's this mature stud with all these young babes at his beck and call.

Tammy's look is sort of goth hooker, straight black hair, black boots, all shiny and crinkly, with heels so high her feet are practically vertical … studs all over her face, lips, nose, and a row of silver rings along the edge of her left ear. Doing this pose, with her hands on her hips, watching Sergei.

This girl is definitely a step beyond, possibly a step beyond Alison, meaning, she is not just going to be degrading Sergei, she's going to draw blood. But she could also be a step beyond Kristina, meaning Sergei is looking forward to a quiet evening of spattering the walls with her blood. Which is probably deep purple, to go with her eye shadow. Anyway, who knows, this Tammy person is hard to read, she could go either way. Or both ways, because, as Mickey and Sylvia say in their timeless R&B classic, love is strange.

I go over to the sideboard, lift the champagne out of the ice.

"Anybody ?" No response from Tammy but Sergei starts bellowing, he's upset because I'm dripping ice water everywhere. So I slap the champagne bucket onto the floor, there's this big glittery waterfall of ice, and Sergei is charging at me like a stripe-ass baboon.

I step aside and clip his shoulder with the bottle as he stumbles by. He's on all fours now and I hit him again, on the head this time. It's like teeing off on a golf ball. Not that I've ever played golf, all I know is that it must be the most incredibly boring game in the world, just thinking about it makes me yawn. But once I was fooling around at a golf club up in Connecticut and this guy told me I had a natural swing. Which I guess I do, Sergei is stretched out on his stomach, in a deep coma, obviously, and Tammy is poking at him with her toe.

No reaction from Sergei. Or from Tammy, for that matter. She shrugs and leaves on those high heels of hers, like some weird combination of a stork and a vulture. I find a towel in the kitchen, wipe off the champagne bottle ... hmm, a little blood ... so I retrieve the ice bucket, fill it with ice from Sergei's refrigerator, ram the bottle back in, and I'm off, holding the bucket in front of me and thinking, wow, Fiona the Homicidal Maniac ... now there's a Fiona I never knew existed. Which isn't entirely true, of course. I always had my suspicions.

Fred is sitting in the Aston-Martin, as calm as ever, through the labyrinth at the end of the Avenue, then over to Second, while I give Fred an abbreviated account of events.

"So he's out cold?"

"Totally."

"Not dead?"

"Not quite."

"Will the guy in the lobby be able to identify you to the cops? I mean, give them your name?"

"No. Well, I guess some of them know my first name. But ..."

"But what?" says Fred.

Now Fred looks over at me, with the champagne in my lap. He's smiling again but also shaking his head. A little drained, maybe, from all the suspense and now he just cruises along until he sees a deli, at which point he double parks and pops out, pops into the deli, gets a couple of paper cups and then he finds this parking space on East Seventh Street. Not a parking space, actually, we're at a hydrant but who cares?

Fred twists the cork out of the bottle, pours bubbly into the paper cups, which I'm holding for him, and then we have a toast. Success at last, so here's to whatever.

It doesn't take us all that long to get to the bottom of the Dom Pérignon, watching the menagerie of kids drifting along the sidewalk, all these looks ... neo-punk, suburban cowboy, hippie from the time-warp that time forgot ... I see this slim girl gliding by in combat boots and a black leather bustier, a raggedy petticoat for a skirt ... it's all so glamorous, in a down sort of way ... I mean, glam should be up, hot, dazzling, full of glittering pinwheel excitement, but, OK, that's just my opinion, live and let live ... because everybody's got a look, even people who think they're way beyond all that, so where's the percentage in developing all these attitudes about looks you would never be caught dead in?

Not that I'm a percentage player.

"You know, Fred ..." I want to thank him, but not in some way that's going to embarrass him. "You know that time you asked me why I dropped out. Went on hiatus."

"Uh, no, actually … or …"

"Well, you did, and I was thinking, I don't really have an answer to that question. I mean, who would do that? It was fun but so ridiculous right at that point in my life. My career. Meaning, I am basically a fuck-up. Which you already knew. But I'm not completely useless, I guess, because here we are. We outsmarted the smart phone. Of course, there were a few glitches."

Fred is looking through the windshield, nodding his head.

"Which were entirely my fault. And, um …"

Fred looks over at me, his face very serious. But sweet, like, I'm not going to help you here because it really isn't necessary for you to say whatever you're trying to say.

Anyway, I think that's what his look means, so I'm just, like, "I never could have done it without you."

He smiles, saying, "Ditto," then gathers up the paper cups and the champagne bottle and gets out and tosses them into a trash basket.

I'm slouched in my seat, savoring the buzz … half asleep, Fred driving me over to my place … we get there, he gives me a kiss on the cheek, I give him one in return, and pretty soon I'm in bed, naked, wondering who's kissing him now …

It's nearly noon, I know that much, but I'm wondering why I woke up. Then I realize it's my phone, which is still ringing.

What?

It's Viktor, meaning, double what?

"Sergei has been recycled."

Big sigh of relief. Like my whole brain suddenly realizes it doesn't have to be tensed up anymore. "That's great. Thanks for letting me know."

A long silence, then "Good-bye, Fiona." It's the first time he has ever said my name.

So I say, "Yes. Good-bye. Good-bye, Viktor."

And that is that.

Plan B has done the trick, which I thought it might. Because Fred called me yesterday, saying that he gave the smart phone to Tom the tech guy, who has been playing around with it and now he has some news. So we should all meet later on tomorrow, meaning today, at Allesandra's.

When I showed up, he and Fred were already there and, and true to form, Tom had the back off this thing that sort of looked like an iPad, but wasn't. There were bits and pieces all over his table, next to his coffee cup.

Sitting down, I said, "Isn't coffee bad for that stuff?" Because some of the bits and pieces were swimming around in these little coffee-lakes Tom had created. Inadvertently, no doubt. But he said, no ... no sweat, you dry them off and you're good to go.

"But these ..." He held up some other bits and pieces. "You have to keep these dry. Or else." And he grinned, like he had just revealed some basic principle of the universe, which maybe he had, how would I know?

"Anyway." He set the non-iPad aside and frowned. Really hard. To make sure that he was completely focused on the subject of the purloined smart phone. Then he said, "This Sergei was an idiot."

I nodded. "True."

"For one thing, there was no encryption. Not that that would have stopped me, necessarily, but, as it was, all this data was just sitting there. Waiting for me to show up with my trusty UFED."

"UFED?"

"Universal Forensic Extraction Device. Plug it into the phone and it slurps up the data. Even stuff that's been deleted."

Tom was so happy talking about his data-slurper I was afraid he'd go on and on about it for the next hour, so I said, "Data? What data?"

"Financial stuff. All these accounts. With account numbers that mean offshore. The Caymans. Also, Panama, which a lot of people don't think of, but it's a very friendly and convenient place for people who want to stash money. Anyway, there is nothing illegal about it. Anyone can have an offshore account."

"Gosh," I said. "This is fascinating."

Tom looked a little hurt, thinking I was being sarcastic, so I said that Fred had told me it was a fascinating story and, guess what, it is. Really is. So Tom started in again, saying that Sergei's accounts, per se, may not have been illegal but, according to what he got from Fred about hide-and-seek with the smart phone, the money was obviously funny. So he extracted the info, zipped it over to the District Attorney's office. And then he posted it on these websites people read in Brighton Beach.

"Even gangsters?" I said. "Russian gangsters go on the web?"

Tom shrugged. "Sure. Who doesn't? The ploy is to get the data out there and let everyone know it's out there. So I make sure the D.A. knows it's spreading through the Russian community, which it will definitely do, and the Russians know the D.A. knows."

Fred compared it to lighting a fuse. Tom considered this, seriously, tilting his head to the side and scrunching up his face, like this is how you show you're considering something really seriously, and finally he said, "Uhnn, no ... it's more like scattering a whole bunch of bread crumbs. Like, here are the dots. No matter how you connect them, they're going to lead you to the conclusion that this Sergei idiot was hiding a huge heap of money for reasons that would be of interest to certain parties. And of course the moment the info about the money comes to light, the certain parties in question are going to grab it with both hands."

I said, "I'm impressed." Which I was, flashing back to what Fletcher Marks said about dishonor among thieves.

Tom smiled and went off on this tangent about making sure that the emails he sent could not be tracked back to him, not ever, no way. I had no idea what he was talking about, IP addresses, remailer apps, server logs, and so on and so forth, a total snore, but I kept the boredom out of my face because Tom said all this anonymity was not just for his protection. It was also for mine, because we wouldn't want anyone, good guys or bad guys, figuring out exactly how the data was obtained.

Which I appreciated, obviously, but it was also obvious that Tom liked talking about this stuff. For him, it was sexy, not that he was doing any heavy breathing, but tech was his turn-on, the thing that got him to the place where everything is really real. Which is what sex does, right? So that's what sex is, the same for everyone. And different for everyone, needless to say. But how different? I mean, had Tom really taken sex into this digital universe, way beyond anything fleshy?

For a second I had this weird urge to ask him, then I didn't, of course, I'm not completely insane … and of course, when these odd thoughts occur, it helps to think of something sensible to say. So I told Tom I thought the bread crumbs had worked.

He nodded, very confident and smug. "No doubt. The guy's goose is cooked. We'll just never know who cooked it."

I've always figured it was Sergei's Russian pals. Because who else? The D. A.'s office doesn't move that fast and if it wasn't the Russians why did I get that call from Viktor? On the other hand, who cares? Sergei was no longer a factor. Everything's great.

Except for Brenda.

And just to remind me how ungreat the Brenda situation is, after Allesandra's I was wandering around in the Village, deciding whether or not to browse for a while at Intermix, when I got a call from Bennett, my shithead ex.

"What the fuck do you want?"

"What do I want, Fiona? I want to give you an opportunity to apologize for your shitty behavior."

"Why don't you drop by, Bennett? Give me a chance to teach you another lesson."

"Oh, I've learned my lesson."

Really?"

"Absolutely, Fiona. I have learned that you're a violent psychopath."

"Flattery will get you nowhere."

"Fiona, that is so dumb. Flattery got me where I am today."

"Which is nowhere."

"Is that your theory?"

"Pretty much."

"Here's my theory, babe. You need a good spanking."

"Are you volunteering?"

"No. I've been thinking that's a job for one of your girlfriends."

I laughed.

So did Bennett, saying, "Look. Fiona. I called to apologize. I'm sorry you were scared that time I sort of kidnapped Brenda. And I had a great time with her. One of the highlights of my miserable existence."

"It's not that miserable."

"No, it's not. On the other hand, yes, it is, but I'm not complaining. It's just that I wanted you to understand ..."

"Understand what?"

"That I understand. About you and Brenda ... you know ..."

"Yeah. I do know. I know that you know. I mean, what can I say, Bennett, you're one really insightful guy."

"No need to be unpleasant about it."

I laughed again. "You're right. No need whatsoever. Thanks for calling, Bennett."

A couple of nights later I was at this big party in a big private room at Bacchanal, all dark with spotlights sailing all around, sort of caressing people, and the music was so smooth and luscious, never too loud to keep anybody from yakking with anybody else, but loud enough so that if somebody came up a minute later and said, what were you talking about with so-and-so, you wouldn't be able to say, because it wasn't about that, it was about the vibe everyone was feeling.

Which was so up and fun and it was so great that everybody was there, including Alison and Maisie and her husband Jake and that beautiful friend of hers, unattached and stunning in black tights like super-tight skin and this white Issey Miyake blouse, semi-sheer with no bra, kind of flirting with everybody but not at all desperate ... this sheer female energy just zapping people.

Including me, which was great, but only for a minute, there were so many other people to see ... Ian Vrdolyak and his brother Trevor, with their ultra-hot babes, and lots of girls I run into all the time on shoots and go-sees and their boyfriends or girlfriends or whatever. Significant others, I guess, though it began to feel at a certain point like everybody was everybody else's significant other, the feeling was so totally perfect.

Even Abigail was there, being really nice to me, mainly because Cora Burke had decided my suspension was a little premature. Or unnecessary in the first place. Or something. Anyway, according to Fred, Cora saw a picture of me up on stiletto heels wearing nothing else but a blue blazer and these tiny pink shorts. And I remembered it immediately, which picture he meant, I mean, my god, those legs!

Those eyes!

I'm staring into the camera like what I'm seeing is about to make me come, it's slightly terrifying, I look so there. So hot. But dignified. Like I'm this sexy girl who's about to lose control except that I've got everything totally under control.

Anyway, Cora decided, fuck the rules, we've got to get her back to work, so I'll be making the rounds again next week and I was really careful at the party not to overdo it, booze-wise, and, actually, it wasn't that difficult to keep the drinking to a minimum, I hardly felt like having anything at all, it was just such a thrill to be in the midst of all these handsome, pretty, adorable people, just everybody, as I said, except for Mike the security guy, who was invited but did not show up, except that he was there in spirit, as far as I was concerned. Because this party was for me and it never would have happened if not for him.

I told Mike what happened to Sergei, the Cliff Notes version, because I thought he should know. For security reasons and also, let's face it, because I hoped he would tell Brenda. Which he did, thank god, and then Brenda got in touch with me, saying, darling, I'm sorry, really so sorry, I was just so scared, so I went over to her place and we sat around and talked, so we could both realize that everything was OK again.

It was the usual chitchat, nothing, really, except that it was everything, I could feel this massive thing taking place, the stars getting realigned or something ... you know that movie, *The Day the Earth Stood Still?* Well, this was the day the earth got back on track, my world reappeared, the same as it ever was, with me loving Brenda, which of course I did even during the dead days when I wasn't feeling anything, but now I was feeling what I always felt, that Brenda is this lovely presence, this loving presence, right at the center of my universe.

It was so amazingly fabulous, which Brenda must have agreed with, I know she did, because, to celebrate how great things were again, she threw this party for me, getting me to tell her the names of all my friends, with one of the assistant-assistants writing everything down. Then they all got invitations and everybody showed up ... Bill was there, of course ... and Fred ... and Tom the tech guy ... a bunch of other people from the agency ... plus all sorts of people I didn't know but was just so happy to see ...

Needless to say, Brenda was there and she was the star. It was my night but it was all about her. Which was absolutely OK. In fact, it was right in line with my idea of heaven on earth, now that the out-of-whack earth had been whacked back into shape, and Brenda must have been feeling it too, understanding in her strange Brenda way everything I had done. Because she asked me to drive off with her, after the party, while everybody, and I mean everybody, tried to get close to her and say good-bye, and she was so sweet about it, not leaving anybody out, and waiting while people said good-bye to me, too, it was this endless serial hug.

We finally got away, both of us sort of sinking back in the seat of her car, really exhausted and happy and then she turned to me and held me and kissed me on the lips, sexily, and this was it, more than I ever dreamed of, so warm and lovely and breathtaking, and it wouldn't have taken much more for me to come, it was beginning, not a full-body orgasm, more like the full-being kind. You come and you feel like the universe itself is crazy about you. Your very existence is totally satisfied, down to the very last molecule.

Then there was this strange rush in my head, like a fast forward, but actually it was just a second later and I was pulling away, with Brenda staring at me, so shocked and so totally hurt. And surprised, which I also was. Totally.

Because I had done it, I had restored the balance of the universe, end of story, all the loose ends tied up, everyone safe and sound. Everything was perfect now, except that Brenda was taking perfection to the next, unbelievable level, coming on to me, I mean, the very heart of my universe was taking me back, wrapping itself around me, and I was backing off. Rejecting her. It was heartbreaking, this look on her face that is always going to be nagging me, even when I'm, like, ninety, doddering around in the sun room, blissed out on all the wisdom and serenity I've achieved, and it'll hit me. Brenda wanted to make love and I pulled away.

Like I was driving in the country, it's late at night and suddenly there's this fawn in my headlights, its eyes looking right into mine, but it's too late, I kill it, just totally dead, and I feel terrible for the rest of my life. But it had to be done. Which I don't know how I knew but I did, absolutely. It had to be done so I could step out of the Brenda cosmos into this previously unimaginable one. This brand-new cosmos with me at the center.

Brenda told the driver to take me to my place, and we got there, finally, silent the whole way, then giving each other girly kisses goodnight, all sweet and sad, and I could feel her hand on the side of my face all the way upstairs. Then I was taking off my blouse and my slacks, looking in every pocket, trying to find the card the woman in the Issey Miyake blouse gave me … remembering her face … all sculptural and gorgeous … and when I found the card, finally, in my purse, I stood there for a while, looking at it.

HELEN BENJAMIN
VICE-PRESIDENT FOR DEVELOPMENT
ARETÉ PRODUCTIONS

Hmm. I wonder what that means … I take off my bra and panties and call the number on the card, as late as it is, absolute silence from the street, nothing but the phone ringing, and then Helen is answering, knowing it's me, I can feel it as I'm saying hello, and she says it is so great to hear from me, really meaning it, I can just tell, really, she means it, it's like this light is filling my head, my whole body, and now I know I'm in the Fiona cosmos because I can practically see it, the future that is opening up just for me and it's just as naked as I am, even nakeder, if that makes any sense, and so promising it's slightly scary.

About the Author

CARTER RATCLIFF is a poet who writes about art. He first published his poetry in *The World* and other magazines in the orbit of the St. Mark's Poetry Project, in downtown Manhattan. In recent years poems of his have appeared in *The Sienese Shredder, The Mississippi Review, Cimarron Review, Hudson River Art, Vanitas, Cover Magazine,* among other journals; and in *In|Filtration: An Anthology of Innovative Poetry from the Hudson Valley* (Station Hill, 2015); *The KGB Bar Book of Poems* (New York: Harper Perennial, 2000); and *Poetry After 9/11: An Anthology of New York Poets* (Brooklyn: Melville House, 2001). His books of poetry include *Fever Coast* (New York: Kulchur Press, 1973); *Give Me Tomorrow* (New York: Vehicle Press, 1983); and *Arrivederci, Modernismo* (New York: Libellum Press, 2004). A Contributing Editor of *Art in America,* Ratcliff has published art criticism in leading journals in the United States and Europe, as well as catalogs published by the Museum of Modern Art; El Museo del Barrio; the Guggenheim Museum; the Royal Academy, London; the Stedelijk Museum, Amsterdam; and other institutions. Among his books on art are *The Fate of a Gesture: Jackson Pollock and Postwar American Art* (New York: Farrar, Straus and Giroux, 1996); *Out of the Box: The Reinvention of Art 1965-1975* (New York: Allworth Press, 2000); and *Andy Warhol: Portraits* (London: Phaidon Press, 2006). Since 2003, Ratcliff has lived with his wife, Phyllis Derfner, in the Hudson River Valley.